# ADDICTIONS

# ADDICTIONS

*Horrors of New York City in the '80's*

by Douglas James Miller

Wire Road Press

Rogers, Arkansas

2015

ISBN-13: 978-0-9909657-2-5
ISBN-10: 0990965724


Cover artwork and layout by noir33.com
Photographs by Douglas James Miller
*Hell-Wings* Latin text by Chad Kiefer


Wire Road Press
820 South Fourth Street
Rogers, Arkansas 72756

To my friends who did not live to grow old: Kevin, Arthur, Timmy.

*Je puis dire que je vivais en ce temps-là avec les morts plus qu'avec les vivants.*

Lamartine

# C o n t e n t s

# ADDICTIONS

# Hell-Wings over Loisaida

## i. Feeding the Habit

Night was falling over the Lower East Side as Jésus slipped around the corner from East Houston onto Suffolk and warily made his way toward Stanton, eyes roving continuously and fingers unconsciously beating a rhythm against his palms. He was uptight and anxious to score, but proceeded with the measured pace of a man who wants to know what's going to happen before it takes place. One down, one to go: he had only moments before copped four bags of Poison on the corner of Clinton almost without slowing down, and now, once he got a couple nickels of cocaine, he could go home and get high. And he hadn't seen any Five-O yet.

At Stanton, the corner was deserted and he saw no one in the long empty block to Rivington, so he made his way toward Norfolk. The cocaine he'd injected just before going out made everything sharp and clear; the world seemed slowed, as if he were somehow moving faster than everything else. He was alert, even a bit paranoid, but it paid to be careful. You couldn't be too careful. You had to have eyes in the back of your head. Jésus had been around: he'd been threatened, beaten up, robbed by another junkie with a knife, robbed at gunpoint by a confederate of the dealer who'd sold him the dope; he'd been junk-sick in the lock-up, which was maybe the worst of all. Now, making his way along the street, scanning for police or trouble, he'd begun to feel nervous, that uptight feeling that served him as a warning, some sixth sense obscurely sensing danger. It wasn't good, and he began to re-evaluate. Certainly he wanted to get it over with, cop the shit and get home, but he could always forget about the cocaine or come back later if things weren't cool. But at the corner of Norfolk a guy in a leather jacket said, "What you want, Miami Vice?"

Jésus nodded. "Yeah, yeah, Miami Vice."

"Up there, past the church," the guy said, pointing his chin toward Houston. Jésus nodded, hurried past. The church was abandoned, a burned-out derelict at least a hundred years old, little more than a pile of crumbling brick and petrified wood, its shattered windows boarded up from inside. Perhaps it wasn't a church at all: its doors and windows were capped with high pointed arches like a cathedral, but over what had been its main entrance was a six-pointed star within a circle, and the inscriptions, now obliterated and nearly illegible, might have been in Hebraic. Its current use was uncertain, obscure. Jésus had remarked a certain activity there, and guessed it was a shooting gallery, for which he had no use, but maybe now it had become a spot. Things were always changing and moving around in the neighborhood.

Up the street he saw a face peek out from around a corner, then disappear again. He glanced back: no cops, no one. He was still uptight, but told himself to get it over with. In the empty lot was another guy, watching both ways and chanting quietly, as if to himself, "Miami Vice, Miami Vice." Jésus went to him.

"How many, how many," the guy said, looking down the street.

"Two," Jésus said, pulling out a ten. The guy took it, put it away, and pulled out a bundle. Jésus held out his hand palm-up, waiting. Then something whipped around his neck and pulled tight, choking him, cutting off his breath. The pain was intense. He floundered about, tried to get his fingers under it, but the garrote was too tight; he gouged his own flesh, couldn't get hold. Black spots exploded before his eyes, his chest was bursting; the blood pounded in his head, swollen veins roaring like surf. He fell to his knees, lips writhing, and the cracked and broken sidewalk of Norfolk Street was the last thing he ever saw.

## ii. The Dream of the Dope House

Often, even when D slept, he slept badly, plagued by obnoxious dreams. All too frequently, these centered on the Dope House, each dream a variant, composed of common elements: a furtive, anxious approach; the lookouts; hurried passage of the vestibule; exchange of money for tiny packets, loose grip of nervous fingers; the mask-like face of the dealer, an Hispanic Fu Manchu. But for all of these constants, other elements remained variable, among them a curious shift in the population of the dreams, the number rising and falling to no discernable pattern: now, he waited behind one or two others; the next time, he stood in line, behind dozens of people, nervous and wary; again, and he was utterly, desolately alone…

But on this occasion, the dream, though not unlike the dreams of the Dope House, was entirely unique. The dream's beginning awoke him; he came to himself with a nervous spasm of his muscles, breathing shallowly. It was not yet dawn, still dark, that hour when even the Lower East Side is quiet, and the sound of a car on Houston is like the wind in dry leaves. He shuddered at what he had seen, but slipped again into sleep, and the dream resumed its course, as the branch of a tree carried on a swollen current may be momentarily snagged, only to be swept along with greater force. He woke again shivering and soaked in sweat, gasping for breath as his heart pounded in terror. Pale light of dawn seeped beneath the dusty blinds. He looked wildly about, fingers clutching the sheets, and then —oh God! What mercy! —the realization that it had only been a dream brought physical relief like the uncoiling of a spring. Tears came to his eyes. He had been, what, a priest! The heavy vestments, so hot, stifling! And that place —a great church, a cathedral —its air thick, choked with incense, and glimmering with the uncertain light of tapers. The congregation —robed and hooded figures, their outlines inhuman —and their faces! —horrible —mouths like open wounds —he couldn't think about it! No! But it haunted him, wouldn't go away, he'd never had such a horrible dream, never experienced such terror. He'd performed the ritual, reading from that insane book, obscene and blasphemous —he couldn't remember the alien words, except for one phrase over and over again... But no, it slipped away. And then those —*things!* —rose from the pews! And queued before the altar, staring at him with depthless black eyes, mirrors to the void of their souls —waiting —*waiting*— He'd pushed the left sleeve of the vestment above his elbow and taken up that curious knife, as they waited —watched and waited —waited as —No! —*he'd opened a vein that they might drink!*

Somehow he slept again. And dreamed again. At last, he was alone. In a strangely luxurious chamber, like the cell of a voluptuous monk, he removed the heavy vestments and hung them in a wardrobe. His left arm was pale and bruised, a shriveled husk. He sat at the desk for a time, reading in an ancient book, medieval Latin in clumsy black-letter print, a text of the most revolting, soul-blasting horror —memory could never sustain it. But after a time, as if the hour had come, he rose and left the room, passing silently along narrow corridors half-paneled in ancient wood beneath yellowed plaster, up and down flights of stairs whose stone steps were worn hollow by the tread of innumerable feet. And it seemed to him that his way traced a symbolic figure through the maze of the ancient structure —a sign of dreadful portent. At length he reached a heavy door, and opened it; beyond was a dark street wet with fresh rain. His errand urgent, he set off at a hurried pace, following a labyrinthine path through city streets at once disturbingly familiar, and unknown; he feared to lose his way, anxious, and uncertain. He saw no one, met no passers-by, and as he pressed on, the night fled, marked by the distant tolling of spectral, dissonant bells. At last, dawn approached, greyish light filtering through the phantasmal streets, and still he passed through block after block, driven on, oppressed by dread, until he turned a last corner to find himself before –the Dope House.

### iii. Norfolk Street: The Synagogue

A reek of mildew and rotting wood pervaded the nave of the ruined synagogue, the air perfumed only slightly by the numerous cheap candles that burned in the alcoves about the room —candles that cast a weak and febrile glow over a few inches of scabrous walls and shattered floor, as they guttered, and threatened to blow out. The fire that had gutted the building years before had badly damaged the roof, and the harsh Manhattan elements had hastened the structure's dilapidation; though surreptitious repairs kept out the rain, the place was dank and drafty, morbidly cool even on a hot day. For years the sole occupants had been the shifting population of a shooting gallery; but now the addicts were gone, banished to some other rat hole, and their heaps of rubbish and waste —empty bags and cast-off clothing, broken needles and stained mattresses —had all been quietly gathered and taken away. The dark lofty space had now a skeletal air, like the shell of some creature from which all flesh has been stripped.

Donatien-Alphonse Levêque, the master of this place, a magus and passing wise in black and forbidden lore, looked about in satisfaction. He stood on the cusp of momentous change. Now this empty shell should serve as a new home, for That which he himself would call forth and install there; and just as his work would give this ruin new life, redeem and transform it with new purpose, soon, once the Guest elevated him to the summit of his powers, he should redeem and transform the world –after his fashion. He was pleased, yes, very pleased indeed. For it was dusk on that signal night, the night the stars showed as propitious for the Opening of the Doors, and the initiates were at work, as Severin, his assistant, directed the last preparations for the rite.

All was progressing apace. The initiates, carefully selected, had all demonstrated exemplary skill and devotion, but even among such as these, Severin seemed to inspire obedience chiefly through fear. His brooding, taciturn presence was invaluable to Levêque. The man's very gaze could bludgeon; his black eyes bespoke the abyss. Levêque himself was certain he had not plumbed their depths. For all that, he was satisfied with his pupil, of whom he had no fear: Severin was his bound acolyte, held by frightful vows of loyalty, and the fate of he who broke faith would be horrendous.

Levêque turned from the great hall and slipped away downstairs to his private sanctum. Having dictated that the more mundane preparations be readied to await him, he would appear when it was time to perform the intricate ceremony. Thus he underscored his dominance over them all; moreover, he had a certain errand, a need that might only be satisfied *in camera*. He bolted the door, took out a set of keys and unlocked a small cabinet. From here he removed a curiously-figured ivory box, yellowed with age, and placing this near the light, took from it two glass vials, a darkened crucible that stood on three legs, an eyedropper, a length of rubber hose, and a syringe. Measuring with a practiced eye, he poured grains of white powder from each of the vials into the crucible, added a few drops of distilled water, and briefly applied the flame of a match until the mixture liquefied. The heroin was of such purity that it dissolved immediately, but the cocaine almost always had to be heated. He drew the colorless liquid up into the syringe, threw off his robe, and rolled up his shirtsleeve. Using the rubber hose to distend a vein, he injected the solution, released the tie-off, and taking a bottle of alcohol from the desk, he sterilized the injected vein even as the speedball surged along the bloodstream to his brain. A soothing warmth flooded through him, and he leaned back in the chair, granting himself a brief rest, just for a moment. He had worked so hard. Closing his eyes, he floated away on a Lethe-like phantasmagoria, wherein, the master of delicious and intoxicating powers, he had become a magus without equal –a master of life and death –become, indeed, almost a god. The rabble, as awed by his power as they were ignorant of its first principles, kneeled at his feet, and worshipfully elevated him, master first of New York City, and then the world.

A knock came at the door; he started, sat up. "Master," Severin's voice called. "The time is near."

"Yes," said Levêque. He rose, a bit disoriented. "I come." The words rasped out, his mouth like cotton.

iv. The Habits of a Scholar

Like a fresh polaroid only by degrees revealing its image, his consciousness resolved slowly, then with increasing speed and clarity, into the demands of habit, the raw need of narcotics-starved cells. D —translator and poet; expert in the Gothic, a specialist in Poe and Baudelaire; an occasional writer of weird fictions; a man out of time; and a heroin addict —D awoke to the familiar sickness: the pain in his muscles and stomach; a feverish, swollen tongue; his nerves, jumpy, starting to fray. He stretched a pale hand to the bed stand and grasped the small silver tray there —a gesture, to his mind, stamped with a lifetime's custom, but which was really only the index to a recent few of his thirty-three years —retrieving the tray with exquisite care, for it bore, like a sacrament, the instruments of his self-poisoning, and remission from pain: an antique pocketknife, a gift from his father, its yellowed celluloid handle like archaic crystal; a short length of plastic straw; and a small glassine envelope, sealed inside a transparent plastic jacket. With practiced efficiency he opened the bag, split it in two, and snorted up half the bitter, alkaline powder. The familiar taste hit the back of his throat; he carefully put away the other half, and lay back with his head on the pillow, closing his eyes.

His yet-mild withdrawal symptoms disappeared quickly but he allowed himself to remain indolently in bed from perverse dread of what the day had in store: guests. An old university friend, and his girlfriend, of whom D was not fond, were coming to stay the day and the night and very possibly a good deal longer: they were apartment hunting. Malcolm had said they would arrive at one, and D knew he would have no real peace until they were gone again; nor, once he actually got up and about, would he be able to relax until they arrived, for he was nervous, and high-strung, and the anxiety of waiting for someone, the simple knowledge that someone was expected, made him restless, and unable to concentrate. Besides, the mail could not have come yet, and though before his visitors arrived, D had errands of his own to complete, the precise nature of these depended on what came in the mail. And so he stayed in bed. He didn't have to get up yet; he could wait.

A buzzing sound roused him —calling to him —as, weightless, he floated in infinite depths of lightless space. The awful noise filled him with anxiety: did it seek to warn him before he drifted, irrevocably lost, into some ultimate and frightful abyss? or did it but lure him on to perdition, the siren song of some predatory creature, buzzing with delight as it sought to draw him to its hungry maw? He floundered about, confused and disoriented, the sound growing louder and louder —until at last, with a terrible effort, he opened his eyes: No! The alarm clock! What time was it?

Ten-thirty. For pity's sake! He'd overslept. He sat up, passing his hands over his face. Had it been ringing for half an hour? He stood, groggy and a little shaken, and walked like an automaton into the kitchen to put on the teapot.

After drinking some coffee he more or less awoke. He got dressed to go out and went downstairs, but the check hadn't come and he trudged back upstairs, dejected. What would it be this time, the pawnshop or the Strand? But something inside him rebelled against selling any more books. He still had his camera, and though it pained him, he took it out, checking for film —empty, of course —got the subway fare from the change jar, and went out again, determined both to do what had to be done, and to get it over with as quickly as possible. He didn't want to be late, though he knew it didn't matter: Malcolm and Becky would be, they always were.

The pawnshop gave him forty-five dollars, almost twice what he expected, probably because he was a good customer. That plus the twenty he still had made sixty-five, and he decided on the spot to go to the coke store. The forty-five would get him through the day and first thing the next morning. After that —well, the check had better come.

At the subway entrance, a ragged youngish man had books and such for sale, spread out on blankets. D stopped to look. It was mostly uninteresting, mainstream horror and science fiction, with one curious exception: a vinyl LP, at least twenty years old, a spoken-word recording of Lovecraft's *Haunter of the Dark*. D was fascinated, he'd never seen anything like it before, but the fellow wanted five dollars and he wouldn't come down. Afraid of needing some cash while Malcolm and Becky were here, D went on without it, regretfully, thinking about it all the way home.

The train took forever, and when he finally got back he was thirty-five minutes late, but they weren't waiting outside on the street and he found no messages on the answering machine. He assumed they hadn't been there, which was good, for he didn't want to get off to a bad start, especially with Becky. Sitting down to wait, after a moment's hesitation, he took a small snort of cocaine, and opened the book he was reading, Ewers' *Vampir*. The doorbell rang, starting him from his concentration. He looked at his watch, surprised to see it had been over an hour. The bell rang again: it was them, they were here.

## v. The Opening of the Doors

Levêque fumbled clumsily with the latch, and found Severin waiting in the narrow corridor, a candle flickering in one hand, the wan light playing over his features. Deferential, yet somehow distant, he had a singularly grave mien about him. For a moment, he said nothing.

"Yes?" Levêque said, disconcerted by the man's gaze, penetrating, appraising. He turned away, back to his desk, as if he sought something, gesturing vaguely with his hands and patting his pockets, and said again, "Yes? What is it?" His voice caught, choked, and he cleared his throat, dismayed: for the first time, it occurred to him that his assistant –his subordinate, his acolyte! –might know everything about him, his weakness, his addictions... The thought was terrible, appalling! Suddenly he felt irresolute, almost paralyzed.

"Master," Severin said behind him. Levêque felt a bitter urge to laugh. "Yes, what is it?" he snapped, trying to assume a dominant tone.

"I am concerned that there is a problem," Severin said.

Levêque composed himself, turned. "What problem?"

"The offering we took this afternoon?"

Levêque didn't understand: "Offering?"

"The provender? The man, the drug addict?" Severin's voice stressed this latter attribute.

Levêque flushed. "Ah, well, what about him? Go on, what is it?"

"He's dead."

"Dead!" Levêque shouted. "What do you mean, dead? What happened to him?"

"I'm uncertain," the other answered. "I had the initiates bind him. They are unfamiliar with such work, and were perhaps over-thorough. His mouth was taped to keep him silent. I believe he choked to death, on his own vomit. Perhaps he had gone into withdrawal…"

"You idiots!" Levêque banged his fist on the desk, raging; this might ruin everything! But he forced himself to calm down, guard his composure, above all not lose control of the situation. He sat down, glaring harshly at Severin, whose expression was unreadable. "This is very grave. Close the door." When Severin had done so, he said evenly, "I relied on you; you've disappointed me. There is no time to get another, and despite all, we must act now. How long has he been dead?"

"No more than an hour," the other said. "Master, I…"

"Hold," Levêque said. "Have him brought up and placed before the altar, and assemble the others. We begin at the appointed hour. I will not lose this opportunity."

Severin hesitated. "But the ritual…"

"I *know* the ritual." Levêque's voice was cold, as he clearly enunciated each syllable. This was too much; when the moment came, he would destroy this insolent neophyte. "Kindly proceed."

When the other was gone he stood, paced about the cramped little room, returned to the desk, sat again. His hands mechanically took out the ivory box, but he was staring, agitated, into the void, and gnashing his teeth. This was a catastrophe; he couldn't believe it. What an idiot, this Severin! Must he do everything himself? His hopes were vanishing like spectres before a cold and hopeless dawn.

*No!* –he slammed a fist on the desk, and shook himself. Such thinking only engendered failure. He had to gather himself, muster all his concentration.

With no time to prepare another shot, he spilled out piles of dope and cocaine, and snorted them off the desk. But something bothered him, nagged irritatingly. He hesitated –after all, who knew the texts better than he? Certainly not Severin! –and turned to the bookshelf. The ritual contained nothing that would clarify the question, but there was a passage in the *Cultes des goules...* In a moment he found it:

> *Or, à ne jamais oublier, Celui qui vient, le Convive, se nourrit et sera nourri de la chair fraîche; car quand Il arrivera Il aura faim et Il exigera de quoi se satisfaire; de même après et assez souvent, quand il Lui plaira. On ne saura pas le Lui refuser.*

That was all –but what did it mean? How was one to interpret *de la chair fraîche?* How fresh? He returned the book to the shelf, looked at his watch, sat down again. The time was nigh; nothing could be done.

He rubbed his temples, and sat holding his face in his hands, trying to think. From overhead came creaks and muffled steps: the others were assembling. The time had come. He was reaching for the *Liber ivonis*, his mind turning over the problem, when the answer he'd been seeking, which had been just beyond reach, and was yet so obvious, revealed itself: if the Guest rejected the offering, he would give it Severin.

He laughed with delight, and stood. The thing was so simple! After all, he really didn't need the other man any more, once the Guest arrived, and the others would only be that much more under his control.

He had just time for another speedball. The powders bit harshly into his nasal membranes, and he winced, tears coming to his eyes. What a waste! –such a dose, and he scarcely felt it. But time was precious; he had to hurry. He returned the drugs to the cabinet, and carefully, gingerly removed the precious and venerated casket –its strange carven wood and locks of archaic design the only vessel that might contain and occlude the blasphemous figurine and seal of Azathoth –and set it with infinite care on the desk, before donning again the great robe, heavy over his clothes. His skin was crawly and itchy, and he realized he'd taken a bigger dose than he'd thought. He heard steps again in the corridor, followed by a knock: Severin again. The acolyte bowed. You miserable hypocrite, Levêque thought, you're as good as dead.

"Master," Severin said. "As you bid, I have arranged the provender. Some of the others seemed... disquieted."

"And so?" Levêque snapped.

Severin bowed again. "All is as you wished."

Levêque ignored the obvious irony. "Here," he said, and thrust the wooden box into Severin's hands. "Take care: that box is more precious than your life. You will bear it before me, in the manner of a sacrament. See that you assume an appropriate mien." Taking up the moldy, crumbling copy of the *Dhol Chants*, and urging his assistant on before him, he passed out of the sanctum, and they mounted the steps as might two wraiths moving to fulfill some uncertain doom.

At the foot of the scabrous brick walls supporting the arched nave of the synagogue, a myriad of candles burned. The room flickered with their feeble light, the smell of burning wax mingling with a heavy odor of incense, as curious shadows moved across peeling paint and ruined plaster. To one side the body of a man was slumped in a folding chair. Apart and away from it, the eleven initiates stood in a nervous, expectant group, completely silent as Severin emerged, bearing the strange and dreadful casket, so tiny and yet so forbidding. In a moment Levêque followed, stepping into view and pausing, that they all might gaze upon him in awe and wonder; aware of his own vanity, he deemed it unnecessary to contain it. He held clasped to his chest the precious, impossibly rare volume, holding the page where were found the complex formulae. Serene, solemn, disdainfully haughty, and high as a kite, he mounted to the altar and posed the repellent book before him, throwing back his cowl and glaring awfully into the abyss.

Severin genuflected before him and placed the casket on the altar, his fingers caressing its surface with a mix of reverence and dread, then stepped away and stood apart in hieratic immobility. Levêque raised his hands, arms extended, and said in a low voice that carried throughout the great room:

"My friends, and initiates, darers of the blasphemous and forbidden, fellow voyagers in what is known and unknown, dreamed and undreamed, we have waited long for this night." His eyes swept the hall, falling on each of the faces that looked with fearful eagerness into his own, and pride flushed through him like a drug. "Waited long, and labored much; waited long, and kept much faith. The moment of our reckoning is at hand, and it is time to reap the fruit of that which we have sown." Replete with his own power, in a moment for which he had waited years, he spread his arms wide and said, "Let the ceremony begin."

It went perfectly, the initiates well rehearsed, each one clever in his way, and a practitioner of the arts. The rite was long, rich in chanted lyrical passages of shocking imagery, alternating with the seven responsorials, each one a Key to those extra-dimensional Doors, through which would arrive the Guest, He who will come. The first three Doors opened unremarkably, but at the fourth Levêque felt something untoward, a vertiginous change like an abrupt slippage or sliding, as if some disjunction in the fabric of time and space.

By the fifth Key, it was clear the others felt it, too: as the Door opened, the effect was like a mild nausea, and Levêque saw their eyes shift about uneasily, their attention distracted. He pressed ahead, excited and flushed with anticipation, struggling to maintain the focus of his own energies. As the sixth Door opened, the hall grew perceptibly dim, light itself now somehow suppressed. A singular draft sprang up, blowing about the room with mounting intensity, like a vortex, as chillingly cold as if it blew from the depths of frozen space. The candles guttered, and went out, but now the room was neither dark nor light —or rather, dark *was* light, as in a photographic negative —and the wind was roaring now, howling and shrieking as it must in the infinite, maddening void between the stars. Levêque was exultant, shouting the last incantatory phrases of the Key in a voice to rival the gale, and holding his fists toward the sky, in triumph. There came a tremendous crash like a thunderbolt —and all was quiet again, and dark.

Yet it had happened, they were no longer alone: the *Guest* had come. Even in the darkness, a *presence* could be felt —powerful, awe inspiring. A fresh smell pervaded the room, so strong one could almost taste it, a curiously reptilian odor, innately revolting. And Levêque heard a sort of rustle, like a great pair of wings unfolding, then settling again. He shuddered involuntarily, but with an effort mastered himself. After all, had not *he* opened the Doors, and bid the Guest enter? "Light," he said —but his voice was like a croak.

vi. Apartment Hunting

"Hello?" D said into the intercom.

"It's Malcolm and Becky," Malcolm's voice said.

"I'll be right there."

Could they hear the lack of enthusiasm in his voice? Did he himself even hear it all? Was it only that? He didn't want to be cold to them; it wasn't Malcolm's fault if he picked the worst girlfriends in the whole world. D went downstairs, saw Malcolm through the little window, smiling just like always. Feeling guilty about not wanting them around, he opened the door.

"Hi, come on in!" D said, and at the same time Malcolm said, "Hey D, how are you? Good to see you, man!"

Becky had changed little, though perhaps the predatory air, which had always pervaded her every act and spoken word, had reached a certain maturity. Malcolm looked tired and drawn, even leaner than, what, a few months before? D wondered if the time with her had drained his friend, as an illness might –or perhaps Becky herself sucked the life from him, like a vampire. She hugged D amidst exclamations of greeting. D tried to mask his revulsion at her touch –at her very presence –and hurriedly ushered them upstairs.

As they all sat down, Malcolm was making excuses for being late: it seemed that Becky had overslept. Becky herself sprawled in the one easy chair and began to peel away the various layers of rags she wore despite the fall warmth, revealing at last an antique dress of rotten lace and faded velvet, and untied her battered combat boots. D assured Malcolm that everything was fine, he'd only been reading, and settled in to listen to an afternoon's monologue, more often than not about Becky. Becky needed help to get settled, Malcolm was leaving for Louisiana to begin graduate school, New York was such a difficult place to find an apartment, and he had to help get her settled and make sure she would be okay. She wanted to find a place in the neighborhood, she didn't want to live in Brooklyn anymore, but in the Lower East Side, where she knew people, like her friend Charlene, and D (the hell you say, D thought): on and on about how she needed his help, with her sitting through it all silent and satisfied, like a cat with a mouse wriggling beneath its paw. After a time, D began to think that Malcolm wanted her as firmly settled as possible before he tried to get away, lest she decide after all to go with him.

The previous day, D had prepared for their coming, with a fifth of vodka. After ten minutes he made everyone a stiff drink and sat sipping his while Malcolm rambled on, the alcohol lowering a sort of curtain between D and his own irritation. Becky guzzled hers while the monologue on the arrangement of her circumstances went on unabated.

At length D excused himself and went into the bathroom. He carefully shut the door, closed the lid of the toilet and sat down, listening for and hearing the murmur of their voices. Satisfied, he poured two small piles of cocaine on a pocket mirror and as quietly as possible snorted them up with a straw. He stood, raised the lid and flushed the toilet, stashed everything in his pockets again, washed his hands and went back out, to find Malcolm waiting for him, waiting to begin talking again.

Malcolm had asked when he'd first called about using the phone, and now when he mentioned it once more, D was only too happy to tell him to help himself. Malcolm got out a big sheaf of papers, some marked-up pieces of the *Times*, and a large, overstuffed memo book and shuffled through it all, then began a series of calls, speaking to everyone very politely, while Becky looked on with a somewhat critical air. Finally she said, "You're too nice, Malcolm. People are going to take advantage of you because you're too nice."

Malcolm looked at her strangely, half-smiling, and D wasn't sure if perhaps he weren't reflecting on the accuracy of this remark, but finally he said, shaking his head, "Just trying to find a place for you, Becky."

D thought this servile, accommodating tone was the most appalling thing he had heard in a long time. He went to the bathroom again and had some more cocaine, looking at his reflection in the mirror for a while, then snorted part of a bag of dope. When he came back, Malcolm was shuffling papers and muttering. Becky fixed D with a penetrating look and said, "So, D, have you been doing any drugs lately?"

D marveled —not only at her acumen, but at her sheer nerve. Perhaps he had underestimated her, but she could go to hell anyway.

"No," he said, in a wistful tone. "Not in a long time. Things have really changed around here. I'm not even sure where you'd get any now. The social club got busted a long time ago, and since then…"

He trailed off. Becky was looking straight at him. He shrugged. Her eyes bored into his, accusing him of lying. He looked away, thinking, I don't owe you anything, bitch.

Malcolm had kept his head down during this discussion. D couldn't blame him: a doped-up Becky was a hundred times worse than a regular Becky. And once she got started, she would only wheedle all his money out of him, just to blast it up her greedy nose.

vii. Body Bag

With the quickness of a spring uncoiling, the *Guest* stretched out a taloned hand and snatched up Levêque, audibly breaking his neck. The master's head lolled to the side, a stunned expression fixed on his face; his limbs convulsed, then went still. The initiates flinched and drew back, sickened, and so terrified they visibly trembled; some looked to the door, weighing their chances; others stood still, gaping stupidly. Severin was shocked, his mind reeling. He watched in horror as it gripped Levêque's head with one hand, talons seeking purchase in eye sockets and jawbone, and ripped away the top of his skull with the other. The bone tore like cardboard, exposing the brain in a spray of blood, and the Guest popped the brain free and devoured it. Severin, nauseous, wanted to turn away, run –but he couldn't move. The Guest glared about, looking at each of the cult in turn, fixing each of them with a malignant stare. When it came Severin's turn, he felt something probing his mind, sucking at his thoughts and memories.

"Brains," it said at last in a low voice more like a croak –or had it spoken at all? "I want more brains."

They stood there dumbly, looking at it, oppressed by fear, and something else, a vague sapping of the will; though afraid for their lives, it was now impossible to run away, the very idea beyond their strength. The hideous thing, whose calling up was clearly now such a rash and foolish presumption, already exerted a certain ineluctable power over them. Watching them closely, its hateful head and burning eyes moving incessantly, it dropped Levêque's body, which fell awkwardly into a pool of its own gore, a heavy mannequin, broken and soiled. Severin looked from the corpse to the others ranged about the nave: a grimace of mortal terror distorted every face; they sought Severin's own eyes, mutely begging him to do something, to save them; one sank to her knees, shaking, her hands clasped before her in supplication, sobbing and incoherent. The thing ignored her.

"You," it croaked. Severin knew it meant him before he even saw the claw extended toward his head. Great unblinking eyes burned into his, boring into his soul, and the croaking voice (but was it only in his mind?) said, "You shall see to it that my needs are met. Henceforth, you shall govern these – *others.*" Its tail flicked like a finger, pointing to them. "See to it that my provender be supplied, lest I take you in its place. Serve me wisely if you have the merest wisdom; but serve me you shall, in one fashion or another. I am not to be denied, and shall not hesitate to take what I require if it be not willingly, and quickly, proffered me. You others..." and the predatory head whipped about, its glance raking them all as its talons flexed in the air, "shall follow his command as he shall mine. Fail not –you are committed to that from which there is no turning back. There are fates far worse than *this.*" It indicated Levêque's lumpy corpse. "And seek not to hide nor flee from me, for I should find you where you hide, and follow close upon your flight, and none of you can even imagine the storm of my wrath, much less suffer it.

"Now go!" Its voice, like a chorus of demons, echoed through the vaulted room, and through the empty spaces in Severin's mind. A shudder of madness passed through him; he was eager to obey. "I hunger, and would feed.

Go, bring more, and quickly! And take these carcasses with you. Dispose of them, their unclean reek offends me."

And it settled there, great membranous wings folding bat-like, and its eyes half-closing. Severin started, as a man who wakes from a dream, and turned to the others, oblivious to their imploring looks. "Get some garbage bags," he said.

### viii. Something Overheard in a Tenement

As Malcolm laboriously arranged a few appointments for the next day, it seemed to D that time had hideously elongated, the passage of minutes and seconds perversely slowing. Restless and unbearably bored, he peered out at the sun, frozen in place to infinitely prolong this hellish afternoon, and racked his thoughts for a plausible errand he might claim to get himself out of the house for even a little while; yet a suffocating awareness of his faltering hospitality oppressed him, clouding his mind, and he stayed where he was. But in the midst of half-listening to another droning tale of tree planting and cab driving in the Northwest, a happy thought occurred to him, and he interrupted: "You know, I'm sorry Malcolm but I just thought, there's two buildings right around the corner that have apartment-for-rent signs on them."

"Really?" Malcolm said. "Where are they?"

"On Suffolk Street, right around the corner. One on each side, I don't know, maybe halfway down."

"Why don't we go see?" Malcolm said. "Maybe we can look at them right now."

"Maybe we *can't* look at them right now, Malcolm," Becky said. "Why don't you go write down the numbers and call them and make an appointment? Don't you think that would be better than all of us going over there and expecting to be let right in, all maybe for nothing?"

"I'm sure you're right Becky," Malcolm said. "That would be better."

D gave Malcolm the keys, and made intermittent small talk with Becky, who in the lapses sang softly to herself and fussed with her skirt. Malcolm was back in a surprisingly short time.

"We can go look at them right now," he said, somewhat winded. "I talked to the super and he can show them to us now. We don't have to call."

Becky neither spoke nor moved, except to look peeved. Malcolm was still standing.

"We should go now, though," he said. "Because the guy is there and I told him we'd be right back."

Becky looked away. D went to the bathroom and quickly did some more coke. When he came back, Malcolm was sitting by Becky with his hand on her arm, saying:

"Come on Becky, I just think we should go ahead and go now since it's right next door and most of these other appointments are for tomorrow."

When she saw D re-enter the room, she said, "Alright, Malcolm, we'll go in a minute. Just give me a minute to get ready."

She stomped off to the bathroom. Malcolm turned to D.

"We'll go in a minute," he said. "You know, I'm really glad, since I'm going to be in Louisiana, and Becky doesn't want to go there, I'm glad she's going to be in New York where she knows some people, like you."

"I think I'll come with you to look at the apartments," D said. "Out of curiosity."

When Becky came out of the bathroom they went downstairs. The sun was still bright and warm, but a chill was in the air. The usual afternoon dealers were out. Seeing D, they called, "Poison! Poison!"

Becky stopped. "Poison," she said. "What's that?"

"Dope," D said, heading for Suffolk. At the corner, he looked back to see Becky slowing Malcolm to a crawl as she tugged on his sleeve and spoke intently into his ear. When they caught up to him, Malcolm said, too loudly, "Alright, Beck, it's right down here."

D let them pass and fell in behind them, taking care to walk in the narrow band of sunlight. In the shade the day was really quite cool.

Someone was copping in the setback at the daycare. D, daydreaming, relaxed now that he had escaped the claustrophobic atmosphere of the apartment, was surprised when they stopped at the group of men who worked at the tire shop. Oh no, he thought, the super is one of these guys?

"I'm looking for Clay," Malcolm said.

"Just a minute," one said, and another turned his head and called, "Clay! Clay!"

"Just a minute," said one of two men standing together some distance away. D saw him put something in his pocket. In a moment the other man walked away, and Clay came over, a short man but hard-looking and muscular. Chewing gum, he glanced appraisingly at each of them in turn, and said at length, "So you're looking for an apartment?"

"Right," Malcolm said.

"Are you all three, I mean, how many people do you have who want to occupy this apartment?" Clay said.

"Me," Becky said.

"One person," Malcolm said. "My friend here, I'm helping her look for a place. Something nice but inexpensive." He noticed Clay looking at D and said, "We're staying with our friend here who just thought he would come along."

D nodded. Clay gave him a long look that D couldn't interpret, but he looked back at Becky and smiled.

"I have to go in the office here for a minute," he said. "Then I'll take you upstairs."

He turned and walked away. D watched him go past a vacant lot to the next building south where, using a key from an enormous ring that might have held a hundred or more, he opened the door to a shabby storefront whose windows were covered with plywood, and disappeared inside. The door shut behind him.

"Okay," Malcolm said. "I guess we'll go up in a minute."

Becky chewed her thumbnail. With D prodding, they sauntered slowly away from the men at the tire shop, and paused by the empty lot. D, trying to ignore Becky's fidgeting, studied the traces of the demolished structure that remained on the walls of the adjacent buildings, while Malcolm stood waiting as patiently as an ox.

Presently the office door re-opened and Clay returned, and led them back to the building with the tire shop. This tenement looked very old to D, the street door opening immediately onto a narrow staircase, which rose precipitously to the foyer door. Beyond this was a tiny hall, its walls wainscoted in dark paneling, with plaster above, and the doors to the first floor of apartments. Another narrow staircase led giddily upward, its ancient banisters and rails, incredibly, made entirely of wood. As they filed up this stair, Becky said, "Oh I remember this now: this is Charlene's old building."

Though he'd seemed relaxed, Clay stiffened and said darkly, "Oh, you know Charlene, do you?"

"Sure," Becky said. "I've been here before."

At the next floor the landing curved back on itself and they passed several doors, turned, and headed up the stairs again. Clay seemed to have forgotten about Charlene, and was slowly mounting the stairs in the lead with the same relaxed demeanor as before.

"Malcolm, do you remember that story Charlene told us about this building?" Becky said.

"No," Malcolm said.

"Remember? Charlene told us that in one of these apartments these two guys lived, who were gay, and one of them was a lot older than the other, and he got sick, the older guy, and died. The other one, the younger one, was afraid he'd lose the apartment, because his name wasn't on the lease, and so he didn't tell anybody that the other man, his lover, was dead, but instead just put his body in the refrigerator. And nobody knew, until the *smell* got so bad, that finally somebody called the police, and that's when they found out. Because, see, a body won't keep in the refrigerator forever, it'll still go ahead and *rot*. I wonder if that's the apartment we're looking at? Hey!" She called to Clay. "Is that the apartment we're looking at?"

"No," Clay said. He stopped in front of a door on the next level, but had trouble for a minute getting the key to work.

They went in and looked around. The apartment was terrible, narrow and dingy, the kitchen opening left and right onto grim, nearly lightless rooms. A moldy bathtub stood in the corner. D went into the right-hand room, past a loft with a ripped mattress, and pulled open a sort of door, which revealed a filthy toilet of antique design. The wooden floor appeared to be rotting away near the plumbing lines.

D went back to the kitchen. Clay was standing with his hands stuck in his pockets, just looking at the floor and slowly swaying back and forth. Is he high? D thought.

Malcolm and Becky were standing in the other room. Clumsy accordion-style window grates blocked most of the light. Malcolm looked doubtful.

"Well," he said. "It's an okay apartment, I guess."

Becky didn't answer. D maintained a disconnected neutrality.

"It needs to be cleaned up," Malcolm said.

Clay ambled in and said, "This apartment isn't quite ready. We're still doing, uh, some work."

"There's no shower?" Becky said.

"No," Clay said. "Bathtub. Just a bathtub."

"And the management, could they install a shower?"

"Well, they'd charge you for it," Clay said.

Becky pouted and walked past him into the kitchen. Malcolm and Clay followed her, Clay explaining the rental terms. D stood in the dismal room, looking at the wretched place. He had always considered his own apartment a slum, but in comparison it wasn't bad, almost respectable.

He heard the door open and realized they were leaving. As Clay locked it behind them, he said, "The other apartment has a shower stall."

Becky went down the steps speaking in a low voice to Malcolm, with D following behind, peering at architectural details and other curious tableaux. Clay was last, now so carefree and loose-limbed that D was convinced he was high as a kite. That must have been what he had to do in the office, D thought. They spilled out onto the sidewalk and reversed order, following Clay through stopped traffic across the street to another tenement building a few numbers down. This one was larger and of slightly more recent construction, one of those with two storefronts, one on either side of the tenant entrance. Each of these was sealed by a locked steel grate. A long row of garbage cans stood along the curb, and the three steps up to the door were flanked by concrete planters which held only shabby plastic flowers and accumulated refuse: candy wrappers, cigarette butts, paper cups, empty glassines. It struck D that the building was very like the Dope House. They passed quickly through a foyer illuminated by a bare light bulb, and into a broad hallway dominated by the stairs up into the building, a cast-iron stairway with marble steps that reversed at a landing between floors. Each floor had some six apartments, their battered steel doors mounted with a miscellany of knobs and locks, no two alike.

At the fifth floor Clay turned toward the rear of the building and opened what a hand-painted number and arrow designated as number twenty-six. They filed down a narrow hallway, no more than three feet wide but at least thirty feet long, and came into the kitchen. The room was very dim, and Clay went to a breaker box on the wall and flipped switch after switch until the lights came on.

It occurred to D that it might have been better had he left the lights off. The place was filthy, maybe the dirtiest apartment he'd ever seen. It was shocking: he couldn't believe the super would even show it like this. Trash was littered everywhere —old newspapers and magazines and junk mail, fast-food containers of every type, empty beer and soda bottles, some filled with cigarette butts, dried animal excrement, soiled diapers and discarded clothing, bits of shattered plastic and broken glass, plus much more that was less recognizable – and the reeking air, soured with mould and rot, was hardly breathable. A tremendous water stain had destroyed the ceiling above the sink; the damage continued down the wall, passing behind the doorless cabinets. Nearby was a metal shower enclosure, partially consumed by rust, and unpleasantly suggestive of a gas chamber, whereas the refrigerator, door hanging open, stood alone and forlorn in the middle of the floor.

Malcolm and Becky wandered about, exchanging words in low tones. Clay leaned against the wall and his eyes rolled up in his head. Jesus, he's wasted, D thought. What was *that* stuff?

A room opened to the left, and through the doorless frame could be seen part of a large clothes rack made of plumbing fittings and wire. D turned into the room on the right, apparently used as the living room by the last occupants, and was surprised by the view from the window. Just beyond, so close that from the fire escape one might almost reach out and touch it, was the rear wall of the abandoned synagogue on Norfolk Street, which he had so often admired. A Gothic ruin, its picturesque decline had arrested his attention even in this slum neighborhood whose prevailing tone was dissolution and decay, and whose inhabitants pursued their lives like vermin squirming through a corpse.

D was fascinated, his aesthete's eye studying the structure from this novel angle. He was enthused by the great roseate window unseen from the street, with its flanking lancet windows, narrow upthrust arches that must once have held stained glass. In all, the design was pleasing; he admired its emulation of Gothic organization on a tiny scale in cheap brick, the structural elements reduced to surface detail, buttressing functions supplanted by piers in the load bearing walls barely four stories high, the roof's pitch increased to augment integrity. Like something from the Middle Ages, the thing was so soundly constructed that it still withstood New York's terrific forces of entropy. It had burned, for the evidence of fire was everywhere: charred eaves and smoke-blackened window frames, the paint peeled from fire-scorched masonry; yet it still stood, still housed activity, gave shelter. He wished he might have seen the fire, and remembered –a thing he'd not thought of for a long time –the fire he had seen, during his student days, in Baltimore. Near his flat had stood a great English-Gothic church, whose square corner tower loomed over the uniform mass of three-story row houses, a dreary neighborhood of working poor drifting gradually into alcoholism. One frigid December night, a great clamor and din of sirens had drawn D and his mistress –a pale brunette, easily bruised –to a third-floor rear window, where they saw it had caught fire. They sat there watching till nearly morning, rapt by the sure and unstoppable process of destruction and disintegration. Even then, D had known he should never forget the flames licking up the tower's broad stones, outlining in silhouette the four gargoyles at its summit, if if to loose their prisoning shackles and free them from frozen immobility. In the cold dawn that followed, D walked over to see the ruin, now coated with ice, and though the nave had collapsed and the chancel and sanctuary were obliterated, the blackened tower still stood and the frightful silent creatures yet strained at their bonds.

A fluttering burst of wings broke D's reverie: pigeons bolting from the rotting eaves of the synagogue. Clearly they nested within. But he remarked something curious: this building, which from Norfolk presented a dilapidated and condemned appearance, with chain-sealed doors and boarded windows, and which he had assumed was a drug spot of some kind, revealed from the rear unostentatious but definite evidence of repair and rehabilitation. The roof had been patched, along with certain structural portions of the masonry. This completely overturned D's assumptions about the place: no one repaired the roof on a shooting gallery. So who in fact did occupy it?

He moved back and forth at the window, trying vainly to get a better vantage. The synagogue had something strange about it, quite strange, and not entirely comfortable: it exerted a sort of attraction on him. He couldn't stop looking at it, and though he had always been curious about its interior, now he found himself considering possible means of ingress. A narrow walkway ran along the building's southern wall, leading from a high cast-iron gate at the sidewalk and giving access to a low door, sunken three steps down, which must lead to some sort of basement; the relative tidiness of the area suggested this was the entrance in use. Of course the sidewalk fence would be locked; nevertheless, one might climb it, or use a fire escape –*this* building, for instance, had a fire escape. As he peered again at the synagogue's scabrous masonry and rotting ornament, his mind following these thoughts, of a sudden more pigeons burst from some roost in the eaves, fluttering and panicked, their heavy dull bodies crashing into one another as they uttered dolorous squawks and cries.

The place was suddenly touched by malignity, and D had an acute apprehension of menace, all the more startling because without reason or cause –for what was there to fear? He shuddered involuntarily, trying to pull himself together. Yet an irrational feeling persisted that he was standing at the brink of an abyss, an immeasurable gulf of terror and annihilation that waited eagerly to consume him. He looked around, wishing the others would hurry, that they might get out of there. But Malcolm and Becky were talking to Clay, and he felt awkward and ashamed before them, unable to just walk out.

There followed one of those instances of sudden quiet which occur so strangely in Manhattan, a moment when all the usual noises cease and there is nothing but an unsettling void. In that brief pause he heard, or *thought* he heard, a sound, an unpleasant sound like the rustle of great membranous wings, folding and unfolding. He went cold, wanted to get away, but couldn't. And it seemed that *something* touched his mind, probing his thoughts and memories, while he stood helpless. But a siren moaned, car horns honked, the city's normal sounds resumed, and he shook himself. What had it been? But of course it was nothing –nerves –his imagination, playing tricks –his nerves were wound up...

Still, he was ready to get out of there, to go home –and yet he continued to gaze with irresistible fascination at the synagogue. Was that –a *shadow* – against the window? He wasn't sure, but his heart was racing, his mouth had gone dry, he was grinding his teeth. Something moved at the periphery of his vision, and he leaned against the glass, looking down. Two men, faces hidden by hooded coats, had come through the street gate below. They struggled with a heavy burden, something in a black garbage bag, which they carried to the basement door, and with difficulty bore inside. The whole incident was unaccountably disturbing. For the life of him D couldn't imagine what might be in the bag.

"Hey, D!"

D jumped; he turned, flushing. Malcolm stood there.

"Come on, we're done," Malcolm said. D followed them out, moving rather mechanically, and for all his curiosity, he experienced overwhelming relief once they escaped from the place.

ix. The Word on the Street

Waking early the next morning, D rose and dressed quietly, taking his last ten-dollar bill and putting on his jacket. He still felt okay but he had no time to waste. In the middle room, Malcolm and Becky were sprawled on the cushions from the couch; he crept through, trying not to wake them. But Malcolm's eyes opened.

"Back in a minute," D said without stopping, and went out, locking the door behind him.

The morning was cool and bright, just the kind of fall weather he liked, and the street was quiet. Only a quarter to eight: he hoped it wasn't too early to cop.

He intended to go down Clinton but a sector car was at the corner and he went instead to Suffolk; and as soon as he turned the corner he could see the building where he'd had such a curious experience the day before. No one was around, the sun was shining, and in the clear sparkling light the place looked harmless, but D felt again a touch of something dimly sinister, mingled with the strangely compelling attraction that had exerted such a powerful hold on him the day before.

He was still looking back at the building from Stanton, and thinking of walking over to Norfolk and the synagogue, when someone called out, "*Holà!*" He turned, saw Juan-Bautista. "Hey, what's going on?" D said, and they shook hands.

"Ah, you know, same old thing," Juan-Bautista said. "You?"

"Got to see the doctor."

"Me too," Juan-Batiste said. "Listen, I'm short, can you spare me a buck?"

"Listen man, I'm sorry but I'm just barely making it myself, you know?" D dug in his pocket and looked at the change. "I got fifty cents, that help you?"

"Anything will help me, man," Juan-Batiste said, smiling, his hand out. D gave him the fifty cents. "Hey, you tried that Grim Reaper yet?"

"No," D said. "I usually get Body Bag, that's where I'm going now."

"Well, listen man, be careful down there, there's Five-O all over the place. I just saw somebody get busted."

"A sweep?"

"I don't know, I don't think so." Juan-Batiste lowered his voice. "Somebody tell me, I don't know if it's true, but somebody said they found a body over on Attorney Street this morning, early."

"A body?" D said. "So what?"

"Yeah, but check this out. They found it inside a garbage bag. Somebody saw a big puddle of blood, coming from it, and when they open it up, there's this guy. And the top of his head was just gone, man, like it was torn off."

"Unreal," D said.

"And people are saying it ain't the first, man."

"No? How many others have there been?"

Juan-Batiste shrugged. "I don't know. But not the first. So there's cops everywhere." He clapped D on the shoulder. "Got to go, man. Thanks a lot. You be careful."

"You too," D said.

D turned and headed back down Suffolk, alert now and watching for police. What his friend had said was very intriguing but out here you had to stay focused. He scanned the street ahead, peering at the men hanging around on the corner of Rivington, but couldn't tell if he knew any of them or not. Three-quarters of the way down, he stopped at the end of the vacant lots, turned and paused momentarily, as you might to examine something on the ground, and looked quickly back: the street was clear. Sticking his hands in his pockets, left hand taking the ten, he turned again toward Rivington, moving more quickly now. Just then his regular dealer Chris came around the corner, his quick eyes and easy smile on D even as he finished with another buyer.

"Yo!" Chris said. "How you doing, man. Walk with me." D fell in step beside him.

"Got to be careful, it's super hot," Chris was saying. Even he looked uptight –which was unusual. "Five-O all over the place. How many you want?"

"One," D said, "but I'll be back later when I get some more money together."

"Cool," Chris said. They made the exchange. D put the bag in his shirt pocket.

"Listen man, if I was you I'd put that stuff in my underwear, man. Unbelievably hot this morning."

"What's going on?" D said.

"I don't know," Chris said. "I heard that the cops found a body on Delancey or something, but you know what crap people are always talking. Just the Five-O leaning on people, I think. Election year, you know, all that."

"Somebody I know said something about a body –a weird murder, somebody's head torn off."

"Yeah, but come on," Chris said scornfully. "Body Bag, Body Bag!" he called to two Latino kids going past. They stopped.

"I'm going but I'll be back," D said to Chris. "How long will you be out?"

"I'll be here all day, but if it's too hot, look for me in the restaurant. I don't want to take any chances."

"Okay, see you later."

Chris nodded, turning his attention to the two kids.

D walked back to Houston quickly but not hurriedly, with his studied air of nonchalance, and went in the deli below his apartment. He had enough cash left for a pint of milk, but after that he was broke again. But perhaps the check he awaited would come today. He wondered about borrowing some money from Malcolm, but the possibility seemed very doubtful. In any event, there was always the Strand, where they bought books. He began a mental inventory of his remaining library, considering what he could afford to lose –but the thought was like the dread of a recurring nightmare which makes one avoid sleep. If only the check would come.

The counter man and a customer were engaged in a spirited discussion. The rapid Spanish was opaque to D but he thought they too were talking about a death or a dead man: the customer acted particularly agitated, and the counter man interrupted himself only to mumble thank you as he returned a few pennies in change. But D largely shared his dealer's skepticism about the things people said, for the city thrived on rumor and exaggeration, scandal and gore. He went upstairs. Malcolm was washing dishes and the teapot was whistling shrilly on the stove.

"Hey man," Malcolm said. "I'm making coffee."

"Great," D said. "I got some fresh milk."

He left it on the counter, went into the bathroom, shut the door and paused, listening. Malcolm was making a racket, but Becky was stirring, and D turned on the faucet before sitting down quietly on the lid of the stool. He opened the bag and snorted up half the stuff, leaning over against the wall as warmth soothed down his spine, and his nerves eased. The acrid taste in the back of his throat was like a familiar friend. That was fine: he would be alright until they left for their appointments. When he heard Becky's voice, sleepy and complaining, he hoped their first appointment would be soon. Besides, he needed to get back to work. But he couldn't hide in the bathroom all day, and he made himself get up, combed his hair and looked in the mirror. He needed a bath –but not as bad as Becky. He grinned at his reflection, went back out into the kitchen.

Malcolm was pouring out coffee that looked as thick and poisonous as crude oil. "Milk, right?" he said.

"And two sugars," D said.

Malcolm raised his eyebrows and spooned sugar. They took the coffee and went into the middle room, Malcolm serving Becky the way one might a baroness.

"Where did you go, D?" Becky said.

What right have you to question me? D thought, and lied: "I had to go by a friend's studio, and then I ran into a couple people I know. You wouldn't believe what everyone's talking about."

"What?" they both said.

"Murder and mayhem," D said. "Heads torn off, and bodies in garbage bags."

"Oh, just another day in New York," Becky said.

x. More Bodies, More Bags

Trepidant and pessimistic, he opened the door to the mailbox —and the check was there! At last! He opened the envelope as he went up the steps: a business check, for slightly more than he had estimated. Today was his lucky day.

He sat down on the couch, took out the last half-bag and snorted it up as he considered what to do. First, obviously, was to cash the check. He would go to the check-cashing place down Essex, come back and hide most of the money in the apartment, and then go back out to cop. But he found himself looking at Malcolm and Becky's bags littering the floor, and decided to do it all at once and get it over with. If he had to go out while they were here, she would start questioning him again, picking at him and prying. He really didn't want everything just set out in front of Malcolm, after all. Why, he asked himself for the hundredth time, had his old friend had chosen such a vampire for a girlfriend? —but at least she made little pretence of being anything else.

He put the check in his jacket pocket and went out. The afternoon was nice, and he felt relieved at not having to worry about money for a while. He could relax, and do some work —at least as soon as his guests were gone —and thereby generate some more income before this sum ran out. He had plenty of work to do, if left uninterrupted. Of course, things would be even better if he could get his daily life on a steady course. The cycle of feast and famine was wearing him down. Most importantly, he had to temper his somewhat runaway appetites. And he would. But just now he had a bit of a splurge coming —one he had earned, and deserved.

Essex Check Cashing was as dismal and dehumanizing as ever. He waited in the long line of government assistance recipients and day-laborers, re-reading the myriad signs concerning forms of identification and the delays in crediting utility payments, and thinking how it hadn't been so long ago that he'd been unable to imagine how people could allow themselves to be exploited in such a way. But what did the bank charge for its services, the privilege of waiting for days on end before a check might clear? Here you walked with the cash. He and everyone else there willingly paid the maximum allowed percentage to the check-cashing store because each and every one of them needed the cash right then.

Once he had the money he went east on Rivington but the corner at Suffolk was deserted. Was it still hot? Feeling apprehensive, he went on to the Castillo de Jagua restaurant, peered through the door, saw no one there he knew. He kept walking, went around the block: no one. This was bad.

He couldn't just stand there. He kept walking, turned up Norfolk, trying to decide what to do. Chris had said it was hot, and though he had yet to see a cop, or at least a cop in uniform or a car, he somehow felt eyes watching him, following his movements. His skin crawled, and he began to sweat. Something was wrong here. A sort of malaise gripped him, and he hustled on, turned the corner onto Houston, and found himself among other pedestrians, some of whom looked at him oddly. His breath was short, his heart going too fast. Shaken, he tried to calm down, but he could not escape the conviction that something bad had been about to happen, something that he had just barely escaped.

Still apprehensive, he glanced back, and saw the ruined synagogue looming in the midst of the block, its blocked-up windows like blind eyes, sealing out the light. A malignant desolation hung over it like a pall, even in the brilliant afternoon light. And yet...

With effort, he turned away, and headed west toward Eldridge. That was the only possibility left during daylight, and anyway he wanted to put some distance between himself and whatever it was that had disturbed him. He didn't really want to take all that money down to Eldridge, but he had his self-imposed rules, and he stuck to them no matter what. And one of those rules was that you had to trust your intuition.

Just his luck, to finally have some money, and there be no one around, the spots as empty as a desert. He turned south at Orchard, crossed Delancey, and while waiting on the light at Allen discreetly pulled a twenty from the roll of cash, and put it in his shirt pocket. While he was here he might as well get two, who knew, the stuff might be good. He'd bought some of the best dope he'd ever had on Eldridge, while it lasted, and there had been the run of twelve-count bundles –what a happy fluke –but in general the place was just too out of control. After the two sellers he knew had drawn guns over his business, he'd stopped going there with any regularity, and used it only, like now, as a back up. His nerves tightened up as he turned the corner –but it was only nerves, not the sixth sense whose warnings he never ignored, and he went on.

The street was quiet. In fact no one was around at all, and his apprehensions faded before disappointment, and concern: what was going on? But a face appeared in the window of a door across the street, and he crossed between parked cars; the door opened and the seller, who looked familiar, glanced up and down the block, and ushered him inside, saying, "How many?"

"Two," D said.

"Okay," the seller said. "Just a minute." He was still looking out the door.

D wished the guy would get going. He looked down the hallway of closed doors, at the stairs leading to more above. He hated waiting in such places, like a rat in a trap. Let's go, he thought; come on, hurry up!

But the guy didn't hurry up; instead he kept on looking out the door, waiting. D was looking too, past him; they both saw the blue and white sector car turn up the street, and ducked back as it rolled past.

"Whoo-ee," the seller said, rolling his eyes exaggeratedly. "Many police today."

"Yes," D said.

"Many police today," the guy repeated, gently pushing D back and opening the door again. A woman hurried in, Caucasian, older than D, dressed in a shabby overcoat buttoned to her throat. She looked bad: skinny and haggard, very pale. "Hi," she rasped in a ruined voice. "How many?" the seller said.

"Four."

"Okay, just a minute. You have to wait a minute."

What were they waiting on? The cops? It never failed —but D was trying to relax, not even look impatient.

"How you doing?" the woman said to D

D nodded and smiled a little. "How you doing."

"Oh, jeeze," she said. "I need to get straight, I'm sick as a dog. I got the shakes…" and she held out her hand, which was shaking, "…and my stomach is killing me, I feel like I'm gonna throw up. I need to get straight."

D nodded, trying to look sympathetic.

"You know how it is. And I missed my appointment at the clinic so it's twice as bad. Listen," she said, taking a more confidential tone. "You shoot, right?"

"No," D said.

"What? Come on. You're kidding me, right?"

"No," D said.

"What, you mean, you just sniff it?"

D nodded. She looked at him incredulously, as if he were lying. "I don't like needles," D said.

"Huh," she said. "I remember when I used to be like that." She shook her head, peered off into space. Was she remembering? But she looked back at D, and said, "Well listen honey, the reason I ask is I need to go somewhere to fix up. Do you live around here? I wouldn't ask except I can't go home right now. I got my own rig and everything and I don't want to impose but I really need to get straight and I got to go somewhere you know and I can't go home right now."

D felt bad for her, and his natural impulse was to help people, but all he wanted right now was some peace and quiet, and he could just imagine her never leaving, or passing out on the couch and turning blue. He shook his head, appalled by both this pitiful woman and by himself, and lied: "I'm sorry babe but I'm just out at lunch and I got to go back to work."

"Oh," she said, seemingly aware that he was lying and as if she had expected as much. "That's okay honey, I know how it is." She turned to the seller as she took a cigarette from her purse, and said as sweetly as her wrecked voice would allow, "Hey there, what's the hold-up?"

"Just a minute," he said without turning. He opened the door again and another man hurried in. D had seen him before, a nervous little guy in a flannel shirt and a baseball cap, hands in his pockets.

"How many," the seller said.

"One." The guy nodded at the woman, who seemed to know him, then at D. The seller stuck his head out the door, glancing up and down the street, closed it again and turned.

"Wait here," he said, and went down the hall and quickly up the stairs. Finally, D thought. Let's get this show on the road.

"How you doing," the woman said to the newcomer.

"Okay I guess," he said. "Be better when I get out of here."

"Yeah," she said. "I'm really sick, I got to get straight."

"Lot of cops around," he said. Every time somebody said this, D cringed inside. "You hear about what's going down?"

"Must be a sweep."

"No, no," the man said. "You must not have heard. I'm telling you, this is fucked up." He looked at D, sizing him up, but went on: "People getting killed, man. Murdered. Like, really sick shit. Cops have been finding two or three bodies every day for, I don't know, a week, or more. Stuffed into garbage bags and left on the street. Found one in the park, right over here in Forsythe Park, a block down, just this morning."

"Jesus!" the woman said, chewing on a fingernail between puffs on her cigarette.

"No shit. And, like, they ain't been shot or stabbed or nothing —it's like something just tore the tops of their heads right off. Is that fucked up or what?"

"Jesus," the woman said again.

"Fucked up. And, like, I heard that they don't got no brains left, none of 'em got any brains left. Top of their heads torn off and the fucking brains just *gone*. And I heard something else."

The woman and D were staring at him, transfixed by his words, as he glanced back and forth between them.

"The word on the street," he said, his voice hushed, "is that every one of 'em was a junkie."

They all exchanged glances. No way, D thought, his blood running cold.

"Every one of them," the guy said again.

"Shit," the woman said in a small voice.

xi. Norfolk Street Again

D hadn't been home half an hour when Malcolm and Becky returned from an appointment to announce they were leaving to stay with some friends in Williamsburg. It wasn't clear if they'd found Becky an apartment or not; D did not press the question. They made vague assurances of seeing one another again before Malcolm left, and that was it: of a sudden they were gone. D was surprised, not unpleasantly.

He went out and scored a bundle of dope in less than five minutes, stopped in the coke store on the way back, and bought two quarter-grams. Alone once more, he was his own man again.

Quite seriously intending to get to work, he snorted up a fair-sized speedball, sat down at his desk, and sorted through some personal writings. The time was ideal: too often he neglected his own work in favor of what would make money, but now, with the afternoon unexpectedly free, he could devote an hour or two to himself. But he read without attention, his eyes passing over the words while his mind was elsewhere. His thoughts returned again and again to what he'd heard on Eldridge Street. He found himself unable to get the varying but similar rumors he had heard out of his mind, though all conclusion eluded him, seeming to recede just beyond his grasp, like a half-finished thought, or a forgotten name. He made notes, writing down the different versions as he remembered them, but the results told him nothing, banal words that one might hear every day in the city; no coherent meaning emerged, and the whole thing remained as much an enigma as before. The afternoon passed. He knew he should be doing something else, something useful. But this was provocative; his sense of the macabre was titillated; it had such an immediate, personal interest –he always eagerly followed any drug-addiction horror-story – and his usual tendency to boredom was absent. Craving more information, he went down to the newsstand, but there was nothing in the papers, nothing on the television news. Restless, strangely anxious, he paced from window to window, looking out at nothing. Now night was falling, and each of the periodic sirens that normally passed wailing but unnoticed, now suggested the possibility of another victim, and the furtherance of the horror.

Speedball after speedball focused his mind on this curious question in a way normally associated with his intermittent periods of work. In vain, he told himself that in all likelihood the whole affair was ultimately uninteresting and a waste of time, not to mention potentially dangerous. The most likely explanation was that the murder spree was the work of some serial killer, one whose sheer volume of crimes would lead to early apprehension, and quick oblivion. Now, D was largely uninterested in true crime stories, and if in fact the reported demographic of the crimes were true, he was a potential victim. Caution and prudence suggested that he forget the whole business, and get back to work. But something in all this troubled him, and wouldn't leave him alone. And for no good reason, or none that he could articulate or even clarify in its outlines, it seemed to have begun for him with his visit the day before to that horrid tenement on Suffolk Street.

At length the room grew so dark he could no longer see. He turned on the lights and closed the blinds, sat down on the couch, and mechanically chopped up another line of cocaine. In broad daylight one might both relish the talk on the street, the accounts so curiously at odds yet not exactly contradictory, and dismiss it as hearsay and imagination, concocted and exaggerated by the chronic paranoia of drug addicts. But with the fall of night, certain disquieting notions, not yet well formed or very clear, arose in his thoughts, and impressed themselves with all their force. A sort of conviction had taken possession of him, and however baseless or irrational it might seem, it would not be denied. No: something else was at work here, something monstrous and uncanny, which surpassed the common reckoning of things and events. *What* it might be yet eluded him, for he lacked enough positive information to even begin to construct a theory. The whole was still too incomplete, the few indications aberrant, more or less unreliable –although they could not for all that be dismissed, no more than could his presentiment, and intuition. But he had *felt* it, a malign influence so strong, it were foolhardy to deny it. What was at work here was something truly outside his experience, some violation of the normal, an irruption of irrationality.

He sat quietly for a time, staring uneasily into nothing, as acceptance settled gradually through his mind, coloring his thoughts anew, and giving them a logic and an inevitability they had not known before. At length, compelled by something he hardly understood, he got up, and looked about for his jacket. He had spent his life in weird reading and arcane studies, in assiduously following little-traveled paths, in delving the obscure by-ways of the nightmare city, and here, at last, he had stumbled upon some festering, noxious horror. It was as if one of his own stories had come to life. Such an opportunity might never present itself again; he couldn't waste it. He would go see what he might learn. Turning for the door, he hesitated a moment, sat down on the edge of the sofa, and quickly cut up another speedball –to fortify himself and steady his nerves. The harsh powder bit into his nostrils and he got up again, and went out.

As the front door closed, the street's hustle and noise enveloped him. With no real plan, no clear idea where he was going or what exactly he intended to do, he turned toward Norfolk Street. Best to return to where the previous day it had all begun for him: the ruined synagogue. After all, that was the key, wasn't it? –the key that might unlock the whole affair. For why had he received such a curious impression the first time, from his vantage in that scabrous tenement? And why had experienced such a strong presentiment of danger when, unthinkingly and unawares, he'd walked past the place? And what was the heavy, lumpish object –carried in a *garbage bag* –which he'd seen those men struggle so to carry inside?

He went down Suffolk, turned west on Stanton, slowing his pace as he neared Norfolk. Thinking it best to survey the situation from across the street first, he crossed to the west side between parked cars to the dim and shaded sidewalk next to the elementary school. The block was deserted, as it almost always was. The synagogue came into sight; he felt his stomach tighten, a lump appeared in his throat, but now he was more excited than afraid –as if he had entered into some weird fiction, and none of this were real.

The prospect, however, was rather unremarkable. Viewed from the front, the building was utterly lifeless, evincing no sign either of the curious repair work that might be glimpsed from the rear, or of the sinister activity D suspected within. Instead it presented the same appearance of decrepitude and vacancy that it always had: here were the same blocked-up windows; heavy steel doors, padlocked shut, still sealed its arched entrance doors; the same heap of trash and refuse lay reeking at the foot of the steps behind the high medieval-styled wrought-iron fence. Dark and silent, the place was exactly the same as it ever was, the wreck of a once-lovely structure abandoned and left to rot. He walked slowly past, trying to dissimulate his interest, although he felt obvious and exposed. But he didn't see how anyone could be watching him –and indeed now he doubted, felt less certain, though he had been so sure; he knew less than ever what to think. From the street side it hardly looked like the same place. Was he wrong about it all? But those men had gone *inside*… Was this rather the perfect façade, an appearance of neglect and inactivity that masked the awful reality behind? He continued up the street, keeping an eye on the place but seeing nothing more, stopped at the corner of Houston, unsure what to do next, and turned west. But it seemed unwise to loiter near the corner of

Essex, and he turned back, retracing his steps, wondering if he'd already been noticed. But he didn't know what else to do.

Going back the other way, he saw no more than before, though he took the east side and went right along the front fence. Dawdling past, he tried to open his mind to whatever awful influence harbored within. The impression of malignance had been so strong, the other times –that sense of awful and impending *menace*. But now he felt nothing, nothing at all. What did it mean? Was he wrong? Yet his conviction remained: despite all appearances, something was going on within there, something hidden, secretive –and ghastly. Only in Loisaida, he thought, where the studied indifference of others was absolute.

He turned the corner –as unwilling to linger, as he would be to hang around at a dope spot –and went a block west on Stanton, to avoid the dealers who operated on Norfolk north of Rivington, then stopped again at Essex. Dope was everywhere –ahead, Hangman and DOA, to the left Grim Reaper, to the right the corner he had just left. He turned back, trying to find an approach, to do anything besides just walking the street, hoping something would happen. The night was extraordinarily quiet, and he recalled with a little shudder that, reportedly, all the victims of the killings were junkies. He asked himself if perhaps he participated in the unfolding of his fate; was he implicated in that which might destroy him? But nothing about the idea was really new. Very well: if from the street he could learn nothing, he would go back to where he had received such a disturbing impression the first time: that leprous tenement. He turned, explicitly accepting the risk, and headed back the way he had come.

The evening air was growing cooler. As he walked, he considered various means of ingress, but it didn't matter, luck was with him, for a couple just ahead turned up the steps, and he simply followed them inside, smiling and nodding thanks as they held the door. They stopped before a door on the third floor and he continued on, taking a nonchalant and neutral air. Pausing for a moment at the fifth floor, he considered the sinister apartment whose door yet seemed to guard some malevolent secret. The idea of going back *there* both revolted him, and exercised a powerful attraction, an evil allure. But he recalled with regret, mixed with relief, that the junkie super had locked it behind them, and as he deemed it prudent not to go about trying closed doors –at least not yet –he proceeded on up. The sixth floor closely resembled the fifth, but after another flight, he found himself at the door to the roof, which, though mounted with a heavy fire-exit lock mechanism, was standing conveniently ajar. He slipped through, careful to not let it shut behind him, and was on the roof itself.

The sky's vault arched overhead, its deep blue but little pierced by stars, and the traffic noise was muted like distant surf. He picked his way across the roof, clambering over tar-covered obstructions and ridges, trying to tread lightly lest his steps be heard below, and crouched by the rickety fire escape ladder, gripping one of its pitted and rusting supports as he peered over the roof's precipitate edge. From there, quite motionless, he stared down for a long time at the synagogue, scarcely even breathing.

Dark, utterly silent, the structure looked smaller from this height, shrunken and hollow, like the shell of some creature long dead. In the gloom, he could see little of what had struck him on the day before. Now his impression was of something subtler, of quiescent horror, like the merest trace where something had passed, something –*loathsome*. D had never experienced anything like it. He wondered: had others noticed it? How had they explained it to themselves? Or had they simply fled from it –as his own instincts urged? But instinct and reason alike had become unimportant before the fascination he felt, and the steadily mounting excitement. If only he could be sure… Uncertain what to do next, he crouched there, watching and waiting, hoping for something to happen.

He didn't know how long he'd been there when a man appeared at the sidewalk gate, opening it with a key and passing through. D held himself quite still, wondering how visible he might be from seven stories above, but the man hurried along the passage without a glance upward. To D's surprise, he passed the low door to the basement, turned the opposite direction, and passed through a narrow walkway behind the adjacent tenement to a door in the next building to the south, which D had not noticed before, and disappeared inside. D was intrigued.

For some moments nothing else transpired, and at length D rose and moved along the roof, intending to identify this second and seemingly associated structure. What he saw surprised him, one of those rare anomalies in lower Manhattan: a hidden building. Obviously quite old, and only four stories high, it was buried in the middle of the block formed by Houston and Stanton on the north and south, and Norfolk and Suffolk on the west and east, without fronting on any of those streets. This holdover from previous and now-obliterated street boundaries had stubbornly resisted the imposition of a subsequent pattern already at least a century old, and was left imbedded within a grid of more recent construction. Its location was perfect, ideally suited to serve whatever covert purpose or end that sheltered in the synagogue behind a façade of ruin and decay.

The appearance of two more figures at the synagogue's street gate startled D, and he ducked back before he could think that it might perhaps have been better to stay still. But these two, a man and a woman this time, moved to the basement door quickly and quietly, perhaps to avoid attention themselves, and failed to notice him. Nevertheless, D's heart was pounding – for such secretiveness unnerved him, and he had already begun to speculate somewhat wildly on what might happen to him were he to betray himself and reveal his clumsy surveillance. Thereafter he did his best to remain absolutely still as yet more shadowy figures arrived; and these, alone or in pairs, moved as silently as wraiths between the walls below, to vanish down the steps into the synagogue.

Aside from some ambiguous thumps and a shuffling-like step which might or might not have come from within the place, he had yet to hear any sound emanate from there, and it was still silent when he perceived that a dim light, weak and unsteady, now filtered from the great rose window, a faint glow whose source could only be candlelight. His suspicions, however inchoate and vague, were in some sense confirmed: something was taking place here, however little he might be able to guess its nature –furtive activity that occulted itself, masking both its workings, and its ends. He felt sure now, although he had seen nothing terrible or even overtly illegal, that all this strange, clandestine conduct was linked to the dreadful rumors on the street; yet this very certainty traced a chill of fear along his spine.

The door to the hidden building opened. He hesitated for a moment, more loath than ever to be discovered, torn between apprehension and curiosity; but his desire to know prevailed, and he rose cautiously, to peek over the parapet. As he stared, gooseflesh rose on his skin.

Below, emerging from the hidden building, two men were struggling through the doorway with a lumpish burden, something like a rolled-up carpet, but perhaps even heavier, that seemed to move on its own a little, as if it contained something alive. For a long moment, they were clearly outlined in the harsh fluorescent light from within, before the door slammed shut. D squinted, trying to pick them out of the gloom, shadowy forms whose grunts and shuffling footsteps were disturbingly clear, then saw them again as they crossed the passage to the street before bearing their burden down into the synagogue.

Now horror took hold of him. It was a body; there could be no doubt. He had seen too well to deny what that dreadful bundle held. They were transferring a body –a *living* body –from the hidden building to the synagogue – but why? He couldn't think about it, he had to get out of there –and he turned away, reeling toward the stairway, revolted by a world in which such things might be. His own steps ringing in his ears, he glanced back, irrationally afraid of some pursuit already behind, and tripped noisily on a tar-covered ridge, just saving himself from falling on his face. But he gained the door and staggered through like a drunken man, going down flight after endless flight of steps, past halls and doors as the echoes pursued, until he found himself alone and out of breath at the bottom of the stairs.

He stopped, breathing hard, straining to catch any sound from above, but the place was as still as death. What now? He told himself to get away, go home. Yet he was strangely afraid to go outside, and lodged the inner door open before peeking fearfully from the outer one. He had no idea even why he was afraid. After all, no one had seen him, and it was only a block or so back to his own building. Still, he hesitated, trembling slightly, unable or unwilling to move, until he saw a woman approaching with key in hand, obviously about to enter. Apprehensive, he went out, thinking that if she had come for him, he would get clear into the street where he could make a run for it. After she entered with only a semi-curious glance at him, the door slammed shut with the clash of a closing tomb. He fled around the corner onto Houston and back to his own apartment.

After a dose or two his nerves steadied; he even felt rather ashamed of himself. What kind of reaction was this? He'd lost his nerve, and left the task unfinished. What had he learned? —nothing. Irritated, he paced up and down the room. Only a few minutes had passed, twenty-five or thirty. He still had time —time to go back, to find out what was taking place. Norfolk Street: he would try that side again; perhaps he might see something there. But going out on the street was like stepping into a hallucinatory dream: he didn't feel sure of what he was doing, which alarmed him, and made him feel vulnerable. Nevertheless, he was calm, very calm, though this was probably due as much to the last bag of dope as anything. But what mattered was that he concentrate — and he made an effort to put his radar up, to muster all the caginess, the crafty focus of purpose he had learned in a thousand games of cat-and-mouse played with the police and the narcotics squad.

But, of course, on Norfolk Street nothing had changed. He stopped in front of the synagogue, near the passageway, listening, but he couldn't hear anything beyond the usual street noise from Essex and Houston. He hesitated, unsure of himself, almost doubtful now of what he had just seen. But he looked at the gate, and remembered, or thought he remembered, that the first man to enter had unlocked the gate, whereas those following simply passed through. Disconnectedly, he saw his hand reach out, as if it belonged to someone else, and push the gate, which of course opened easily at his touch. For a moment he did nothing, only now realizing that he hadn't quite wanted this to happen. But the way was open. Now it was only question of his nerve.

He glanced quickly up and down the block: still quiet. The passageway gaped open; what madness lurked there? Mouth dry, he slipped through and pushed the gate shut behind him. An open padlock hung to one side. He left it alone. Curious thoughts passed through his mind, only to vanish.

He scuttled to the corner of the building, but then moved slowly and cautiously along, one step at a time, acutely conscious of the sound he made. Away from the streetlamps, it was very difficult to see. The walls soared up closely on either side, framing a narrow strip of sky, and the windows were far overhead; he would have to go around to the back. Above, a pigeon stirred, flew away. Tiny rivulets of sweat ran down his temples. He thought he heard a sound, a sort of muttering, indistinct; he kept going, picking his steps, trying not to betray himself. As he reached the back, the sound clarified itself: voices, chanting together. The words, unfamiliar and strange, were in no language familiar to him. He thought he discerned the pattern of some ritual: it had a formulaic, incantatory quality, and cycles of repetition, like a responsory. Now the leading voice wavered, become weak —or fearful? He strained his ears, trying to listen, but now he noticed a smell, pungent enough to penetrate even his numbed and shattered nostrils, and he was surprised at what it recalled to him – the heavy, dank stench of the reptile house at the zoo.

His mind reeled; awful possibilities presented themselves to him. There came again that sinister rustling he'd heard from the tenement, as of great wings folding and unfolding, terrible in its suggestion of tremendous span. Now, at last, he was truly afraid. Why had he come here? —so that whatever devil or nightmare that stirred about inside these walls might discover him, rip off his skull, and tear out the brain? Yet in his heart he still didn't believe it. Would anyone have? So he skulked for long minutes in that narrow brick chasm, as in a lightless abyss between worlds of madness, turning over in his mind the few and unlikely options for getting a look inside; as all the while the muted chanting continued, and the reek of reptile intensified, seeming to congeal in the air about him. He was trying to recall what he had read on those sects whose rites centered on snake handling and speaking in tongues when the chanting reached a sort of crescendo, and abruptly stopped. In the silence that followed, he distinctly heard a grating shuffle suggestive of considerable bulk, and a sibilant respiration, decidedly inhuman. There came a thick snap as when a tree branch breaks, followed by a curious sound as of something being torn open. No one could have mistaken the sound that followed: heavy jaws snapping, tearing flesh and engorging it.

He lost his head then –forgot all need for stealth, overwhelmed by the irresistible compulsion to run away. Afterwards, he couldn't remember, was never quite sure how he had gotten home.

xii. The Horror in the Box

He'd been up all night, pacing from one end of the narrow apartment to another, now obsessively looking from the windows, and now shunning them, lest he be seen, though by *whom* or *what*, he couldn't have said. Dawn came, as he was running out of cocaine; a bundle of dope too was almost gone, and soon he'd either have to get some rest, or go out and cop some more. He knew he should forget about it all, and sleep —but he *couldn't* —couldn't get it out of his mind, for even a minute —and at length he simply gave in to it. He'd suffered such demonic urges to keep going before —up all night and on through the day —but the morbid fascination that now held him in its grip had less to do with the drugs, than with the ruined synagogue and the lurking, malignant horror it concealed. So as the eastern sky brightened and the pale streets filled with light, he snorted up the last lines of cocaine, put some money in his pockets, and went out.

Traffic was already busy along Houston, small swarms of cars moving past, trucks rumbling heavily along, double-parking to make deliveries, and the few people on the sidewalks were bleary-eyed and irritable, hurrying toward the subway. D let them pass, and fell in behind. When he turned down Norfolk, the street was deserted: the school wouldn't open for another two hours, and no one else was visible for blocks. He had a little time.

The synagogue loomed before him, mute and sardonic, leering from blocked-up windows. At the sight of it, he keenly recalled what he'd seen and heard the night before, and fear touched him, a cold finger tracing his spine. He had abrupt second thoughts —this was madness, what was he doing here? —but he shook them off, kept going, slowing down as he passed the front doors, listening intently. But now there was nothing. For a moment, he had a vague sensation of being watched, though by whom he couldn't tell, and he dismissed the sensation as a nervous reaction. In fact the block was desolately quiet, and he could hear the traffic behind him with odd distinctness.

The gate opened at his touch —as if it had been left open for him. He went through, closing it behind him again, his heart beginning to pound, and crept down the narrow space, newly strange in the early morning light, pausing here and there to listen intently. As he neared the back of the building, sounds drifted down from above: mingled voices and laughter, the clatter of dishes, the cries of infants and small children in the apartments above. He shuddered: unknown to everyone around, even those in the closest proximity, hidden by the anonymity of the vast city, some malefic horror festered here —festered and hungered, fed and grew strong. And it might go on and on, indefinitely, for it seemed all too likely that only D even suspected that the synagogue was where it lurked.

The east wall soared above him, a reversal of the first perspective he'd had, from the tenement on Suffolk, in the crisp light its decrepitude strangely beautiful. No one was visible in the little tangle of interior courtyards. Very nervous now, for who knew when they might return, he went down the steps and examined the basement entrance. The doorframe was badly weathered and decayed, and the door itself flimsy, cheap laminated wood; it had no deadbolt, and apparently only locked by the button on the inside handle. He took out his driver's license, inserted it lengthwise next to the knob, forcing back the bolt, and pushed. The door opened. The building was quite dark inside, and what little light filtered in only accentuated its obscurity. Feeling as if something stopped his breath, he stepped through the doorway that gaped wide for him like an open mouth.

He found himself in a broad empty space, the air cool and musty. There was a box of candles next to the door. He took one and lit it, stuck another in his pocket, and then, sure it was best to conceal his entry, he reluctantly shut the door.

The way was clear along the south wall, and he turned this way, holding the candle high and listening carefully, although he felt somehow sure no one was there, that the building was for the moment unoccupied. A disused hall took up most of the basement, which held little more than some refectory tables and chairs, a battered desk, boxes with jumbled papers and files. The place reeked of mold. Ahead, through a door in a partition wall, a corridor led toward the front, doors opening from the interior walls: a water closet, an empty storage room, and a second, transverse corridor, leading to a private study or office. This cramped, windowless room was clearly in use: here was a great wooden desk, piled with papers and books, two battered chairs, and a coat stand, from which hung a heavy robe, like a vestment. A metal filing cabinet stood to one side, drawers ajar and files stacked haphazardly on top, and one whole wall was lined with shelves, crammed with battered and worm-eaten books. These on examination proved to be an astonishing collection of esoteric and arcane writings –the rarest of tomes, forbidden and proscribed. D was stunned: among them was the *Book of Dyzan* and the *Liber ivonis*, the *Seven Cryptical Books of Hsan*, ex libris Columbia University, as was the *R'lyeh Text*, a coverless copy of *De Vermis Mysteriis*, von Juntz's *Unaussprechlichen Kulten* in the Düsseldorf edition, and much more, some of which D could not even identify. For the most part he had never seen such books, had in fact doubted their very existence. He moved to the desk, where, its spine broken, lying open to one terrifying page, was a crumbling copy of the *Dhol Chants*.

His mind reeled as he struggled to come to terms with the horrific reality that this room exposed. That these books in fact existed was already a revelation, but the obvious implication was that the cult employed them in its degraded rites. This opened new vistas, dissolving distinctions he'd long held as to what was real and what fiction; it shook his hold on reason and sanity. Staring at the open volume, the bizarre symbols and characters wavering in the wretched light, he turned a page, then another, but the thing had a vile and loathsome feel beneath his fingers and he took his hand away, the leaves returning to their original place.

His eyes fell on a small box next to the sinister book, and he bent closer to examine it. Intricately carved, from some wood whose like D had never seen before, and in perfect condition, it had nonetheless an air of incredible age; its design, moreover, was indescribably bizarre –alien and unearthly. The thing was repulsive, even nauseating, yet D felt an irresistible urge to touch it: unable to stop himself, he saw his hand stretch forth, his fingertips brushing the curiously warm surface. Then –it must have been his nerves –the box seemed to *twitch* beneath his touch. He snatched his hand away, recoiling in horror and glaring down at the thing.

But this was ridiculous. He turned to the door, irritated. How absurd! – and he was wasting time. There was nothing here; some shelves full of old books meant –nothing. And yet his eyes returned to the horrid box, repugnant but fascinating.

At the end of the corridor was a stair, soundly repaired and solid beneath his feet. He mounted to the main floor, and found himself standing at the entrance, now sealed with heavy steel doors chained shut. From here spiral steps continued up to a narrow balcony above. Sunlight filtered in, and he moved toward the altar, blowing out the candle and letting his eyes adjust. The place was quite empty; there was nothing to see. The interior was gutted, the evidence of fire everywhere, scorched brick and blackened plaster, though the floors were neatly swept. Two of the ceiling's heavy spandrels were missing, and the great roseate window was terribly damaged. There were no pews or furniture of any kind. He proceeded slowly, looking for any evidence or clue, some trace of the nightmare cult that lurked in this forsaken place, conducting its ghastly rituals, but found nothing, nothing at all. Even what served for an altar was merely an old packing crate. The copious stains on the wrecked wooden floor might as easily have been made by water as by blood. Only once, as he stood alone in the chancel of this pitiful wreck, did he catch the odor of something unclean and vile –but then it vanished, and he wasn't sure if perhaps he hadn't imagined it. He was tired after all; he'd been up all night, come all this way, and found nothing. He didn't know whether to be disappointed or relieved. Though he'd expected more, wasn't it better after all that he hadn't found it? It was time, perhaps, to re-evaluate the whole affair.

He stood looking about at the crumbling walls, the shattered roseate window, just now touched by the morning sun, its flanking lancets boarded up, as blind as the orbits of a skull, and it struck him that it was all like so much else: when you reached the center, the very heart of it, there was nothing there. Of course, he was coming down now, and beginning to feel quite low. Time to go, he told himself; no matter what secretive cult the place harbored –and, were it not for the curious books he'd seen, he'd have been inclined to think it something perfectly banal –he didn't want to get caught here by anyone. Time to go home, and get some sleep.

He relit the candle and made his way back down the stairs. Anxious to leave –clearly the wisest thing to do –yet he paused near the study, thinking of the books. He was reluctant to leave without at least examining them once more, carefully; this might be the only opportunity he would ever have to see their like.

Kneeling by the shelf, trying to make out the titles in the feeble light, he was astonished anew. He opened a photostat of the *Eltdown Shards*, but the text was baffling, unlike any language he had ever seen, and he replaced it, took instead the tattered copy of Prinn. This was the little-known Latin edition, published in Prague in 1809, an impossibly rare volume. Beside it stood the *Cultes des Goules*. His first love was French, and he'd long been curious about this aberrant and discredited book, written in a tortuous and decadent style, and filled with the most depraved, noxious ideas. He opened it to where a slip of paper marked the page:

> *Or, il n'est pas le cas que toutes les clés soient irréparablement perdues. Bien des clés physiques ont péri avec le temps ; mais il en reste d'autres, dont la nature est plus éphémère, et liée à la rite. Certainement, même à nos jours, il existe des adeptes capables d'ouvrir les portes, si seulement ils ont assez de force. Les portes sont éternelles et les Convives attendent patiemment par-delà. Il suffit que la porte soit ouverte et l'invitation faite, pour que le Convive passe à travers.[1]*

This was disturbingly suggestive, and seemed to bear directly on the problem. Now, clearly, he would have to read this book, for it might unlock the whole enigma. But he felt nervous, alone here in this isolated room, unsure how long he'd been there, and concerned lest someone arrive and discover him. He would have to take the volume along, photocopy it, and somehow return the original –for were its absence noticed… He set it carefully on the desk, scanned the shelves for anything else. There: the *Liber Ivonis*. This book, bound in curiously smooth, tanned leather, was of uncertain provenance, though it likely reproduced the Latin text printed in Rome in 1662. After a woodcut frontispiece, sadistic and revolting, and a title page blank but for the name, the text simply began on page one. D read:

> *Mundi finis ad nos venitus est. Mors sors hominis. Morituri omnes amplexum sepulchri et basium vermum scient. Sunt autem isti qui non pereunt. Fatum istis tolerantia est et perdurant manentque. Aditus ad istos clausus est quamquam olim apertus, necesse igitur remanere est. Sed si vir audaciam magnam scientiamque habet, si*

---

[1] But in no way are all the keys irretrievably lost. Many of the physical keys have perished with time; but there remain others, whose nature is more ephemeral, and linked to ritual. Certainly even in our day there are adepts capable of opening the doors, if only they have sufficient strength. The doors are eternal and the Guests wait patiently beyond. It suffices that the door be opened and invitation made, for the Guest to pass through.

*omnia audet praesumitque, via iterum aperta de parte nostra erit, ut manentes transirent tamquam diutissime antehac.*[2]

Shuddering, D put the volume on the desk with the *Cultes des Ghoules*, and took off his glasses, passing a hand over his eyes. He was tired, and in a suggestible state, undeniably more and more uneasy. It was time to go. He stood, taking the two books, but the candle had burned too low to hold. He lit another, but when he reached for the books again, he saw, next to them, the dreadful box. He looked at it, aware that it frightened him, yet somehow subject to its weird and powerful allure. Holding the candle close, he bent over it again. The thing resisted comprehension, remained as baffling as before. Indeed, his mind felt dulled in its proximity, and he had to force himself to concentrate, to study it: a rectangular box, approximately six inches by four, three and one-half deep, made of an unfamiliar wood, dark and close-grained, with corners and hinges and a simple latch formed from some unidentifiable metal, and of curious design. Its decoration —and here D's descriptive and analytical powers failed him —was of indeterminate provenance, related to no style or tradition with which he was familiar, and not even clearly definable as abstract or figurative — yet for all that, appallingly grotesque, and profoundly disturbing to look upon. D could hardly take his eyes away, yet it shocked and dismayed him. Like something in a dream, and though mindful of the previous experience he'd had, he saw his fingers stretch forth, pass over the thing gently, caressingly. Did it not still seem warm to the touch? Or was that but his own feverish hand? Somehow compelled, he took it up, examining every surface, then returned it to the desk. His fingers went to the latch: it would open easily. He felt a powerful

---

2 Upon us the ends of the world are come. Man's lot is death, and all shall die, and know the embrace of the grave, and the kiss of the worm. Yet there be those who do not die. Their lot is patience, and they abide, and wait. The way is closed to them, where once it was open, and so must they wait. But if a man have courage, and great science, if he will dare, and risk all, the way may be opened again, from this our side, so that those who wait might pass through again, as they did in time immemorial.

impulse to open it —but he resisted, apprehensive, afraid of what he might see. And yet he wanted to know… For a moment he wavered, but the urge was too strong. He turned back the latch, opened the lid. Inside, on a cushion of something like velvet, was a tiny figurine. D brought it close; the vile thing made his flesh crawl. That it represented some sort of *creature*, he could not doubt, but a creature so obscene the mind could scarcely support it —a blasphemy and an abomination. He had never seen anything so execrable; the accursed thing blasted his soul.

From overhead there came a heavy thump, followed by a sound like the shifting of a large bulk over the floor, and something else: a rustling in the air, as from vast, membranous wings folding and unfolding. D froze, listening: it came again. Trembling, he put the box back on the desk, staring down stupidly at the insane, repellent figurine even as nightmare moved restlessly about above his head. A certain odor began to filter to his nostrils. He felt as if he were falling, plunging wretchedly into the void, as the winds of the abyss whispered atrocities in his ears, blighting his reason. His will almost consumed, only some last access of sanity made him slam the box shut. He reeled, moaning as in pain, snatched up the still burning candle, and fled panicked from that hellish place.

xiii. Finis

He should have been working. D knew that. He certainly needed to be working, and thereby earning some money, for what little he had was draining like sand through his fingers. Inquiries awaited an answer; he had final corrections to make on a translation that would pay upon delivery; two express packages sat unopened. He had dutifully sat at his desk in the afternoon, but now, as dusk turned to night, he had done little more than sort through a few papers and stare out the window.

He had now been up for much of the forty-eight hours since his guests' departure, wired on speedballs, and fatigue was contributing to his perverse inability to concentrate. Or, rather, to concentrate on anything but what was rapidly devolving into an obsession. Time, money, his responsibilities and work, had all assumed a certain unreality since his excursion to the synagogue the day before.

Nevertheless, that adventure had itself become somewhat unreal. He had replayed what he remembered in his mind till it had grown stubbornly mute, the memories so familiar that they resisted all effort to make them reveal any new detail or association; and he had proposed so many interpretations that he ended by becoming lost in them, unable to discern the plausible from the fantastic, or deem one theory more likely than the rest. He could think of nothing else, and now he knew only that he had to go back there –that very night.

He had to know. It came down to that: he had to know. The initial trip had taught him nothing, however suggestive it may have been. He'd found nothing, so, in fact, he knew nothing. At one bad moment the night before, he'd almost called the police –had the phone in his hand, ready to dial. But what could he have told them? And so he hung up. He hadn't *seen* anything – which meant, for all his suspicion, he was as ignorant as before. But he had to know, and he intended to find out –and thus he was going back there, that night.

Before going out, he put an extra bag and a straw in his jacket, just in case. He had a pocket flashlight, as well; its illumination was steady, and he could turn it on and off quickly. Calm, wired-out but quite calm, he felt ready for whatever might come. Quite by chance he had been drawn into a terrifying enigma of bloodshed and horror. But had he not always believed that there existed more in the universe than that which man knew? This *thing*, whatever it was, this blasphemous secret, hinted at in those terrible books, and apparently all too real in its appetites, proved that he was right. And in the unfolding of this dark mystery, he had found his own rôle: the scholarly recluse turned investigator, driven not without shuddering to seek out a cosmic malignity beyond mere evil. Such an abomination might perchance only be exposed by a man who, having spent his life in cryptic and arcane studies, was singularly prepared to unlock such an hideous secret and gaze upon the nightmare thus revealed.

Once on the street he felt focused, clear, able to grasp every detail around him. Up till now, only one approach had proved successful, and that was the front. He would have to try it again; were it locked this time, he'd have to climb the fence. He was going back inside: if they were there, he would surreptitiously observe; if not, he would hide himself, perhaps in the balcony, to await their return.

At Norfolk the block was deserted. He stopped before the synagogue, listening. To all appearances it was not just quiet but empty, vacant —for the moment. He was nervous now, apprehensive and unsure, but he had to risk it; there might be no better opportunity.

The gate was locked. He looked up and down the street, saw no one, and began to climb. The fence could not have been more than ten feet high, but it made hard going, for he wasn't athletic, and he had forgotten to change his shoes, he was wearing loafers. As he scrambled over the top, he thought he heard steps. It startled him; his foot slipped, he slid over and down, metal biting his hands; his knee banged the fence, pain slamming through him. He scrambled, found a toehold, and lowered himself to the ground, looking around. There was no one, he'd imagined it, but his knee hurt badly; he could hardly put his weight on it.

He crept down the dark and silent passage, favoring the leg. All was quiet. Pausing at the corner, one hand palpating the aching kneecap, he peered around in both directions, but he still sensed that the synagogue was empty, that for the moment he was quite alone. The opportunities that presented themselves now sent a rush of adrenaline through him, racing along his nerves and exhilarating him more than any drug. His fear was gone; it was as if he'd never been afraid. He slipped down the steps and tried the door: locked. He jimmied the door as he had the first time, took out the pocket flash and shut the door behind him, enveloped now in the most perfect silence. Passing again through the corridor, he mounted the stairs, continuing past the deserted main floor, and up the stairs to the balcony. Here he had to move with care, for they had not been repaired, and appeared unsound. The balcony itself was entirely ruined, one whole side so decrepit it might have fallen in at any time, and D was sure it could not support any weight whatsoever. He crept forward along a relatively substantial area, wary and alert. Though it held, every step, every shift of weight or position produced a betraying amount of noise, and left the fire-scorched, powdery wood splintered and pulverized. From the balcony's edge, he could see the altar perfectly, but given the angle, D was apprehensive, lest he be too visible here; he moved back. He had to choose his spot with care, for once *they* returned, his slightest movement might be detected. At length, he settled in to wait.

But it was uncomfortable there, the air musty and hard to breathe. Time crawled, and he wished he had brought some cocaine; he was beginning to doubt this plan; he might wait there all night, and they never arrive. At length he began to feel rather foolish, sitting alone in the dark, and the hasty, ill-considered aspects of the scheme weighed on his mind; abstracted, he took out the bag he'd brought along, and snorted up half of it –without, however, feeling much relief. Finally, after more than an hour, convinced that no one was coming, he stood, dusted himself off, picked his way to the stair, and went down.

He played the light through the shell of the nave, indecisive and out of ideas; the void mirrored his thoughts. Doubtless he should leave at once, and watch from the street, or even go home, and consider the night a failure. He turned away, descended again, dismayed by the ready crumbling of everything that he had, after all, just as facilely constructed. But once in the basement, he thought again of the books –those rare and forbidden volumes that he'd forgotten the first time in his panic. Like the siren's song, they exerted a greater attraction than ever. He could take them with him now, carry them away; he would have no better opportunity. After a moment's hesitation, he turned again toward the study.

The two volumes were just where he'd left them, on a corner of the desk, as was the hateful box. D was both surprised and relieved: apparently no one had noticed their displacement. Seizing them eagerly, he would have left right then, but for the thought that he might have missed something precious. Quickly: he turned again to the shelves, playing the light over the grimy, flaking spines, admittedly feeling some misgiving, and determined to hurry.

And he *was* hurrying, scanning the titles, and pulling out a book here and there to page through it, seeking the illustrations and plates, or checking its edition or provenance —when he heard a sound, distant and muffled. Unable to identify it, he froze, holding his breath and listening hard, but it was not repeated. After some moments he told himself, gratefully, that everything was okay. But now a fresh noise, clear enough this time and all too close, imposed itself and disallowed every doubt: footsteps, more than one person, moving through the passageway between buildings, headed for the rear of the synagogue. D's heart began to pound, and sweat broke out all over him. He stuck the book he'd been examining back on the shelf at random, and rose up, trying to think: if they went on, to the hidden building, he'd get out and away immediately, but if they came into the synagogue itself... How had he let himself get caught in here? And he thought desperately of the empty room, but he couldn't make it, he hadn't time.

Now the steps grew faint, and he eased the door open a bit —to hear with horror the sound of a key in the lock, the basement door opening. He was cornered —trapped! —and now afraid for his life. Enervated, feeling as if his legs might fold up beneath him, he looked about despairingly for a place to hide. Behind the desk? —useless! What would they do if they found him? Faltering, paralyzed, he stayed where he was, frozen by fear, hoping against hope that they would pass by, and go up the stairs. As they came nearer, the beating of his heart grew louder and louder, so that they must hear it, and fall upon him; he tried to hold his breath, but his ears were ringing, and he felt he might pass out. Time slowed, as his doom came close upon him. But the steps passed by, and mounted, shuffling, to the main floor of the synagogue.

Weak with relief, he swung open the door, determined to get away. But now there were more sounds outside: others passing in turn between the buildings, headed for the basement entrance. He closed the door again, realizing now that they were assembling, doubtless to perform the ceremony. He didn't even know how many of them there might be. But that was nothing before the fact, now abruptly clear, that he was trapped in the only room of the building that might serve as a repository. And he looked with horror at the *Dhol Chants*, lying open on the desk, and next to it, that awful box containing the loathsome figurine.

Time elongated fantastically. Listening with dread as footsteps trudged past, proceeding to some appalling and loathsome rite, D sweated in trepidation, lest one of those who passed unseen should turn his way and come upon him. It was not pleasant to imagine what would result. Yet strangely, inexplicably, in the midst of all his terror and dismay, his thoughts turned again and again to the horrid box, and its frightful contents. Long moments passed in contemplation, a sort of reverie, which began with the box, and its idol or god, but then transcended it, as if vast new dimensions were unfolding, strange but alluring, an unsuspected cosmos of wonder, and delight. He forgot how many of the cult he had counted, or how long it had been since the last had gone by. Instead, he turned from the door, snapped on the light, playing its beam about. The sight of the box made his blood ran cold, some part of his mind cognizant of what horror fascinated him, but he couldn't help himself, no longer had real control of his actions. Stepping closer, he stretched out his hand, filled with an irresistible desire to open it and gaze upon that which was within, although he'd never seen anything more abhorrent.

He took it up, holding it under the light and looking once again upon its frightful, alien carvings –repelled by them anew yet horribly aware that his will had quite ebbed away, like that of a dreamer who cannot awake, who cannot make himself awaken. Even as his fingers sought the latch, the box pulsed and squirmed with febrile life. But his fear was fading now, vanishing before the dawning recognition that his sole great purpose in all eternity was to open the hateful box and set free that which was cruelly, wrongly imprisoned within.

The lid opened easily; his enthrallment deepened, intensified. His soul tumbled –away from the sane world –through the box, as through a trapdoor – falling and falling –past whirling mad planets and black nightmare suns –cities of doubtful geometry –the dust and ruin of immemorial civilizations, dead for millennia –on and on, through ghastly realms of gibbering, noisome horror.

This trance, if such it were, might have prolonged itself indefinitely, slowly emptying his soul and voiding his reason, had something not reached him; as if roused from a drugged, unwholesome slumber, he came to a thick and torpid wakefulness. Was it the apprehension of a dank, reptile-like stench? Or a *whoof!* of hell-black wings, beating, slowly beating in the void? Or was it the muted cries of terror and dismay, which passed with difficulty through the ceiling, from the synagogue above? Or was it the sound of footsteps hurrying down the corridor, approaching quite near now?

D reeled, as on the brink of an abyss. The door opened; the light of a candle fell into the room, and he heard a cry. Startled, he turned guiltily, the box slipping from his fingers. He saw a tall man, powerfully built, dead eyes framed in a grimace of surprise and anger, as the box fell to the floor, its ancient wood smashing irreparably apart, the figurine tumbling away into a corner. The tall man stared at it; a horrified, piteous look crossed his face. D hesitated, unsure what to do, for the other blocked the door. But the cries above had turned to screams of agony and death, amidst other noises, still more terrible: the tearing of flesh and bone, and a crushing and grinding, of monstrous, powerful jaws. They both froze, listening, but the tall man turned murderous eyes on D. "You idiot," he whispered.

He lurched forward, powerful hands reaching for D's throat. D dodged to one side, flinching away, and the other man missed him, his momentum throwing him off balance. D shoved him, hard, and the other crashed into the shelves, knocking books and papers to the floor. Adrenaline racing, D jumped for the door. He scuttled down the corridor, blindly crashed through the next door, desperate to escape from that maddening place of nightmare and its hell-spawned occupants, and hurled himself toward the rear of the building, smashing past obstacles, bruising arms and legs. Above, the screaming, like a chorus of damned souls, mounted to a climax of suffering and terror. The disembodied sounds followed hard on D's heels, threatening to coalesce and engulf him; his reason was almost unhinged, a state of which he was morbidly aware; he gabbled words and phrases, incoherent: "Hurry... Can't... No!"

Fumbling open the door and staggering through, he pulled it shut behind him, as if it might do any good, and stumbled up the steps. His heart was hammering like it would burst through his chest; he gulped in the cool night air. The screams were still audible —at least to him —couldn't anyone else hear? He had to get away —but now *something* rattled at the gate, barring the way to sanctuary, and sanity. "No," he said in disbelief —but the gate was thrust open. He heard a shout.

Time elongated aberrantly, every moment crystallizing like an element precipitated from solution. He glanced around, desperate; no good, he was trapped. Was his life not running out, as the last few grains of sand fall through an hourglass? He had one chance, just one —heavy steps coming toward him, crashing through the passageway —one chance: the fire escape of the tenement opposite, whose ladder dangled just out of reach and which led up the rear wall of the building which he recognized now, appalled, as 157 Suffolk.

He could climb or die —of that he was certain. He scrambled across the obscure and narrow space. The ladder was partly extended, its lowest rung only a few inches beyond his reach, apparently rusted in place. He had never been physically strong, but now fear goaded him on, madness shrieking in his ears, and he made a running jump, grasped the bottom rung, and pulled himself up. He got one foot on the bottom rung —and this alone saved him —when the ladder suddenly broke free, plunging toward the ground with a sickening lurch, and banged to a stop at the end of its span. The rasp and clang of metal rang through the air. Somehow D held on, though the jolt racked his bones, the pitted rung to which he clung tearing the flesh of his hands.

Appalling noises followed close below and behind him. D shook himself and climbed wildly, like a frightened monkey, gaining the second floor and wriggling through the open space to the landing. Running up the stairs without looking back, heedless of the noise he made, and concerned only with getting away, he passed apartment after apartment, some lighted and awake —here and there a curious or frightened face peered out at him as he went by —others dark, their windows closed, staring like blind eyes. The flights seemed interminable.

Feet ringing on the metal, he struggled upward, hauling himself along by the rail, forced to greater effort than he'd ever made before. But at what must have been the sixth floor, the stairs ended; leading further up was only a metal ladder, the very one from whose summit, now above him at a sickening height, he had first spied on the synagogue at the beginning of what was clearly the single most foolhardy endeavor of his life. Winded, gasping for breath, he paused on this landing, and took a terrified glance back. Below, at a vertiginous depth, the synagogue had gone horridly, deathly quiet, and he could see nothing. He turned away, began to climb the rickety ladder to the roof.

The steps were an awkward distance apart, and as he heaved himself up, away from the relative security of the stairs and landings, he felt horribly exposed, like a fly crawling over the wall. Swearing that if he got out of this, he would never do anything so foolish again, he visualized his escape: over the parapet, through the roof door, down the steps, to run like hell for home. Never, in all the times that, his pockets stuffed with narcotics, he had walked past the arrogant and knowing scrutiny of the New York City police, his radar scrambled and nerves screaming —never had he so longed to get home, lock the doors, and hide himself from the dreadful, nighted city.

But from somewhere behind him came a great *whoof!* —as if hell-spawned wings of terrific span beat in the night air. He gave a start, and his feet —slickly shod in the loafers he had idiotically forgotten to change —his feet lost purchase. He slipped, nearly fell, holding to the ladder with all his strength. And for a moment, a moment only, he glanced back.

Now —even as his feet scrabbled for a rung, and he hauled himself up the last few feet of ladder that banged and creaked as its struts pulled at their straining screws, threatening to tear free and send him plummeting to the ground below —were matters not clarifying for D into a reality too insane for belief and yet too dreadfully real to be denied? As he threw himself over the last rung and between the uprights onto the roof, stumbling, falling, staggering up again, and reeling toward the roof hatch and the door to escape below, had not the answers to all the ill-conceived questions which had led him here suddenly revealed themselves? Had not mundane, inadequate logic collapsed, obstinate denial wilted, had not nightmare burst from the bonds of sleep and erupted all about him into awful, horrific existence? For in that one glance back, even as that appalling *whoof!* repeated itself again and again, beating on the wind and wafting toward him that squamous reptile odor, what he had seen looming in the night air had shocked him profoundly, and shown him what it was to be truly afraid. Those leathery, hell-black wings! Those rows of teeth flashing in a greedy, gaping maw! Those talons like curved knives, flexing in anticipation! And those eyes –those burning, lustful eyes! "God help me," he murmured. But no help came. Stumbling, he fell again, pain stabbing through his wrists; he scrabbled heedless to his feet and ran on.

Now he was at the roof-hatch door, and he flung himself upon it with a sob of relief, so blind with terror that he did not even see it was closed until it refused to budge at his frenzied grip. Shut –locked from the inside –and he wasted precious seconds tugging at it in disbelief, a curse dying on his lips as the fact of his doom sank in. *How could this happen to him?* And his mind skated on the edge of madness till a black shadow rose above him, blotting out the stars.

"Goddamn it!" he screamed. He threw himself over the edge of the next roof, a drop of several feet, and landed heavily, shattering pain tearing through his injured knee. Picking himself up, he stumbled on, limping and gasping for breath, the air all about him full now of that loathsome stench. With a *whoof!* something hooked his jacket and jerked him back. He wriggled free and staggered on, feet unsure, leather soles slick on the unseen tar roof. Behind him –*whoof!* –came an accelerating beat of hell-black wings. Dope, he thought (comprehension flashing through his mind –useless now –the time left to him running out –last seconds ticking away, one by one) –it wants dope. Maybe it's hooked now –strung out –it needs a fix. He thought with dismay of all the cheap and potent drugs that had gone *whoof!* –No! –up his nose –*whoof!* –headed straight for his brain –*whoof!* –gram after gram of bitter white powder saturating the cells –*whoof!* –No! (last precious seconds slipping into the void) –and his mind screamed, *Why don't you feed your own goddamn habit!?!* There was a little breath of air behind his neck —*whoof!* —something brushing past —*whoof!* —just that close! —and he realized that was exactly what it was doing—

# Rock-n-Roll Will Never Die

They were glitterpunk nobodies, superstarlets of the Lower East Side, hierodules of rock-n-roll: Dreamwhip. They were a chick band but they played so loud and hard that nobody could say they didn't rock. Besides, they were hot as hell, the guys' teen creem dream: four babes laced into skin-tight PVC-jeans and hot-pants, stuffed into lacy push-up brassieres and spiked bustiers, adorned with great feather boas, fishnet stockings, star- and skull-dusted scarves, cheap 'pearls', fake jewels, hoop earrings, bangles, leather bracelets and anklets with rings or locks like sadomasochistic restraints, they stomped across the tiny stages in spiky 'dom' heels and shiny thigh-high boots that encased lick-me legs; and with their teased hair, sometimes under top-hats or Nazi officer's caps, their gorgeous eye-makeup and false lashes, their scarlet or black lips full with promise of exquisite delights –maybe for *you* –it was a near-overdose of glamour. At their shows, couples quarreled, guys got into fights, or stood open-mouthed, gaping at the one they'd most like to fuck, or imagining themselves with two, three, the whole band. For Dreamwhip was pure sex onstage, the focus of an overloaded feedback circuit of raw lust. Their music –'maximum glitter-punk', like a '70's muscle-car blown, supercharged and painted metalflake pink –might have found an audience on its own; but when the guys saw them perform, saw these half-naked super-sluts manipulating their guitars, saw the singer, Koy-Toy, stroke the microphone squeezed between her double-D breasts, shaking her hips to the beat, and stretching her tongue down to *almost* lick the bulging metal head –then a sort of delirium shuddered through them all, a hot flush of desire, expressed here and there in grunts and muttered curses. Dreamwhip were stars –of the noxious, decaying slum from Fourth Avenue to Avenue D, 14th Street to Delancey.

It wasn't enough; they wanted more. They wanted the fame that had first lured them years before: the stardom you saw in fan magazines and on TV: money, gold records, limos, screaming fans; expensive clothes, expensive guitars, expensive drugs; a big house, fancy cars, a swimming pool. They wanted to cut an album at the Record Plant, or out in Hollywood somewhere. They wanted to play Madison Square Garden, be on the late shows, the cover of *Rolling Stone*. They wanted it all.

In many ways, they were just like most bands. They argued and fought, nursed grievances, formed shifting alliances, struggled for control of various issues. They were together too much to really be friends, though after a good show, or when getting loaded, they grew sentimental, made declarations of loyalty and affection, swore undying vows. The rest of the time, no one really trusted anything that anyone else said, and some questions were subjected to intense analysis, with confederates in the band, or outside confidantes. Not one was exactly as she seemed: the singer propped up her confidence on a mounting heroin addiction, now mainlined, to save money; the guitarist had constructed a mask of cool intensity copied from record album photos, which hid a natural bookishness and an Ivy League degree, as well as a profound shyness; the drummer maintained a rigorous barrier between the band and her private life, in which she staggered painfully toward the bitter end of an affair with a much older, married man; and the bass player –and this was the greatest difference between Dreamwhip and other bands –the bass player was a vampire.

*               *               *

"Backstage" at CBGB's amounted to just two dinky rooms, one slightly larger than the other, right behind the stage, usually just a place to leave guitar cases and coats and stuff —but after the Dreamwhip show backstage was packed, with more people trying to crowd in every minute, and everyone was talking at the same time, convinced that whatever he or she had to say was very important. Koy was trying to talk to three people at once —a middle-aged woman with a background in management, who said she was interested in booking the band; a big guy in a Hawaiian shirt, very patient, whose card named an indie label she'd never heard of; and a pimply kid in an NYU shirt, stammering his admiration —when a message came from the doorman.

"Yeah, he's on the list," she answered.

"Your list is full," the guy said. "Over-full. And the show's over."

"Well, ah, we'll pay for it," Koy said. "Let him in —please." Fucking JT, she thought, turning back to the others. He missed the whole goddamn show.

She could see Kaci Valentine and Trish Trash, putting away their guitars. Kaci's back was turned, but Trish was sweaty, her makeup had run, and she looked tired. Some guy was hitting on her, but she was smiling, a little. In a minute the two guitarists joined Koy, still trailing fans, looking for their boyfriends. Barbi Crash came over.

"Good show," she said, hugging each of them. "I've got to go... See you Tuesday, huh?"

"Yeah, sure," they said. "Good show."

When she was gone, Koy said, "There she goes again."

"Where do you think she goes?" Trish said.

"Oh, it's got to be some guy," Koy said. "The question is, why doesn't he ever come to one of the shows?"

"Ha! Come on!" Kaci said. "No one's ever seen him."

"It's her mystery date," Koy said. "He must be really cute, that's why she doesn't want us to meet him.

"Here," she said, handing Kaci and Trish each a stack of printed cards.

"Passes for our show at the Bunker. Try to give them to people you don't know, just don't let anybody from CB's see you." She looked around, spotted the pimply kid. "Check it out," she said to him. "Free passes for our show at the Bunker. Bring some friends." She winked at him, and made her way toward the door, working the crowd.

"Jeeze," Trish said. "It never stops."

"That's right," Kaci said.

Dizzy squeezed his way in, wearing a tuxedo coat and looking like the king of the punk-rock prom. He pushed his way through to Koy. "Hey, good-looking," he said, kissing her on the cheek.

"Hey yourself, hot stuff," she said.

"Can't get enough," Dizzy said. "Wow, you really had them going."

"Thanks," she said. "How was it, really?"

"It was a good show," he said. "It rocked. The sound was good, and loud. And you were smoking. The mic thing was great... like watching a porn star, or something. Except that you're *much* better looking than any porn star."

"Mmm, you're such a doll," she said and kissed his cheek again. Trish joined them. Koy said, "Trish, where'd you get such a good boyfriend?"

"Found him in the trash," Trish said. She pinched Dizzy, kissed him.

"Good show," he said to her.

"Yeah?" she said, frowning.

"Oh, yeah!" he said. "It rocked. The crowd was really getting into it."

"Did you hear my mistakes?"

"Did you make any?" he asked. "Is this a trick question? Oh, and you looked great, I mean it, *super* hot."

She just smiled –unconvinced, but skeptical as well of her own doubts – and brushed her lips over his ear, making a kissing sound.

The room was thinning out as JT came in. He nodded hello to various people, before making his way to Kaci. "Hey, babe," he said. "Guess what, the house is empty. The Gobstoppers are playing to an empty room."

"No way," Kaci said. She told Koy, who was passing by with the record guy.

"Everyone left after us," Koy said.

"Listen, I'm sorry I was late," JT said to Kaci.

"Oh, that's okay," Kaci said. "Did you see much of the show?"

"Well, not as much as I wanted to."

"How was what you saw?" Kaci asked.

"Oh, you really had them going," he said. "It was rocking."

She just looked at him. Where had he been? She was sure he had missed the whole thing. It was always so obvious when he was avoiding the truth. She glanced around and flushed: Koy was looking at her, pity on her face. JT, turned away, was talking to some guy he knew. You bastard, she was thinking. Can't even make it to the show. How could he treat her like this?

Koy went out, saw Trish and Dizzy watching the other band. But they were terrible, and Koy walked through to the bar. The place was almost empty: a few people standing at the front, and two homely rock chicks at a table –band girlfriends, probably. Thankfully, there were only a couple songs left in their set. When they finished, Koy applauded a little, to be nice, then went to find out what they'd get paid *this* time. This was the part she hated; they needed a manager, somebody who *liked* arguing with people. Maybe that woman she'd talked with –let her get them a gig, and see what came of it. But if not her, *somebody* –somebody who'd take care of all the shit, and let her concentrate on what was important: being a rock star.

\*                 \*                 \*

The cabbie waited while Barbi loaded her drums into the hall. They were always twice as heavy after a show. When she finally got them upstairs and stacked in a corner of the tiny apartment, she collapsed on the sofa, exhausted, her ears ringing. At times like this, she couldn't listen to music –she'd had enough of that –and she couldn't put up with the television. She would have preferred to just crash out, but she was too wound up; after a show it took a while to relax. She flipped through a catalogue that had come in the mail, and tossed it aside, bored. But he'd left her a message before the show, wishing her luck. On impulse she called him back.

"I told you not to call me at this time of night," was the first thing he said.

"Is she there?" Barbi asked.

"No… Well, yeah, but she's asleep."

"So what's the problem?" Barbi said.

"I can't take any chances."

She found herself wheedling just to get him to talk for a couple of minutes. She felt disgusted with herself but she couldn't stop. In the beginning he had been the pursuer. Now she suspected that he had come to regret the affair, or anyway would prefer to keep it all entirely at his own convenience. It was maddening, and she found herself responding in ways she never could have imagined herself doing –before.

He asked about the show, then didn't seem to listen. Abruptly, at a pause, he said, "Look, I have to get off the phone. Are you free Tuesday night?"

"Well, not really," she said, taken back. "I mean, Tuesday is our practice night."

"Oh, that's right," he said, then went on crossly: "You never have any free time, you're always busy with your band."

"What?" she said, abruptly angry. This was too much! "I have more time than *you*," she said. "You're *married.*"

After they hung up she was proud of herself for a while, the way she'd tried to wound him by spitting out the hated word like an insult, but the feeling faded and she just felt ridiculous –childish, even. After all, she'd known that almost from the beginning.

*              *              *

"Now for the glamour side of rock-n-roll," Dizzy said as the cab pulled up in front of their building on East Houston. Trish paid the fare as Dizzy shifted the stuff inside from the sidewalk –all except for the big cabinet, which took both of them to move. Once they'd gotten off the street, they carried it all up the two flights to their apartment on the third floor. The cabinet with its eight ten-inch speakers was always last, as no one could possibly steal it, but it had no castors, the handles crushed your hand, and it felt like it weighed two hundred pounds. They stopped, out of breath, on the second floor. "Not far now," Dizzy said, leaning on the banister.

"I can't wait till I have roadies," Trish said.

"I can't wait for you to have them, either," Dizzy said. "Then I won't have to carry your stuff."

When they finally got it all upstairs, Dizzy flopped down on the sofa and turned on the TV. Trish wandered around, walking from room to room, still wound-up from the show. From the kitchen, she called, "Do you want a drink?"

"Sure," Dizzy said. "Whatever you're having."

When she brought the drinks, he was cutting up a big line of cocaine. He snorted it up, took the drink from her hand, and sipped it. "Do you want a line?" he asked her.

"Maybe a little one… It's late," she said. "Don't you have to work tomorrow?"

He shrugged. "Oh, sure. But I promised myself this back at CB's and I'm going to have it now."

He cut her a line. The cheap coke bit into her nasal passages.

"Jeeze," she said. "That stuff burns."

"Yeah," he agreed. "It's kind of harsh. I got it at the candy store up Avenue B. The count is good but it has that gasoline taste." He did up another line and drank off half of his drink in one go. "Ahh," he said, and grinned.

"So, tell me, what did you think of the show?" she said.

"It was good," he said seriously. "It was a good show, better than that last show at the Bunker. It was tighter, and of course the sound was better. I think we need to work on your sound: there's a lot of bottom end, which is good, but not enough definition; it gets muddy or rumbling at times... I wonder if we should add back some highs on the EQ." He went on, as always analyzing and critiquing every aspect of the performance, meticulously and thoroughly, all the while cutting more lines and snorting them up. In a few minutes he finished his drink, and interrupted himself to say, "Hey, you want another drink?"

Trish looked at her half-full glass. "No, you go ahead," she said.

He came back in a minute with a drink that looked like ninety per cent alcohol, and went back to both his analysis and the bag of cocaine with equal enthusiasm. Trish found herself getting sleepy; her eyes kept closing. The night was catching up to her. When he paused to snort another line, she said, "Hey, do you think we could talk about this some more tomorrow? I'm feeling like I might need to go lie down."

"Sure, that's fine," he said. "You look tired. Go ahead, I'll be there in a little while." He stood up, went to the closet. "I think I'm going to do a bag. I'm feeling wound-up."

*                    *                    *

JT wheeled Kaci's amp out to the street, Kaci following with her guitar and bag of stuff. She felt tired and dirty after the show, and the cool night air was welcome. A cab was waiting down the block. They flagged it, loaded the gear in the trunk and climbed in. Kaci sank into the seat.

"Man," she said. "I am so tired."

"Yeah," JT said.

The night streets slid by and they were there in minutes. When they got the stuff upstairs, she went in the bathroom. She looked terrible: her makeup had run and her hair was stringy and limp. She brushed it a little and washed her face, without much improvement. She gave up, went back out. JT had turned on the TV and was flipping through the channels. "You want a drink?"

she asked.

"Yeah, sure," he said.

She made two drinks, brought them back out. JT kept flipping channels; you couldn't tell what was on. She stared at the screen for a while, not really watching. Finally she said: "So how come you were late?"

"Oh... my mom called. I had to talk to her."

"Your mom called? At eleven o'clock?"

"Yeah, well, she's worried about my sister... You know."

His little sister was reportedly doing poorly in college, partying all the time and skipping most of her classes. But his mother had never once called after eight o'clock at night.

"So what's up with your sister?" she asked.

"Oh, it's just more of the same."

"And your mom is upset?"

"Well, yeah! I mean, I think she just needed to talk about it, you know. So what could I do?" He looked at her: "Anyway, I'm sorry I missed your show."

She just nodded, thinking, So he's no longer even making a pretence of having seen any of it.

"So how did it go?" he asked. "I mean, how did you feel about it?"

"Oh, okay," she said, talking despite herself. "The set went well, but Trish had problems with her sound again, she just doesn't seem to have it together with her equipment. Koy forgot the words to the new song again, just like the last time, and besides she was so late it was almost time to go on before she got there. And my playing, I don't know, it was so-so... I botched an intro, a couple leads didn't go right, I had trouble staying in tune..."

He looked bored, didn't really seem to be listening. She trailed off, irritated, but sick of her own self-criticism and anxieties. What was the point? Nothing ever changed: the others never learned from their mistakes, just kept repeating them; and she too felt stuck, going around in circles, never making any progress, never getting better.

On the television, late-night-show idiots, fatuously self-confident, were blabbing as if they were the most fabulous things on earth. Incredulous, she watched for a while, floored by such arrogance and self-conceit. What was wrong with her, after all? Why couldn't she have a little more confidence?

But JT had begun to snore. She got up, went in the kitchen, about to make another drink, but stopped herself. What was the use?

*   *   *

Koy-Toy was lounging on the sofa in the living room of her crummy little apartment on Delancey, the TV on, while she enjoyed the first flush of her post-show fix. She wasn't really paying attention to what was on, it was just background noise as she floated in warm well-being thanks to the two bags she had fired into an ankle vein. But a funny commercial came on, a sex line: "Hot co-ed nymphos can't wait to hear from you," a lascivious voice declared, and she giggled, lit a cigarette. Phone sex: what a boy's fantasy. But wasn't she selling pretty much the same thing? Nympho rock star Koy-Toy and her band of bitches will suck and fuck you dry. And that's why they loved her, all those sweaty boys stretching their arms toward the stage and shouting hoarsely...

But the show came back on and she thought, Wait a minute, what time is it? Already after one; she got up and went in the bathroom to put away her works. Johnny would be there soon, he got off at one. He'd felt so bad when he told her he had to work that night, that nobody else at the pizza place would cover for him, and he would have to miss the show. She'd tried to sooth him, saying she understood perfectly and he shouldn't worry. Maybe it was for the best: afterwards wasn't always a good scene. Sometimes after a Dreamwhip show, he could hardly control himself, he was so hot for her; but more often he was sullen and morose, victim to some absurd jealousy he fought unsuccessfully to control, as if he couldn't stand all those other boys looking at her and getting hot for her. And yet wasn't that why he wanted her for himself? Really he could be such a child sometimes; still, for all that, he was so sweet.

\*                    \*                    \*

Trish and Dizzy's apartment was a rock-n-roll/horror-movie junk heap in a tenement on Houston, near Avenue B. Like a voodoo hut, everywhere were little skulls, toy monsters, shrunken heads, incense burners in the form of curious idols, oddly-shaped mirrors, innumerable candles. A couple of guitars were always sitting around, and a stack of weird books no one had ever heard of, and the TV was usually on –they just turned the sound down if the stereo was playing.

The night after the CBGB show, Dizzy was sitting in the living room playing the guitar when Trish got home. "Check this out," he said. "It's called 'OD'd on You'." He played a chugging riff, at the change singing:

> *I'm overdosed on you*
> *Overdosed on you*

over and over, before going back to the chugging part.

"What do you think?" he said.

You could never tell much from these early demos. Sometimes in the beginning they were horrible but turned into good songs. Sometimes they never went anywhere.

"It's cool," she said. "You can do something with that."

"Yeah, maybe," he said.

"That's all you've got, right?"

"Yeah, right now… It's just a beginning."

"Right," Trish said. "Well, I think if you want to use it, you should finish it yourself. Don't give it to Danny to finish, you know, the lyrics. Not after what he did to *Too Tight*."

"No, you're right," Diz said. "You know, we don't even play that any more."

Trish just looked at him.

"No, I get it," Diz said. "You're right."

"So what's up?" she said. "Are you guys practicing?"

"Yeah," he said, getting up and putting the guitar in its case. "In fact, I better get going or I'm liable to be late."

"Not be the first one there, you mean?"

He gave her a look.

"Sorry," she said. "I don't mean to rub it in."

He got his stuff together, put it by the door, and came back for a bag from the stash. "So what are you doing tonight?" he asked her.

"Oh, Koy wanted me to call her so I'll probably do that... I might practice a little, watch some TV... I'm still pretty tired from last night."

He nodded. "Okay, I'll see you when I get back."

Traffic was quieting down on Houston and the sellers were coming out. As he passed by, he could hear them chanting: "Poison!" "C and D!" "Works! Sealed!" He crossed Allen, stopped at Sal's and bought two slices. The pizza wasn't the best but it was right on the way. He ate one slice before he got to the subway, stuck the other one in his bag and went down into the station.

The platform was empty. That wasn't good; had he just missed a train? He ate the other slice while he waited. Gradually a few other passengers came down but the train was taking forever and he was already late. When it finally came, it was almost full, as if there'd been a delay, and he pushed his way on with the guitar, ignoring people's evil looks.

At West 4th he could see the lights of a train he'd missed, disappearing uptown. He put his stuff down to wait, wondering if the others were already there. Another train came quickly enough, though by the time he got to midtown it was getting dark. He hustled the two blocks to the building and took the elevator up. But the door was locked: no one else was there.

He went in, put his stuff down, looked at his watch: half an hour late, and he was the first one there. He opened up the windows, and after a minute went back out in the hallway, into the adjacent bathroom, and snorted up half the bag, then looked in the mirror, trying to distract himself, and not feel irritated before the others even arrived. But it was hot, even hotter than in the stupid room, which despite its two large windows on 8th Avenue, always seemed airless and stifling. May as well get ready, he told himself. That way when they finally get here you can go have the other half bag while they set up.

He pulled the half-stack from the closet, turned it on to warm up; got out the various cords, the fuzz box and wah-wah; tuned up his guitar. Still no one. He plugged into the Marshall, played a couple chords and adjusted the tone, then cranked out the new riff he was working on. But it sounded terrible, he wasn't sure if he could do anything with it, and in a minute he flipped the amp to standby, set the guitar on a stand, and, after hesitating a moment, sat down on the windowsill to wait.

Traffic was light down below, moving slowly but steadily up the avenue. He regretted not having a book; he'd meant to bring one, but forgot; from now on! He could probably read a book a month in the time these idiots made him waste.

A couple of rock-n-rollers came around the corner and he looked down, trying to see if he knew them. He couldn't tell from five flights up but he thought one of them was that red-haired guy, the drummer T-Bone knew... That guy was a good drummer, a real rock-n-roll drummer, who laid down a good beat without a lot of fills and shit every other bar. He knew what to do and he did it. And Diz began once again to muse on one of his most common daydreams, the 'supergroup'. Every band he'd been in since he came to New York –even those with the most promise –had been crippled by one or two members, for any of a number of now-predictable problems: flawed musicianship, poor taste, bad attitude, lack of team spirit, wrong look, drug or alcohol abuse... And such people simply repeated their mistakes even as they moved from group to group, wrecking one band after another. One day it struck Diz that the answer was to put together a 'supergroup' –musicians who were a proven quantity, who already had it together and would do their job right. That drummer, for instance... And he already knew a couple of bass players who looked great and played what you wanted to hear on bass, but for whom –for whatever reason, but usually because of the other people in the band –things just hadn't worked out. The big problem was a singer. That was

91

hard to find: it had to be somebody good, with experience, but who didn't have an impossibly huge ego…

He heard a noise at the door, looked at his watch: an hour late, they were finally there.

*       *       *

At the rehearsal studio, the clock was already running. Kaci got there five minutes early –typically she was ten minutes early for everything, but she hated hanging around the studios, where the guys stared and mumbled stuff to one another –and found Barbi Crash already there, talking with Jeff, the manager, about something they'd seen on the news. Kaci didn't watch the news: it was depressing and you couldn't do anything about it anyway. She had other things on her mind.

But now at ten past, they were still the only ones there. Jeff set the levels on the PA, checked the mics, and very patiently walked Kaci through the use of the recording deck and the video cam, had even loaded it and left the whole thing on pause. Kaci set up her gear, tuned her Les Paul and adjusted the Marshall, cranking out a few riffs and messing with the knobs, trying to get a decent sound, while Barbi ran through the kit, shifted it around slightly, and then sat quietly without banging on it –unlike most drummers –just waiting with that angelic patience that was mostly so endearing. They made small talk and looked at each other through the viewfinder on the video cam, and Kaci was retuning her guitar when at a quarter past Trish Trash rushed in, all flustered and apologizing before she even got through the door, "Hi you guys, I'm totally sorry but I couldn't get a cab," and blah blah blah. "It's okay," Kaci heard herself saying although what she really wanted to say was, Why the hell can't everyone just get here on time? "Koy-Toy's late too."

Trish was getting out her bass. "Well, at least I'm not the last one here," she said, like that made it better.

"How you been, Trish," Barbi said sweetly.

Exasperated, Kaci turned away. Why the hell did Barbi always have to be so nice?

Trish was telling some stupid story when Koy-Toy finally walked in, twenty-five minutes late.

"Hi darlings," she said in her superstarlet voice. "I'm *sooo* sorry I'm late. But I just couldn't help it. Do you hate me? Don't hate me." She was rummaging around in her bag. "Listen, you're really going to hate me but I might have to leave early."

"Koy!" Kaci said, pissed off.

"I'm sorry, love, but… well, it's work, I might have to work."

Kaci's cheeks flushed. "Goddamn it Koy, you're already half an hour late and we're paying thirty dollars an hour for this room!"

"I know, I know," Koy-Toy said. "I'm sorry. And I'm not sure, it's just that I might have to. I'll call them in a little while." She paused while nobody said anything. "So let's get started. Is everybody ready?" She peeked through the video cam's viewfinder. "Is this thing on? Wow, Kaci, you look just like you're on TV!"

"It's on stand-by," Kaci said. "If we ever get going, all we have to do is push the button."

She could have left right then, just packed up her guitar and walked out. It was the same way she'd felt, what, a dozen times before, in the last year alone? Over and over again the whole thing had struck her as hopeless, a waste of time. But Koy came up to her.

"Don't be angry," she said quietly. "I'm sorry. Let's have a good rehearsal."

"Yeah," Kaci said. "Okay. It's okay."

"I am sorry," Koy said. "It's just, like, things are really hard for me right now. You know." She was looking sadly into Kaci's eyes.

You're such a little girl, Kaci thought, and you think that because of that, everyone will take care of you, and put up with anything. But in spite of herself,

Kaci's heart melted and her anger faded away; she just felt tired and down.

Koy started telling some crazy story to Barbi while Trish messed with her bass. Kaci, trying not to listen, warmed up silently. But in a minute she realized everyone was looking at her. "Well," she said, "uh, why don't we do a cover to get going?"

They'd played the tune dozens of times, but before they even got to the verse, Kaci called a halt. "Trish, you're way too loud," she said.

"Sorry," Trish said, flushing. She cut her levels, too much. "Sorry."

Kaci watched her fumble with the unfamiliar studio gear. "You know, that reminds me," she said, trying to keep her voice even, not come on too strong. "At sound check, before our next show, we need to see if we can get a better tone from your amp."

Trish looked at her, trying to read her expression. "Okay, what's... What were you thinking?"

"Well, it has lots of low end, which is good," Kaci said. "But it's boomy, like there's not enough definition."

Trish nodded, as if she understood: "Okay, yeah... We'll, ah, work on that..."

They started the song. Trish seemed rattled; she kept screwing up the simple changes. Kaci decided to ignore it: the new girl couldn't stand too much scrutiny —yet. At the end, Kaci looked around, nodding and trying to look positive. It hadn't been very good, but she wanted a good run-through on video; that was why they'd rented this expensive room.

"I just remembered, I've got an idea for a new song," Koy said. "What do you think of this: *Maximum Stimulation?*"

Kaci laughed. "Koy, that sounds like some kind of weird condom."

"Like from a truck stop!" Barbi said.

Koy made a face, stuck out her tongue. Kaci just grinned and looked around; she had to try to keep them focused. "Okay," she said. "Let's turn on the camera and try to run through the set. Trish, turn up your volume. We want to hear you."

It went pretty well. *Supersonic* was rough, and Koy forgot the lyrics to the new song —again —but Kaci bore down on her guitar, tried not to let her frustration affect her. As the last notes died away, Koy leaned into the lens and said, "That's all folks!" —and shut it off. "Cool!" she said.

Kaci checked her watch. "Just over forty-five minutes."

"And not much down time between songs," Barbi said. "But we've got to keep it that way. No messing around, just one song after another."

"I forgot the words to the new song again," Koy said.

"Yeah, that happened at the last show, too," Kaci said.

"Well, it's the new song," Koy said. "Don't worry, I'll get it."

Kaci nodded, thinking that the song wasn't all that new: they'd been working on it for six months. "Let's do it again —that and *Supersonic*."

"Yeah, I messed that up," Trish said.

They wasted the last ten minutes watching the playback, amused to see themselves on video, although the static camera angle was boring. As they were leaving, Trish said, "Hey, Koy, I thought you had to leave early."

"Yeah, well, I'm going in late," Koy said. "I'll tell them I got stuck in the subway."

Kaci turned away so no one could see her expression. They came out of the building onto 30th Street, a long black empty canyon: no cabs, no traffic at all.

"Let's go over to Seventh," Koy said, and they turned east, all of them tired and dragging, when Barbi said: "Hey, did you guys hear the weird news?"

"What?"

"Well, it happened down where you two live," she said, looking at Koy and Trish. "Somewhere in the East Village, I think it was on Avenue B. But anyway, this was really weird. They found a body…"

"So what else is new?" Koy said. "A guy I know told me somebody found a decapitated corpse in the trash the other day."

"That's really losing your head!" Trish said. Kaci snorted.

"So anyway, they found a body," Barbi started over, "and, you know, the police department wouldn't comment, but the news people managed to dig up the person who found it, this hugely fat Puerto Rican lady…"

"The body, I mean, victim or whatever?" Koy said.

"No, no, the fat lady found the body —it was the body of a man —and anyway she found it this morning, in a dumpster. So anyway, she said that when she saw the guy her heart almost stopped. It wasn't just that he was dead, she knew right away something terrible had happened, because he was Latino but he was so pale, paler than a white person."

"No!" Kaci said, laughing, as Trish said, "No, she did not!" Koy repeated, "Whiter than a white man!"

"I swear!" Barbi said. They were all giggling. "So," she went on, having trouble getting it out, "the newswoman said, 'New York City Police will neither confirm nor deny that the victim had been drained of blood'."

Gradually they all stopped laughing.

"No way," Koy said.

"Hey," Kaci said. "Maybe it's a vampire!"

"It's probably one of the Degenerates," Koy said.

"Talk about bloodsuckers," Trish said.

"Rock-n-roll vampires!" Kaci said. They all laughed again.

*        *        *

They caught a cab downtown, dropping Kaci at 17th and Barbi on Second Avenue. Trish opened her mouth to say East Houston but Koy cut her off with a look.

"Second Street and Avenue A," she told the driver. She leaned back and said in a low voice to Trish: "Will you come with me? I have to go by the Dope House."

"Yeah, sure," Trish said. They were there in moments. Koy paid the driver with Kaci and Barbi's money as Trish got her guitar out of the trunk. When they were alone on the sidewalk, Koy said: "I've got to work tonight and I've got to do a little. Or I just can't stand it. I really don't want to, especially with Johnny and all. But I have to, I need the money too bad. And if I do a bag, you know, I don't care so much. It's like pulling a curtain down between them and me, and then I don't care as much. Do you know what I mean?"

Trish said she did. Privately she was uncertain as to what kind of work Koy actually did that was so unbearable, and she rather suspected, without really caring, that all this was just Koy rationalizing her habit. And Trish had nothing against anyone's habits. But Koy was still talking: "I really just feel like saying, fuck it, you know? But the last time I blew it off –well, last week, Johnny had a night off, and we were having such a good time, and he didn't want me to go, he's so sweet, and I didn't feel like it –I mean I really love him, I do –and so I called in sick, you know? And my boss was really pissed off, and she bitched me out, and gave me this lecture that I was putting them in a bind, and I had responsibilities, and they would have to call in some other girl to fill in, and what if she didn't, like, do such a good job, and anyway, if I didn't show up for my, well, if I started not showing up that they would, uh, fire me."

"What a bitch," Trish said. "But, listen, your job can't just fire you because you call in sick. That's illegal."

"Well I don't know," Koy said. "Anyway I can't take a chance on it. I need the money too bad."

Trish was about to press her point but they were there and Koy said:

"Okay, you want to just walk on by and wait for me down the block?"

"No," Trish said. "I'm coming in too."

Koy gave Trish a look but said nothing and led the way. Trish had a quick glimpse of a face at the window as they mounted the steps. The door opened and the face, which belonged to a tough-looking Puerto Rican, broke in a wide grin.

"Hi!" Koy said sweetly, smiling her stage smile as she passed.

"Hey beautiful," the sentry said. "Who is your oh-so-good-looking friend?" Trish flushed, uncertain what to do.

"This is Trish," Koy said over her shoulder, walking past. "She's in my band."

"Hey-y-y, Treesh," the sentry said. "Man, you must have some kind of band."

"Hi!" Trish said, following Koy down a long hallway. They stopped at the stairs behind another buyer, a short nervous guy with straggly black hair and worn-out rock-n-roll clothes. The seller was standing on the first stair, counting bags into the buyer's hand with painful slowness. A stocky man of medium height, easily forty, whose heavy eyelids and goatee weirdly reminded Trish of Fu Manchu, he looked so high that he might have nodded off at any minute. Trish wondered how he could possibly work. As soon as the rocker got his bags he hustled for the door without so much as a look at the girls, and Koy moved up.

"Hi cutie," she said. "How you doing?"

The seller brightened without perceptibly opening his eyes, and he smiled, nodding and moistening his lips with his tongue in acknowledgement.

"Give me four D, honey," Koy said, proffering two twenties. Fu Manchu nodded and took the money, carefully counted it, and added it to a large roll he drew from one pocket of a fanny pack strapped around his waist. He put the money away, and drew from the other pocket a bundle of bags. With slow and deliberate motions which he must have practiced thousands of times, he pulled off the rubber band and dropped it to the floor, and counted Koy's four bags into her palm as if concerned he might make a mistake.

"Thanks," Koy said, and moved aside for Trish.

"Two D and one C," Trish said, holding out the money.

Koy giggled. "You and Dizzy gonna have some fun?"

The sentry opened the door for them, his tongue lolling out and his eyes stripping off what few clothes they had on. Koy just smiled and said goodbye and Trish did the same. As they went down the steps, an Oriental babe scooted past them, her heavily made-up eyes giving them a quick scrutiny before she slipped inside, and Trish glanced down at herself to see if she were popping out of her top or something. Suddenly a cry went up from the corner of Avenue B: "Mikey! Mikey!" —repeating up and down the block. Koy hissed, "Shit! Be cool!" Trish looked around, said, "What is it?"

"It's the cops," Koy muttered. "When they yell 'Mikey' it means a cop car's coming."

"Great," Trish said. They were nearing the gas station, its high wall of scrap metal sculpture looming dark and ominous along the street. Behind, a bunch of misfit artists and punk rockers were standing around a fire burning in a fifty-gallon drum. Sparks flew into the night sky and expired like falling stars. Trish started to look around for the cop car but stopped herself. "What do we do?" she said.

"Just be cool and keep walking," Koy said, calm now as the cop car turned the corner, slowly cruising their way. "They won't stop us, and even if they do, we're just going home after rehearsal. We don't know nothing."

Stop us! Trish thought; vague but terrifying notions flashed through her head. But already the cop car was passing without slowing down. Koy let out her breath and said: "Ha! It's cool. We weren't even near the place. They have no reason to stop us. The building has lookouts at both ends of the block. They don't want to get busted even more than we do."

I doubt that, Trish thought. They turned down Avenue B.

"They see the cops coming and give the alarm. All you really have to worry about is you don't want to be inside when it happens. But really, there's no way to avoid it, sometimes. I've been in there when it happens. Used to they would let you wait in there. Once me and a couple other people all ran upstairs and waited on the second floor, and the whole time I was thinking how was I going to explain what I was doing there. But nothing happened, and lately they've been running you out of there as soon as the alarm goes off, and then you've got to walk up the block acting cool. Of course as soon as the cop goes by, everyone turns around and goes back. It's pretty funny, in a way, but you get sick of the cops messing with you."

Trish was only half listening, her mind elsewhere. When they got to the corner she looked towards her building and saw the lights on: Dizzy was home.

As they crossed Houston, Koy was still telling harrowing stories, but Trish wasn't listening; she had another score to take care of.

\*　　　　　　　\*　　　　　　　\*

JT hung up the phone when Kaci came in the door, and he looked uptight —guilty. She couldn't help herself, and said, "Who was that, JT?"

"Huh?" he said. "No one —a wrong number." She just looked at him, knowing she hadn't heard the phone ring as she was coming upstairs. He looked back with nervous defiance, turned away, and lit a cigarette.

She put her bag on the kitchen table, and went into the bathroom. She could be alone there, at least for a minute, while she washed up and brushed her teeth. For some time, life at home with JT had been strained; he was increasingly distant and withdrawn, she subdued and anxious; they spoke little, seemed to avoid each other. But the wrong number... Lately, she'd begun to have certain suspicions that both angered and frightened her. He was up to something. That wasn't right, he shouldn't treat her that way; but she had begun to look at herself very critically: was she not pretty enough? Or maybe she wasn't good in bed? Though she knew she shouldn't think like that, she couldn't help herself. Her face was showing her age, her skin dry, lines at the corners of her eyes and mouth; worse, her hips looked broad and she was afraid she was gaining weight. And she hardly ate —didn't even feel hungry anymore.

She went back out to the living room. He had changed his shirt, was putting on his jacket. "I'm going out," he said. "Got to meet some guys." That was all.

"Okay," she said. "See you later."

"Yeah," he said. She watched him go out the door.

\*　　　　　　　\*　　　　　　　\*

The Contusions were at their rehearsal studio in midtown. Nothing was happening: Ratso was fiddling with his drums, banging out different beats and adjusting stuff; Diz, whose nerves couldn't take the noise, had tuned his guitars and gone out to the bathroom; and Danny was sitting cross-legged in the corner, reading a paper. They were waiting on Mick D.

Diz didn't like to hang out in the bathroom long: it was filthy and it stank, badly. As he snorted up a couple of pops in the one dingy stall, trying not to touch anything, he was thinking of the stories he had heard about musicians living in this building. The thing was unimaginable. Out in the hall, you could hear different bands practicing on the various floors, the sound coming up and down the stairs and elevator shafts and blending to a thumping, dissonant roar. Shabby-looking rock-n-rollers were always going in and out of the place, moving equipment, talking trash. When could you possibly sleep?

He snorted some water up his nose and went back to the studio. Mick was finally there; his eyes were pinned out, he was obviously messed-up. "Oh man, listen to this," Ratso said.

"What?" Diz said.

"I was just telling these guys," Mick said. "I just got this call from Howie Zero."

"What?" Diz said. "Oh no."

"Yeah, man," Mick said. "Our gig with the Degenerates is cancelled."

"Goddamn it," Danny said.

"Why?" Diz asked Mick.

"The Degenerates cancelled," Mick said.

"They're *trying* to screw us up," Ratso said. "Jeeze, this pisses me off. How many times has this happened?"

"They don't want to play with us."

"I think they're *scared* to play with us!"

"This sucks."

"Yeah, this sucks!"

Mick rambled on, slurring his words and repeating himself. Diz went over to one of the windows and sat down on the ledge, not listening anymore and watching the traffic flowing up the avenue. How many times had this happened? He tried to recall: three or four at least, before now. What was the use of it all? The guys in the Degenerates had been around forever, and had played in a bunch of bands; they ran a monthly house party, so they knew everyone; their songs sucked but they had connections; and now they were the lords of the Lower East Side, and here he was, stuck with these losers.

"This never would've happened," he said finally, "if we hadn't played that party."

Ratso and Mick just looked at him. "Huh?" Danny said.

"The end of last summer, we played one of their house parties," Diz said. "That was when we still had T-Bone. Those guys didn't even have a band then. They were just running the thing. But they saw us there. Remember how they just stood and watched the whole set? Well, something made them get their shit together. By Christmas they had their first gig, and now they're out to fuck us up. We're still better than they are, even if they do know everyone in the neighborhood, and they don't want to play with us or have anything to do with us. I think all they want is to see us go down the toilet."

"You're right," Ratso said. "I never thought of that."

That doesn't surprise me, Diz thought. He just nodded.

Danny looked pretty dejected. Diz went on, talking to him: "You'll notice that nothing much happened until they kicked your buddy out of the band. What was his name, George? But once they got rid of him, this is, what, the fourth gig that's gotten screwed up."

"This was our gig, too," Mick mumbled. "I set it up, and asked them if they wanted in. Then they cancel and the whole thing's off."

Diz stood up. "I can't believe it. I just don't know... You guys want some beer?"

"Uh, I don't have any money," Mick said.

"I'm buying," Diz said. "Get out your guitar. I'll be back in a minute."

But the first thing he did was go back in the bathroom and snort up most of another bag he'd saved for later. It took the edge off some. He'd been about to have a fit. Now with that familiar bitter taste in the back of his throat, the warmth coating his nerves, soothing and dulling them, he just thought, the hell with it. He left the stall and went over to the mirror, studied his reflection. You know you're going to have to get out of this band. You knew that already. It just isn't happening –there's too many problems. You've got to start figuring out your options. And he couldn't believe it, for in the beginning it had seemed like this would be it –that they would make it this time.

He leaned forward and stared into his own eyes. The pupils were the size of pinheads. He would have to start over again. How many times had *that* happened?

Going down the stairs he lost count after ten or eleven, and he decided to think about something else, and not try to count it again.

When he got back with the beer, Mick was trying to tune up. Ratso and Danny were still complaining about the cancelled gig. Diz strapped on his guitar, checked the levels, and waited. When they finally got going it sounded pretty bad. After the third song they came to a stop.

Ratso beat on the high-hat, then adjusted it. Without the blasting guitars, the sound was like a file rasping Diz's eardrums. "We need some new tunes," Ratso said.

That's your answer to everything, Diz thought; he just shrugged. "Aww, everybody's just depressed because of the gig," Danny said. "Let's play a couple cover songs, maybe we'll get into it."

"That's cool with me," Diz said. They ripped through one as if pouring their anger into making the worst possible noise; it would have been good if there hadn't been something wrong with it, some slight wandering from the single-minded expression of pure rage. Diz started another one, chopping metallic slabs of guitar anchored by deafening drum strokes. It was cool; he was getting into it; they were all getting into it, he thought, until Mick muffed the bass part, on a song he had played a thousand times, and couldn't get back on.

Diz looked over: Mick's eyes were shut, like he was falling asleep. He shook himself; they got to the end of the song.

"Damn, it's hot in here," he said, scratching himself on the chest and arms.

"It's not that bad," Danny said. "We got all the windows open."

"No, man, it's hot," Mick said, still scratching.

Ratso counted off another one. This time Mick just nodded out in the middle of the song. His hands were still on the bass but he wasn't playing; the strings were ringing, a low tone that kept getting louder and louder; he was swaying from side to side, eyes closed, mouth half-open.

Jesus Christ! Diz thought, and quit playing. Ratso came to a stop, confused, as Danny yelled, "Mick! Mick! Wake up!"

Mick's eyes opened; he looked around, scratching himself again. "What's going on?" he said, scratching.

"What's going on?" Danny said. "You fell asleep in the middle of the song!"

"Sorry, man," Mick said. "Take it easy. I'm sorry. I'm just really tired. Let's do it again."

They made it through that one but he nodded out again in the next one. "Let's take a break," Ratso said. They were all disgusted. But Mick went to Ratso, appealing to his sympathy, like he always did.

Danny came over to Diz and said, "Like, what kind of drugs is he on?"

Don't you know? Diz thought. "I don't know, man," he said.

"This sucks," Danny said. "What a waste of time."

Diz couldn't argue with that. After another twenty or thirty minutes, they went reluctantly back to their instruments. Mick had woken up now but he could hardly play, wasn't good for anything; everyone else was irritated and bored. They couldn't get anything going, finally just rushed through their set, to get it over with, and quit.

Nobody had much to say in the car. They dropped Danny off at Port Authority and headed downtown. "Mick, you want me to drop you off?" Ratso said.

"No, man, drop Diz off, I'll ride with you," Mick said.

There was no radio in the car, just the noise of traffic: horns honking sporadically, drivers racing from red light to red light. Ratso made a couple of dumb jokes; Mick was rambling about the Degenerates and the cancelled gig again; Diz just stared out the window, tired and ready for some coke. It always took forever to get downtown. Sometimes Diz thought he couldn't listen to them any longer, it would be better to just get out and walk; and sometimes he imagined what it would be like to go on tour with them, to be stuck in a van with them for weeks, slowly dragging from one city to another all the way across the country, like a nightmare from which you'd never awake. That night, they must have hit every red light for forty blocks.

*   *   *

Dizzy was at rehearsal: that made things easier, anyway. But Trish needed to score. As dusk fell over the Lower East Side, she paced restlessly through the stifling rooms of their railroad apartment, going again and again to the dirty windows as if by vigilant attention she might accelerate the coming of night. Her need was very strong now, and increasing momently: it claimed the best part of her attention and would not be denied. Yet she waited, tormented by the cravings of her appalling addiction and helpless either to satisfy them or to even think of anything else —waited with clenched teeth and fretful hands, stomach hurting, for the sun to sink safely below the western skyline. Experience had shown that it was the sheerest folly to venture out on the mission before the city had grown quite dark. The dangers of going too early were simply too great. And so she waited.

When the light grew dim and the streetlamps came on, she stripped and went to the jumbled and overstuffed closet to find something to wear. She'd learned to do her make-up earlier, before her hands should begin to shake so badly that she couldn't use a mascara brush or eyebrow pencil, and only made a mess of herself. Now she squirmed into a pair of silver lamé Capri pants, holding her breath and sucking in her stomach to get them buttoned, squeezed her 38-D silicone breasts into a black leatherette push-up bustier, and zipped her feet into spike-heeled ankle boots; and standing before the mirror, she reverted to her normal self long enough to frown at a tiny roll of fat puckered above her waistline. But finally it got dark, and she grabbed her frayed denim jacket and went out.

On the street the air was cooler and she put on the jacket, trying not to attract too much attention, but every few moments, all the way up Avenue B, guys hooted at her from bicycles or honked from passing cars. She gnashed her teeth, cursing, all the strain from her agonized nerves amplifying her impotent fury into hellish fantasies of murder. She would have liked to slaughter them all, smash every lust-crazed mouth, gouge out their leering eyes, choke the words in their throats —and then she'd have strewn the avenue with dismembered limbs, stained all Loisaida blood-red. She imagined severed jugulars spraying blood, still-beating hearts torn free and pumping in her hand as she sucked on the broken arteries like straws; and these orgiastic visions made her giggle for a moment, then shudder.

Take it easy, she told herself. Calm down. You've got to think about what you're doing. You can't take any chances. Indeed, she was almost there: Seventh Street was only a block away. She slowed her pace and felt for the ten-dollar bill in her pocket.

Poor Dizzy had explained how things worked at Laundromat but still imagined she had never been there. By now she was enough of a regular that the lookouts always recognized her. Ahead came a sharp whistle and she squinted to see what was going on. The spot operated from a tenement in the middle of the block, where the seller waited behind a high entrance door for the signal to go to work, or go back inside. Another whistle answered just as she approached; above a half-flight of steps, the door opened, and a man stepped out, a middle-aged Puerto Rican with his hands thrust into the pockets of a money apron, looking for all the world like a taco vendor at a street fair. Trish went to the side of the steps, and held up the unfolded bill, saying, "One D." The seller glanced left-right, took the money, put a small blue glassine in her palm, and glanced left-right again. Trish hurried away as the next buyer stepped up.

So far so good, she thought, slowing her pace as she headed back toward Avenue B. Of course, now was the hard part.

Luck was with her, for a likely prospect appeared immediately: a rock-n-roller, skinny and rather short, with badly dyed blonde hair and ragged clothes. She had never seen him before but he was unquestionably there to cop. When he was quite close, she made a show of hiding the bag of dope in her cleavage and looking up surprised, smiling as if embarrassed. He grinned back and went past her toward the spot.

At the corner she took off her jacket and lit a cigarette, dawdling by the window of an antique clothing shop. In a couple of minutes the guy was on his way back. She made eye contact, smiled and said, "Hi."

"Hi!" he said in a gross nasal voice. "I've seen you around, haven't I?"

This should be easy, she thought, and it won't keep me up nights.

"I think so," she said. "Aren't you in a band?"

"Yeah," he said, swelling up, "the Rat Boys."

"Oh yeah, cool," Trish said. "I've seen you guys play somewhere, I'm not really sure where." She laughed an airhead laugh.

"Yeah! Probably at the Bunker," he said.

"Yeah, probably," she agreed. "Listen, I wonder if you could help me. I mean, like do me a favor?"

"Yeah!" he said, moving closer. "I mean, I'm sure I'd be glad to help a beautiful lady like you –if I could."

"Well," she said, "I just copped, right? and like, I can't go home right now, and I wondered if you had someplace we could go to, um, get off?"

His eyes shone wolfishly and he grinned. "Sure," he said, "come on, we'll go to my place."

"Is it far?" she said, following alongside him.

"No, no, it's right in the neighborhood."

"Oh, that's great," she said breathily.

They went down to Third and turned west toward Avenue A. Trish was keeping a careful watch, checking the street ahead and behind them, and he must have assumed she was nervous about the cops; he started talking about how hot it had been lately. He told her about a buddy who'd gotten busted and spent forty-eight hours in jail, going through withdrawal, and another who'd been grabbed by undercover cops as he came out of a coke store, and how they'd taken him down by the East River and beaten him up till he told them what he knew about the place, which was mostly just that you could buy coke there. Next was a long and rambling theory that the cops were using taxi cabs now for surveillance and operation, because all these out-of-service cabs were always driving around the neighborhood, and sometimes both the driver and another guy were sitting in the front seat, with no passengers, nobody sitting in the back. Trish wasn't really paying attention at first, but the longer he went on about these cabs, the more paranoid she got, and her nerves were fucking screaming now too, it was all she could do to keep a grip on herself. Finally, thank God, they got to his building. As best she could tell, nobody saw them go in. It was just another dilapidated tenement like dozens of others, smelling of dust and decay, and everyone else in the place must have either been gone or engaged behind locked doors in their own secret vices. They had to go almost to the top, and Trish was starting to feel very weak.

"Alright," he said, unlocking the door and ushering her in. "Welcome to my nightmare."

The place *was* a nightmare: a narrow one-room rat-hole with a tiny kitchenette at one end and a sort of closet for the bathroom at the other. There was one window, with the shade drawn. Most of the space was taken up by a big sofa, sagging and split at the seams; a TV faced it, sitting on a milk crate, near a couple of mismatched chairs, and a box that served as a table. An electric guitar leaned against a cheap combo amp. The guy went to a battered stereo and turned on the radio. "Sit down," he said.

Trish sat down in front of the TV and took out a cigarette. "Do you have a roommate?" she said.

"No," he said. "There's no room. I used to have one when I had a bigger apartment, but the other guy never paid any rent and I had to move in here." He had taken a set of works from a shoebox on the floor and was cooking up a shot. Trish wasn't really listening to him. He had his sleeves rolled up, and she was fascinated by the pattern of scars, some healed, some fresh, that mapped his veins.

"But I like it better without a roommate," he said, drawing the solution up into a dull-looking insulin syringe. He squirted a drop into the air and grinned at her. "You have your privacy, you can be alone. You don't have to worry about when somebody else might come in."

Trish nodded and smiled. She was thinking that he didn't know how right he was.

"Listen," he said. "Don't be shy, go ahead and fix up. You got your set?"

"Umm, no," she said. "It's at home. Maybe I could borrow yours, after you get off?"

"Okay, that's cool," he said. He tied his arm off, trying to distend a vein, and was probing with the needle. Trish couldn't take her eyes away. When he finally found one and a scarlet thread shot back up the syringe's neck, she could almost taste it. He pushed the plunger home, released the belt, sighed deeply, and sank back into the couch.

"Alright," he said. His eyes closed; he put the needle down, mumbling something. Trish smoked her cigarette, waiting.

It was almost too easy. When he was quite nodded out, she took the arm nearest her and raised it to her face. There was something singularly arousing about this ravaged flesh, this pathetic arm, which might have been that of a leper, or a victim of the plague. She ran her lips over the scabbed and spongy skin in the crook of the elbow, then tore open his veins. In moments his life ebbed from him.

She sat back, calm now, suffused with a certain euphoria, luxurious and enervating. Some time passed, she wasn't sure how long. When she came down some, she started thinking about getting home. The nervousness and pain were gone. She could deal with things. Everything was cool: she was all right for another day.

She turned off the stereo and the lights and locked him in, careful now to touch nothing. The halls of the building were still deserted. Outside, the night was cooling off, and a light breeze came from the East River, slightly foul but refreshing. The air tingled deliciously over her skin. She smiled in satisfaction, tossed her hair, and strutted back toward Avenue B like the Queen of the Lower East Side.

*    *    *

JT was already irritated when Kaci hung up the phone, since he'd heard part of it already, and when she told him the tentative arrangements Koy had made with some indie guy who wanted to put them on a 'Downtown' compilation, he simply scoffed: these deals never happened, the guy probably had no money, he probably just wanted to get into Koy's pants. In the first flush of hope, Kaci asserted that no, this one was for real —even though she had no good reason to believe that, herself. He laughed at her, asked how many times before had these deals been for real; he counted them off, naming each one. She was surprised that his memory of these things was as good or better than hers —why? He wanted her to acknowledge that this one too would come to nothing. When she didn't answer, he acted offended; spitefully, he added that it was all just as well, since Dreamwhip wasn't ready to release something anyway. Kaci wanted to know why.

"Oh, come on," JT said. "You need more practice. You need to refine your material. You've got to work out some of those parts where people aren't together or don't know what they're doing, where it doesn't sound *good*, where it doesn't sound *tight*. The rhythm section has to get it together. And *you* have got to get your shit together."

Oh man, she was thinking. Why is it always like this? But she couldn't help herself. "What do you mean?"

He acted more and more irritated, like something was making him mad.

"What do I mean?" he said. "Well, let's see… Your rhythm parts aren't distinct, they need tightening up and your execution is sloppy. Your timing is bad. Your leads are simplistic, clichéd and repetitive, and what's worse, they don't go anywhere, there's no excitement. And your sound, well, your sound is just terrible."

Kaci was taken back, stung. "Jeeze," she said. "Have you been wanting to tell me this for a while?"

He shrugged, looked away. "You asked me."

"I didn't ask you to put me down."

"Just trying to be honest with you."

"Honest about this, right? This one thing, once."

He didn't answer, just shrugged again. She already mistrusted him, but this criticism of her playing was really too much; it made her mad, and she lost her mind a little. "No, I believe you're sincere, JT," she said. "I just wonder why your views are what they are. Last week all you had to say was that we had to make a recording, a good recording, if we were ever going to get anywhere. Here some guy is talking about recording us and putting it out, but now according to you, we couldn't possibly do that, we're just not ready. Well, those ideas don't fit together very well, do they? They're contradictory. Why is that? I mean, I wonder why?"

He looked really angry now but Kaci didn't care, she was getting carried away. He said, "Look, I don't have to listen…"

"It's because you're jealous, that's why! Whenever anything good comes along for me, you get jealous and you turn completely negative."

"That's bullshit," he said.

"It sucks being jealous of your *girlfriend*, doesn't it?"

"Go to hell."

"You're jealous!" Kaci repeated.

"*I'm* supposed to be jealous of *your* band?" he said, like he was spitting on it.

She was furious: "You're fucking jealous!" He laughed at her, theatrically, and turned his back.

"The problem is this," she said evenly. "When was the last time anyone wanted to put out a recording of *you*?" She saw him tense up –she probably shouldn't have said that. But it was too late, she'd said it. "All you do is put me down," she went on. "I can't play, my rhythm's bad, my timing's off, my leads are dumb, my sound is bad, I don't stand right… Basically, I'm terrible, I suck."

"I didn't say that."

In spite of herself, tears were forming in the corners of her eyes. She hated that, and rushed on: "But what do you know, somebody is stupid enough to want to record us. It must be the tits and ass, right, JT?"

"The hell with you, Kaci. I didn't say that."

"But that's what you think, isn't it? That's how you explain it to yourself. If anything good happens to us, it's because we're bimbos, not a band!"

He shrugged, plainly no longer denying any of it. At that she completely lost her head. "Well, the hell with you and your superior attitude! I'm sick of it! And you know… I notice you don't have any put-downs for Koy! Or Trish! Why might that be, I wonder?"

"What are you talking about?"

"I've seen you ogling Trish. You're totally obvious, like a teenage boy. You'd like to get your hands on those big boobs of hers, wouldn't you?"

"Whatever, Kaci!"

"It's just too bad Trish has Dizzy. There's somebody else you don't like. Why is that? At least he tries to help us. Why don't you like Dizzy, JT? Are you jealous of him, too?"

JT spluttered. "Me? Jealous of that guy?"

"Well, JT, are you? Why do you dislike him so? His fancy shirts that you hate so much? His sparkle guitar? Or his blond bimbo girlfriend with the big boobs… who happens to be in *my* band. What is it exactly, JT?"

He said slowly and coldly: "You're a bitch. You'd be nothing without me. I've taught you everything you know, and you turn around and spit on me."

"A magnificent speech, JT."

He grabbed his coat. "Since you won't need me to plan your platinum album, I'm going down to the bar." He stalked out without another word, slamming the door behind him.

She had tears in her eyes, which only made her resent it all the more. What a bastard, she was thinking. Taught me everything I know…

\*                    \*                    \*

The Deuces were playing at Cafe Bustello, a real toilet of a place on Avenue C, and Koy was hanging out with Dizzy while the band was on stage, blasting through its string of more or less inane rockabilly songs, like 50's delinquents strung out on amphetamines. She was thinking that Dizzy must like this stuff, although he didn't seem to like Johnny all that much; or maybe he was there to repay some obligation; or maybe, like her, he just had to get out of the house sometimes, driven out into the night city and obscurely searching for something. They were almost alone: no Trish, no Kaci, no Kamikazis or other Contusions; all in all a poor showing for people who knew so many other musicians –virtually no one there.

So she hung out, flirting a little with Dizzy, though not much, for she knew Johnny always watched her from on stage. But the Contusions' guitarist seemed distracted, and when the last song was over he excused himself, went up and shook hands with Johnny. She watched them together, the tall skinny glamour boy with the smaller, wiry greaser-punk: neither really smiled, and they exchanged only a few words before Diz came back, said goodnight and left. Johnny put away his guitar, the big black hollowbody that seemed slightly too large for his frame, and was winding up cords, frowning. The house sound came back on, jarring.

She looked at her empty drink, went back to the bar. They'd be out of here soon. She thought for a second, and ordered a lemon drop; when it came, she downed it in a gulp and lit a cigarette. She wanted to be ready to go when he was.

Johnny was talking to the other guys. It took a while. Apart from the bartender, the place was empty. She looked at her watch: one-thirty, no wonder.

Finally they were leaving. Johnny wheeled his amp across the room and carried it carelessly up the steps, banging the cabinet and the casters here and there. His mouth was drawn into a tight line. She shook her head –this didn't look good –went over to the stage and got his guitar. "Hey guys," she called. "Good show." They all said 'Bye' or 'Thanks', and that was about it. She felt sure something was going on.

She passed back by the bar and said goodbye to the bartender, went upstairs and did the same with the doorman, a huge tattooed biker wearing a silly leather cap, his grin missing teeth. "Alright darlin', see you later," he answered,

Johnny was outside, looking around. "Hey honey," she said, and pointed to a waiting sedan. "There's our car right there."

Johnny loaded his stuff and got in the back without a word. Koy got in beside him, anxious and uptight –and hurt, too, for whatever was bothering him, it wasn't her fault.

The driver was watching in the mirror, waiting. "You want to drop your stuff off?" Koy asked. "Yeah," Johnny said, and gave his address. The car moved off.

"Hey, you were good," Koy said.

"Thanks."

Silence! Jeeze! What was the matter *this* time?

"The vocals sounded good tonight."

"P.A. sucked," Johnny said. It sounded like a contradiction.

They didn't say anything else all the way back to Johnny's. He was glaring out the window; Koy didn't want to get snapped at. The driver double-parked in front of the building and Johnny unloaded his gear and took it in. Koy asked the driver to wait. He nodded, set the flashers and turned up the radio. They knew her: she had an account, was a good customer.

When Johnny came back down he didn't get in, just opened the door and stood there. "Come on," she said. "You don't want to stay here alone." With a little more coaxing she got him in the car and they set off again.

"Tired?" she said, gently.

He grunted yes, took out a comb and combed his duck-tail. "What a waste of time," he said finally.

She reached out, rubbed his hand. "No way," she said. "Like you always say, a show's better than a rehearsal, and it doesn't cost as much. Besides, it was good. You rocked."

He just shook his head and looked away.

When they got to Delancey she paid the driver, doubling the tip and giving him a big smile. He smiled back, his eyes holding hers. It gave her a tingle –he reminded her of one of those hot Latino singers, she didn't know which one.

Johnny was brooding by the door. They went up, and she let them in. "Beer?" she said.

"Got any vodka?" he said.

"Yeah, sure," she said, surprised. He followed her to the kitchen. She took the bottle from the freezer and he poured off a big shot and drank it straight. She could see it hit him. He poured a second one and drank it.

"Ahh," he said. "What do you got to mix it with?"

They went back to the living room. He flopped down in a chair and glared at his drink for a while, and then began to rant. Everyone was against him. No one acknowledged his work, his good ideas, even his leadership anymore. They had wreaked havoc with the tempos, forgotten everything it had taken them two weeks to learn; Pronto ignored him, Fast Freddie had gotten drunk again; they'd screwed up every song. He couldn't believe they were such idiots. How had he gotten involved with such idiots? He was the idiot, for getting involved with them.

On and on. Koy found herself getting drowsy. He was complaining about the others' vocals, and their clothes, and something else, she couldn't quite follow; after a bit she wasn't trying anymore. But when she felt her eyes closing she sat up quick. *Wake up!* she told herself, knowing he was in no mood for *that*. But it was late, and she'd worked the night before... She sat up again. He paused, but went on. She knew he'd get even more irritated if she fell asleep. Finally she excused herself. He nodded, hardly even looking at her.

In the bathroom she had two quick snorts of coke, flushed the toilet, fluffed her hair and touched up her lipstick. He was still sitting just like before in the now-silent apartment.

Somewhere in the building somebody was listening to salsa. She turned on the stereo, took his drink in the kitchen and freshened it, sat down again and waited. "What do you think you should do?" she said finally.

He shrugged. How was he supposed to know? He knew one thing, though: either things were going to change, or he would look for something different. There were other bands out there, looking for guitarists.

She was awake now, she definitely wasn't sleepy. But she wasn't listening any better than before; her mind kept drifting off and she'd find herself thinking of other things. She tried to force herself to concentrate but he wasn't really making much sense, just letting off steam, and besides, the vodka was catching up to him: he was repeating himself, stumbling on certain words. But he kept swilling it down, going back to the kitchen for refills. She kept thinking it would run out, she hadn't thought she had all that much.

It was late. She'd begun to yawn again. He'd fallen silent, more or less, after formulating the utter hopelessness of it all, and repeating, "What's the use? What's the fucking use?" She turned on the TV, gave him the remote. Of course there was nothing on.

He fell asleep with the drink still in his hand. She took it away, put a blanket over him. The lights in the apartment were getting pale: it would be dawn soon. She got up, stirred about a bit. Johnny was snoring, his mouth hanging open. Some rock star. And hadn't it been a fun night. Talk about sex, drugs and rock-n-roll.

It was so late, she decided to go ahead and fix up; maybe in the morning she could sleep late. For all she knew, Johnny had to make pizzas in the morning. She considered trying to ask, but let it go: that was *his* problem.

She went in the bathroom to cook up a shot. She hated having to sneak around in her own place. It didn't seem right. Sitting on the toilet with the lid closed, it took her a while to find the vein. When she finally did, the stuff was such a relief –she hadn't even realized she'd been so uptight.

*         *         *

Trish got out of the car-service car in front of the photographer's loft and unloaded her stuff: a fun-fur, two jackets, her bass, a big suitcase, and three smaller bags stuffed with hats, belts, shoes, make-up, lingerie and sunglasses. The driver helped her get it all inside; thankfully, the place had an elevator.

Upstairs everybody else was there, doing their hair and trying on different clothes. At the other end of the big loft, Robert was setting up lights and reflective screens. "Hey, Trish," he called. "How you doing?"

Trish smiled and waved. Koy-Toy came over: she'd had her hair cut, and she was wearing a leatherette push-up bra and silver hot pants. "Hi!" she said. "Let's get your stuff. Do you like my hair? I just got it done, I'm not too sure about it. And I want you to help me pick out my shoes." Her eyes were totally pinned-out.

"Your hair looks great," Trish said. Now she wished she'd gotten hers trimmed. Koy could have said something, told her; but she had to be the star.

Kaci was sitting in a chair, already dressed and playing her guitar. Trish was glad Koy wasn't ready. Barbi kept having trouble with her contacts; she'd gotten eyeliner in one eye, and kept going back and forth to the bathroom, muttering, "I hate this stuff."

Trish rummaged through her things, trying to figure out what she could wear that would both go with and be different from everybody else. Koy couldn't decide; she kept changing; she tried one pair of shoes after another –it was incredible, even Trish didn't have so many; she couldn't make up her mind. Every other minute she interrupted Barbi or Trish to ask their opinion, then hardly listened to the answers. Kaci seemed withdrawn, saying little; only her hands moved over the guitar as she looked off into nothing. At the other end of the loft a large and expensive stereo was blasting rock-n-roll.

"The photos are in black and white," Trish said, already sure of the answer. "Not in color, right?"

"No, both," Koy said. "I mean, we're doing black and white, but, well, Robert suggested that we shoot some in color in case we got some interest by a slick magazine."

Barbi was passing by. "Like what?" she said. Koy didn't answer. Trish was stripping off her clothes again, she hadn't counted on color, and now Koy was digging through *her* stuff!

"Oooh," Koy said. "Trish, can I wear your Nazi hat?" She was already trying it on.

Irked, Trish didn't want to say yes, but what *could* she say? "Sure, but it'll flatten your hair."

"Not too bad," Koy said. "And it'll make me look like a real 'dom' bitch." But in a moment she tossed it aside, and sat down, abruptly quiet, a strained look on her face.

Trish went to her and said lowly, "Don't be nervous –you know, because of *him*."

"I'm not nervous," Koy said, but she looked at Trish thoughtfully.

She pulled off her shoes and tugged on a pair of thigh-high platform boots. Jeeze! Trish thought, that's what I was gonna wear! She opened her mouth to say something, stopped herself, and waited. Sure enough, Koy no sooner had them on than she took them off again.

Trish looked around. Sitting on a rolling chair next to Kaci, chatting and twirling a pair of sticks, Barbi looked like a rock-n-roll cowgirl: black leather jeans, black girly cowboy boots with white musical notes, a baby doll T-shirt with the *Club* porno-mag logo. Next to her on the floor were a leopard cowboy hat and a half-empty bottle of tequila. Kaci had on a black micro-mini with bondage buckles up one hip, ripped fishnet stockings, black patent-leather platform pumps with gouging spike heels –Koy's shoes? Trish wondered –and a see-through top over a black patent push-up bra. Trish felt a pang of envy over the guitarist's flat, well-defined stomach.

Koy reappeared, bursting from the bathroom even more messed-up than before. Now she was wearing silver lamé chaps over tiny black stretch shorts, black patent-leather sling-backs, matching silver lamé opera gloves, and a triangle top crusted with fake diamonds. "What do you think?" she asked breathlessly.

"Wow!" Robert said, passing by.

Koy rolled her eyes, looking at the others.

"Fantastic, you look fantastic," Barbi said.

Trish made a snap decision, stripping again. What did she care about Robert? She squeezed into black PVC hot pants, holding her breath to zip them up, and pulled on black patent-leather knee boots. She threw her top back in a bag and changed to a leopard-print push-up bra, and slipped on a cropped motorcycle jacket.

"Whoa, that's some cleavage," Kaci said.

"Yeah, Trish!" Barbi said approvingly.

Trish just smiled, catching Koy's envious expression. "Alright," she said. "I wonder when we start shooting?"

"Five minutes," Robert said from the other end of the studio.

Things moved quickly after that. Robert's assistant Angie fussed over them a bit, then ushered them toward the other end of the studio. Trish recognized her from the rehearsal studio, where she sometimes worked the front desk: always friendly and outgoing, efficient and capable, she was also quite attractive, in an understated rock-chick way. Trish had the idea –she wasn't sure why –that this Angie was also Robert's new girlfriend, noting that she and Koy treated one another with a cordiality that was definitely cool.

Robert seated them on an old sofa in front of a white ground. He studied the composition a moment, then had Trish and Kaci change places. At a look, Angie switched on the lights, and Bob shot some tests. Under the blaze of lights, it got hot fast. "Just relax," he said in a deliberately soothing tone. "Act naturally." But Trish had the impression that she was anything but relaxed and natural, although the others seemed quite at ease –which only increased her anxiety. What was more, she couldn't get it out of her head that sitting on this sofa was making her look fat. Surely they could do some shots standing up?

The lights snapped off again and they went to look at the tests. The others were pleased but Trish hated how she looked, especially her expression. Once again, she told herself the whole thing wasn't all about her, that she was still the new girl; but going back to her seat she felt nothing but dismay.

As he sighted through the camera, Robert began a strange monologue, partly encouragement, partly direction: "Great... Oh yeah... Everybody move a little... That's it... Koy, chin up a little... Good... Fantastic... Kaci, drop your right shoulder some... That's it... Great, great... Love it..."

He straightened, smiling. "Alright!" he said. "I think we got some good shots. Okay: everybody up, Angie, let's get that sofa out of the way, we're going to reset for some standing shots."

When the lights snapped off, leaving them like the sun had gone behind a cloud, Trish followed the others to the mirrors and checked her reflection. She was relieved at the change of scene but felt trapped by her own anxiety. But Koy had shifted into prima donna overdrive: she stripped off what clothes she had on, leaving them in a pile on the floor, and pulled on a pair of black latex short-shorts, a large zipper through the crotch front to back –a pair of fence-net thigh-highs, black patent bedroom mules with white feathers, and a tiny French-sleeved T-shirt with the word COCKSUCKER in big letters. She threw a pink boa around her shoulders, tossed her hair and said, "How's this?"

Kaci looked bored but Barbi just laughed and slapped the singer on her ass. Robert was waiting patiently; doubtless he'd endured countless such situations before. He placed them together, tried a couple of compositions, shot the test. Angie was frowning as they got set to shoot. "Hey guys, try to relax a little bit," she said. "Like, you know, have fun with it."

"I always do real well when somebody tells me to relax," Trish said, trying not to move her lips.

"Me, too," Barbi agreed. "Hey, Koy, say something funny."

"I can't *think* of anything funny," Koy said. "When I'm wearing this shirt, all I can think about is sucking cock."

When they got done laughing, the spell was broken. Trish felt better; even Kaci was grinning.

"Okay," Robert said, firing the shutter. "Great... I like it... Koy, a little closer to Trish... Look this way... Good, good..."

Kaci as usual was all focus: she had practiced posture and poses at home in front of the mirror, when JT wasn't around. But the damned boa kept tickling her or getting under her nose, making her want to sneeze; and of course Koy kept throwing it around like a pilled-out movie queen. Finally she couldn't take it any more, and hissed, "Koy, get that thing out of my face!"

Koy looked hurt. Everyone was silent.

"Kaci," Barbi said sweetly. "You need to relax... Just think about sucking cock."

Kaci was about to say that was some people's answer to everything but she started laughing too.

"Okay, girls," Robert said, handing the camera to Angie. "Take five, then we'll go up to the roof."

Koy had asked for some shots with the skyline behind them; they were a New York band, after all. Kaci thought it might be more appropriate if they stood in front of a burnt-out building or a long row of trashcans but she said nothing, just checked her makeup while Koy changed again. This time the singer squeezed into a rubber dress, bright red, squirting some kind of liquid shine all over it, which she got Trish to help her buff to a high gloss. The thing plunged in front to her navel, and laced across the back, and though not much bigger than a tank top, it looked incredibly expensive. Everyone waited while she tried five or six pairs of shoes.

They came out under a sky that was bright but completely overcast. Robert frowned, sent Angie back for a different camera. Kaci walked to the parapet, looking away at the sea of roofs, the hulking skyscrapers. Seen from here, the city was impossibly vast, a great anthill bustling everywhere with activity. Something about it made her think of when she'd first come to New York, full of ambition and naive confidence, ready to make it hers, to get her bite of the apple. Such feelings were far in the past now, as if they came from a previous life. The city looked implacable, forbidding. She envied her younger self, a little. Where had all her confidence gone? She turned back toward the others: Robert and Angie were setting a reflective screen as Koy talked trash, making Barbi and Trish laugh. Beneath the gray sky, their finery was tawdry and cheap, their makeup overdone, clownish.

When the roof shots were done, they went back downstairs. "Great!" Robert was saying. "That was good work. I think we got some really good shots, some very usable shots."

"When can we see them?" Koy asked.

Robert looked at Angie. "Oh, I think we can have some proofs… day after tomorrow?" Angie nodded.

They made an appointment, and Robert said, "Well, great shoot, guys, great shoot. Now, Koy, you and I were going to do some solo shots… The rest of you are welcome to stick around, if you want."

"No, I'm out of here," Kaci said. "Barb, you want to share a cab?"

"Sure," Barbi said. "Trish?"

"You guys go ahead," Trish said. "It'll take me some time to get my stuff together."

As she packed up, Koy sat nearby, smoking a cigarette she'd bummed from Angie. "So what are these solo shots?" Trish said.

"Oh, you know," Koy said. "Robert thought we should do some because sometimes an editor just wants a picture of the singer, you know, if it's like an interview or whatever. Plus, we're going to do some soft-core," she went on, lowering her voice.

"Really?" Trish said, intrigued. "Like what?"

Koy shrugged. "I don't know, topless… Maybe I'll do the mic thing." She squeezed her breasts together. "And we talked about me naked in, like, feathers maybe, or dollar bills. That was Robert's idea but I like it. And see, he knows people at some of the skin magazines. I mean, you never know."

Robert heard her and came over. "Trish, you want in? We can do the same type of thing with you. It doesn't have to cost you a cent, we'll just do it on spec."

Trish blushed. "Oh, maybe not."

"You sure?" Robert said. "I mean, it's worth thinking about. And you don't know where it might lead. There's lots of money in skin."

Trish just giggled, embarrassed. "Cut it out, Robert," Koy said.

"Hey, you're turning down a gold mine," Robert said. "Guess, just *guess* what I'd pay you and Trish for a girl-girl layout."

Koy didn't answer.

"Just guess –it's probably double what you'd think. Or more –if we throw in a strap-on, show a little pink, some penetration…"

"Robert, you need to get out more," Koy said.

*      *      *

The phone rang; it was Koy. Diz rolled his eyes. Trish shrugged, picked it up. What else could she do? She listened for a couple minutes, told Koy to hang on.

"Koy wants to go to CBGB's to see Electric Mistress. She thinks it's important. Do you want to go?"

"No," Diz said. "You just go ahead and go."

"You sure? We can get in free."

"No, I've got something to do."

Trish nodded, thinking, something to do. She told Koy she'd be ready in a few minutes, went in the bathroom and fussed with her makeup, teased her hair. How long had it been since they went anywhere together? He never wanted to do anything. But maybe he just didn't want to go with Koy.

You're just making excuses for him, she thought. She went back in the other room and rummaged through her clothes. "Sure you don't want to go?" she asked. He was chopping up a line of coke.

"No," he said. "I don't like Jizzo's band, and I don't really feel like going out with Koy tonight. And I do have to take care of something." He snorted up the line. "You want one?" he said.

"No, thanks," Trish said. She changed clothes, kissed him 'bye, and left. As soon as she was gone he snorted up another, bigger line, and then paced nervously through the small apartment, back and forth, occasionally peeking through the blinds.

The street looked pretty quiet. He didn't want to go out, he was dreading it, but he'd put it off about as long as he could. He looked at his watch: nine. Both the Dope House and Laundromat were probably open, and they were safer. On the other hand, the better stuff was at Clinton and Rivington –Body Bag was particularly good, he really got off on that –but riskier: more cops, and you could get in trouble. He'd been mugged before –what, three, four times? – south of Houston, and he couldn't afford that now. Which reminded him.

He went to the closet and took down the bank envelope with the rest of his pay in it. It felt appallingly thin, and this was only Monday. Might have to go to the pawnshop before Thursday. Without looking, he took out three twenties, and felt of the envelope again. Still some left: he found some reassurance in that.

He took one bill, put it in his shirt pocket, folded the other two in quarters and put them in a pocket of his skin-tight black jeans. All right, he told himself, get it over with, and then you can come back and relax, play the guitar.

Finally at nine-thirty he took a deep breath, put on a coat, and went out the door. By now he was so wound up he could feel one corner of his mouth twitching periodically. You really don't need any more coke, he told himself going down the stairs. But maybe if I get one, I'll just have a little more tonight and I'll save the rest to get through the day tomorrow. But you've really got to save it this time. Dump it all out and divide it up, and put away two-thirds for tomorrow.

He hated his job, but since he'd been on the stuff, it had become a lot easier to deal with. It made a lot of difference. He just worked steadily and most of it didn't really bother him. The place was always either flush with cash or else on the verge of going bankrupt, but mostly the latter, and there was always a lot of screaming and shouting and scheming and a great need to blame somebody for any and every problem. Before the dope, he'd thought it was going to seriously affect his nerves, or give him an ulcer; and of course the worst had been when he was on-again, off-again, because he was always sick and vulnerable. But ever since the day he had quietly and passively accepted the fact that he was addicted, things had smoothed out. Except in the case of some unforeseen accident, he was almost never sick; the need to quit, to kick once and for all, had receded to a dull and vague necessity, to be met, like death, at some uncertain time in the future, which was, again like death, just as indefinite and unthinkable. On the speedballs he could work like a mad dog, and the whole day just went more quickly.

He went to the candy store and bought a quarter-gram. They made him take one of the little drinks, even though he tried to say he didn't want it: the guy just took one out of the refrigerator, put it in a paper bag and handed it to him. Diz always felt more suspicious with one than without; it was like a sign that he'd just copped. At least without it you could say that they didn't have what you'd wanted. One of the stores sometimes gave away real Cokes, but this was just junkie juice: colored sugar-water –you could've fixed in it. As soon as he got out on the street he threw it in the nearest trashcan.

He turned the corner and walked right into the middle of a raid. It was a nightmare; his heart jumped into his throat. The cops were everywhere:

uniforms, plain-clothes men, special agents from the Mayor's task force, big guys in blue windbreakers with yellow letters on the back. You could see their shoulder holsters through the thin material. They were frisking people, holding them against walls, cuffing them, walking them away to waiting cars and vans – the haul a sorry-looking bunch, men and women of every race, buyers and sellers, regular people, hard-core junkies, bums, rock-n-rollers. Diz just kept walking as purposefully as possible, right through the middle of it all, sure that at any second he would get grabbed, but he just kept going. Whether they were done, or didn't notice him, or he looked like he genuinely belonged there, for whatever reason he walked straight through the whole thing and nobody stopped him.

The other side of Rivington the street was empty, absolutely nobody on the whole block. He kept going straight toward Delancey. His heart was pounding so hard he could have fallen over. He couldn't believe it. He'd thought he was a goner, for sure. Why shouldn't they grab him too? The thought of the jail was just too much; he tried to put it out of his mind. What a nightmare.

At Delancey, since he had a couple extra dollars, he went in the Chinese restaurant and ordered some fried rice. Carrying it around seemed like a good excuse for being out, and besides he could eat it later. When it came, he didn't really want to leave yet, and he dawdled around getting soy sauce and duck sauce and extra napkins and stuff; but he wanted to get the mission over with and now he really needed a bag. He hated this shit, he really did: the cat and mouse game.

Let's go, can't hang around here all night; but instead of going back up Suffolk, he turned toward Clinton, mingling with the crowd and taking it easy. Better to not go too fast. A lot of people were still out: couples, people buying food, whole families with armloads of bags from the discount stores, kids admiring the jewelers' displays, or wandering slowly in and out of the clothing shops. The restaurants were busy, the kitchen doors open to the street; the shouting of the cooks and waiters, the banging of the dishwashers, mingled with the smell of steam and fried food. But Rivington was deserted: away from the corner no one could be seen in either direction. That was bad. He kept going. Here the stores thinned out, it was calmer, mostly just people going home. He didn't see anyone he knew; the hallways where he sometimes copped were empty, or their doors shut; it looked like the raid had been very thorough. Stanton was empty. Feeling like an idiot now with the fried rice, he turned back. A woman went past, glanced at him scornfully, and looked away.

The hell with you, he thought. He had to cop. He'd try Rivington once more before walking all the way to Laundromat: who knew what was going on up there? Now the dread of it taking an hour or more to cop some dope surpassed the fear of getting busted. But on his way back toward Rivington he saw a sector car coming north up Clinton, and his nerves wound up again. It rolled slowly past him, the cops looking him over; he looked back calmly, as calmly as he could manage, as if he wasn't doing anything wrong, although the bag of cocaine in his pocket was burning like a hot ember against his chest. Go to hell, he thought as the car passed on and away. This is my damned neighborhood, I belong here.

At Rivington a big black guy was standing to the side of the restaurant where the sellers hung out. Diz made eye contact, casually crossed the street and went over to him.

"How many?" the guy said quietly.

"What do you got?" Diz said.

"Body Bag."

"Okay," Diz said. "Give me four."

"Come inside," the guy said, opening a door behind him. Diz didn't much like this but he followed. Inside was a dingy, narrow hallway leading to a set of stairs. In the dim light, Diz could just make out a hand-made sign stuck to the wall. *WARNING*, it said, over a crude drawing of a pair of eyes. *DON'T BUY OR SELL DRUGS HERE. I KNOW AND I'M CALLING POLICE.* It made Diz snicker; at the same time, he felt pretty uptight.

"I only got two," the guy said.

"Okay," Diz said, thinking, Jeeze, that's just great. "You gonna get any more?"

"Not tonight. You want it or not?"

"Okay, sure," Diz said, getting out one of the twenties. He put the two bags in his shirt pocket with the coke.

"You shouldn't put it there, you should put it in your underwear," the guy said. "Lots of Five-O tonight."

"It's okay, don't worry about it," Diz said.

"Put it in your underwear!" the guy said, glaring at him.

Diz shrugged, stuck the bags down his pants. He turned to go.

"Wait," the guy said, putting a huge hand against Diz's chest. Oh no, Diz thought, his heart jumping. But the guy just opened the door and looked out. "Okay, go," he said, and pushed Diz out the door, slamming it behind him. Diz hurried away, wondering who was watching, as if those eyes from the sign were looking at him, staring from every window on the block. He joined the flow of pedestrians on Clinton; everyone ignored him. Were they ignoring him? He felt completely vulnerable. No, no, he told himself; he was just paranoid.

The bag with the fried rice, completely saturated with oil, was starting to come apart; drops of oil were slowly gathering to fall from the bottom; one splashed on his jeans. He took hold of the box by the sides, but even through the paper his fingertips got coated with grease. He removed a paper napkin and wiped away the excess, not wanting to stain his clothes, and when he looked up for a trashcan, two beat cops were standing in his path, looking at him.

It took him by surprise, and something must have shown on his face, for when he swerved to go around them, as if they were just another obstacle, one of them stepped into his path and said, "Hey, man. What's going on?"

"What?" Diz said. He hated it when they called you 'man' or tried to sound cool, but he could feel the blood flushing his skin. His heart was racing. This was bad, he had to get out of this.

"I said what's going on," the cop repeated in an irritated tone.

"Going home," Diz said.

"What's in the bag?"

"Dinner," Diz said. "Chicken fried rice."

"Where do you live?"

"Houston Street."

The cop was studying him. He had a smug air of power, and looked vaguely familiar. Diz hated the sight of him.

"Don't I know you?" the cop said.

"No," Diz said. "I don't think so."

The cop kept looking at him. "Yeah, I do," he said. "I know you. I busted you for pot, right over there." He nodded at the corner.

This is crazy, Diz thought. "You must be thinking of someone else," he said.

"No, it was you," the cop said. "I remember. It was you, wasn't it? Don't lie."

"Somebody else," Diz said.

"No, it was you, I remember, just there was something different about you. You had red hair then. Didn't you used to have red hair?"

"No," Diz said, starting to feel angry at the unjust stupidity of all this. He'd *never* had red hair.

"What, you got a brother?" the cop said, irritated now too.

"No, I don't got a brother, and I'm trying to tell you, you've got me mixed-up with somebody else."

"You don't got a brother?"

"No."

"Then it was you. Don't lie to me."

"Look," Diz said. He sighed, trying to keep his cool. "I don't have a brother, and I've never had red hair, and I've never been busted for pot here or anywhere else, and I don't remember ever seeing you before, so I'm afraid you've mistaken me for someone else."

"No," the cop said. He was tapping his stick against his leg and staring at

Diz. "No," he said again. "It was you." He glanced at his partner. "Okay. You can go." As Diz turned to leave, the cop said, "See you around."

You son of a bitch, Diz thought as he headed up Clinton. Trying to goad me to the point he could search me. Diz was mad, but he was also trembling from the close call, so bad he could hardly walk. When he got home, he put the fried rice in the refrigerator. He wasn't hungry anymore. It took most of the first bag of dope before he calmed down. *Son of a bitch!* he thought, I've got to go out again! Only this time I'm just going to Laundromat.

*          *          *

Koy and Trish walked out of CBGB's with their ears ringing. Even the Bowery and its stench of stale urine and vomit were refreshing after the stifling atmosphere of the club.

"Alright," Koy said, looking around at the deserted street. "Well, what did you think of that?"

"Jizzo," Trish said, "can't sing." Koy giggled. Trish went on: "I mean, she's just not a singer. And the band was terrible."

"She sure is skinny, though," Koy said. "And don't say shit like that. That's JT's band."

"Big deal," Trish said, imitating Jizzo's gravelly voice. "Jizzo can't sing. And she's such a prima donna." Koy looked at her, and Trish added pointedly, "It's pretty uncool to bitch and moan while your guitar player tries to tune."

Koy rolled her eyes, but said, "You're right. She could come up with something else to say."

"Or just wiggle her ass and try to look cute. I'm sure the boys would like that a lot more than her griping."

"Want to go to the Bunker for a minute?" Koy said, still looking around.

"I don't know… I ought to go home," Trish said vaguely.

"C'mon, we don't have to stay long. It'd be a good thing to do."

Trish looked at her watch. "Okay, but just for a little while, or Dizzy'll get worried."

"Dizzy, schmizzy," Koy said. "He should've come with us. Come on. Let's take a cab."

She was waving her arms at one on Houston. Its turn signal came on.

"I'll pay," Koy said, adding, "We can split a bag on the way."

"Whatever you say," Trish said. The cab pulled up and they got in. The driver frowned at the destination, but when Koy said they were afraid to walk at that time of night, he shrugged and took off. By the next light Koy had the bag ripped open and half of it snorted up without any fuss, but when she passed it over, Trish thought her half looked rather small. Still, who was she to complain? —and she honked it up and gave the empty glassine back to Koy. That familiar, delicious glow spread across her nerves, and she sighed, settling back in the seat. The car pulled up at St Mark's Place.

The club had a cover charge but Koy knew the doorman so they cut the line and went in free. To Trish, it seemed like Koy knew almost everyone there, but the music was so loud that although the Koy shouted introductions, she couldn't hear a word, just smiled and shouted hello. They gradually made their way to the bar where Koy kissed the bartender on both cheeks with great effusion. When their drinks came he waved Trish's money away. Koy clinked glasses with a wink that said: See? It's who you know. She downed hers at a gulp. Another round appeared as soon as she put down her glass, and she leaned back, posing like a film starlet and scanning the crowd.

Trish was watching the band, a bunch of pretty boys. As usual the singer couldn't sing and the rest played in a silly macho way that said Look at me! —but sounded terrible. All the songs were alike, which could be a good thing but wasn't this time. The singer kept rubbing his crotch while he howled into the microphone; mercifully, he couldn't be heard very well over the blaring guitars. For the finale he knocked down the rest of the band, and the song ended with everyone lying on the floor. The lights went down and the house music came up at a more tolerable level.

"Thank goodness," Koy said, finishing her second drink.

"Really," Trish said. "They were worse than Jizzo's band."

"Cuter, though. I liked the drummer's red hair. You know," she went on in a lower voice, "I heard that Jizzo is a slut."

"Well, I don't like that word," Trish said, "but I'll tell you what I heard from Diz."

They were talking tête-à-tête now, oblivious to the admiring stares of the passing rockers.

"What's that?" Koy said.

"Well, it's not like it's a big deal," Trish said, "but it's funny in a way. Dizzy said that T-Bone told him –you know, Timmy from the first Contusions –that he was out on the avenue one night, all fucked up I suppose, and he ran into Jizzo coming out of the Fuzz Box, and she was definitely all fucked up. So T-Bone hits on her, for lack of anything better to do, he said, and she went for it; so they walk down to the Dope House and cop a couple of bags, and go back to Jizzo's, she lives right around the corner on Avenue B. So T-Bone, as he put it, just 'one-nighted' her and tells her the next day that he'll call her, and he never does, and after that, every time he sees her, like out on the avenue, he just turns around and goes the other way." Trish took a sip from her drink.

"So?" Koy said.

"Well now wait a minute, I'm only getting to the good part," Trish said. "So, in this neighborhood, it's not so easy to just totally avoid someone, right? But whenever he does run right smack into her, he's like, 'I'll call you.' And you'd think Jizzo would get the message, right? But she never seems to understand." Trish rolled her eyes.

"Yeah, so, go on," Koy said.

"So one night the Contusions have a gig over at the Underground, and Diz and T-Bone always used to help each other move; and when they finally get done and it's like three in the morning, they take a walk over to the building to cop. And when they get there it's one of those times when everybody's standing in line and they only let you in one or two at a time. So they get in the line and they're all burned-out and the line is piling up behind them and all of a sudden the person right in front of them turns around and it's Jizzo!"

"Oh shit!" Koy said.

"Yeah! So when they come out, there she is waiting. T-Bone's about to tear his hair out and Jizzo just gloms onto him, so Diz bails and comes home; but T-Bone told him later that she followed him all the way from Second Street up to Thirteenth where he lived. Now T-Bone's girlfriend Emily who lives in Connecticut had come down to see the show, and she's waiting for him upstairs, and he's trying to get rid of Jizzo but she just won't take the hint, and she follows him right into the foyer of his building, and he stops there, like, trapped, and unwilling to go any further. So she's like going all out now, and to convince him, I guess, she just gets down on her knees right there and starts giving him a blow job."

Koy giggled.

"Now right next door is a big coke spot," Trish said, "and all the time she's going down on him people are going past left and right, copping, and he's afraid somebody's gonna find them or his girlfriend's gonna come down right as Jizzo's sucking him off, and he's both desperate to get rid of her and kind of into it. So Jizzo's wearing something like what she had on tonight, that denim vest over a push-up bra, right? So finally as he's about to get off, he yanks his cock out of her mouth and spurts cum all over her boobs!"

"No!" Koy said, cracking up.

"Yes!" Trish giggled. "And she just sits there for a second, stunned, looking at him, with jism all over her and her expensive brassiere, and then she screams and jumps up and slaps him and runs out down the street, crying, with cum dripping off of her."

They were both giggling uncontrollably, spluttering and trying to stop, when a male voice said, "Hey, just what are you girls talking about?"

Koy and Trish turned around. The guy was a rocker: leather jacket, dyed-blond hair. He was pretty cute but he looked stupid —or maybe just really fucked-up.

"Huh?" Trish said. "Oh, we're just talking about somebody we know."

"Hey, like, I know who you guys are," he said. Koy looked at Trish and reached for her drink, smiling her show-biz smile.

"Yeah, I saw you the other night at CBGB's," he went on. "You're Dreamwhip, right?"

Trish and Koy both nodded.

"Cool," he said. "Like, I really like your band a lot. You were really good. I totally got into it."

"Cool," Trish said. "Thank you."

"Yeah, thanks," Koy said. She was digging around in her jacket pocket. "Listen, we're playing here in a week. Next Thursday. Here." She gave him a couple of discount passes. "We'd be glad for you to come. Bring a friend. It's gonna rock."

"Cool," he said. "You guys were rocking the other night." He looked around, bent closer. Trish could smell the alcohol on his breath. "Listen," he said. "I was just going out to my car before the next band to do some blow. You guys want to come with me?"

"Um, no, thanks," Koy said. "I'm trying to stay away from it."

Trish thought fast, made up her mind. "I'll go, sure," she said, standing up. She finished her drink and put the glass on the bar.

Koy was looking at her. "I'll wait for you here," she said. As the guy turned toward the door, she whispered, "Be careful!"

Trish winked at her and followed the guy out. Third Avenue was quiet, only a few people hanging around outside. "It's up here," he said, turning toward Ninth. "Right around the corner."

But really they went nearly to the end of the silent one-way block. As the traffic noise faded behind them, he said, "Yeah... You guys are cool, your band... You're like, uh, the guitar player, right?"

"No," Trish said. "I'm the bass player."

"Oh yeah, right, right," he said. "Yeah. Like, I'm here to see my buddy's band, you know, but, wow, after that last band I needed something stimulating, you know?"

Trish laughed and nodded, thinking, What an idiot. The car was a four-door sedan with New Jersey plates. They got in and he turned on the radio, took out a vial and a metal plate, and dumped out two big lines. They snorted it up. Trish giggled as the stuff hit her: good, much better than you usually got.

"Alright!" she said. "Cool!"

He was grinning at her, nodding his head. "Yeah, it's pretty alright, isn't it?"

"Mmm-hmm," Trish said.

They sat there for a minute, high, listening to the radio. "Wow," he said. "You want another line?"

"Okay," Trish said.

They each had another big line. Trish was high as a kite. "Hey," he said. "You know, it's really cool, getting to know you like this… I get this great feeling being around you." He leaned closer, said hoarsely: "You know… you're really beautiful."

Trish just smiled at him. He kissed her, tentatively, then again hard. His hands squeezed her breasts; she arched her spine, thrusting them up and toward him, turning her lips away from the foul taste of his mouth; he plunged his tongue into her cleavage. She looked down at him, at the blood pulsing beneath the skin of his neck, his face smothered in her warm flesh. Then he pinched her nipples too hard and it hurt; she bared her fangs and tore open his veins.

\*           \*           \*

Then there was the dinner. Suzanne Knickerbocker, Kaci's old friend from college, called. She'd brought her boyfriend –a Yale guy –home to introduce him to her family, and while they were there, she wanted Kaci and JT to have dinner with them. At first JT had agreed, probably just to placate her, and at the last minute he claimed conflicting plans, trying to get out of it. She'd more or less pleaded with him, so that in the end he grudgingly complied, a concession she was sure to pay dearly. That night, he came home high, started drinking before they left, and refused to change his ratty clothes. They'd agreed to meet for drinks before dinner; at the bar JT out-drank everyone easily two to one; and if at first he was sullen, even surly, by the time they reached the restaurant he'd become quarrelsome and insulting. They hurried through the meal as if by mutual accord, and afterwards Kaci's friends jumped in a cab, leaving her on the sidewalk almost without saying goodbye. Furious, she turned on him, demanded to know how he could embarrass her so. He just sneered at her.

"What do I give a shit about your snotty Ivy League friends? They fucking look down on anybody who didn't go to Harvard or Yale. I bet you never told 'em I dropped out of college, did you?" He spit on the sidewalk. People going by were staring.

"JT, they don't care about that…"

"The fuck they don't –that's the only thing they do care about. Well, I'll tell you something: that Susan or Suzanne, she's a tight-ass, frigid bitch, a neurotic who couldn't get by in the world without daddy's money, and her boyfriend's a closet case, he probably sneaks off at night with the stable boy, to get fucked up the ass."

"JT, you're such a jerk."

"I am, aren't I? And your friends don't like me. But your girlfriend's probably jealous of you: at least I ain't no limp-wrist Ivy League faggot."

He was so proud of himself, it was laughable –pitiful –except she lived with him. How had things gotten to this point? The whole thing was too horrible –unbearable –she couldn't stand it all, just wanted to run away. A taxi was coming.

"I'm going home," she said, and waved for it.

"Suit yourself," he said, and was walking away, headed downtown, before the cab even stopped.

\*　　　　　\*　　　　　\*

Koy thought she might go by and see him at work —just pass by, say hi. The day was beautiful, cool but warm in the sun, the air clear, just enough of a breeze; she had been shopping, up on St. Mark's, and decided to walk home. She kept seeking her reflection, checking herself out: she was dressed a little like Daisy Duke, in halter-top and cut-offs, but she had on her new knee boots, and she felt good.

Everywhere people were selling stuff, a rag-tag bazaar spread out on flattened cardboard boxes and dirty blankets. Koy scrutinized it all carefully but found nothing she really liked. She never found anything. She'd heard of people who found incredible stuff, Versace dresses, diamond earrings, shrunken heads —but her, never.

The pizza place had all its doors open and the radio on. When she came in everybody looked up quick; a couple of them said something she couldn't really hear. Johnny came walking toward the front, wiping his hands on a towel. He glanced around at the others, looking cross, but smiled at her. He looked cute in his apron with flour on it and his hat cocked to one side.

"Hey," she said, winking at him.

"Hey," he said. "What's going on?"

"Nothing," she said. "I'm just on my way home, thought I'd say Hi. You guys busy?"

"No," he said. "Not right now. We were earlier."

Koy nodded. Johnny seemed uptight, glancing around at the shop. She wasn't sure why, but she didn't want to irritate him.

"I better go," she said. "I know you've got to work." She kissed him quickly on one cheek. "Call me tonight?"

"Sure," he said. As she went out, she heard the others begin to hoot and jeer, razzing him about her.

He called her that night, all right. He was already pretty mad when he called, but before long he was just being mean. She wasn't quite sure why; he wasn't very articulate, he must have been jealous of something; she gathered she'd caused quite a stir at the pizza place. She felt exasperated: this was New York! –and besides, just because she liked him didn't give him the right to tell her anything. How she dressed was her own business –and anyway, he used to like it.

After a while she told him she had to go. Which was true, she had a date, she had to get ready. But he wouldn't stop, just kept after her. It all went on forever, but when she finally got off the phone, it had only been about fifteen minutes.

She wasn't exactly angry, she just felt exhausted by it all, upset and depressed. And after all, what had she done? It wasn't fair.

Little Johnny. He really needed to grow up.

*   *   *

Trish had decided on the gym because it was raining –always a bad time to score –but she had to be careful, she could never leave with someone: not only might you be noticed by the employees who took care of the front desk, but video cameras were all over the place, at the entrance, downstairs in the lobby, and in the elevators too, for all she knew. The cameras were a nightmare, they were everywhere; you couldn't imagine how many there were until you looked for them –and then they were everywhere you went, bewildering, capturing your image and your voice, date-stamping and recording them, forever.

From the exercise bikes, she could easily survey the room. Detached from others by the music in her headphones, going hard with the beat, her mind clear, she felt elevated, powerful –and it was easy to select a score, to time her routine to his, catch his eye, finish at the same time, and leave right before him.

She had her umbrella open, trying to hold on to it and digging through her purse, as he came out of the elevator. He stopped short, came on out the door. The rain was blowing in little gusts.

"Hi!" he said.

"Hi!" she answered, still going through the motions of looking for something.

"Do you need some help?" he said.

"Well," she said. "This is stupid, but I can't find my subway tokens or my money. I was in a hurry, I must have left it all home."

"Oh!" he said, and laughed. "That could happen to anyone. Look, my car's right down here, why not let me give you a ride?"

She put on her gloves as they walked to the car. He opened the passenger door for her, got in, started the engine, buckled his seatbelt. She was fumbling with hers, couldn't get it to work. "Could you help me?" she said, giggling. "I can't figure it out."

He leaned over awkwardly, hampered by his own belt, stretching his neck right in front of her —it was just that easy.

*     *     *

Mick and Diz were hanging out at the Fuzz Box, talking about the band, the conversation just going around in circles, like always. But Mick came back from another trip to the bar and said, "Hey, like there's a guy here that I know, and he's got quarter-grams of blow, if you want to split one." "Oh yeah?" Diz said, thinking that this might be better than the usual stuff he got. "How much?" "It's thirty-five but he wants to split and said he'd give it to me for thirty." "Well," Diz said. "I guess so, if you want to." "Yeah, sure," Mick said. "Why not?"

Diz gave him some money and Mick went back to the bar; he was back in a couple of minutes and said, "Alright, we're happening. Where should we go?" "Do you want to go down to my house?" Diz said. But they were both psyched-up and didn't want to wait, and Mick said, "No… Let's just go in the bathroom."

They jammed into the tiny space, entirely covered with graffiti and rotting from filth. "Stand in front of the door," Mick said. "Wow, where can we do it?" But the only place was right in front of him, a narrow shelf over the toilet, incredibly dirty. Mick opened up the aluminum-foil packet, dumped out the powder and scraped it into two piles with his driver's license, took a rolled-up bill from his pocket, and loudly snorted up one. Jeeze! thought Dizzy. All at once? Somebody thumped on the door, wanting in. "Just a minute," Dizzy said. He took the bill, changed places with Mick, and bent over the stuff. The pile looked huge: if it were really good, he'd probably die. He snorted up half; the stuff hit the back of his throat, burning like Drano; he choked, shook his head. The door thumped again, louder. "Wait a goddamn minute," he said, and snorted up the other half.

Mick took his bill back and they filed out. A soft-looking fat kid with a mohawk was standing in the hall. "Like, c'mon man, what is this?" the kid said. "I'm about to piss in my pants."

"Suit yourself," Mick said.

They went back to the bar. Dizzy's heart was pounding, going a hundred miles an hour. "Oh man," he said, and sat back down. "Wow."

"Yeah," Mick said.

They sat there for a while, Diz wasn't sure how long. He wasn't feeling very good: he was jacked way too far up, his heart was racing, breath short, nerves wound tight. "Look," he said to Mick. "Do you think you could get me another drink? Here's some money."

"Sure," Mick said. "Hey man, you all right? What's the matter?"

"I'll be alright," Diz said. "Get yourself one, too. Get me a double."

But he was uptight, grinding his teeth and looking around, just wired. When Mick brought the drink, he drank down half of it straight off; in a couple minutes he was feeling a little better, but not much. Jeeze, I should have known better than to do so much at once, he was thinking; I shouldn't have done that,

I should have saved some. I *know* better than this. And here was Mick, rambling, trying to talk to him about the band again, but he couldn't follow it.

"No man, really, I think the deal is that we had a different sound when we had T-Bone," Mick was saying. Diz was nodding but he really couldn't concentrate, he was thinking he wasn't going to be able to take it. But he hadn't brought anything with him...

"Yeah, see, Ratso and I have been talking, and he and I agree that, you know, having the focus of a singer is good," Mick was saying. Diz really wished he were paying attention, he wanted to pay attention, this was probably just more of the same as always, but he wasn't sure; the trouble was, right now, it just didn't matter, all that mattered was that he really had to come down, he had to go take care of it now, right away. After that he could sit down, have this discussion, think about whatever it was, no problem, he'd be glad to, but right now, he had to come down first.

"But, like, I guess it's the interplay of the two guitars, which frees the bass and drums to, well, to get to the next level. That's how you take it to a higher level."

"Hey, listen, man," Dizzy said, quietly, and leaning forward, trying to get Mick to do the same.

"What?" Mick said.

"Look," Diz said. "I got too high, I've got to come down a little... Do you want to take a walk over to Laundromat?"

"Uh, yeah," Mick said, seeming surprised. "Okay."

Diz finished his drink and stood up. Mick was grumbling –did they have to go this very second? –but he finished his own drink and followed Diz out the door. They headed east, Diz going pretty fast, and Mick still trying to talk about the band.

"Remember those gigs with T-Bone where it was just like a wall of sound? At the very first one didn't Trish say we were like a machine, huge and unstoppable? And that demo, man, that demo we made at Danny Savage's, that thing sounds big."

They were about halfway to Avenue B when Diz thought he saw a cop car coming their way; his heart sank. Yes: rolling slowly west, just approaching B now. This was bad; he never came here this late on Friday, he didn't know – maybe there was always a lot of heat; or then again, maybe they'd open right back up. But when they got to B and crossed over, the block was empty.

"Shit, they look closed," Mick said.

"Let's walk on past," Diz said. "You never can tell when they'll open."

"Yeah," Mick said. "And sometimes they look open from here, but you walk up and it closes."

"Oh, yeah, I hate that," Diz said. "Usually that means there's a cop *right there.*"

But the block wasn't empty, just very quiet. They passed one lookout sitting in a car with the window open. "Keep walking," he said.

They kept walking. A small man, standing next to a tree, seemingly oblivious of them, without looking at them at all, said, "Keep walking."

"Jeeze," Mick said after they passed. "You'd think they'd know that we know, that if the guy ain't standing up there, it ain't going on."

It definitely wasn't going on, but Diz kept watching the door at the top of the stairs, hoping it would open, and the guy would step out, hands in the pockets of his apron –it had happened before, just that quick, the door opens and there's the guy, and they're open for business.

But nothing happened. They went on by. Fifty feet on the other side was another guy, stationed silently in a doorway. "Keep walking," he said. They kept walking, reached Avenue C, turned the corner and stopped. "Now what?" Mick said.

What's there to do? Diz thought; he was checking the avenue for cops. "Wait a minute and go back, I guess," he said.

No cops –at the moment –but he hated Avenue C, it made you feel obvious and exposed –nowhere to hide. And tonight there were lots of people out, which just meant they stuck out all the worse. "Let's cross the street, go up here," he said, turning uptown.

"Man, this ain't a good place to hang out," Mick said.

"Relax," Diz said. "What do you think's going to happen to you?"

As he crossed he could see there was still nothing going on. They walked on slowly. This always happened when you really wanted to score. You just had to be cool, wait it out. Somewhere, right now, they were selling dope; in a minute, they'd be selling it *here*.

Mick coughed and said, "Look man, I just don't think we should be hanging out over here."

"Okay," Diz said. "Let's turn around at the corner, go back and see if they've opened up."

He tried to drag it out –although, of course, sometimes, when you tried not to go back too soon, you got there just as they were closing *again* —but Mick was anxious to get moving. And his own nerves were crawling, the cocaine riding him relentlessly. As they turned the corner, he could see the place was still closed. They went down the opposite side of the street –with the straight people –hoping to see it open up. Nothing happened.

"Well, shit," Diz said when they got to the corner. "Now what?"

"You want to go over to that bar and wait a few minutes?" Mick said.

The corner bar was usually packed, and painfully loud; Diz had only been there a few times, he didn't think he could stand it. "Not really," he said.

"I know," Mick said. "There's a guy that's sometimes on Sixth Street, maybe he's out tonight."

"Let's check it out," Diz said. "Is it any good?" He'd never heard of this.

"Yeah, it's pretty good," Mick said.

People were out on Sixth but Mick couldn't tell if any of them was the guy. Twice he thought he saw him, but then no. "Well, maybe he ain't here," he kept saying. Diz was trying to decide: Laundromat again, or walk all the way to the Dope House?

But a guy came walking toward them –a regular, more or less normal-looking guy –and Mick said, "There he is. Hey man, what's going on?"

The guy stopped and said, "What's up?"

"Hey, this is my buddy," Mick said, indicating Diz. "He's cool. We play in a band together."

"How you doing," Diz said.

They guy nodded, said, "So, what's up? Looking for something?"

"Yeah," Mick said. "You got any of that I got last time?"

"That shit's gone," the guy said. "But this is better anyway. How many you want?"

"Uh, like, one for me, but…"

"Three," Diz said.

"Wait here a minute," the guy said and walked away. This had started out weird; Diz was glad to see it turning into a drug deal. The guy retrieved something from the base of a lamppost, came back, took the money, and gave them the stuff. "Later," he said and walked away.

Diz stashed two bags and opened the third. "What's up?" Mick said. Diz ignored him, looked up and down the street, stepped into a doorway, pulled out a length of straw, and tore off the top of the bag.

"You're gonna do that now?" Mick said.

Diz snorted half the bag up each nostril and held his head back, pinching his nose shut. Relief oozed slowly down his spine. Though not real strong, it did the job. He put the straw away, tore the bag open, licked up the residual powder, and tossed it away.

"Ahh," he said. "Much better."

"Man, you're too much," Mick said. "You ought to be more careful, you'll get us both in trouble."

Diz ignored him. He was starting to feel all right for the first time since the Fuzz Box bathroom –even starting to feel good! What a relief! Finally! Okay: he could deal with it now, with –whatever.

"Wow," he said at last. "You know, we shouldn't have done all that coke at once."

"Man, you ought to be more careful," Mick repeated. "You're starting to remind me of T-Bone."

*     *     *

The day before the TV interview, Kaci decided that the best plan, both as far as her nerves were concerned and just in terms of general organization, would be to order a car service to take them out to the college: it could pick her up first, and head downtown, picking up Barb then Trish on their way to Koy's, which would give Koy plenty of warning and maybe that way she could be ready on time. Or at least close. Kaci hated to pay for the car service but she didn't really know anyone who owned a car, and a taxi would cost even more. She called Koy first. "No way, that's tomorrow?" Koy said. "Damn it, Koy," Kaci said. "I'm just kidding," Koy said. "The taping's at five, right? When's the car picking you up?" "Three," Kaci said. "Okay," Koy said, "so, tomorrow, when it picks you up, just call me to say you're leaving." Kaci had anticipated this.

She called the others: Barb said fine, Trish wasn't home. Kaci left a message, thought for a minute, and ordered the car. Trish wouldn't argue: she was still the new girl.

The next day, they were almost late anyway. The car service man called at five to three; Kaci told him she'd be there in a minute, and called Koy. Koy wasn't home. Kaci left a message, thinking, I'm going to kill her if she's late. On the way to Barb's she tried not to think about it.

At three o'clock, Koy was out trying to cop and it had really turned into a big hassle. She should have taken care of it the night before, or at least earlier in the day, but one thing led to another; and when she finally went out at two-thirty, nobody was around. Clinton was absolutely deserted, no one at the school or the playground, nobody on Rivington even playing dominos, much less selling dope, and only one little old man drinking beer by the bodega on Suffolk. The streets were empty, and even some shops were closed. What was going on? Where was everyone? Was it a holiday?

Time was getting away from her, and she still hadn't copped. This was bad. But no way was she going out to Brooklyn somewhere, without any; who knew how long it would take? She kept walking… Finally, desperate, she went all the way to Ludlow, and just as she came around the corner, a guy was peeping out one of the doorways, and he waved her over and let her in. Of course she had to wait while he went upstairs. She didn't have her watch but it had to be three.

On her way back she kept trying to figure out what to wear. Why hadn't they talked about this? She was the only one to think about their image in an overall way —though when she tried to suggest something, they acted like she was giving orders. The hell with them, she'd just upstage them all… If you wore the right thing, no one watching would see anyone but you. But she had to hurry; she didn't want to make Kaci mad again.

Barbi was waiting downstairs and just came out and got in the car when Kaci pulled up. "Hey, how are you?" she said as they took off again. "Good," Kaci said, trying not to sound uptight. "How are you?" "Fine," Barbi said. "You talk to Koy?"

"Uh, no," Kaci said. "Not today. But I talked to her yesterday and she knows when we're going." The words sounded strange to her ears, somehow wrong: they were *already* going. "That's cool," Barbi said. After a minute she said, "Do you think we ought to call her and tell her we're on our way?" "Well, I already did," Kaci said, trying to sound cool. "That was right before I left my place, but she didn't answer. Who knows," she added, "maybe she was in the shower." She laughed; did it sound forced? —it sounded forced to her. "I left a message."

"Oh," Barbi said. They rode a couple blocks before Barbi said, "Well, she'll be there."

"Oh, yeah," Kaci said.

At Trish's, Kaci jumped out and rang the buzzer. "I'll be right there," Trish's voice said. Kaci went back to the car; they waited close to five minutes, watching the traffic on Houston; finally Trish came out, carrying a huge suitcase, another bag like when you buy a hundred dollar's worth of makeup, a big handbag, and her bass. Jesus Christ, Kaci thought, Trish has got all this stuff and I didn't even think about bringing my guitar? What is the matter with me? The driver scrambled out to help Trish, who beneath her fun-fur was about to pop out of a leopard-skin brassiere.

When Koy got back to her apartment it was quarter-past three. She checked her messages: Kaci sounded pissed-off. Well, there was nothing she could do about that. She just had to get ready really fast. They weren't here yet, were they? She looked out the window. No, if they were already here, they'd have already called.

She cooked up a shot quick and booted it. No one had called yet; that was good; but it was three twenty-five. She grabbed a travel bag and stuffed clothes into it, helter skelter. You could never tell what the others would wear. Did she need shoes? Wear a pair of boots, and take some heels in the bag. Stockings, some lingerie. The live footage! They didn't have a real video but they did have the footage from CBGB's, where was it? That was better than nothing. This was a TV show after all: they needed some video footage; otherwise, what were they going to do, just sit there and talk?

The phone rang; Koy answered it. "Koy, we're downstairs," Barbi said. "Okay," Koy said. "Just hang on. I'll be down in a couple of minutes."

Where *was* it? She really had to get the place cleaned up, she couldn't find anything. She threw on some clothes, hated them, changed. One look in the mirror and she added more clothes to the bag, knowing she'd want to change again when she got there. Makeup; Trish would have hairspray and a blow dryer, she didn't have to mess with that; was there any coke left? While she was looking for the vial, she found the footage, buried under a pile of stuff, of course, and then the coke, enough for a couple of lines. She snorted a pop, looked around, worried that she'd forgotten something but also anxious to go, afraid they'd call again before she could get out the door. "Oh hell," she said out loud, "as long as I've got the video and I look good, what else matters? What else do I need?" But still feeling like she'd forgotten something, though at a total loss for what it might be, she zipped up the bag and ran downstairs.

Kaci saw Koy coming out the building and looked at her watch: ten minutes to four. "There she is," Barbi said, and tapped on the window at Trish, who was outside, leaning against the car and smoking a cigarette. The driver jumped out again, popping open the trunk, and rushing to help Koy, who was struggling with a huge bag that was apparently stuffed full. "Hi!" Koy said, as he loaded it into the car. "Are we ready to be on TV?"

"If we ever get there," Kaci muttered. Koy and Trish squeezed into the back seat, the driver jumped in, and they took off. "Well, I'm excited," Koy said.

"Me too," Barbi said, and Trish said, "Oh, yeah… Kaci, where is it we're going?"

"It's on the other side of Brooklyn," Kaci said. "Near Coney Island."

"Wow, that's like saying the other side of the world," Trish said.

"Have you ever been to Coney?" Koy asked. "No, never," Trish said. "Really?" Barbi said. "Oh, you ought to go sometime, it's fun." "Yeah," Koy said. "I can't believe you've never been there." She started telling the story of her first visit. Kaci was watching the traffic and tuned her out. She was sure now that they would be late; the show wasn't live, but she hated to waste other people's time: it wasn't right and besides, it usually made them mad. The car crossed the Brooklyn Bridge and zoomed down the BQE, and it made her nervous how the driver kept staring at Koy and Trish in the rear-view mirror; she wished he would watch the road.

"So when I came back with my belly-button pierced, Robert just flipped out!" Koy said. "It was like all of a sudden like he was my dad or something."

Trish and Barbi laughed. Koy was about to go on when Barbi said, "Well, listen, while we're on the way, why don't we figure out what we're going to do? I mean, well, this TV-show thing is different, you know?"

"That's a good idea," Trish said. "Like, what's it going to be like? And what are we going to do?"

Koy laughed. "We're going to be Dreamwhip!"

"Well, yeah, right," Barbi said, "but, I mean... Kaci, why don't you tell us what you know about it?"

Everyone waited, deferring to her, and finally she said, thinking that she'd already said all this before, "Well, there's this guy, Jake, who's the host... It's like one of those celebrity talk shows, right? Like a rock-n-roll *Tonight Show*. It starts off with him making some jokes, and then we come on and we're the guests. And we'll talk about the band... I mean, it's stupid, but this show's on public access all the time, over and over again..."

"No, no, it's cool," they said. "Yeah, I'm excited," Barbi said. "I just wanted to know how we were going to... What we were going to do."

"I brought the video footage from CBGB's," Koy said. "Maybe he can use some of that."

"Wow, that was a good idea," Trish said.

For some reason this irritated Kaci; she wasn't sure why; but this whole trip was getting more and more aggravating. She couldn't wait to get there, just to get out of the car.

The road made a broad turn, and they saw Coney Island. Everyone was looking; Trish wished they could go there; but really, outlined against an overcast sky, it was unattractive, ugly even —remarkably dilapidated and cheap-looking. After they passed, it just disappeared from sight, as the road turned, following the shore. The driver left the expressway and zigzagged through a large residential area. Every block looked exactly alike, suburban and plastic.

"I hope we're going the right way," Barb said. But soon they saw a sign with the name of the school; everyone was looking around, though they had no idea what they were looking at; the car stopped at a security gate: the college. Behind a big wall, the campus wasn't particularly impressive; really it looked more like a mid-sized high school. They pulled up at the Communications Building. It was just five o'clock.

Kaci got out and looked around as the driver helped unload their stuff. The campus was quiet, which seemed strange; no one was around; next to the building was a big parking lot, empty except for two beat-up old cars. She hoped this was the right place, and wondered if they should ask the guy to wait until they found out, but he was already driving away.

"Well," Kaci said. "We're here, let's go be on TV!"

Just then a guy came out the main door, saying, "Hey, alright! You *must* be Dreamwhip!" He was medium-height and muscular, with short dyed-blonde hair, and had a sleeve of tattoos on each arm.

"That's us!" Koy said.

"Had to be," he said, grinning and winking. "Which one of you is Kaci Valentine?"

"I am," Kaci said, noting Koy's slightly put-out expression. "Hi!" he said, offering his hand. "I'm Jake." Kaci was pleased to be treated like the leader, for once, and she smiled and shook hands, saying, "How do you do... This is Koy-Toy, our lead singer." "Hi, Jake," Koy said, smiling brightly. "How's it going," he said, clearly pleased to have such a bunch of babes on his program. "And this is our rhythm section," Kaci said, "Barbi Crash, our drummer, and Trish Trash, our bass player." "Alright!" he said, shaking hands all around. "This is great! Come on in. I'm really excited that you guys are gonna be on the show!"

He ushered them in, and they followed him down a short hall, past the journalism and print media departments, and a broadcast center, to a large double door marked Studio B. Inside was a small plain sound stage with a set of drums.

"Okay," Jake said. "Usually everybody likes to start with what's most familiar –I mean more or less. So, we thought we'd get you guys on stage, and we'll get some footage of you, like, you know, pretending to play."

"Huh?" Barbi said.

"Look, I know," Jake said. "But it's all we have facilities to do. We're hoping to get set up for live recording –it's a question of money, getting a good sound is just incredibly expensive –but anyway, for right now, well, just think of it as like being on *Soul Train*: those groups aren't really playing either. I'm going to tell my partner, the cameraman, that you're here."

When he was gone Barbi said, "I still don't get it. What are we going to do?"

"I think we're going to lip-synch," Koy said.

"Oh, okay," Barbi said.

"I don't have a guitar," Kaci said.

Everyone turned to her, but she didn't say anything more. For a minute no one else said anything either. Finally Koy said, "Don't worry, we'll ask Jake. He's got to know somebody with a guitar." And when she asked him, it turned out he kept one in his office.

When he came back with it, Kaci was taken back: a B.C. Rich Mockingbird, cherry red, with a neck-through body, abalone fretboard inlays, and a deluxe whammy bar as smooth as silk. She would never have touched it in a music store, never even looked at it, but it was an excellent instrument, balanced, lightweight, and its action super fast; she couldn't believe it.

Jake was watching her try it out; she glanced up at him, and he smiled. "Like it?"

"I've never played one before," she said. "It's really nice."

"You look cool with it," he said. "And hey! Here's Bobby, our cameraman."

They all turned, and Bobby said hi. He wasn't tall, really on the small side, but he wore a Misfits shirt and his cap backwards, a flaming skull was tattooed on one arm, and he had a certain crazed air about him, like he would do anything. He was already filming them with a mini-cam; everyone introduced themselves; when he smiled, you could see that two upper teeth were missing. Koy rather liked him, she could already tell he was getting the right sort of footage.

"Okay, so you've got your demo, right?" Jake asked her. She gave him one with a new cover in mock-up ("Excellent," he said. "We'll get a close up.") and the live footage from CBGB's ("Yes, fantastic, the more visual material, the better —usually all bands have is a disc."). He asked if they wanted to change for the video clip. Koy said she thought so, and he left, dragging away Bobby, who had been telling Trish jokes, trying to get her to laugh.

"Wow," Trish said. "I think all he shot of me were my boobs."

"Shake your moneymaker," Koy said.

"So what are you going to wear, Koy?" Barbi asked.

"I don't know," Koy said. "Wow… I guess if it's for TV, I should wear the most outrageous thing I've got."

They were all looking at her. "Which is what?" Barbi said, finally.

"Huh?" Koy said. "Oh! I don't know, I can't decide. This happens to me every time!"

*   *   *

They quickly found it wasn't so easy to pretend to play your own song. Everyone kept making mistakes, especially Koy, who had rewritten the lyrics since the recording, and couldn't get the old ones right, and Trish, who hadn't played on it, hadn't even listened to it since she joined the band. Kaci, distracted, cringed at the high-decibel playback, where every flubbed pick attack, every waver in tempo was audible. Only Barbi fell right into it, pounding the beat as the camera rolled. The first take, they were so stiff that after a word with the cameraman, Jake asked for another run-through without moving the camera. "Alright," Jake said encouragingly. "Weird set-up, huh? I know it sucks… but hey! Rock out! Don't be camera-shy!"

Rock out, Koy thought, yeah. She wished to God she had thought to bring a pint of something –a couple of shots and they might all have loosened up. She looked around: Kaci was bitching about the recording to Barb, as Trish fiddled with her bass –like it mattered!

They tried it again: at best, mediocre. Koy could see Jake and Bobby exchanging glances; she flushed, embarrassed and irritated. What a bunch of bimbos! Why did it always come down to her?

Because you're the leader. And she made a face, took a long breath, and waved everyone back toward the drum kit.

"Look," she said quietly, but with force. "We're fucking up! But there's no reason to, it's all attitude! We don't have to know what we're doing, we just have to look good. Forget about what's on the recording, just shake your ass, come on!"

"That's right," Barbi said.

Kaci nodded, Trish looking vague.

As the other two went back to their places, Koy said to Trish: "Hey, you didn't even play on this. It doesn't matter. No one will ever know. They're only going to think of how *hot* you looked." She winked, blew a kiss. Trish giggled.

But, thank goodness, this time it worked, they were loose, sexy. Kaci, who'd gotten used to the guitar, was super-bad, sneering, but strutting. Trish gave up trying to look like she was playing, and just danced with her bass, shaking her stuff and getting down. Barbi had yet to miss a beat, but now she twirled her sticks, tossed her hair, smiling like a beauty queen. Koy, over the top, did a stripper routine, shedding her clothes, peeling away her lingerie.

Jake and the cameraman grew very serious. They did another take: Koy did another stripper dance, getting almost naked. The two guys were obviously into it. At the end, Jake shut off the music and said, "Alright!" He was grinning broadly.

"Do you want the spanking bit?" Koy asks.

"What?" he says.

"Well, normally in the show, during the guitar lead, I spank Trish."

"Oh, absolutely." As they set up the shot, he said to Bobby, "This is going to be hell to edit."

"I live for my work," the cameraman said.

*                    *                    *

Jake wasn't a very good interviewer. Koy did her best, but it everything just kept going flat. She was hoping that got fixed in the editing. They each said their names in a close-up, and, after trying to get it right a few times, they all said together, "And we're Dreamwhip!" Jake did his introduction; he chatted with Koy about the scene in New York, about where they'd been playing, and with whom (Koy even mentioned the Contusions, Dizzy better remember that); then he went on with questions like, Where did you grow up? and, Who was your favorite band when you were fifteen? (and every one of them had lied, Koy was sure of it). He might as well have asked, What's your favorite color? Kaci was pretty good, mouthing off and being a smart-ass; Trish didn't say much, just kept giggling, but maybe that was good; but Barbi was quiet, camera-shy. Koy kept blabbing –what did she care? –but she thought her own voice sounded stupid, and certainly the others could have been more lively.

Jake was asking Trish if she had any tattoos. She laughed, shook her head.

"But you're into piercing, right?" he said.

"Oh yeah," she said. Stretching, she pulled up her top and fingered a large belly-button ring.

"Cool!" Jake said. "Got any more we haven't seen?

She stuck out her tongue, wiggled it.

Jeeze, that's as big as a marble, Koy thought. No wonder she can't talk.

"Koy, do you have any tattoos?" Jake asked.

"Not yet," she said. "I'm going to get one the first time I go to Hollywood."

"Oh yeah? What's it going to be?"

"It'll say *Dreamwhip* of course," Koy said. "We're all going to get one." The others were nodding agreement. "Oh yeah," they said.

"What's it going to be?"

"It's a secret," Kaci said. "Only our most *hard-core* fans will ever see it."

"Alright," Jake said. "I think it's time everybody got a chance to check out your music, so let's go to the video! We're rocking with Dreamwhip, and the tune is…"

"*Spank Me*," Koy purred.

"Good!" Jake said. "Let's keep it going with the second half." He cleared his throat, took a sip of water. "Everybody good? Alright, let's go… That was

Dreamwhip, with their song *Spank Me*. Koy, what's the story behind that song?"

Oh Jeeze, Koy thought. "Well, I can be a very bad girl."

"Oh, I'm sure," Jake said. "Alright, let's talk zodiac signs. Kaci, what's your sign?

"What, you want a date?"

"Trish?"

"Take your pick."

"Barbi?"

After a moment of silence, Barbi laughed. "I don't know."

"Koy?"

"I'll tell you when I get to know you better."

"Alright," Jake said. "How did you get into music? Kaci, why did you start to play?"

"Come on, Jake," Kaci said. "Everybody knows it's cool to play the guitar."

"That's true. Trish?"

"This boy I knew played guitar," Trish said, "and I wanted to play with him."

"Barbi?"

"I don't know, it just seems like I've always played the drums."

"Cool... Koy?"

"So I could be a big rock star," Koy said. "With a limo and a jet."

"Alright. So what's the worst job you ever had?"

"I worked in the cafeteria at..." Kaci stopped, went on: "I worked in a cafeteria."

"Where?" Jake asked.

"In Boston," Kaci said. "A place no one ever heard of."

"Trish?"

"I was a waitress."

"But you made tips, right?"

"No," Trish said. "I was a bad waitress. I mean, I was really bad, I was terrible. Finally they fired me."

"Uh-huh… Barbi?"

"I've had a lot of terrible jobs," Barbi said. "Umm, but I think the worst was when I worked at City Hall. Working for the government is a special kind of hell."

"What did you do there?"

"Oh, I checked forms. They all had to do with automobile accidents. Just imagine all the accidents. A mountain of work came in every day. You could never get caught up, never in your whole life."

"Wow," Jake said. "Koy?"

Koy's mind went blank, all she could think of was what *not* to say. Why these dumb questions? Say something, answer!

"All of them," she said. "Every job is always so boring. They're just a waste of time."

Tastee-Freeze. La Mode. The Dollhouse. The Pink Pussycat. The Kama-Sutra. New York Nites.

"You can say that again," Jake was saying. "And now, let's check out some video footage of Dreamwhip *live* at CBGB's!"

He took a sip of water, grinned at them, and turned back to the camera: "Alright, I'm Jake LaRue and we're back with Dreamwhip. Koy, when you were little, what did you dream of doing when you grew up?"

Koy laughed harshly. "Getting married and having kids. But I got over it."

"Barbi? Did you dream about the same thing?"

Barb was looking surprised. "Well, yeah, I guess I did." They were all looking at each other now.

"Trish? Kaci?"

"Yeah," Trish said finally. Kaci just nodded.

Koy didn't like this. "Hey, man," she said. "Look, that's just what you're *programmed* to think when you're a woman."

"Exactly!" Kaci said. "But we're here to say, you can be what you *want* to be! *Anything* you want to be."

"Alright!" Jake said. "Koy, where do you see yourself in twenty years?"

"Well, after I get out of rehab, I'll probably start working on the Dreamwhip reunion tour and comeback album."

"Barbi?"

"Oh, I'll be playing the drums, man." She laughed. "Probably waiting for Koy to call me about that tour."

"Trish?"

"Suing the tabloids, getting a face-lift. And I have a concept for a celebrity psychic game-show. It's going to be huge."

"I think I'll just have an interview show," Kaci said.

"That's where the money is," Jake agreed. "Alright: what's the best thing about being in Dreamwhip?"

"Getting an audience really turned-on," Koy said.

"Yeah, playing live," Barbi said. "Definitely."

"Playing in a band with these guys," Trish said. "It's fantastic."

"I would have to say it's the audience," Kaci said. "We've made some fans and we hope to make lots more, and they're all great, we really love and appreciate them."

"I'd like to show each and every one of them just how much," Koy said, winking.

"Well, I know we all hope to get that chance," Jake said. "Alright, we're running out of time, but a couple last quick questions. Tell me, have you ever had sex in a car?"

"Of course," Koy said. "Everyone has." The others were all nodding, saying yes.

"Where was the first place you ever had sex?"

"In a car," Koy said.

"A car," Barbi said.

"A van," Trish said.

"A van," Jake repeated. "Trish, did you count the van as a car, or did you mean both in a car and in a van?"

Kaci started giggling.

"Both," Trish said. "In a car and in a van."

"But which was first?"

"The van."

"Kaci, first place you ever had sex?"

Kaci was still giggling: "In a car."

"Koy, where was the best place you ever had sex?"

"Mmm, backstage, after the show."

"Barbi?"

Barbi looked put out. "In a car."

"Trish?"

"I don't know… Do you mean, a place you remember? I don't know. It's still to come. The next place is the best place."

"Kaci?"

"In a car and in a van," Kaci said.

"Kaci!" Trish said.

"Kaci, what's your favorite position?"

"On top."

"Trish?"

"On top."

"Barbi?"

"Oh, I don't know…" Plainly exasperated, she looked around. "What did you guys say? On top."

"Koy?"

"Doggie-style." She winked again.

"Alright!" Jake said. "There you have it, from the luscious lips of Dreamwhip themselves. Look for them rocking your favorite club soon! I'm Jake LaRue –see you next time on New York Rock Scene!"

"Alright!" he said, standing up and stretching. "Good job! It's going to be a great show!"

*       *       *

They watched themselves on playback, giggling. Kaci couldn't believe how cool she looked with this weird guitar, she wondered if maybe she should get one; Barbi was hoping no drummer she knew ever saw this show; Trish worried that she looked fat, scrutinizing herself every second; only Koy seemed truly satisfied, laughing and flirting with the guys, though she really wished she had been wilder, more out there. You had to keep pushing, you couldn't let up.

"Okay," Jake said, scooting back from the console. "Looks good. So… we've got the lip-synch, we've got the live-from-CBGB's footage, and the straight-up interview. I think we're good, unless if you want to do some outro footage."

"What's that?" Koy said.

"Oh, like, something to run while the credits are rolling."

"We can do that," Koy said. "What do we do?"

Jake shrugged. "It's up to you… Like, if a band does it at all, they usually just fool around. You know, goofy stuff."

"Okay," Koy said, turning to the others. "We can do that."

They went back to the little studio. Kaci sat down behind the drums, and Barbi picked up the guitar. "Roll our demo," Barbi called to the cameraman. In a moment, *Alone With You* begins to blast through the speakers. Kaci and Barbi pretend to play as Trish dances. Koy comes up with two Tootsie-Roll Pops, hands one to Trish, pops the other in her mouth. She watches Barbi strutting and shaking her hair to the heat, then sticks her face into the camera, licking the sucker lasciviously. "We're Dreamwhip," she says. "Call our chat line and see how nasty we can be!"

"Get in close on Trish's tits," she says in the ear of the cameraman. He nods, moves up. Trish is shaking it, her breasts filling the monitor screen —as

Koy whips up a can of Silly String and sprays the sticky gobs of stuff all over them. Trish's look of surprise closes the next show.

*       *       *

Trish picked him out in Sounds on St. Mark's Place. She brushed past, making sure he got a look at her ass, caught his eye, and smiled. But in a couple of minutes, she left. When he came out, not long after, she was sitting on the steps, smoking a cigarette. She smiled at him again as he went past. He stopped, said, "Hi!"

"Hi there," she said. "Didn't find anything? Me neither."

"No," he said. "Nothing good."

"Hey," she said. "Do you like to go see music? I'm in a band and we're playing in two weeks at Limelite. Take this, it's a free pass. Take two."

He looked at them, saying, "Wow, cool... Dreamwhip. What do you play?"

"Bass."

"Wow, that's really cool," he said.

Now, Trish thought.

"Listen," she said. "Somebody was supposed to meet me for a drink but they stood me up. Do you want to have a drink with me?"

"Sure! Where do you want to go?"

"Oh, I don't care, anywhere you like is fine with me. But first I'd like to go put this bag in my car. Walk with me?"

She led him back to Third and turned south, letting him talk but moving quickly. It was quite dark. The sidewalk traffic thinned out fast, and they turned back east on Sixth. He was saying something or other as they passed under a sidewalk-shed; the block was empty. She stopped.

"What is it?" he said. "Lose your car? What is it?"

"I thought it was right here," she said. "It's a Civic. Blue." She put a hand on his arm, to keep him from stepping away. "I thought it was right here." She pointed; he craned his neck, looking for the car that wasn't there: really, it was just too easy.

*   *   *

Kaci watched the broadcast of the TV interview with a certain unease. This was the first chance she'd had, since all the other broadcasts had been during the day. The band looked stilted and nervous on-camera, especially in the beginning, and the lip-synched song, though edited with loving care, was just poor. The live footage from CBGB was cool, though the sound wasn't great, and she found herself laughing out loud at some of the later parts of the interview. But what worried her was Koy: to her eyes, the singer was obviously messed-up, and at moments, especially during the performance segments, she was beginning to look fat. Both of those things were very bad.

When it ended, JT chortled at the Silly-String, then turned off the TV. When he didn't say anything, she said, very seriously, "So, what did you think?"

"That," he said, "is the stupidest thing I've ever seen."

Kaci looked at him. "Why do you say that?"

"Because it's true!" he said. "How do you expect anyone to take you seriously? You look like a bunch of clowns."

She sighed. "It's great how I can always count on you to be supportive."

"What do you expect? I mean, that was sad. If I were you, I'd just hope nobody else ever saw it. And what the fuck is Koy on, anyway? Jeeze, she looked fucked-up!"

So he'd noticed it too –but the rest was just mean. "Oh, come on, that's just part of the act. She's just doing her bimbo routine."

JT snorted. "She doesn't have to *act* to come across as a bimbo."

"Oh, come off it, JT. Do you always have to put down everyone and everything?"

"Hey, you asked me what I thought.

"I guess that was my mistake."

"The truth hurts, Kaci."

"The *truth*?" she said, angry now. "Since when have you placed such a high value on *truth*?"

"I don't know what you're talking about."

"Oh, you don't," she said. "Well, let's see. Since you're being truthful right now, JT, tell me: why did you miss the show at CBGB? And what have you been up to while I'm at rehearsal?"

He didn't answer.

"And your little mystery calls? All those wrong numbers? You sure get a lot of them. Are they wrong numbers, JT? Or are they calls you don't want me to know about? Maybe from *somebody* you don't want me to know about?"

"That's a lot of bullshit," he said. But he wouldn't look at her.

"Is it?" she said. "Okay, tell me the truth: have you got a girlfriend on the side?"

"I don't have to put up with this."

"Not exactly a yes or no answer, JT. Come on: the *truth*, you were being *truthful*, remember?"

"Stop being such a bitch, Kaci."

She knew she had him. He wasn't a good liar, so he usually just avoided stuff. But she was sick of avoiding it —of letting him avoid it.

"You may as well admit it," she said. "Because it's not exactly the first time, is it? For instance… there was Betty." Betty Benzene had been the singer in his last band.

Now he was glaring at her, defiantly.

"Go on, admit it. That would be truthful, anyway… I know all about it, JT: I know you went to bed with her."

Silence. His face was twisting, his mouth all wrong. Finally he said, "That's not true."

"And now you're going to lie about it? Of course it's true. I heard her tell someone else about it. She never meant for me to hear it."

He didn't answer. Oh, how she hated him at that moment! —as if saying it out loud made it worse. She hadn't wanted to believe it, but now it was obviously true. She could have killed him.

"How about it?" she said. "You want to know what she said? Check this out: she said you were lousy in bed."

"Fuck you," he muttered.

That just made her all the more mad. "Here's *exactly* what she said. She said, 'I feel sorry for Kaci. JT is pretty cute but he's just lame in bed.'"

"Fuck her and fuck you."

"You said it. Do you want to hear what she said about your dick?"

He turned livid. Her eyes had dried. In a way, she felt relieved; at least she wasn't keeping it inside anymore. But now, between them, was this horrible and stupid thing that he had done —and she was beginning to see that she couldn't go on. That was what this fight was all about. And he too was using the breakup talk: "You're going to wish you hadn't acted like this. You're going to be sorry. I'm the best thing that's happened to you in a long time."

"Oh, yeah," she said. "Right."

"You haven't had that much luck with boyfriends, have you? Starting back in college…" The way he said *college*, it was pitiful.

"That's all right, JT. I think I'll take my chances being alone."

She couldn't believe she had said it —and neither could he. In a rage, he grabbed his jacket and left, slamming the door. He didn't come back that night, and when she got home from work the next day, his stuff was gone.

\*           \*           \*

Dizzy snorted up the bag, licked it clean and flushed it down the toilet. Coming out of the stall, he went to check his hair in the mirror, but the light in the Bunker bathroom was so bad, he couldn't see. Instead, he sniffed some water up his nostrils, and went back out to where Ratso and Danny were standing. The band was about to start, checking volumes, skronking out a chord or two and banging moronically on the drums. One of the guitarists was

Danny's friend George. They'd played together in the Cherries, a pretty cool band —Diz had heard the recording —that had done all the usual stuff: write some songs, play some gigs, make a demo, and split up. Somebody had theorized that the most common time for a band to break up was right after they'd made a demo —who was it had said that? Danny? He couldn't remember, but he now found the idea unnervingly verisimilar, and for a number of possible reasons. George had since been in the Degenerates for a while, but they kicked him out and that was when the trouble had started for the Contusions.

Danny and Ratso were talking about something, so Diz went to the bar and bought a round of drinks. The cute bartender was there, the large-breasted blonde who always wore little cut-offs and thigh-high boots. She smiled at him. He left her a big tip.

Finally the band got started. The first song was okay; he got bored during the second, and it just grew progressively worse. He was glad —relieved — because they looked so good. They all had good clothes, *expensive* clothes, and great hair. The singer's hair was particularly fine, but he couldn't sing. George was a good player —you hoped that would be the case, so you didn't have to lie —but the other guitarist covered him up, playing too loud. This guy, who looked like a jerk, ruined every song, while smirking inanely; it was just horrible. But what was really unbearable was his guitar: a Gibson Les Paul with a hot-pink sparkle top —an outrageous guitar, one of a kind. Diz could hardly stand to look at it; he couldn't take his eyes away.

After the show they went up to talk to George, who was rapidly tearing down his stuff to get out of the way of the next band. He turned out to be a really nice guy. He and Danny seemed to be old friends, and he kept cracking them up, making jokes about his own band and their performance. As George himself said, if only the set itself had been so entertaining. Diz tried to talk to the other guitarist, complimenting him on his guitar, but the guy just blew him off. It didn't seem like a really great situation for George, but what could you say?

"Alright, we're going to load out," Danny said. "I told George I'd help him get his stuff home. You guys staying here?"

"Yeah, yeah," Ratso and Diz said. "Later." They wandered toward the bar.

"Did you talk to the guy here?" Ratso asked.

"Yeah, I talked to him," Diz said. "He said he'd give us a spot early next month but he doesn't have his book with him. I'm supposed to call him tomorrow."

"Doesn't look like it would be such a big deal, just to give us a date."

"Yeah, well, I don't know," Diz said. "I'll call him tomorrow." Some rock chicks went by, Ratso checking them out: "I wonder who's the next band."

"Who knows," Diz said.

"Not me," Ratso said.

It looked like a metal band. The guitar player had one of those super-Strats —lime green, whammy bar, one knob —and a large molded-plastic pedal board that held a dozen effects boxes. Diz wondered what they all did.

"What did you think of George's band?" Diz asked.

"They were okay," Ratso said. "They were kind of like us. But they were mostly boring. That one guitar player was bogus."

"Yeah, I got sick of him," Diz said. "What did you think of the drummer?"

"He was okay," Ratso said. "I was bored."

Diz nodded. Of course you were, he thought. The guy was keeping the beat.

Ratso was still talking: "Now the bass player... Did you notice the bass player?"

"Yeah?"

"The bass player was good."

"What was he doing?"

"He was doing his job, that's what he was doing!" Ratso said. "He was laying down a solid groove and he was playing in time."

"How rare," Diz said, wondering if Ratso ever reflected on these concepts in regard to his own playing.

"Yeah, man, I don't know," Ratso said. "After all, they played the gig and we're just here talking about it. We've got to get it together! We're just stalling out, we're doing nothing and we're going nowhere."

"I hear you," Diz said. "We've got to do something with the demo."

Ratso looked pained, as if he would disagree.

"You know as well as I do," Diz went on. "The demo's got to be duplicated and sent out. Otherwise we'll never get any action on it. If we send out enough of them, *somebody* will pick us up, for a single, or a compilation, or distribution, or something."

"Man, I'm broke," Ratso said. "We just spent *so much* on that thing!"

"Yes, we did," Diz said. "And you'll remember I said from the beginning that we should go somewhere cheaper, cut it more cheaply. Because there are other costs, lots of them. You're not done when you finish cutting. You've only started."

"And that demo from Danny Savage's studio sounds hotter," Ratso said.

Dizzy shrugged. "In any case, we've got it and it's done. But it's worthless, we may as well have saved the money and never even done it, if we don't get it out. We've got to. At this point we can't afford to be cheap about it."

"I'm broke, man," Ratso repeated. "Got to wait."

Then quit complaining, Dizzy thought.

"Hey man," Ratso said. "Have you noticed that lately Mick seems, uh, out of it?"

"Yeah," Diz said. He waited but Ratso didn't continue. In a minute he said, "Go on, I'm listening."

"I don't know," Ratso said. "What do you want me to say? He's... I don't know, but he seems wasted a lot of the time. I mean like *really* wasted."

"Yeah, I know," Diz said.

"Like that rehearsal last week," Ratso said, getting warmed up. "Who goes to sleep in the middle of a song? It was so loud in there! There's no way! That's no good. And you know, when that happened, when he was nodding out like that, I had this feeling, like when you've seen something before, but you've forgotten it. I think when we played that house party, that last gig with T-Bone —I think he did that same thing then."

"Huh." Dizzy was trying to determine just how much Ratso knew or understood about anything, and from there how much the guy could or ought to be enlightened.

"That was a gig, man!" Ratso shook his head, as if at the enormity of it all. "I guess it comes down to this: getting too fucked-up to play just isn't cool."

Diz nodded. "Mick's been the way he is for as long as I've known him."

"We can't have something like that happen on a gig!" Ratso said.

Diz sighed. Was now the time? "No," he said. "You're right… Look: Mick is a pretty good guy, and we've been playing together for quite a while now. But I've been having some doubts… Not because he's usually wasted, although that's true. It's other stuff. He's not a good songwriter, his vocals are so bad he shouldn't even sing back up, and I don't really think he's a very good bass player. And that's the main thing."

"What are you trying to say, man?" Ratso said sharply.

"I guess what I'm *asking* is, would we be a better band if we had a better bass player?"

Ratso looked upset, and Diz wondered if he should stop now, but he had committed himself, and he might not have this good an opportunity again.

"So what are you getting at?" Ratso said.

"What does it sound like? What were you saying yourself? Is Mick a problem? Shouldn't we think about what we'd do if we had to replace him?"

"And what would we do?" Ratso demanded. "You're the one who's always saying that it's hard to find people, hard to find the right guys."

Diz waited a second, and went on quietly, "It's obviously hard to find the right guys. That's why we've got to start thinking about it now in case we have to do it."

Ratso just shook his head, looking away, and Diz couldn't tell if he were angry, or nervous, or what.

"Look, take it easy," Diz said. "I've got an idea, check it out. This isn't a situation like when we lost T-Bone. We're an established band now. We've played a bunch of gigs, we've got a demo, we've got our sound. We're just talking about a bass player. And I think we should go looking for one, rather than just passively hoping that somebody good will answer an ad."

"Like who? What do you mean?"

"Well, for example, do you remember that guy Dino from the Heart Throbs?"

"The bass player."

"Yes," Diz said. "The bass player. I see him around, here and there. We always say hi. The guy is doing nothing. The Heart Throbs stalled out two years ago —*two years* —looking for a guitar player. They've played maybe three gigs since. In two years. Sure, they've got a deal, but the guy has got to be going nuts. He's an excellent player, he could easily play our stuff. And he looks great. He totally has the look."

"So why would this guy want to join us?"

"Maybe he would, maybe he wouldn't, I don't know! He might, he might not. The point is that he's not doing anything. And we know him."

"We don't know him. We have no idea whether he'd be interested or not."

"I know him, enough," Diz said. "I know him enough to find him and talk to him. That's enough. I know another guy, the bass player from a band I tried out for two or three years ago. He's good too. I saw him on MacDougal a while back. They broke up —looking for a guitar player —and he's playing in a bar band in Jersey. They make some money, but it's not a great gig. The point is that these guys are part of the scene already. They know the score. I'm saying that if we had to, we should try them first, before we just spin our wheels hoping someone will call because they read our ad in the *Village Voice*."

"You know, all this is really a moot question," Ratso said. "I mean, there's really no point."

Diz stopped, waited.

"We already have a bass player," Ratso said.

Diz didn't answer, just kept waiting. Ratso went on, angrily: "I mean, I don't understand this. I just don't get it. I don't even know how we started talking about this! We're talking about Mick, and all of a sudden you're talking about replacing him with this guy from the Heart Throbs that we don't even know! We don't know anything about him!"

Diz opened his mouth to say something, but Ratso kept talking: "What's all that about? And what about Mick? We've done a lot of stuff with him! Are we just going to kick him out? Do you think that's right?"

"Take it easy, man. I didn't say that."

"Yeah, well, what you're saying is crazy. We don't even know these guys, and you're talking about putting them in the band."

"Alright, Ratso, that's fine, forget about it," Diz said, disgusted with it all. Ratso was impossible to talk to: he hated to admit it, but the guy was essentially stupid.

They didn't say much more, and Ratso didn't stay much longer. As soon as he was gone, Diz left too. The evening had really been a waste; he wanted to get home, have some coke, do a bag. As he turned east on Houston, he was thinking again about the supergroup. If only he could find a singer!

*   *   *

Trish was on Forsythe, across from the park, when she saw the girl in the white hot-pants crossing from Allen: petite, dark-haired, she'd left the bar at the corner. Trish stopped where she was, got out her cigarettes and lit one, giving the other girl time to get ahead. The brunette glanced back as she crossed over, heading east on Stanton, then was lost from sight. Trish hustled across Stanton, wondering which spot she was headed for. It turned out to be the closest one. Good, she thought: they always make you wait in there. The brunette was delicious —*smoking* as Dizzy would say —and Trish was rather envious of her platform knee boots.

At the spot —an ancient tenement, elegant even in decay —the door opened for the brunette, started to close again but stopped as Trish hurried up. The seller smiled at the two half-naked white chicks. "How many?"

"Two," the brunette said.

"Two," Trish said.

He nodded, opened the door again and looked out, closed it again. "Wait here," he said, and went up the steps.

This is it, Trish thought. "Hi!" she said, smiling. "I have to tell you, I love your boots."

"Thanks," the brunette said, and whispered, "They're Fendi." She seemed pretty drunk.

"Fantastic," Trish said. "You look great."

The brunette just smiled.

"I wish I were going out," Trish said. "My boyfriend just split on me."

"Men!" the brunette spit out. "Oh, don't *talk* to me about *men*. Although…" She was looking at Trish appraisingly. "There's a couple cute ones in that bar over on Allen. Why don't you walk back over there with me?"

"Oh, I don't know," Trish said. "I'm not really dressed for it."

"That's nonsense, you look great." She got out a cigarette. "I'm the one who's overdressed. But I love to see their little tongues hanging out. Ahh, and here's the gentleman."

They took their bags. "*Gracias*," the brunette said. When they were out on the street, she turned, said, "I'm Brittany."

"I'm Trish."

"Well, Trish, I'd like to stop at my car a minute, but do you want to go with me, back to the bar?"

"Sure," Trish said. She couldn't believe how all this was working out: the woman was just going to sit in her lap. In a way she felt bad: Brittany was so *nice*.

They crossed the park to her car. Brittany was talking; Trish slipped on her gloves. The car was newish, expensive. "Let's get in a minute," Brittany said. "I forgot my lipstick. And we've got our refreshments."

They got in. Brittany checked the mirrors, snuggled down a bit in her seat, tore open one of the bags, produced a tiny length of metal tubing, and snorted the whole thing up. "Oh, yeah," she said, sounding like a porno actress. "Mmm." She passed the tube to Trish. "Go for it," she said, stretching, opening her leather jacket. She was wearing a tiny halter-top, white to match the shorts; her perfume was dense, complex. Trish was hot for it now, her need strong. "Brittany, do you want some coke?"

"Yeah, gimme some," Brittany said, her eyes half-shut.

Trish passed her the vial. "Might wake me up a little," she said. "That dope is strong." But her eyes closed. She murmured contentedly as Trish stroked fingertips across her belly; her lips opened, moist. Her flesh, cool and smooth, tingled against Trish's hands. She shifted slightly, opening her jacket and offering her breasts; her nostrils flared as she drew in breath. Trish scented blood, could almost taste it. She took Brittany's exquisite breasts in her hands, stroking and caressing them, and leaned her face forward, drawing in their fragrant warmth. Her tongue licked down.

"Ahh," the brunette said, gliding skilled fingers over Trish's legs, spreading Trish's thighs, warm and already moist. "Ahh," she said again –and she offered her neck, silky, perfumed, the vein pulsing just below the tender and delicate flesh.

*   *   *

Koy's phone rang just as she was getting home. "Koy, this is Annette from New York Nites. I've been trying to call you since six."

"I was out," Koy said.

"Well, do you want this one, or not? Because if you do, you've got to get moving. Otherwise I've got to find someone else."

"No, no," Koy said, taking off her boots. "I want it. I'm getting ready right now."

"Okay, but he wants you there by nine." Koy took down the information: Mr. Takahata, room 810, Hotel Concorde. "I'll be there," Koy said. "Let me finish getting ready."

Let them wait. They're all the more ready for it when you get there. No one ever canceled because you were late.

She ran a bath and soaked in the hot water for a while, trying to relax and get into the right frame of mind, but it wasn't easy. She wasn't sure what to wear... The look was everything: the more you embodied the client's fantasy, the bigger tip you made. But she was distracted, thinking about the band and worrying about stuff, even while she did her makeup and hair. Things weren't going right, and she was sick of it. There were going to have to be some changes. She hadn't put everything she had into it for this long, to let it screw up now.

She picked through her clothes, still couldn't decide what to wear. It was already nine, but she was vaguely dissatisfied with everything. Finally she put on the red rubber mini-dress, a pair of seamed stockings, and Italian spike-heeled shoes, grabbed her fun fur, and went down to the car-service car.

Mr. Takahata was very nice, elaborately polite. He gave her a seat, offered her a glass of champagne: Moët et Chandon. They chatted for a time. He was in New York on an extended business trip. His affairs were going well but he was lonely; he missed his wife. Koy asked about her. "She is petite, like you, with fine lovely hands and beautiful skin. But she is very modest, from a very traditional family."

Nodding, sipping champagne, Koy smiled sweetly and crossed her legs, leaning forward and gently squeezing her breasts together. He lit a cigarette and asked about her. She told him about the band, and they talked a little about music, its beauty and passion.

He must have liked her, for he gave it to her good, then sent her home with a two hundred dollar tip.

*        *        *

Diz heard the train coming as he was buying a token: the next one would be too late, this was the one. He hustled through the turnstile and went down the steps at a run. It was the uptown. He jumped on as the signal rang; the doors closed, they were rolling –made it! He looked at his watch: 5:20. Change at West Fourth and take a chance? –but maybe save the two avenue blocks? Or stay on the F –but maybe have to run?

He sat down in an empty spot, holding the guitar upright between his knees. He really didn't want to take this one –not that he ever played it, he'd just had it so long –but the three he usually took were already there. He tried to think about something else.

The train came into Broadway-Lafayette and began to fill. Every person on the platform was moving in slow motion. Can't you see that I'm in a hurry, he thought, and laughed, in spite of himself.

The train pulled out again. He refrained from checking his watch. He felt exasperated with himself: he should never have waited so late, he knew better, he should have gotten it over with early. Of course, he would have already spent some of the cash, too. But it was pretty late to cop, especially down on Rivington. He'd have to take the subway back to Delancey –but that meant carrying all the cash. Jeeze.

He hadn't noticed but they were coming into West Fourth. He looked at his watch: 5:27. Change trains, or not? He didn't want to run the two long blocks. On impulse, as the train slowed, he jumped off and scuttled up the two flights to the Eighth Avenue lines.

I hope I'm not going to regret this. But a bunch of people waited on the platform –which could be good or bad –and in a couple of minutes he could

173

see a light approaching, far down the tracks: an uptown train.

It was already crowded, and most of the people waiting jammed on too. Diz pushed his way on calmly, ignoring the irritated looks at his guitar. Won't have it on the way back, he thought, and found a spot where he could grip the pole.

The car held some unpleasant odor, probably because it was overcrowded. Some passengers got out at Fourteenth as even more packed on. The next stop was Twenty-Third. It always made Dizzy think of his first days in the city, when he had stayed at a friend's place at Eighth and Twenty-Second. That was all so very distant now. How he'd loved New York then!

I guess the new wore off, he thought, and looked at his watch: five-forty. Three more stops. I hope they won't care that I'm coming in so late. Just as long as they lend some cash.

Thirty-Fourth: a bunch of people off, before the train slowly refilled. Hurry up!

He hoped that the place didn't have some cut-off, like they stopped letting people in at 5:30, for instance. Surely they took anyone who showed up before 6:00? But he didn't know, he'd never been there this late before. Always new experiences, he said to himself. A shame they were usually bad ones.

At Forty-Second, the car half-emptied, hot air blasting through the door: air conditioning exhaust, chemical detergents, heavy-duty lubricants, human filth. Diz sat down, looking out at the station curiously; unless he couldn't help it, he never got out at Times Square, it creeped him out. No new passengers got on. The doors closed.

Okay, next stop. He looked down at the antique case, its crocodile-print tolex torn and frayed, wondering what they would give him. You didn't want to take too much. A hundred. No, maybe a hundred twenty-five.

As the train braked he stood up, hurrying through the doors and up the steps. Outside, it was getting dark, already cooling off. He came up around the corner, turned back on Eighth, going fast and looking for the sign, right on this block and —yes! —it looked like they were still open.

It was 5:50 by their clock when he came through the door, and business was hopping. The loan representatives each had a customer and two more were in line ahead of Diz, but the pawnshop was making deals and moving fast. A couple of chicks were looking without interest at the gold and diamonds, clearly just waiting for their boyfriends to pick up some Saturday night cash. Diz kept smiling, minding his own business, relieved that he'd made it; everything looked cool.

Two guys got money in quick succession and Diz was next. He went to the window, held up the guitar case. The guy inside —the usual guy —moved to a large double-windowed shelf made of bulletproof plexiglass and opened the store-side door; Diz put the guitar through, his side closed, the pawn shop man's opened and he pulled free the case, laid it on a bench, and opened it. His eyebrows raised, his lips pursed, his head waggled slowly from side to side. He brushed a finger across the strings.

"Where you get all these guitars?" he asked.

"They're mine," Diz said. "It's my collection."

Pawn shop man picked up the guitar, looking closely. "How much you want?"

"How about a hundred twenty-five?"

"No, is too much." He was looking at the finish. "Is cracked. One hundred."

"That's a valuable guitar," Diz said. "Hundred ten?"

"Okay." Pawn shop man put the guitar back in its case and typed up a receipt, whereon the checked finish and worn hardware of the ES125TDS were carefully noted. Diz signed it, said thank you, took the cash and split. It was 6:05.

Still time to get to Rivington. If he took the Sixth Avenue, he could change at Broadway-Lafayette, or even walk. He set off for the station two blocks east, moving fast and trying to make time.

*   *   *

Saturday evening, she'd been out shopping, and somehow it got later than she realized. Now, no matter what, she couldn't go home, drop off her packages, and go out again, what with Dizzy probably already waiting for her. No, better to find something on the way –but how? As she walked slowly toward the subway, a group of kids went by, hooting at her and saying crap, but she just looked at them thoughtfully.

Sure enough, as she went down to the F train, a guy hanging with some buddies noticed her, called out, "Hey mama, what you got going on? Oooh, ain't you fine!" But instead of ignoring him, she glanced his way, looked him up and down, and said smoothly, "Matter of fact, right now I ain't got nothing going on, I'm just going home."

He followed her down to the platform, and stood there, talking trash mostly, trying to be cool and come on like a big player. She didn't have to do much, just laugh a little here and there, but she was nervous, not sure what to do, both wishing the train would come, and dreading it. People passed them, heading for the other end of the platform and leaving a wide space. I wonder if they think I'm a prostitute, she thought. For some reason, this made her mad, although she had no reason to think it so, and some privacy was welcome anyway. You're just uptight, she told herself. Be cool. Focus.

The train came. Although it seemed bizarre –and she had been worrying about what to do –he got on with her as if it were the most natural thing in the world. The car was mostly empty, and she went to the back and sat down where he could sit next to her.

The train always went dark when it left Second Avenue. She left him sitting up, eyes closed as if he were asleep, and got out at East Broadway, catching a glimpse of him one last time through the window as the train rolled away. Who knew how long he might ride like that? —maybe all night.

*    *    *

The first couple nights after he was gone were the worst: Kaci could hardly sleep, and she sat there, flipping channels, just miserable. After that, things didn't really get any better; she just got used to it. She wasn't even sorry, she was sure she was better off without him, but for some reason knowing that didn't help. Instead, she went over it all again and again in her mind, that last fight, his faithlessness and cruelty, their first dates, her happiness when they first moved in together, the gradual deterioration of their relationship —all in no meaningful order, just a jumble, a confused mass of memories whose only common element was the pain they caused. She hated the weekend now: going to work was easier, it took up most of the day, and forced her to think about something else. On Saturday and Sunday the emptiness of the hours oppressed her like a weight; she lay in bed, hardly ate, and spent the whole day in her robe, or the clothes she'd slept in. She'd once read voraciously, but now her books lay untouched; there was nowhere she cared to go, even her guitar gathered dust.

Once a week she dragged herself to rehearsal. Somehow, Koy knew about the breakup, and tried to be nice, in a low-key way. Kaci couldn't tell if the others knew too. For some reason she felt ashamed, didn't want people to know, as if she'd been scorned, as if JT had somehow marked her with the sign of rejection, and unworth.

What was really bad was that she suffered from some basic sense of inadequacy on the guitar, an insecurity that JT had typically tended to encourage. He was a fine player, technically proficient and smooth, the notes just flowing beneath his fingers. Although, over time, he didn't have much luck with bands —as far as Kaci could tell, he tended not to stay in any one group very long, for whatever reason, and they were quite varied —his evident ability was intimidating. And he had no patience. She'd finally given up asking him to show her anything. Now that he was gone, she decided this was all mystification, but somehow his presence lingered on, belittling her efforts to write songs and become a better guitar player.

Nevertheless, the band had gigs coming up, and the recording date wasn't far off at all. Feeling pressure, she tried to concentrate. She ran through the songs at home, but flubbed them with the group; she consciously experimented with her tone, as she'd seen other players do, but all her results were equally atrocious; in rehearsal she bore down on her guitar, trying to take out her anger on it, only to misfire, fingers slipping, pick flailing uselessly. Curiously, the others seemed not to notice, looking about and nodding, satisfied, after each botched song, saying the same encouraging stuff when parting each night. Were they deaf? Too doped-up or dull-witted to notice? Or maybe they were just trying to be nice? Frustrated, she pushed herself: she picked up the guitar when she got home from work, ran down all the band's material; she learned songs off albums, and studied leads she liked, not so much copying them exactly as figuring out how they worked; she left the guitar lying around all the time, picking it up here and there when she had an idea, jamming distractedly on it while she watched TV. She never felt like she got any better, but she was playing constantly. Time passed more quickly, and at least she wasn't always thinking about JT.

Yet when the phone rang, a horrible sickly feeling went through her, a dread like a physical shudder that it might be him; and once there had been someone at the door and she cringed from the insistent, repeated buzzing of the doorbell, only at length making herself answer. It turned out to be someone else's pizza. Galled, she grew furious with her own reaction, accused herself of weakness, of still being a slave to him, or worse, to his shadow. She was often angry now, had a certain reservoir of anger that was inexhaustible yet whose only clear object was herself. It might boil over at any time, poisoning her mood and usurping her concentration: she brooded on what she saw on TV, fumed over something her boss said, lost her temper when someone shoved her on the subway.

She had real problems too, most especially money. She didn't make enough. The rent was the biggest drain: exorbitant even when she'd split it with JT, now it was impossible. It took her three weeks to put it together, leaving next to nothing to live on. She needed to move, but she was only six months into the lease, and breaking it would mean losing the security deposit, which she'd need for a new place, and besides, about a fifth was JT's. He'd already left two messages, reminding her about it.

Of course, the band worried her too, as if once she'd accepted that she was a loser with men, everything else in her life became suspect as well, and more than suspect, the object of harsh and unforgiving analysis. She had reached the point where she was convinced of the band's ultimate and inevitable failure: not only was it charged with a complex of flaws whose sum formed a mass it would be impossible to change, but it was also subject to destructive, ineluctable forces she was powerless to resist. For example, drug addiction: she was sure Koy was becoming increasingly mired in some sort of drug habit, a conviction that alternately infuriated her, and filled her with a certain horrified pity. Thank God it wasn't her. Nevertheless the fact of the problem remained. Certainly she didn't consider herself uncool or some kind of goody two-shoes –not at all. In her college days, she had sometimes been quite wild, a Saturday-night Vodka Queen, hanging out in the rock clubs with the musicians, and downing shot after shot; but she had calmed down, gotten serious about herself and what she wanted to do. She might have a beer at rehearsal, or a drink or two at a gig, but that was it. The band was a serious business; she had a responsibility to the others, expected them to respect that too. A drugged-out screwed-up superstar singer was the last thing she wanted to deal with…

\*　　　　　\*　　　　　\*

The phone rang; Koy answered. "Koy, this is Annette." "What's up,"

Koy said, yawning. It was six o'clock; she must have been asleep for a couple of hours. "What are you doing tonight, do you have any plans?" Annette said. "Well, yeah, sort of," Koy said. "Why, what's up?" "Well, I'm sorry to call you this late, and don't feel obligated, but I just got a really good offer that I felt like I had to tell you about," Annette said. "Your client from a week ago called, Mr. Takahata, and asked specifically for you. I told him that was irregular, and it was probably too late to reach you, and he said he regretted any imposition, and offered to double the fee if you could meet him tonight." "No way," Koy said. She calculated: six hundred, plus he would surely tip her, which would cover things till the end of the month, including dope; and if she could get just one more date, there would definitely be no problem. "So I told him I would let him know," Annette continued. "If you're coming, he asked you to call him, I have the number. It's up to you, Koy. I know it's terribly short notice, but it is a lot of money. But, now, I don't want you to feel any pressure about this... What do you think? You've got other plans?" "No," Koy said. "I'll do it. What's the number?"

When they'd hung up, she sat for a while holding the number, trying to decide whom she should call first, Johnny or Mr. Takahata. Johnny would be mad. She wandered around the apartment, indecisive, but looked at the clock and ran a bath. Six hundred dollars! He'd just have to be mad. She couldn't very well tell him about the money, of course; what was she going to say?

She went to the phone and dialed the number Annette had given her. "Hello, Mr. Takahata? This is Koy, from New York Nites."

"Ah, no, sorry," a man said. "Please hold one moment for Mr. Takahata." Who's this? Koy thought. Another one? How many of them were there? The phone picked up again.

"Hello, Koy," Mr. Takahata said. "Thank you for calling. I am delighted to hear from you. In fact, I am dining with a business associate tonight, and we would like to invite you to join us. He is intrigued by your musical career, and would take great pleasure in meeting you. Would you care to come?"

"Why, yes," Koy said. "I'd love to."

"I will send a car for you." He took the address and they hung up. Koy was confused: what was all this about? Was it just a double? That was okay, but they should have told Annette. And what was this stuff about her career? What if… She couldn't, she wouldn't let herself think about it.

The bath was ready. She shut off the water, gazing into it. What if… All she needed was one chance.

She had to call Johnny. Better do it now, then relax. She didn't really have long to get ready; the car would be there at seven-thirty. She picked back up the phone, dreading it.

He was mad. He wouldn't really talk, just said okay, she could call him later. She tried to say she was sorry, that it was important; he said little, barely responding. She didn't have time to lose. Finally she said, "Okay, I'll call you… And anyway, I'll see you Sunday night at Limelite, right?"

"Yeah, maybe," he said. "As long as nothing *important* comes up."

That was just to hurt her, of course –like she didn't already feel bad about it! When she hung up, she asked herself, what else she could do? You had to do what was necessary. Johnny worked at the pizza shop! The truth was, things with him weren't going well, but she had to put that out of her mind right now; she had work to do.

She'd been a stripper when she first came to New York, completely alone, crazy about rock-n-roll, and almost entirely without job skills: she couldn't type or use a computer, had never handled a phone or even waited tables. But she was hot, young, new on the scene, and she made a lot of money in the topless bars. The trouble was she'd spent most of it on cocaine. The job was weird at first, uncomfortable and unsettling, but she came to enjoy it, the pure sweaty lust, the intoxicating power of having what every man there wanted. She learned how to play an audience. In a strange way, it was good experience, but it wore her down. She tired more and more easily, found it harder and harder to get in the mood, and they could tell when you weren't into it; so only by snorting ever-increasing amounts of cocaine could she do it at all, and that ate up all the money. It had been a bad time, and of course that was when she met Robert; really, hadn't marrying him been just a way of running away from the problem?

Thank God all that was behind her now. If she hadn't been in such bad shape she'd never have let him get hold of her. And he wouldn't let go either; he couldn't accept that their marriage was over. It was so clear at the photo shoot: he still clung to her, still thought of her the way she had been, back then, and he still wanted to control her, still hoped to make money from her. But to her, it was already so long ago, as if it had all only taken place in a bad dream that was beginning to fade away.

The bath felt nice; she stayed longer than she should have, had to hurry around. At quarter-past seven her hair and makeup were pretty much done, but she was still only wearing her robe, with no idea what to put on, and she still needed a fix. Better get that out of the way first, she decided; she could always throw something on. Still, she worried about it all the time she was cooking a shot, thinking about what Mr. Takahata had said. Clearly, she had to look like a rock star. Maybe that was all they wanted, a date with a rock-n-roll slut, a real-life bimbo out of a music video; if that was what they wanted, she could provide it; but she kept thinking that there might be something more…

Feeling relaxed in the glow of the dope, she put on some lingerie, black lace and fishnet stockings. "Looking good," she told herself in the mirror, and winked. Hell, she was ready to bang every record executive that came her way if they'd give her a record deal…

She had to wear a dress, definitely; they were going out to dinner. She didn't want to scandalize them. But she couldn't decide. The phone rang: the car-service driver. "I'll be there in a couple of minutes," she told him. This was ridiculous. If only she hadn't worn the rubber dress the last time. But maybe the knit one with the cut-outs…

When she was finally dressed, she snorted up a little line of coke, put on her fun-fur and went out. It was a quarter to eight. The car-service guy was pacing up and down, watching the traffic on the Williamsburg Bridge and smoking a cigarette. "Hi!" Koy said. His eyes almost popped out of his head.

They took off. The car was outrageous, almost a limousine, and Koy sank back: the seat was more comfortable than her own couch, the soft leather cool against her thighs. The blocks flew past as Koy looked vacantly from the windows, enjoying the luxury.

They stopped somewhere in the sixties, in front of a small Japanese restaurant. Koy dug in her purse, looking for some money, but the driver shook his head. "No, no, the client, he take care of everything." He jumped out and opened the door for her, staring at her cleavage. Koy winked at him.

The restaurant was quiet, dark; everything bespoke discretion and expense. The maître d' approached, a severe Japanese man wearing a tuxedo, and bowing, said, "This way please." The two men rose as she approached, Mr. Takahata smiling and holding out a hand toward her. He introduced Mr. Akimoto, a business associate and close friend. Mr. Akimoto bowed: he was rather smaller than Mr. Takahata, and very reserved. Both men were impeccably dressed. Mr. Takahata helped her with her seat, and the gentlemen sat down. Mr. Takahata had just the time to thank her for joining them when a waiter appeared with a bottle of Dom Perignon: would she care for a glass of champagne?

"I'd love some," Koy said. She couldn't believe it. This was the way to go —these men didn't mind spending their money. They chatted pleasantly as the waiter brought a tray of appetizers. Mr. Takahata hoped she didn't mind, he had ordered for them, and hoped she would find something she liked. The food was outrageous, though she had no idea what she was eating; dish after dish arrived at an easy pace; Mr. Takahata poured more champagne. Koy was feeling a bit light-headed —not drunk, just pleasantly tipsy. Mr. Akimoto ordered sake, which he consumed with delicate avidity. They were asking about the band. She explained her concept of it, some of their history, her plans, what they had coming up. Both men seemed interested, or perhaps they were merely polite. Mr. Takahata seemed to watch Mr. Akimoto, who said little, merely nodding from time to time —never taking his eyes from Koy, as if he'd never seen anything like her before. Feeling somewhat self-conscious, she told herself to play the role.

"And have you made a recording?" Mr. Takahata said.

"The only demo we have is rather, umm, outdated, and it doesn't represent us well," Koy said, "but in fact we're going into the studio in a couple of weeks to make a new one. I'm very excited about it." She smiled.

"That's very good," Mr. Takahata said, nodding. Mr. Akimoto was nodding too. "Very good," he repeated. "And when is your next performance?"

"Sunday night," Koy said. "At Limelite. It's Rock-n-Roll Church, really the biggest venue we've played yet, very high profile."

"What time does your show begin?"

"Ahh," Koy said, surprised. "About eleven-thirty."

"Very good," he said. "Koy, I'd like to offer you my business card. You see, Mr. Akimoto and I represent certain financial interests that are often seeking to diversify. Perhaps you could provide me with a copy of your recording once you have completed it." He took out a card case, adding, "And perhaps we will be able attend your performance Sunday."

Koy took the card mechanically. She couldn't believe her ears; her mouth went dry; she swallowed some champagne but it didn't help.

"Great," she said. "That would be great."

They were both smiling but her head was in a daze, she couldn't think; her dreams seemed to be turning to reality; who would have expected this? She had to get herself together!

"Yes..." she said, "yes, if you would like to come to the show on Sunday, I would be happy to... That is, please be our guests, they'll expect you at the door. I would love for you to attend. We would be honored. You could meet the band..."

"Very good," Mr. Takahata said. "We too would be honored."

"Yes," Mr. Akimoto said. "Honored."

They left the restaurant not long after that. Another big luxury sedan waited outside. Koy settled back as they headed downtown, half listening as the men exchanged a few low words in Japanese. It was all so strange, she felt as if she were in a dream. The radio was playing and she was drowsy from the meal... Would it really happen? Or would she simply awaken to the same wretched reality? The blocks flew past; they stopped; coming out of a rockstar fantasy, she got out, slightly disoriented. I'd better have a snort when we get upstairs, she thought.

Mr. Akimoto's suite was on the twenty-sixth floor; the windows looked uptown toward Times Square. Koy excused herself and went in the bathroom. She did up a couple rails off the marble vanity, thought it over and snorted up a bag, too. When she came out, they were pouring more sake. Later, it was like something out of a porno movie: the one banged her doggie-style, then fucked her up the ass while she gave the other one a blow job... Koy had never done anything quite like it before; she almost got into it, a little.

*    *    *

Koy was thirty minutes late to rehearsal and the others were fed up: even Barbi Crash, exasperated, had ventured a critical remark or two, but Kaci fell silent. She was sitting cross-legged on the floor next to her guitar, glowering, half-listening as she picked at the holes in her fishnet stockings. Irritated as much by Trish's hypocritical condemnation of tardiness as by anything, Kaci was darkly musing over how long she ought to go on putting up with this shit. Other girls were out there, trying to put bands together. She had been with Koy from the beginning, almost three years now, and it was hard to say exactly where they had gotten in that time. And she wasn't getting any younger. Why go on wasting her time? She could have a new gig with another group in a week, she was sure of it. The trouble was, thinking this way made her feel bad. When she and Koy had started out, they were completely inexperienced: she hardly knew three chords on the guitar, and neither one of them had the slightest idea how to write a song, or run a band. All they'd had was enthusiasm, and some shared tastes; but a month or so after they met, they'd gotten drunk one night listening to old albums, and they'd sworn to stick together and go for it, and each thought that if they kept this promise and put their hearts into it, they would, finally, *really* make it. And Kaci had held up her end, just as Koy had more or less held up hers: they were on their second drummer, their fourth bass player, but Koy and Kaci were still, like Jagger and Richards, the essential core of the band. But now… Koy was daily more unstable, prone to mood swings, and sometimes she acted so fucked-up –all of this coincident with trips to the bathroom. Whatever anyone might think, Kaci was not naive. What was more, Koy was putting on weight, and a fat singer would destroy them, especially since her voice was only mediocre. But this very criticism left Kaci feeling bad, as if guilty of disloyalty. Though she defiantly tried to believe that she had to look after herself, the uncertainty, worry and guilt entailed by any rupture, no matter how justified, all combined in the end to plunge her into a depressing confusion.

Trish had noticed Kaci's gradual withdrawal from the discussion, and consciously attempted to moderate her criticism of Koy; as Barbi had made but few comments anyway, they all lapsed into silence. Finally, at quarter till nine, Koy burst into the room. Everyone looked at her but no one said anything.

Koy shut the door. "Look, I know," she said, "and I'm sorry. But it was for a really good reason this time."

"What, you couldn't decide what to wear?" Kaci said.

But Koy just laughed and said, "No, silly. I've got great news –for all of us. For the band."

"What is it?" Barbi said.

"I just got off the phone, and you're not going to believe it. This guy I met, well, this man, really, he's a Japanese businessman, he called me just as I was about to leave, and he's got connections to certain corporations in the entertainment industry –like, maybe Sony –and he's talking about backing us!"

"What?" "No way!" "Really?"

"Yeah! Can you believe it? He said stuff about going to Japan and making an album! He's going to come to the show at Limelight, and we have to give him our new demo as soon as we get it done, and I guess if everything's cool, he'll talk to us after that about contracts and money and stuff!" She threw up her arms, laughing; it was her triumph.

They all began talking at once. This was *it*. Their big chance! It didn't seem real. Koy watched them, a smile on her face. They had no idea what she'd gone through for this –they'd never know –but no one could mess with her now. But Kaci picked up her guitar, put it back down.

"We've got to think about this," she said seriously.

"What?" Koy said.

"I mean there are things we've got to do if we're going to take advantage of this. We've got to get it together."

"Well, sure," Koy said, a bit irritated but trying not to show it. "And we will… But I couldn't wait to tell you! Pretty cool, huh?"

Trish and Barbi began talking again, and Koy was laughing and nodding her head, while Kaci looked on, wishing she felt so excited. She didn't really blame them, but she was just burnt-out on it all, the hopes always followed by disappointment, the days and weeks going by, every day things getting just a little worse. Koy looked high, and Trish didn't act too straight either; she wondered what Barb thought? Barb was so nice she sometimes seemed naive, but she wasn't stupid. The other two, though: they weren't living in a real world.

\*　　　　　　\*　　　　　　\*

Nobody was out. Nobody. It was terrible, Trish couldn't believe it. Avenue B was just *empty*, void, for blocks, in both directions. The last guy had gone by ten minutes before, and he had just shrugged, shaking his head. This made her nervous, really nervous. She had to get something going, *soon*.

Maybe she should go back down to the Dope House –but that was a long way, and maybe for nothing. She decided to walk around the block again, although that meant she had to go past Laundromat one more time. She didn't want to get their attention. But she couldn't just stand there, either.

Back down to Sixth and around the corner past the rehearsal studio. The same band was still playing, a rumble of guitars over a muffled beat. She went back across the long block to Avenue C –no one out here either, this was getting worse all the time. She didn't like it. A couple of cars on Avenue C, not much. Back west again on Seventh –and now a cop was coming! She was jinxed.

She watched the car go by from the corners of her eyes, but the cop only glanced her way and kept going –*that* was good, anyway. But the street could have been hit by a disintegrator ray: everyone had disappeared. Laundromat was shut up tight.

She went slowly on toward Avenue B. This was bad, it could go on all night. And she didn't have all night.

Back down? The Dope House, Clinton Street, Rivington? Something had to happen, somewhere.

Then a guy came around the corner in a hurry, with that look she'd seen before, and knew. She slowed down; as he came up close he glanced at her, then back down the street, squinting.

"They're closed," she said.

"Shit!" he said, and stopped, turned back. "Nowhere's open tonight. I've been everywhere. It's impossible."

Trish waited a second, said, "Listen… Do you have a place we can go, to get straight? Cause I got two, right before the cops came, but I need a place to go."

He looked suspicious. "Why don't you go home?"

"Cause I *can't* go home right now," Trish said.

She could see him thinking, calculating. "And you'll give me a bag?" he said finally.

"Yeah, if you've got someplace we can go… Someplace private."

"Well," he said, "okay, we can go to my place, but you can't stay very long. My girlfriend will be home after while and you have to leave before she gets there."

"That's fine, I won't stay very long," Trish said. "I'll just get straight and leave."

He led her quickly up Avenue B and across Tenth, not saying much. Trish didn't try to talk either; she needed it, bad. The streets were still deserted, but he was agitated and nervous, as if watching for the cops every minute. They crossed Avenue C, to a dilapidated tenement on the north side, and went into the vestibule. He fumbled about for a moment –and turned, holding a knife, and looking mean. "Okay, bitch," he said. "Give me those two bags, and then you can just fuck off."

Trish was surprised. It took her a moment to realize that this idiot wanted to rip her off –and then it made her *mad*. She knocked away the knife – it clattered to the floor –and clubbed him across the temple with the side of her hand. He crumpled.

The dirty bastard –but his blood was sweet. When she was done, she thought about leaving him in the dumpster across the street, but it was too much trouble. On the way home, though, she felt a little bad about the girlfriend. If that part were even true.

*       *       *

Sound check for the Limelite show was at eight. Koy talked to everyone the day before, arranging to meet at a quarter-till. At seven o'clock, she was at Laundromat, and copped as soon as they opened. She called Trish from the corner to say they'd get a cab.

Upstairs, Trish was a nervous wreck; she looked terrible. Dizzy was tuning the basses, but didn't seem to be helping things much. Koy went in the bathroom and cooked up a quick shot. When they finally got a cab the traffic was heavy, but somehow they arrived on time anyway; Koy was relieved. The other two pulled up right behind them. Now everybody looked nervous. Jeeze, Koy thought, what is there to worry about?

The stage door was unlocked and they just went in. Down a short corridor, past a couple of rooms, they found the stage, the soundman connecting microphone cables. The backline was pretty nice, the equipment all set up and ready to go, even the amps turned on and warming up. Koy watched Kaci and Trish tune as Barbi ran through the kit.

"Alright," the soundman said. "Let's check the vocal mics."

Koy walked to the front of the stage, looking out into the darkened empty space that had once been a church. She felt strange up here where she'd seen so many bands, disconnected from her own voice as she spoke into the microphone. They ran through two lackluster songs: Koy distracted now, the guitarists uptight and out of tune, and Barbi struggling to keep time. But the soundman was satisfied and sent them home, saying to be back at eleven and ready to go on at midnight.

They filed back out onto Sixth Avenue and stood in a group. A passing car honked; somebody yelled something. Koy blew them a kiss and said, "Now what?"

"Jeeze," Trish said. "It's not even nine o'clock."

"That's good," Kaci said. "It gives us plenty of time to get home and get back here on time."

Koy caught herself popping her gum —she was a little sick of this attitude! —and nodded emphatically. "Right."

Trish still seemed uptight on the way back downtown, nervous and worried. Koy could hardly get a word out of her, although she didn't seem *mad*, and Koy decided she was just scared. Hey, the Limelite was a pretty big deal — especially with the backers coming. Maybe *I* should be nervous, she thought. But for some reason, the sound check behind her and forgotten, she felt as if she were sitting on top of the world. Hell yeah, she told herself, you've wanted this for so long and finally here it is. How many bands have you seen in that place? —and now it's *you*.

When they got to Trish's, Koy decided she didn't need the drama. "Look," she said. "I'm going to walk home. I'll be back for you at ten-thirty."

Trish just nodded, and Koy left.

Clinton was empty —had there been some heat? —and Koy was glad she had already copped. The big question now was, what should she wear?

What would Mr. Takahata like? They might come backstage, to meet the band. In her mind, these men had become almost larger than life. In a way, that's true, she thought: they have a *lot* of money. So what would they get into? She ran through possibilities in her mind, at the same time hoping fervently that the others were putting some thought into this question. Should she call them? —no, maybe not —it would only aggravate Kaci, probably without accomplishing a thing; as long as Barb did her hair and make-up, she was fine. Koy knew she could count on Trish to dress right, the problem was the neurotic look on her face —and there wasn't a thing Koy could do about *that*.

As she turned the corner of Delancey toward her building, she was telling herself for the millionth time that, no matter how hard she tried, there were just some things she couldn't do anything about. Just do your thing, *you're* the star. So: hot pants? A mini? The rubber dress? The lace-up hip-huggers? If only she'd bought those fantastic shoes she'd seen on West Eighth…

*   *   *

Kaci dropped Barb on Second Avenue, saying she would call just before she headed back, and rode home alone, as always. Her street was quiet, the building mostly dark and apparently empty, and after she locked the door and put the guitar in a corner, she didn't know what to do. Finally she went to the couch and just sat there.

After a bit, she turned out the lights, opened the blinds and sat down again, looking out at the night sky. She needed to call home. Not right now. But she wanted to tell them about the Limelite —not that they had any notion what that was —and sooner or later, she would have to tell them about JT.

She got up and paced around but tears came to the corners of her eyes anyway; she got a tissue and dabbed them away, irritated with herself. The last thing she needed was puffy eyes and spoiled make-up. Stupid JT. He could go to hell. But like a specter, the past haunted her, and threatened to persist, indefinitely, into the future.

She wondered if he knew they were playing Limelite. Oh, he knows, I'm sure. He's probably green with envy. Toward the end, she'd lost the feeling that he wanted good things for her; how could he want them now?

She had to quit thinking about it; she had other things to do that were more important. She cleared off the table, took her guitar from its case and laid it there. Working methodically, she wiped it down, polished the finish, cleaned the strings, and carefully put it in tune. The strings were still almost new, just broken in, but you never knew; really, she was just trusting to luck that she wouldn't break one. It would be bad if she broke one tonight. She didn't have a back-up, and she was too proud to borrow one from someone, like Dizzy. Not that he would have minded. He was always happy, even eager to help –though for some reason she didn't really like that very much. But a back-up cost money and she definitely didn't have that, especially now with JT gone.

Money: she didn't make enough. That was more obvious every day. She didn't know what to do. Her stomach tightened up. Stop it, she thought. One thing at a time, and right now the thing is Limelite. She checked the clock: less than an hour till time to leave. She had to get dressed.

*　　　　　*　　　　　*

Barbi went straight upstairs and called; an hour later, miserable and crying, she hung up on him and turned off the phone. He wasn't coming to the show, said he couldn't get away; though probably true, it had happened so many times before, too many, and she had really been hoping he could make it to this one. Lately, when things had gone wrong or weren't working out, she'd manifested behavior she hardly recognized as her own: petulant, exigent, wheedling, jealous, insistent, raging by turns, each confrontation left her exhausted and shocked with herself. She should never have called him tonight, it would ruin everything…

*   *   *

Trish walked upstairs to find Dizzy snorting an enormous line of cocaine. "Hey," she laughed. "Save some for me!"

"You want a line?" he said.

"No… not yet, it'll just make me nervous," she said. At least he had already taken a shower, it would give her more time in the bathroom. She put her stuff down and paced up and down the narrow apartment, about to jump out of her skin.

"Do you want some help with your stuff?" Dizzy asked.

"Yeah, maybe." This was crazy! She didn't know what to do first. She didn't have enough time, she felt paralyzed. And what the hell was this music he was listening to?

"What are you going to wear?" he asked.

"I don't know," she said sharply.

"Okay," Dizzy mumbled, and went into the next room. She didn't mean to be unkind to him, surely he understood, this was really just the most nerve-wracking thing she had ever done. Limelite! She couldn't even think about it. And she had been so bad during sound-check –terrible! Why hadn't she practiced more? Why hadn't she practiced yesterday, and that afternoon?

"I'm going to change the music, you don't mind?" she said.

"No, no, go ahead," he said.

She put on her favorite album and turned it up. What time was it? Did she have time to do her nails? But of course it was too late, she would barely have time to get ready at all. She hurried into the bathroom to do her make-up.

In the living room, Dizzy quietly opened another bag of dope and snorted it up. Jeeze, he was thinking, this is going to be worse than I thought.

\*                     \*                     \*

Getting ready took Koy the rest of the bags she had copped at Laundromat, and she knew she'd better get some more now rather than wait till after the show, but she'd have to move fast. No question of going all the way back to Seventh Street; the Dope House was close to Trish's, but on Sunday nights it often opened very late, and Koy didn't think she could rely on it; that left Ridge Street.

Although the night was warm she put on a thigh-length fun-fur because really she was almost naked, slung the faux-Chanel bag over one shoulder, checked herself in the mirror for the thousandth time, and went out. She looked hot. She knew it. She felt hot. This was going to be good.

Men stared, whistling and calling out to her as soon as she hit the street. She just smiled to herself, and swayed her hips a little more. She couldn't wait to go on –if only the show were about to start now! –she had that feeling, that things were going to *happen*.

Ridge Street was quietly busy. Even there the other buyers, who normally paid no attention to anyone, were checking her out. She copped from the old man she knew as Carmello, who never said a word, just looked around, and fished the bundle out of his underwear. She was headed north, toward Trish's, when the police car pulled up beside her and stopped, the cop rolling down his window and leering at her. Her skin crawled.

"Hey there, blondie," he said. "What are you doing around here?"

Koy reluctantly stopped. "Um, excuse me?"

"I said, what are you doing around here?"

"Well, officer," she said, trying to keep her voice composed, "I'm walking up to my friend's house."

"Oh yeah?" the cop said. He was acting tough but he was obviously checking her out. "And were does this friend live?"

"Corner of Houston and Avenue B," Koy said. She wasn't sure how to play this, and the cop's attitude was starting to irritate her —something she didn't want to show. Take it easy, she told herself. She tried to smile.

"Looks to me like you're in the wrong part of town. What were you doing down there at the corner?"

This irked Koy. "Look," she said. "I live on Delancey, between Attorney and Ridge. Now I told you I'm going to Houston and B, and I didn't want to walk up Attorney —you know what I mean?"

"I'm not so sure," the cop said. "No, I don't think so at all. No, I think you were down there at the corner buying some smack. You been buying some smack, pretty lady?"

Koy didn't answer, she just tried to look disdainful.

"Maybe I should frisk you," the cop said.

Koy saw her entire future —from the show just over an hour from now, and ensuing break-through success, to her long-awaited enjoyment of the pampered and luxurious life of a rock-n-roll star —saw all this snatched away and destroyed by this idiotic cop. She had to get out of here; she took a chance. "Oh, officer," she said, pouting a little bit. "That would be nice, but I just don't think I have the time."

He loved it; for a second, he didn't even know what to say. His partner said, loudly, "Hey, what are you, some kind of musician or something?"

"Yeah," the first cop said, distracted. "You're dressed-up like a movie star."

"I'm the singer in a band," Koy said. She found two passes in the Chanel bag and gave them to him. "We're called Dreamwhip. We're playing tonight. I'm on my way to the show."

"Huh," the cop said.

"Limelite," the other cop said. "Isn't that the place looks like a church?"

"That's right," Koy said.

"Kind of creepy," he said.

"Look here, Dreamwhip," the first cop said. "This isn't a good neighborhood for you. It's not safe, there's a lot of drugs around here. You shouldn't be coming back here."

Koy didn't know what to say. This was crazy, she *lived* around here.

"You understand what I'm saying? Find some other way to get to your friend's. Don't be coming back here. Now get moving." He pointed with his chin toward Stanton.

Koy just nodded and walked away; what else could she do? She could feel them watching her, knew they were talking about her as she went up the street. Cops! What fascists! It was too much! 'Don't be coming back around here.' She *lived* around here!

*          *          *

When Koy got to Trish's, it wasn't quite eleven yet but of course Trish wasn't anywhere near ready. In fact, Trish seemed closer to a nervous breakdown than to being ready; and Koy wondered, once again, about the wisdom of her choice of bass players –but who else was she going to get at the time? She could see that Trish had been crying, and now her jaws were clenched tight as she ground her teeth –nerves, or cheap cocaine, what did it matter? Koy helped her get dressed and pick out two spare outfits, in case she wanted to change; Dizzy had at least tuned the guitars, and checked the other gear; by quarter-past, Koy managed to get them all out the door and downstairs, where the car-service car was waiting. They were making a U-turn to head back west on Houston, when Dizzy said, "Oh no! I can't believe it! Pull over!" "We can't!" Koy said. "What is it?" Trish said. "I forgot the camera!" Dizzy said. "Pull over!" he told the driver. They were already at Avenue A. "Go on!" he said, opening the door and jumping out. "I'll get a cab, I'll be right there." Trish looked lost and confused. "Okay," Koy said. "Just hurry."

Koy wondered if he'd really forgotten it, or if he just wanted a break from the psychodrama. Trish looked like she was about to start crying again. "Hey, don't worry," Koy whispered, giving her friend's arm a squeeze. "Everything's going to be great." Trish tried to smile, as she rummaged through one of her bags.

The blocks flew past in the light Sunday night traffic, but to Koy they couldn't go fast enough. Kaci would be mad about the time, although it obviously wasn't Koy's fault, Trish on the verge of falling apart. What a bunch of jerks! and only Barb didn't cause trouble or give her a hard time, just played the drums and kept smiling. Sometimes Koy really didn't think it was fair, the way things kept turning out, after all the effort she had put in and all the sacrifices she had made.

But the car was pulling up, and though Koy had seen the place, when somebody big was playing, with a long line of people waiting to get in, now the block was deserted and even the doormen had momentarily gone inside, so that nothing had ever looked more desolate. Koy paid off the car and they hustled in. Kaci looked mad but she and Barbi were listening to the promoter, and nobody said anything about the time; in fact, this guy –an aging rocker, gone to fat, dressed in expensive clothes, his long hair pulled back in a pony-tail to hide a bald spot –was telling them in a pleasant but definite way not to even think about going on before twelve-thirty; he would let them know, it would probably be closer to one. He gave them three drink tickets each, but told them to be careful, not to get drunk, then winked and grinned –his teeth were nauseating – and went away, leaving them alone.

"Good Lord," Kaci said. "Now it's more than an hour. What are we going to do?"

Koy looked around. The backstage of the posh Limelite was a dump. Assorted couches and battered, mismatched chairs lined the walls of a dingy rectangular room, and there was nothing else but a big mirror at one end, a pair of cheap little guitar amps for tuning, and a table from a school cafeteria with a couple of bowls and an ice-chest. Koy walked over to it: peanuts, tortilla chips, sodas. She took a diet soda, but put it back.

"What the hell," she said, turning back to the others and holding up the drink tickets. "Let's go to the bar."

Trish thought there was a bar upstairs, where there usually weren't too many people, and they could hang out up there. Down the hall they found the stairs, and went up a flight where they went through a second door, marked, 'Employees Only' on the other side –"Well, I guess we're employees for the night," Barbi said –onto a narrow balcony overlooking the dance floor. The lights were flashing, the music was loud, and people were dancing. "Check it out," Koy said. "I've never been up here before." From here, the stage looked small, and the backline equipment, surrounded by cables taped to the scarred and dirty flooring, looked battered and worn, like so much junk. And how would the band look? The view was too good, Koy thought, anything you did wrong would be immediately obvious.

They went on to the bar, empty except for the bartender, and got drinks, then stood together in a knot, not really talking. Koy finished hers first and got another. Time was crawling; she was afraid she would come down too much before time to go on. If they wanted the band to go on so late, why not tell them so in the first place? But the others were looking at her, expectant. She said, "Okay… Shall we go tune and fluff?"

Trish and Barbi got refills, and they filed back along the balcony to the employee's door, down the stairs and back to the dressing room. Dizzy was sitting there, the camera on the table. "Hey," he said. "I figured you guys were doing something important, so I hung out here and watched your stuff."

With him there they had to act like they knew what they were doing. They milled around, checking the mirror, looking at the guitars. Barbi put a rubber practice pad on a chair and began to warm up, as Kaci and Trish tuned. Koy was fussing with her hair. "What the hell, let's plug in, play something," Kaci said.

They turned on the amplifiers and laughed: the things just made the nastiest sound. Kaci blasted out a couple of horrible riffs, and Dizzy called, "*Sonic Reducer!*" Every one of them had played the old song at least a hundred times. Koy forgot the words; Trish's fingers slipped, she didn't know where she was; Kaci just sounded dinky; at the end, they just fell apart. "Jeeze," Trish said. "Glad we got that out of our system," Kaci said. "Yeah," Barbi said. "It was a little like barfing." Koy had already forgotten it, and headed for the bathroom.

But they felt better, somehow. Trish suggested *Blitzkrieg Bop*. They assaulted it, as if trying to make it sound as bad as possible; when Kaci looked around and Koy wasn't there, she sang it herself. Barbi and Trish looked surprised but they just grinned and jammed harder. It sounded horrible. They were all laughing as it ended.

"Wow, that was like our greatest moment," Trish said.

"We should play it tonight," Barbi said.

Someone wanted to know how long now: maybe only fifteen or twenty minutes. Where was the guy? But it could be a lot longer. Everyone remembered that one gig in Staten Island, when they hadn't gone on till three-thirty. Really, they thought they had waited long enough; but if it were going to be much longer, maybe they should go back to the bar? They were loose now, ready to go…

The guy came back and said twenty minutes or so. "Tell your singer," he said, and left. And in fact, where was Koy? "Well, that's it, I'm going back to the bar," Barbi said. Dizzy went with her to help.

By the time they came back with the drinks, Koy had reappeared, high as a kite. She wandered around, as Trish and Kaci jammed through half a dozen old songs, really getting warmed up now.

The soundman came in. "Okay," he said. "The amps are on and warming up. I'm going up to the booth. Joey will walk you up to the stage. Plug in and get set. When the house music goes down, your mics go up. Are we ready to rock?" They all nodded, serious as a heart attack. "Alright," he said, and looked at his watch. "Five minutes." He left.

Five minutes! They all looked around at one another. This was it! Limelite! Suddenly everyone was nervous again: they had waited for this for so long!

"Are we ready to rock?" Trish said, imitating the guy.

They all cracked up laughing; the touch of panic was gone.

Dizzy left to go out front. Trish ran to the bathroom; Barbi was carefully putting on lipstick; Koy gargled with salt-water; Kaci put on her guitar, walking in a circle and playing with her eyes closed. Trish came back, put on her bass. Barbi was still fussing in the mirror. "How's that hair?" Koy said. "Hey, come on," Barbi said. "All they can see of me is my hair."

They were checking the tuning again when the Limelite guy came back. "About that time," he said. "Are we ready to rock?" Barb giggled, Koy tried not to laugh, and said, "Yeah! We're just, ah, tuning up, one last tune-up." "Great, great," the guy said. "About that time."

Kaci and Trish were ready. Koy said okay to the Limelite guy, and he led them back to the still-dark stage. From here the house music was very loud, filling the luminous arch of the club; but in the backwash of the ever-changing colored lights, they couldn't see anything. The Limelite guy was telling them to go ahead and plug in. Trish tripped over something, almost fell. The Limelite guy told her to be careful.

"So plug in, get set," he repeated. "When I give the go-ahead to the soundman, the house music goes down and you're on."

Koy was standing in front of the drum riser. Diamond light-points from a mirror ball swirled across the stage, over the others. She held out her hands: the reflected glimmers flowed gracefully over them. "Koy!" Barbi was shouting; Koy turned around. "Koy! Are we ready to rock?"

Koy laughed, and now she felt good, so good, better than she'd felt in a long time. "Is everybody cool?" she called. Kaci smacked a pick against muffled strings, nodded; Barbi winked; Trish cranked up the volume, thumped the bass once loudly, and nodded, still frowning at the amp. Koy watched her for a moment, assuring herself that they were ready, then held up a thumb and blew a kiss at the Limelite guy.

He nodded, picked up a phone. The house music went down, and the

DJ's voice came over the sound system: "Alright, brothers and sisters of the Rock-n-Roll Church... Put your hands together and give a very *warm* welcome to... Dreamwhip!"

They heard clapping as the stage lights came up, blinding and hot. "Alright," Koy said, and grabbed the mic. "Mmm", she purrs, "we're *so* glad to be here." Kaci is already counting off, "One... two... one two three four!" and the band kicks off *Alone With You*: thick slabs of power chords, then slinky guitar grinding its hips against the pumping beat. Koy is shaking it good, even if her voice is thin; Kaci pouts, her face in profile, eyes half-shut; Trish, feet planted wide, holds the bass against her hip, pointed at the audience as if aiming a shotgun; Barbi is all concentration and focus, the drums huge. The colored lights –they have never had such great lights before –are disorienting, and they play the first verse from feel and habit. At the dropout the vocals reverberate through the hall

> *When we come together it's a*
> *Ch-ch-chain reaction*

crash of the intro chords, and there's a wall of sound

> *Alone with you, I wanna be alone with you*

At the second verse, the volume drops, Koy tracing a finger down her belly as she sings. A camera flash goes off, then another. Her skin is already damp with sweat, like under an incendiary sun, but the band is rocking, it sounds good, and the crowd starts to move at the next chorus

> *Alone with you, I wanna be alone with you*

Kaci kicks into her lead, hot-rodded licks snarling over the driving rhythm section, her face serious, heavily made-up eyes on the fretboard. Fists rise into the air –the guys love this devil-doll guitarist –and the break ends, the band crashing into the last chorus

> *Alone with you, I wanna be alone with you*

They stop on a dime, silence sucking back into the room, like a vacuum. The crowd hoots, whistles, claps their hands. "Oooh, thank you," Koy says. "This one's called *Tied Up*." Kaci kicks it off, guitar slashing and burning, and Barbi joins in, the pounding drums like detonations. Trish's bass throbs, more felt than heard –here and there in the audience, heads are banging in time –and Koy feels herself up as she dances. The audience presses forward as the band hammers through the first verse, vocals jittering around the icy, brittle riff. Kaci and Trish step up to the mics at the chorus

> *Tied up*
> > *in my leather boots, I'm*
> *Tied up*
> > *like a lace in my shoe, I'm*
> *Tied up, I'm tied down*

The guitar forces its way into the skull like a lobotomist's knife

> *I'm tied up, I'm tied down*

Kaci's lead, a ray-gun burst of fuzz, disintegrates the song. At the end the vocals are obsessive, monomaniac

> *Tied up, you're tied down*
> *Tied up, you're tied down*

The audience thrashes in place, holding up fists; there is a roar at the song's end. "Oooh, thank you," Koy says. "This song is about what you gotta do when I've been real *bad*." Barbi kicks off *Spank Me*. Trish is grinning now, swaying in time to the beat. Kaci surveys the audience, the hint of a smile at the corners of her mouth. Barbi, regulating her breath like an athlete, is beginning to sweat, but Koy is really working, prowling the lip of the stage, wiggling and writhing

> *Why don't you just spank me, why don't you*

Her one goal is to turn the Limelite into a seething cauldron of lust. The audience is digging it –especially the guys. At the lead, Koy spanks Trish, as Kaci strokes nasty licks from the guitar; then the volume drops, Koy on her hands and knees, crawling, whispering the soft-core lyrics

> *You know I want it, yeah yeah yeah*
> *You know I need it, yeah yeah yeah*

As they slam into the chorus, Koy turns her back to the crowd, runs a hand over her ass

> *Why don't you just spank me, won't you just*

*Spank me*

The song shudders to a stop, drained dry; hoarse shouts come from the audience. "Oh yeah," Koy says, strutting like a beauty queen turned stripper. "I like it… Do it some more!" Barbi counts off four; she and Trish kick into *Going Supersonic*: eight bars of crushing drums and bass, a dopplered flyover by Kaci, and the three lock into the groove. Barbi smiles, tossing back her hair; Trish pouts cherry lips at the fretboard; Kaci sways from side to side, cranking out the riff; Koy spins and grabs the mic to start the verse. Under the shifting disco lights, Kaci's white Les Paul turns red, blue, purple, yellow, when abruptly the room goes dark, and strobe lights negate all natural motion, stripping what is seen from what is heard, threatening to disorient even the band. Barbi shuts her eyes; Trish watches herself play, confused by what her own hands are doing; Kaci bites her lip, trying to concentrate but mesmerized by the heaving dance floor; only Koy is into it, bumping and grinding, timing her movements to the pulse of the strobe. The effect shuts off –a moment equally disorienting –as the song locks onto the chorus

> *Ten, nine, eight, yeah*
> *We're lifting off the ground*
> *Going past the speed of sound, our love*

The guitars drop out, leaving only the drums, a titanic backbeat

> *Is going supersonic*

The riff slams back from nowhere, the house rocking. We've got them, Koy thinks. The dance floor throbs, the rockers boogie in place. Koy is pushing herself to the limit. The song freefalls through a second chorus, into a change, like the riff turned inside-out: Koy moans over and over, as stuttering echoplex guitar dislocates the groove; there's a dropout like a gasp; the drums flip, and they reset at the top of the chorus, rocking hard

> *Ten, nine, eight, yeah*
> *We're lifting off the ground*

The strobe is back

> *Our love… is going supersonic*

Koy squeezes the mic like a swollen cock between her breasts, a mask of perverse joy on her face, and the crowd shudders, the air heavy with sweat and musk. Trish blows kisses, runs her tongue over her teeth; Kaci looks over the crowd, a cool dominatrix; and the hypnotizing riff repeats over and over with the monotonous insistence of pure lust. When it ends, throaty yells punctuate the applause.

Trish starts the intro to *Intoxication*, a throbbing, repetitive hook. "Oh *yeah!*" Koy groans; Barbi smacks into a bump-and-grind. "Let's do it *again.*" The crowd is into it, people dancing in place even as they stare toward the stage. Koy sings in a low, husky voice

*Baby I want you so much*

Kaci and Trish grooving to the beat, Koy wriggling like a snake charmer's snake

*And I need your magic touch*

Barbi tosses her hair back from her eyes; she has the look of a runner at mid-race

*You put me under your spell*

There is movement off to the right, in front of Trish somewhere, but Koy can't see, doesn't want to look, doesn't want to lose concentration

*Now I'm caught between heaven and hell*

Kaci comes in, wah-wah guitar swelling over the bass and drums; and Koy oozes into the chorus

*You intoxicate me, intoxicate me*
*Intoxicate me, intoxicate me*

The strobe lights are back, but the groove is too huge to be slowed: the guitar erupts, then vanishes; the mind-numbing bass thumps on, bumping booty with the drums; Koy does her stripper moves with the mic-stand, grinding her hips

*You intoxicate me, intoxicate me*

She wants every cock stiff and every pussy wet: C'mon! Do it! Don't you wanna fuck me? Come *on!*

*You intoxicate me, intoxicate me*

Kaci lashes the riff side to side; Trish, locked in with Barbi, sways back and forth, shaking her hair

*Intoxicate me, intoxicate me*

The guitars fade, dying to nothing over the beat. "Ooohh… yeah," Koy whispers. "You know… When I like someone… I'm pretty uninhibited…"

And Kaci rips out the opening of *Uninhibited*, pure rock-n-roll raunch; she is smiling like she just got laid. Koy, banging a tambourine and shaking her ass, winks at the guitarist, blows her a kiss. Trish and Barb are like a machine, as Koy sings

*Can't can't get me, out of your head*
*Can't can't wait to get you, get you in bed*

*Something* is going on, off to stage right, people pushing and shoving, but it stops. Even Barbi can see the crowd getting down and shaking it. She is going rock-steady, strong and tough, a big grin on her face, the drums huge. Kaci edges up her volume, pushing and pushing

*I'm uninhibited, yeah, uninhibited*

At the guitar lead, Koy simulates fellatio on the mic, the crowd going nuts as she strokes it, runs her tongue along the shaft, licking and kissing the bulging metal head. On her knees at the lip of the stage, rubbing it like a vibrator over sweaty flesh, her pelvis thrusting, eyes shut, she doesn't see the fight break out –but there, in front of Trish, people are pushing and trying to see, then backing away from two guys shoving one another, swinging their fists. Here comes the bouncer, then quickly two more, big men like linebackers, and still the two idiots try to fight. The bouncers separate them, hustle them away, out of sight. Koy squeezes the mic between her breasts, but she's lost the audience.

"Wow," she says when the song ends. "I guess those guys got a little *too excited*, huh?" She looks back: Kaci is tuning, Trish swigging a drink. She goes on: "But like, our music… our band… we're not about fighting, we're about love." There are whistles, shouts of approval. "Yeah, we need to *love* each other… That's what gets *me* excited."

Kaci nods to Barbi; she clicks off four on the sticks, and they come in together on *Automatic*. Koy struts to the juicy groove, blowing kisses and smacking her ass with the tambourine. The sound is louder now, the bass and drums vibrating the stage. Koy plants one spike heel on her monitor, and leans out toward the audience

*Flip that switch*

She is getting tired –they all are –but if they're to get this audience back, it's got to be *now*

*And I go automatic*

Kaci moves up beside her, leaning out and shaking her hair as she cranks her guitar

*Flip that switch*

For a moment –she's not sure –Koy *thinks* she sees the Japanese men –but when she looks back again, she can't tell. And the band is going hard: drops of sweat fly from Barbi, who is trying to keep Trish from dragging; Kaci looks determined but she's wearing out

*And I go automatic*

Koy thinks briefly of the bag she is going to do right after the show; but she is getting down, getting *down* and shaking it, and the audience is digging it again. Stabs of ray-gun guitar –strobes –last chorus –they punch the ending. "Oh, wow," Koy giggles. "I'm always into a quickie... Doesn't everyone like a quickie?"

Kaci is already kicking out *Control Myself*, sticky lube-coated guitar – then doggie-style drums, DP bass; Koy, covering her eyes with one arm, dances enslaved to the beat

*I can't control myself*

Her own skin is slick with sweat, the lights burning hot

*I can't control myself, with you*

Her throat is beginning to go –she's got to be careful –

*I can't control myself*

She holds the mic stand, grinding her ass and looking out at the eyes looking back at her

*With you I can't control myself*

Eyes stripping her, gripping and penetrating her –and a delicious feeling goes through her, she's so turned on, singing to them

*I can't control myself with you*

At the second verse she crawls on hands and knees, moaning and whispering the words; the room pulses with her voice. Red lights flare, burn and fade —and in the beat of their glare, Koy looks demented, ready for self-immolation in lust, her flesh bruised, or over-ripe

*With you I can't control myself*

Singing, squeezing her breasts, she strokes herself

*I can't control myself with you*

At the end, orgasmic guitar spurts, spatters, drips —deep-throat bass and skull-fuck drums —Koy squealing and moaning like a porn star. Stunned at first, torpid with desire, the audience cheers; some yell hoarsely. "Mmm, thank you," Koy says. "That was *so* good for me… I hope it was good for you." At a nod from Barbi, Kaci begins simulating motorcycle noises with the guitar, a motor racing as the throttle is opened. "This song is about the girls in Dreamwhip," Koy says. "It's called *Built for Speed*." Sticks smack skins, the guitar peels out, and they smash into it, going flat out but running on vapor. It's too fast, Koy is thinking, but the throttle's stuck

*When I jam it make the tires squeal*
*Ain't that the kind of speed you can feel?*

Kaci, superb, spanks out the staccato rhythm as she rocks back and forth, looking out over the crowd with an ambiguous, appraising expression. Trish takes a Sid Vicious stance, bass rumbling like a funny car on the line

*Make rubber burn, make your motor hum*
*Maximum speed make your mind go numb*

To Barbi this *is* maximum speed; she shakes sweat from her eyes, almost loses a stick; but the beat is relentless, it's maybe the best show she's ever played, it feels great. The audience is going nuts —Koy has transformed from porn starlet to dragstrip chick, and they're loving it

*Talking bored-out supercharged fuel-injected bad*
*Maybe the best ride you ever had*

Kaci moves to the front, she leans into Koy's mic at the chorus

> *My engine whines*
> *Your ears bleed*
> *Tach's redlined*
> *I'm built for speed*

They spin apart, Kaci circling back as Koy repeats

> *Built for speed, I'm built for speed*

The volume drops for the second verse; Koy's voice is throaty, tired, but nothing can stop her now, she's *got* them. Kaci lays back, building into the bridge; her eyes catch Barbi's, and they smile

> *Talking bored-out supercharged fuel-injected bad*

Trish is shaking her ass as she bangs out the riff

> *Maybe the best ride you ever had*

Kaci prowls up to her mic, she's got to make it to the end –just one more after this–

> *My engine whines*
> *Your ears bleed*
> *Tach's redlined*
> *I'm built for speed*

She stomps the fuzz box and moves to the middle of the stage, guitar over her head, a long bent note rolling over into feedback. Barbi and Trish kick into the break –Koy, far stage-left, gyrating like a go-go dancer –Kaci drops the guitar into place and wheelies into the lead. Fists and devil-horns pump the air, the place rocking. Trish moves up, Kaci turns to meet her and they step up close, whipping their hair –Kaci swings back, trick-shifts, afterburns down the neck, drops out. Bass and drums –Koy back at stage-front, Trish at the mic

> *Red light*
> > *Oooh, feel the pressure climb*

Kaci at the mic, she and Trish just whispering

> *Red light*
> > *Feel it squeeze your mind*

Koy purrs like a phone-sex girl –Barbi pushes the beat forward, slowly building

> *Red light, red light –going blind*

Kaci in on guitar –Koy a demented diva

*Let me loose or I'll lose my mind*

Drum fill like a massive backfire, guitars winding out

*Red light, yellow light, green light —go!*

Pedal to the metal now, Dreamwhip is redlined and overheating, hurtling toward the last chorus —but on the verge of coming apart

*Honey this machine ain't just for show*

Limelite is rocking, men and women dancing and jumping

*Red light, yellow light, green light —go!*

The decibels are painful —mind-bending, subjugating

> *My engine whines*
> *Your ears bleed*
> *Tach's redlined*
> *I'm built for speed*

The chorus repeats —and they slam to a stop, like smashing into a wall. The audience too is out of breath. "Alright," Koy says. "Wow… You guys are great, you're really too much… Mmm, and we'll *show* you how much we appreciate it. This is our last song, it's called *Whip On You*." Kaci wipes sweat from her hands. As Barbi clicks off four, Trish is wondering if she can make it, but Kaci lashes into the deranged riff, a psychotic smile on her face. After two, Barbi comes in like a machine; Trish slides down the neck; Koy picks up the tambourine, smacking it to the beat. The riff repeats, insistent, cruel —and Koy plucks the microphone from its stand

> *Out of my head but I don't mind*
> *I got my whip in my hand and I feel fine*
> *Yeah I feel fine*

Trish is pogoing in place, fighting a cramp in her hand, trying to think of something else; Kaci, stage-left, feet spread wide, cranks out the punishing guitar, sneering at the rockers not dancing; Barbi, sweat running down her face and neck, dripping from her hair, plays like a goddess, superb and aloof

> *Look out honey 'cause it's coming down*
> *Already here before you look around*
> *Yeah, before you look around*

But Koy is intense, cold and commanding as an empress. Her eyes hidden behind mirrored glasses, you watch her mouth as she spits out the words.

> *Saints and sinners in a gothic frieze*

Her lips turn scarlet, then black in the shifting light —her tongue licks out like a serpent's

> *Kneeling at the toilet begging please please please*

The mic no longer a cock or a dildo but a weapon —her fingers splayed, nails jut like knife-tips

> *Aww, whip on you*
> *That's all I wanna do*

The guitarists shout the refrain, Koy lashing back the response

> *Whip on you*
> *You know you love it too*

The crowd *is* loving it, jumping up and down, knocking into one another. Koy goads them on

> *You got yours, now I'll take mine*
> *The cash value will do just fine*
> *Yeah the cash will do just fine*

She glances to the left at her guitarist —then back at the crowd —working her throat, trying to make it last

> *Lover's lips and fingertips*
> *Are all very nice if you got the time*

They stare up at her —smiling and leering —some stretch out their hands to her

> *But I'm sorry honey, 'cause I don't got the time*

She rises above them —her worshippers —she could spit on them —stamp their fingers —kick at them

> *Whip on you*
> *That's all I wanna do*

The band roars, a juggernaut, an ingenious exterminating machine whose task is the annihilation of the world —and Koy's fingers squeeze the joystick

> *Whip on you*
> *You know you love it too*

Her throat is going —got to make it last

> *Whip on you, baby*

Red lights like blood, blue like bruises —hands of the suppliant, eyes of the enslaved —mouths twisted in frustrated desire

*Whip on you*

Kaci's lead like a cat-o-nine tails scars and disfigures, slicing cheeks and gouging out eyes. Koy spins away from the mic, unbuckling her heavy belt and stripping it free. But Kaci never looks around, just slams one foot up on the monitor, and steps up onto it —Koy can't believe it! —balancing there, like a skateboarder, and blasting demently on her guitar. Koy holds the belt high, stretched between her hands, then whips it down onto the stage floor. An approving grunt comes from the crowd. Koy lashes the floor again and again, berserk, her skin flushed and eyes wild, as Kaci leaps down, still playing, and they assault the chorus

*Whip on you*

Barbi is smiling, the grin of a mannequin —a stick flies from her hand and she pulls another without missing a beat

*That's all I wanna do*

Trish pounds her bass mercilessly, shouting into the mic

*Whip on you*

Kaci tosses her hair back and presses her lips to the mic —her eyes languid, half-closed, the eyes of a vicious lover, heartless and beautiful

*You know you love it too*

Still whipping the floor, Koy falls to her knees, convulsed in a paroxysm of sadistic pleasure

*Whip on you, baby*

The audience is jumping around, slamming into one another, trying to get her attention —but she doesn't see them

*Whip on you, baby*

Guitars buzz and whine like torture machines, drums roaring like a bombardment —but Koy is simply demonic

*Whip on you, baby*

As if blind with fury, she drops the belt, reaching out a clutching hand, stretching toward those just in front of the stage, scarlet fingernails seeking their faces and eyes

*Whip on you*

There is a last explosive *whump!* like a detonation —and the music's over. Koy, back on her feet, licks her lips —Barbi, standing, points out to the audience with her sticks —Kaci unslings her guitar, holding it by the neck, one fist in the air — Trish is blowing kisses. "We've got to go," Koy says. "Goodnight! We *love* you! —won't you love us too, just a little bit?" And then they're gone.

*       *       *

"Jeeze," Trish was saying as the fumbled their way through the corridor backstage. "I am *so* tired."

"Yeah, me too," Barbi said. "I'm ready to drop."

Behind them the music came up, and the DJ was saying, "Alright everyone, put your hands together one more time for… Dreamwhip!"

Koy giggled hoarsely. "Put your hands in your pants one more time… for Dreamwhip!"

Limelite guy was in the hall. "Alright, great show. Had the place rocking." He gave them more drink tickets, said he'd call them to set up another date soon. "Hang out a while. Enjoy yourselves."

Koy shared out the tickets. "Hang out," she said. "Enjoy yourselves."

"Hey, look, you guys take my tickets," Barbi said. "I have to go."

"What?" Trish said. "No way!"

"Yeah, come on Barb, you have to have one drink with us, anyway," Koy said. Barbi looked at Kaci, hoping for an ally who'd let her off, but Kaci said, "Yeah… Don't you want to stay for a minute, Barb? You can stay for one."

"Okay," Barbi said finally. "But really, just one."

"Come *on*, let's go meet our adoring fans," Koy said. "Squeeze some flesh."

"Get squeezed is more like it," Trish said.

"Yeah," Barbi said. "That's just what I wanted to avoid."

*                    *                    *

At three a.m., Koy was still hanging around the stupid Limelite; she herself wasn't completely certain why. Barbi had gone home early, of course, after guzzling the one drink. As often before, Koy wondered idly just what the story really was, but she'd decided she would never know and it didn't much matter. Kaci stayed somewhat longer, not saying much, smoking Trish's cigarettes –that was unusual –before she left too. For a while they had creeps and weirdoes all over them, but nobody they knew was there. It was disgusting. Where were the fucking Kamikazis? And the Contusions? Not that Koy could fault Dizzy, though tonight he'd been so wasted; maybe he was jealous of the gig, or maybe it was putting up with Trish. It was a shame, the Contusions would never... Koy stopped herself, she didn't like to be negative about her friends, didn't want to think bad thoughts. But the Kamikazis could have come. And Johnny. Fucking little snot-nosed Johnny never showed up. Still mad, she supposed. Well, he could go to hell.

The big question was if the two Japanese men had come. She'd never seen them.

She couldn't think about it, used up her last drink ticket and called the car service. What good was hanging around there? She didn't even know what she was waiting for, but whatever it was, it wasn't happening. Playing at a club always ruined the place for you: everything exciting or attractive just disappeared like magic during your show and all you saw afterwards was trash and dirt and stuff that needed to be fixed. Probably the next step, she thought, was that nothing ever looked very good again in the first place.

Her car was the only one on the street. Of course it was four a.m. on Sunday. No, really it was Monday. She climbed in, trying to remember if she was working Monday or Tuesday. She hoped it was Tuesday. Tuesday would be better. That way, she could rest all day Monday. She was pretty sure it was

Tuesday; anyway she hoped so.

The car was gigantic, plush. The big leather seat was softer than a bed. She leaned back and closed her eyes. The streets slid by in silence; the trip took only minutes. Going up the stairs she realized how tired she was, how much her legs hurt, and her feet. She was ready for a shot —she'd been snorting bags all night.

*         *         *

A couple nights later, Mick D was shooting pool at the Fuzz Box when Koy walked in. She waved at him and went to the bar; but after she got her drink she felt bored and went to the bathroom. No one was there, so she went in a stall and got out the vial of coke, the good stuff she had saved, and snorted up two spoonfuls. It went straight to her head, and she felt good, like a million bucks. It sure wasn't like that crap you got in the neighborhood. She had one more snort for good measure, went to the mirror and fussed with her makeup, put on some more lipstick and went back to her drink.

But now that she was high as a kite the place was more boring than ever. What did she expect on a Tuesday night? —and she was beginning to wonder if she shouldn't just slam the drink and go on to the Bunker when she noticed Mick D looking at her. She smiled at him and glanced away, but already she had that little tingle she got sometimes and she started thinking about it. Hadn't somebody said his girlfriend had moved away? She glanced back: he was stretched over the table for a shot and she smiled to herself, looking at his cute little ass and imagining going to bed with him. She'd always thought he was good-looking: he had a pretty mouth and nice eyes and he always had such great haircuts. Laughing, she drank down half her drink. She felt like a star when she felt like this. *What the hell?* she thought. Go talk to him.

She walked slowly toward the back of the bar, swaying her hips. He took a shot, straightened. "Hi!" he said.

"What's up?" she said.

"Oh, just letting this guy beat me," he said, grinning. "He needs to build up his confidence." The other guy laughed. "What's up with you?"

"Oh, I just wanted to get out of the house," Koy said.

She drank off her drink, watching them finish the game. He asked if she wanted another one and they went to the bar. He was joking around, making her laugh, telling her how great she looked; it made her feel good. They started talking about the scene, coming inevitably to their own groups. She told him how much she liked the Contusions, he predicted huge success for Dreamwhip; she hoped he was right, he said he was sure of it; she repeated her admiration, but felt reserved in regard to herself, and he seemed to feel the same. Slowly, haltingly, they began to confess their doubts, worries, irritations, vague wishes to make a change. She kept ordering drinks. It felt good to talk to someone, to be able to talk to someone.

They were getting pretty drunk, or anyway Koy was, and the trouble was that she was starting to come down. That was no good, and she seized a pause in what he was saying. "Come with me to the ladies' room."

"What are we going to do there?" Mick said, getting up.

She led him to the bathroom and shut the door, and after he glanced around he put his heel against it so no one could come in. She got out the vial and they each snorted a couple spoonfuls.

"Wow, what is that, blow?" he said.

"Mmm-hmm."

"Wow," he said.

"Keep that door shut," she said, and readjusted her brassiere, squeezing her breasts.

"I haven't done that in a while," he said.

"Oh, I'll bet," she said. They both laughed.

"No, I mean coke," he said.

"Mmm-hmm," she said.

They were still laughing as they went back to the bar. Mick got two more drinks and they sat down on a banquette, side by side and looking back at the rest of the place. Mick sniffled loudly. "Sorry, my nose is running. That's good coke."

Naturally enough, now they were talking about drugs: who on the scene was using, who was strung out, who was a hard-core junkie. Koy asked about the Contusions' old guitar player, T-Bone, though she vaguely knew, and Mick told her the story: he'd been using more and more; he took to blowing off his job, kept having to pawn his guitars; finally he got kicked out of his apartment, and had to go home to Connecticut. Mick was afraid the same thing was happening to Dizzy: he didn't seem to be much into the band any more, he was getting hard to work with; no one got along very well anymore; Ratso, their drummer, was getting all bent out of shape about it.

None of this was very much fun for Koy to talk about, she kept thinking about herself, and Kaci, and Dreamwhip, feeling more and more uncomfortable. And perhaps Mick understood this, for now he was talking about some of the other girl singers, comparing them to Koy and saying how much better Koy was.

"Like JT's band," he said, "and no offense, I like JT, he's good, but he's, like, out of place, 'cause the band ain't that good, and you're so much better than Jizzo…"

"Oh, you call her Jizzo too." Koy laughed.

"Yeah, I don't know, Dizzy started that, I don't know why."

"Oh, you don't know?" Koy said, and she told him the story. They were laughing and talking about sexy stuff now, and he had his arm resting on the back of the banquette behind her.

Mick was funny. Some of his jokes were pretty dumb, but she felt attracted to him. Besides, she was still angry with Johnny. He couldn't show up for her biggest gig ever? Fuck him! She didn't need him. So she sat there thinking about going to bed with Mick –it was like a way of getting even with Johnny. Besides, she *wanted* to.

So after a while, even though it wasn't that late, she said she probably ought to think about going home. He said he would walk her. She objected a little, but he said he had to go down and catch the subway anyway. It wasn't much out of the way and he would feel better about it. She just smiled and said okay.

The night was nice, and they set off slowly. She went on talking for a couple of blocks, but Mick, distracted, was obviously thinking about something else. She waited, and finally he said, "Do you want to split a bag of dope?"

"Sure!" she said. "We can go to the Dope House."

With this new purpose, they sped up, talking and laughing again. She'd been afraid he was about to say something about his old girlfriend, or, worse, about Johnny. As they passed the pizza place, she felt a twinge of guilt but told herself to forget it. Turning down Second, he asked did she want to wait somewhere while he went and copped?

"No, let's both go," she said. "I know them, it's cool." Sure enough, one of the lookouts was a guy she knew, and so was the guy at the door. Mick had never seen anything quite like it: everyone smiled and nodded, and one of them said, "Hey, how you doing?" to Koy in the friendliest way, like they were guests. They went in, back to the stairwell, and the seller, a pudgy older guy with a weird goatee, whose eyes were always half-closed as if he were just on the verge of nodding out, actually brightened up, and smiled.

"Uh, one," Mick said.

"No, two, please," Koy said, and handed Mick a ten. Mick gave the two tens to the seller, who slowly counted both bills, put them away, and counted two bags into Mick's hand.

"Thanks," Koy said. The seller smiled again. As they went down the steps outside, the main lookout said, "Be careful. Pretty hot tonight."

Down the block, Mick said, "Well, that was impressive."

"Huh?" Koy said.

"At the Dope House."

"What do you mean?"

"They pretty much roll out the red carpet for you."

"Oh, that," Koy said. "Yeah, they're nice."

When they got to Koy's, Mick sat down on the sofa, winded from climbing six flights of stairs. The window was open and the noise of a train crossing the bridge was very loud. When it had passed, he said, "Wow, you're just about sitting on top of the Williamsburg."

"Yeah," she said. "It's alright, I like it."

She turned on the stereo and made them a couple of drinks. They each had a line of coke and half the first bag. In a minute they were making out. It was a fun night, although every now and then she felt a little bad about Johnny.

*        *        *

The phone rang; it was *him*. She couldn't stand to hear his voice, it just ripped her apart. "What's going on, JT?" she said, trying to distance herself by saying his name.

"Not much. I wondered what was going on with you."

"Not much," she said. "The usual stuff." He wanted something –but what was it this time?

"Me too," he said. "It's getting me down, I need a break. How's the band?"

"Oh, going great," she said. It was only something of a lie. "We just played Limelite, we had a good show there, it was cool. And we're going into the studio next weekend, to cut a new demo. Plus, Koy thinks she's found someone who wants to back the band financially. I'm not sure what will happen with that, but we'll see. So it's going good. What about you? Are you still playing with Electric Mistress?"

"No," he said. "That ended up not working out. So I've been doing some jamming here and there, and I'm talking to some people."

Kaci was surprised but she didn't press it –she didn't really want to be talking to him at all, it was too painful. Just hearing his voice made her eyes tear up. She couldn't take it. He was talking about his troubles at work –he always had troubles at work –but all she could think was how she could get off the phone. Finally she felt so agitated she just interrupted him.

"Wow, that's terrible," she said. "What a bad deal. But look, JT, I've got to get off the phone –I've got to go."

He stopped. "You've got to go," he said.

"Yeah, I'm sorry but, uh, I've got rehearsal, and I need to get going."

He sighed and said, "Well, okay... Listen Kaci, I just wondered if you'd have coffee with me sometime, maybe later this week."

There, she'd forced his hand. Still she wasn't prepared, and found herself saying, "Well, I don't know, I'm pretty busy this week…"

"Just for coffee."

Her resolve was melting. "No," she said, as firmly as she could. "I'm sorry, but I can't do it. Not right now."

"Oh, come on!"

"No," she said, her voice choking up. "I'm sorry, I can't. It's too soon."

"Well, I guess you're the big rock star now!" Now he was angry, his tone harsh. "No time for me anymore. We only spent a year together, and more! That's great, Kaci!"

"I know how long it was!" She was crying now. "And it's not that I'm some kind of a rock star. It's not even that I don't want to, it's that I can't. I can't. It would hurt too much and you've already hurt me too much, I can't take any more!"

After she hung up she just sat there for a while, crying intermittently. He'd managed to hurt her anyway, and maybe that's all he'd wanted in the first place. He was such a bastard; she hated him, and the sound of his stupid voice on the phone had made her realize all over again just how badly she missed him. It all sucked, it just wasn't fair.

*      *      *

Dreamwhip was at the rehearsal studio. It was the last practice before the recording session –but Koy wasn't there. They had two hours booked; one was already gone.

"You haven't talked to her?" Kaci said again to Barb.

The drummer shook her head. "Not since the show."

"This is unbelievable." Kaci looked furious. "I mean, she knew about it. We booked the time after the last practice."

"Oh, yeah, she knew about it," Trish said. "We talked about it at Limelite. 'Cause I asked her what we were going to record, and she said that we'd make the final decision at practice."

Kaci shook her head. "So where is she?"

"But see, that's why I think something's wrong." Trish was insistent. "She knew about it. She was planning on it. So she *must* be sick, or something."

"You called her," Kaci said. "She didn't answer. If she was *sick*, she'd be *home*."

"Something's wrong," Trish repeated.

Kaci didn't answer, just turned and put her guitar back in its case. Barbi and Trish looked at each other. "Hey, do you want to run through some of the tunes?" Barbi asked.

"What's the point?" Kaci said.

"Well, we've still got almost an hour left."

"Right." Kaci picked up her guitar. "And that's one hour in my life I don't have to let Koy waste. See you Saturday."

When she was gone, Trish said, "This worries me."

"She'll cool off," Barbi said. "Anyway, I hope so."

*   *   *

The stuff was bad, that was all she could think. She hadn't gotten it from one of the usual guys. It looked okay, it was stamped 'D.O.A.', but as soon as she fired it she knew something was wrong. Her stomach cramped up and it was all she could do to stumble into the bathroom. At first she couldn't even throw up, though she was nauseous, the room spinning –just sat there on her knees, chin on the toilet seat, wanting to vomit. Then it started. After a couple times there was nothing left in her stomach but the retching wouldn't stop.

It went on like that for maybe an hour. When the vomiting fit finally passed, she crawled back to her bed and lay there. Her stomach was cramped and sore from throwing up but there was something more, a dull pain that spread itself through her whole body, like she'd been poisoned.

When she woke up, it was dark. She had no idea how long she'd been asleep. She tried to get up but it made her too dizzy; she tripped, fell, had to crawl back to the bathroom and vomit again. Somehow she got back to bed once more.

In the morning the worst was over but she was weak and dope-sick. No way was she doing the other bag. It took all her strength to go out and cop, thank God from somebody she knew this time. Even once she got straight it was like the poison was still in her system. The shit must have been cut with strychnine or something. It was a while before she remembered they'd been supposed to practice the night before. The thought made her blood run cold: how was she going to explain *this*?

*       *       *

Koy needed an ally; she called Trish. "I am *so* sorry I missed practice. I got this shit, I mean, it was awful, it made me *sick*."

"Oh, yeah?" Trish said. "That happened to us, once. I wasn't that bad, but Dizzy… He was still sick the next day. He threw up in the trash at work, and they sent him home. He said he had to hold onto parking meters all the way back."

"That's just what it was like," Koy said. "I was so sick, I thought I was going to die."

"Look, don't worry, rest up," Trish said. She had to go out; she couldn't listen to this all night. "We'll see you Saturday."

"Okay, thanks," Koy said. She called Barbi. There was no answer; she left a message.

Well, that's alright, she thought. Barb won't give me a hard time; she'll understand. It's Kaci who's the problem. Get it over with, she told herself. She called, hoping to get the answering machine. Kaci picked up.

"Hi, Kaci, it's me. How you doing?" She could tell already this was going to go badly.

"Fine."

Koy took a breath. "Listen, I'm sure you're upset with me. I'm sorry I missed practice. I was sick, really sick."

"Uh-huh."

"I guess I had food poisoning, or something. It must have been something I ate. I mean, it was really bad. I threw up so many times, I lost count. I lost, like, almost a whole day. My stomach is still sore from throwing up so much."

Kaci didn't answer. The silence on the line hummed. Koy didn't know what to say. She went on in what she hoped was an appeasing tone. "Listen, Kaci, I know you think I… I'm not always very responsible. But I couldn't help this. I don't know when I've been so sick. There was no way I could come to practice."

"And you couldn't call somebody?" Kaci's voice was icy. "You couldn't make one phone call? You wasted everyone's time. We were there! You never called, you never showed up, nothing. And Trish called you! Why didn't you answer the phone?"

Koy tried to think: had the phone rung? She didn't remember. Why couldn't Kaci understand? "She called? I didn't know. That's how sick I was. I should've gone to the hospital. I was *sick*, Kaci!"

"Okay, fine, you were sick. Now what? That was our last practice before the recording. Now we're screwed! We don't even know what we're going to do!"

"We can do whatever you want." Even as she said it, Koy knew this was lame. "We'll just try a couple and go with what sounds good. Pick a couple you like…"

"That's great, Koy. Just great. Sure. We'll just try a couple and see what happens. That's the kind of pre-production that's guaranteed to produce a good recording."

"But —that's not what I meant—"

"That's what you said. What did you mean?"

Koy had tears in her eyes but she didn't want to let on. "I don't know. You're right. This fucks things up. But there's nothing I can do about it. I was really sick, too sick to practice. If you can't understand that, then I don't know what to say."

Silence. What did Kaci want her to do —bleed?

"Listen, it'll be alright, huh? I'll see you Saturday, okay?"

"Okay," Kaci said.

After they hung up, Koy wiped her eyes and tried to pull herself together. But she had a bad feeling. And after they'd had such a good show! —this had to happen.

\*            \*            \*

Trish didn't feel good about it from the beginning, but she was already sick, it was late, and she needed to score and get home. The guy was a real loser, one of those you wonder how they have an apartment at all. His shabby rocker clothes shone with grime, his scraggly hair was limp and oily, his skin spotty and livid —but she'd glimpsed multiple track marks inside the elbow, some scabby and some fresh, and it set her off: she had to have it. He led her to a vile tenement on East Fourth, all the way to Avenue D, and though the street was empty, she felt dangerously exposed and out of place, following this terminal case down a block of mostly rubble in her baddest super-slut rock-chick clothes. But no one had seen them —she didn't think.

Once inside, going up the stairs, she noticed how bad he smelled, like he hadn't bathed in a week. And he probably hadn't. But his empoisoned blood was pumping sluggishly close to the surface, its odor seeping out from multiple tiny wounds, perfuming him, and maddening her. Her nostrils flared at the scent, her mouth was watering, her lips snarled back in spite of herself —and she almost took him on the stairs, right then —fighting down the urge from fear of raising an alarm. Soon. *Soon.*

His apartment was on the fourth floor of five. Waiting for him to unlock the door, she heard a clatter of plates from the apartment across the hall, and a muffled sound of voices. It smelled like they were eating tacos.

She followed him into the apartment and he locked the door behind them. The place wasn't as bad as she'd expected: tiny, but mostly empty, and clean, at least pretty much. She sat down on a battered sofa, looked around, saw an ashtray on the table.

"Is it alright if I smoke?" she asked.

"Oh, yeah, sure," he said, his attention absorbed by the cigar box he'd taken from a cabinet. He sat down in the chair opposite and methodically prepared a shot. Trish watched, fascinated by his practiced hands. In a minute, without taking his eyes from the task, he said: "Don't you want to fix up?"

"I didn't bring my set," Trish said. "Could I use yours, when you're done?"

"Nope," he said. "But I've got a new set I'll sell you for five bucks." The going price was three.

"Let me see if I've got it," Trish said. She made a pretence of looking through her purse, but he was trying to distend a vein and she couldn't concentrate. The vein wasn't easy to find. She bit her lip as he probed in one spot after another, thick drops of blackish blood oozing from deliciously mutilated flesh. When he finally hit one, the blood spurted, and she gasped as a spray of red drops spattered to the linoleum floor. He pushed the plunger home, his eyes rolling up.

"What's the matter with you, scared of blood?" he said, voice irritated. "What do you do, stick yourself in the ass?"

She didn't answer —trying to act cool —don't scare him! But she was breathing hard, trying to keep control, wait for the right moment —trying to wait—

She stood up. He was staring at her.

"What the fuck's the matter with you?" he said.

"Where's the bathroom?" she said.

"Jesus!" he said. "It's back there. What the hell?"

She walked past him, toward the bathroom. Her head was swimming, she was unsteady on her feet; a terrible aching throbbed in her stomach. Every cell in her body was craving it, screaming for her to do it, *now!* She staggered, clenched her fists and blinked her eyes, trying to focus.

"Why don't you just sit back down?" he was saying. "Jeeze, what the fuck? What's the matter with you?"

He was starting to get up when she fell on him. He let out a yell and she clapped one hand over his mouth. But he tried to fight her: she had to smack his head on the table, then finish him.

It didn't take long, and she couldn't take too much of such corrupted blood, it was too intoxicating. Satisfied, she sank back down on the sofa, shaken and exhausted, both by the too-prolonged wait, and by the adrenaline-pumping rush of the score. Her eyes closed. Noise came from the hall. Someone knocked. Voices. They knocked again. "Mr. Helms?"

A woman's voice: the neighbor. Trish looked down at the body on the floor; her blood froze. She looked around —she had to get out. The two windows were both on the back. One of them had to lead to the fire escape.

Another knock. "Mr. Helms! Are you okay?" They said something to each other, Trish couldn't tell what. She went to the window, pushed it open as quietly as she could, and clambered out onto the fire escape. Down was no good: a closed courtyard, with a door that might or might not open from the outside. She looked up: it led over the roof. She'd have to go that way.

Someone was banging loudly on the door now. She went up the iron steps as quietly as she could. From the top floor she had to climb straight up a ladder. Her heart was pounding, her shoes kept slipping, the iron rungs tore at her hands, but she made it over the top. Better to go down through a neighboring building –but the way was blocked by a chain-link fence, topped with razor wire. She'd have to go past them.

She was scared to death –but the sooner the better. The stairwell door was open. She paused at the threshold, trying to slow her breathing. They were still down there, shouting and banging. She slipped down from the roof to the top floor, followed the stair around and saw them: a large woman, fat and very loud, shouting and pounding on the door, and two men, one medium-height and skinny, hands in his pockets and a cigarette burning between his lips, and a second, older man, much smaller and crippled, supporting himself on wrist braces. This one noticed Trish first, and never took his eyes off her; then the other man saw her, stared. Trish couldn't tell what they were thinking. The woman only looked around as Trish passed; her mouth fell open, she stopped knocking.

Trish made the turn, turned down the next flight. They were all staring at her, silent.

"*Qué pasa?*" she murmured –no one answered –and then they were out of her sight. When she got to the street, she walked for the first half-block, and then ran the rest of the way home.

*           *           *

Even though Trish was over half an hour late to the recording session, when she arrived, Koy still wasn't there. Kaci was sitting in the lobby of the studio, reading a magazine and looking irritated. Trish said hi and went back to the cutting room, where Barbi and the engineer were working on the drums. Diz had said it would take an hour to set the drum mics, and it looked like he was right; why be all mad about anything? The engineer pointed out where she would plug in to go straight to the board, so she got her stuff together, tuned up her bass, and leaned it against the wall. They'd begun the laborious process of getting the drum levels right, and Trish went back to the lobby to smoke a cigarette. Kaci looked even angrier than before.

Trish got a soda out of the machine and sat down next to her. "So what amp are you going to use?"

"I don't know," Kaci said.

Well that's good, Trish thought, and said, "What do they have?"

"Uh, well, a couple of Fenders... and, um, a Marshall, I talked to the guy and I'll probably use that... There's some other stuff, you know, either too clean or too heavy metal, and some old stuff, I didn't know what it was."

"Well, that's cool, a Marshall," Trish said. "I'm supposed to plug straight into the board. After they get done with the drums we can check out your amp."

"Yeah," Kaci said. They sat there for a while; muffled, regular drum hits were audible even through the thick walls; finally Kaci said, "Where the fuck is Koy?"

"Oh, she'll get here," Trish said. "You know, the first hour is mostly setting up the drums. It's better if she's not here, she would've had to sit around and get nervous." Kaci just looked at her. Trish couldn't tell what she was thinking.

Not more of this, Trish thought. It's the truth, and anyway you know Koy and there's no reason to think she's going to change just because we booked some time at this little studio.

It had been more than an hour when the engineer came out and said, "Okay, we've got preliminary levels on the drums, why don't we get your guitar amp set up and we can start micing it up." Down the hall was a big closet full of amplifiers, all shapes and sizes.

"Hey, you've got a Hi-Watt," Trish said.

Kaci looked blank. "What's that?"

"Oh yeah," the engineer said. "That's a good amp."

"It's British," Trish said. "Diz used one somewhere and he really liked it.

I think he said the Who used them."

"Yeah, right," the engineer said. "You want to check it out?"

"No," Kaci said. "I'll just stick with the Marshall."

Yeah, great, the Marshall, Trish thought; you and a thousand other guys. I shouldn't have mentioned Diz, you're intimidated by him. Never mind that he bends over backwards to try and help you.

As the engineer rolled the amp back down the hall, he said casually, "So… where's your singer? What's her name? Koy?"

"Who the hell knows," Kaci said.

"She's on her way," Trish said. "She'll be here any time."

"Yeah," Kaci said. "Let's hope so."

The engineer just looked at them, and rolled the amp into the cutting room. While he went for a mic, Kaci plugged in, played a couple of chords; the guitar was hideously out of tune. "New strings," she said. She tried to tune up; it kept getting worse. Trish turned away and picked up her bass.

"Where's Koy?" Barbi said.

"That's the big question, isn't it," Kaci said.

The engineer came back with a mic and set it up in front of the guitar amp.

"Is it alright if we play a little to get warmed up?" Barbi asked him.

"Oh yeah, sure," he said. "Go ahead, that'll be good."

They put on their headphones; it sounded completely unfamiliar, and wrong. They tried one cover song and fell apart in the middle; the second, easier one sounded terrible. Kaci kept trying to tune her guitar but it wouldn't stay there. Trish had never heard her sound so awful: already, things were going from bad to worse. The other two looked uptight, and Trish herself was feeling more and more nervous.

They were counting off another song when Koy walked in. Even from across the room, Trish could tell by Koy's eyes that she was high as a kite. "Hi!" Koy said. "How's it going?"

"Glad you could make it," Kaci said.

Koy looked hurt. "Were you waiting on me?"

"No," Trish said. "We're just now getting set." Kaci gave her a dirty look and turned away, facing her amp and cranking out an out-of-tune riff.

"Why don't you ask the guy where he wants you," Trish said. "I think he said something about a vocal booth."

Koy disappeared. "Were you waiting on me?" Kaci mimicked, looking at Barbi, who shrugged, staying neutral.

"She's, like, an hour late," Kaci said.

"Yeah, I know, you're right," Barbi said. "You're right. But I think we ought to concentrate on what we're here to do, on making this recording."

Kaci didn't say anything. Trish didn't know whether she should say anything or not; she decided not to. They heard Koy over the headphones.

"Hey, I'm here! Can you hear me? I'm over here!" And there she was, waving through a window in one wall. "I feel like I'm in a cage," she was saying. "Help! Let me out!"

Barbi laughed. Trish thought this stupid but she laughed too. Kaci muttered something. The whole situation was weird: with the headphones, the only person they could hear was Koy, who kept repeating, "Help! Let me out!" Trish took the phones off one ear as Kaci said, "For crying out loud, Koy, shut up!" Trish looked at Koy, drew a line across her throat with one finger. Koy got quiet.

"I can't take much more of this," Kaci said.

The engineer came in and explained that he wanted them to run through one or two of their songs so he could make some adjustments. They all looked at one another. "What should we start with?" Barbi said. "How about *Tied Up?*" Trish said. "No," Kaci said. "How about *Going Supersonic?*" Barbi said. Kaci shook her head.

"Well, what do you want to play?" Trish said.

"I don't care," Kaci said.

"Let's do *Whip on You,*" Barbi said firmly.

"That's cool," Trish said. Kaci nodded. "I'll count it off," Barbi said.

It went okay. They couldn't hear much through the headphones. Beyond the glass, the engineer's eyes were intent on the board as he adjusted the levels, but the sound in the phones just became more and more confused. At the end of the song, everyone wanted to hear more of her own part, but he explained that he couldn't do much about the headphone mix. They cranked through another song without really being able to tell what they were doing. At the end, the engineer called them into the booth; he had recorded the second song. "Check it out," he said. "I want to know what you think of the mix."

The mix was fine but the band sounded terrible. Trish was shocked, and no one else looked very happy either. Kaci got up and went back to the cutting room. The engineer was looking at them. "I think the mix is just fine," Barbi said. "Now we just have to get a good take."

The first take was so bad, they should have just quit in the middle. The second wasn't any better, the third marginally so. After the fourth they switched songs. The four and a half takes of it were dismal. They couldn't get it going; everything was off. Frustrated, Trish said, "Can we take a quick break?" "Sure," Barbi said. "Why not?" Kaci said.

Koy was already in the bathroom, snorting a spoonful of coke. "Koy!" Trish said. "You've got to sing!"

"I'm not doing anything now," Koy said. "We're gonna re-record the vocals later. I'm just singing to keep us at the right place in the song. Want some?"

Trish snorted up two spoonfuls. "We've got to be cool, and we've got to get it together. Kaci's already pissed-off, she's been that way since I got here."

"What's she mad about?"

"Cause you and I were both late."

"What? You've been here. Fuck her!"

"Koy, listen…"

"No!" Koy said sharply. "That's just not right. I'm not late. They said it would take an hour to get the drums and whatever set up. So I was right on time. I mean, I know I missed practice and all, but her whole attitude is really making me mad."

They heard steps in the hall. Koy hid the stuff but no one came in.

"Look," Trish said. "We really haven't lost any time but I don't think we should let ourselves get into an argument right now. We need to concentrate on what we're doing."

"Hey, no problem!" Koy said. "I don't want to argue. I'm ready to rock." She flipped her boa over one shoulder like a movie star, and walked out.

Trish snorted some water up her nose and followed, but the hallway was empty. She hesitated, went back to where Kaci was sitting on her amp, alone and tuning her guitar.

"Where's Barb?" Trish said.

"She went downstairs to get some beer."

"Well, that's probably a good idea," Trish said. "We need to loosen up."

"We need to do something."

Trish went back out to the lobby to smoke a cigarette. All over again, this was starting to look bad. Koy was wandering around, humming to herself. Trish didn't know what to say, didn't know if she should say anything. The elevator opened: Barbi, back with the beer. They all went back to their places, opened a beer, messed with their instruments and headphones. The engineer was sitting at the board, waiting patiently.

"Let's try *Built for Speed*," Barbi said.

They tried it; it sounded awful. Barbi was dragging, Kaci out of tune; Trish messed up a change; Koy sounded like Betty Boop. They did it again, with no better result.

"Trish, you've got to get that change right," Kaci said.

"Yeah, yeah, I will," Trish said, thinking, That's right, take it out on me! "I don't know why I'm messing up."

"We need some energy," Koy said over the phones.

Kaci made a face, but Koy couldn't see her. "Let's try a fast one," Barbi said.

This time Koy messed up. Kaci stopped in the middle of the song, pulling off her headphones. "Goddamn it, Koy, don't you know the goddamn *words?*" she yelled. The band stopped. "What happened?" Koy said.

"You fucked up, that's what happened!"

Koy couldn't hear her. "Huh?"

"I said you fucked up!" Kaci yelled. She put down her guitar and stomped out.

Trish and Barbi looked at each other. "Oh no," Barbi said. In a minute they could hear yelling from the lobby. "We don't need this," Trish said.

"No," Barbi said. "Let's go try to calm them down."

They were both furious, each shouting at once. Koy was stamping her feet, Kaci counting off complaints on her fingers. Trish and Barbi walked up, waited; the argument went on; finally Barbi said, "Hey! Hey!"

They stopped, glared at her.

"Come on you guys," Barbi went on. "It doesn't have to be like this. Look, we may have our differences, but we can work them out, right? I mean, we're supposed to be friends here," she added.

Koy looked embarrassed, slightly ashamed. Kaci flushed.

"*Friends,*" she said, "don't treat friends this way. And besides, this is a *business.*"

"That's right," Koy said. "It's a business, and we've got work to do, and instead you're giving me this attitude. I don't think this is all very professional, Kaci."

Kaci laughed bitterly, exaggeratedly. "So that's it. I'm not professional. *I* am not professional. Well, if that's what you think... but I'm not the one who missed practice, who's always late, who's always fucked-up..."

"Hey!" Koy said, but Kaci went on: "Things have changed, Koy. *You've* changed. It wasn't like this in the beginning. But now that you're the big star... Well, they can crown you Queen of the Lower East Side, but the way things are, this band is going nowhere."

"Oh yeah?" Koy hissed. "Well if that's so, why don't you just *get out?*"

Kaci looked at her for a long moment. "Okay, fine. That's just what I'll do. I'll get out." She turned and walked off, back into the cutting room.

Nobody could believe it. Trish followed her. Kaci already had her guitar put away; she wouldn't listen. When Barbi came in, Kaci said, "Look you guys, I'm sorry. But I can't go on like this. The whole thing's gone bad. You better think about yourselves." She picked up her guitar case. "Talk to you later," she said. "I'll call you." She walked out. Trish couldn't believe she was serious; the whole thing had gone to pieces right in front of her. After the elevator doors shut, Koy started crying.

They sat in the lobby for a while, stunned. The thing was too much; it was unreal. What were they going to do?

Koy went to the bathroom. The other two talked about whether or not Kaci would come back. Trish didn't want to admit, to herself or to Barbi, her very real fear that Kaci would never be back, that this was it, the sudden and unexpected collapse of everything they had worked on for months. She couldn't accept it, but what could she do? But they remembered that they were on the clock, and jumped up. "We better go talk to... that guy, the engineer," Barbi said.

He was still in his booth, waiting. Barbi explained what had happened, and he listened patiently through the whole story, nodding his head from time to time, before explaining that they had taken the studio for the whole time; there was no possibility of getting any money back. That was the policy, and there was nothing he could do about it. "I'd say, try and get some good out of it. Do any of you play guitar? Or do you know anybody who plays guitar?"

They went back to the lobby. "Well," Barbi said. "What about Dizzy?"

"I didn't want to suggest that," Trish said.

"You didn't suggest it, I did."

"I think it's a good idea," Trish said. "Where's Koy?"

Koy came out of the bathroom; they explained it to her. "Fine," she said. "Call him. How much time have we got left?"

"About three hours."

"Call him now," Koy said.

*         *         *

A horror movie was on TV, and Dizzy was sitting on the sofa, watching it, playing the guitar, and looking at a skin magazine, when the phone rang. He was relieved when it was just Trish. She told him what had happened, asked him if he could come and lay down some guitar tracks.

"Yeah," he said. "Yeah, sure... I pretty much know the songs... I'll get there as soon as I can. Let me get it together. I've got to, um, go out first... Then I'll take a cab."

"Fine," Trish said. "Do whatever you need to do, just get here as soon as you can."

"Right," Diz said. "I'll bring the Gretsch and the Junior. Look for me an amp, something small, British. Make sure it has tubes... I better change clothes."

"We don't care what you look like, just hurry. We're on the clock."

"Right," he said, and hung up. He didn't care what she said, he was changing clothes. And he had to go cop –better do that first.

He got some money, put on his coat and went downstairs. One of the Pure Energy guys was right outside. Diz opened the door and said, "Hey, Eddie, what's up?" Eddie came over; they ducked back inside and Diz bought four bags. "See you later, man," Diz said, going back up the stairs. But once in the apartment he decided he should go to the store, too: he didn't want to get all wired out, but he'd better have some coke just in case he did too much dope. He got another twenty out of the closet –they were going fast –and went back down.

The street had been picking up but now a beat cop was standing on the corner, looking around and flipping his nightstick. No going to the store next door. Clinton, he thought, that's far enough down the block. That damn cop is just wasting my time.

Inside the candy store they were watching the same horror movie. "How many?" the guy said without looking away from the screen.

"One," Diz answered. The guy slowly got up and went to the back room, clearly irritated by the interruption. One thing about these places, Diz thought, they don't have to be nice to the customers.

The guy came back with the coke, took the twenty and handed the bag to Diz. "It's a good movie, isn't it," Diz said.

"No," the guy said. "It's stupid, but I want to see how it turns out."

"Okay if I take a Coke?" Diz asked.

"Yeah, sure, whatever."

Diz got a Coke, put it in a bag himself, and said, "Thanks… See you later."

Back outside the cop was coming down Clinton towards him. Great, Diz thought. He unscrewed the lid of the Coke and drank some. Good thing he didn't make me take the junkie juice. The cop gave him the evil eye as he went past but he didn't say anything. Go to hell, Diz thought.

He went back to the apartment and snorted up a big line before getting his gear ready. Luckily both the Gretsch and the Junior had fairly new strings. He checked his bag, put in the wah-wah and a fuzz-box, and went to the bathroom, pulling his hair back to wash his face. Man, you don't look so good, he thought, you really need a shower; but it had already been twenty minutes since Trish called. He rummaged through the closet. None of the clean shirts were decent; he picked through the dirty ones, smelled a few, found one that didn't seem too bad. Some cologne would help.

When he was finally ready, he chopped up the rest of the coke, snorted up another line, and had half a bag. All right, he thought. A cab was sitting right outside the door, and the driver was just walking out of the bodega. Diz stowed the stuff in the trunk and jumped in the back seat. "Ninth Avenue and Forty-sixth," he said, and sat back.

The day was nice and he was feeling cool as they zoomed across town. What a deal! Recording with the babes! He hoped he could remember their songs... This situation with Kaci was a bad deal for Trish, for the whole band. They had shows coming up; maybe he could help them, fill in on guitar till they could find someone else. If Dreamwhip broke up, it would be bad for everyone: the girls drew a big crowd, and if you could go on before or after them, you had a good spot. Dreamwhip was very important to the scene. Really, he thought, grinning to himself, what you really ought to do is forget about the Contusions, become producer and songwriter for Dreamwhip. Make some real money there. Their biggest problem is their songs. If they had good songs, they'd be unstoppable.

He was still picturing himself like a pimp, living the high life off the sweaty flesh of Dreamwhip, when the cab pulled up in front of the recording studio. They buzzed him in, and he went up in the elevator. The girls were sitting in the lobby, looking pretty low. He tried to cheer them up a little, then went in to set up.

Barbi in particular looked like she'd lost her best friend. "I don't know," she said. "I mean, what are we going to play? Diz doesn't know our songs."

"He does, sort of," Trish said. "He's helped me with some of them."

"I've been thinking about that," Koy said. "The most important thing is that we get *something* recorded. Even if it's our older songs, I don't think it matters that much, but I've got to have a demo to give to the backer."

"But without Kaci, it's not really the *band*," Barbi said.

Yeah, but it's *me* singing, Koy thought. Could the other two tell she was thinking that? "Listen," she said quietly. "I know this thing with Kaci is bad... We're going to have to deal with it. Maybe she'll change her mind... and maybe she won't. I'd like to work things out, we've been together a long time, but even if not, we can't let it stop us. We've lost people before, and kept going. If we have to find a guitarist, we'll find one."

"It may be harder than that," Trish said. They could hear Diz warming up.

"We'll do *something*," Koy said firmly. She stood up. "C'mon," she said. "The important thing right now is that we make some kind of recording. Let's go talk to Diz."

They followed her. Diz and the engineer were talking while they set the mics on the guitar amp.

"What do you think, sweetie?" Koy said.

"I think we're about set," Diz said, grinning at her. "Why don't we warm up on a cover song, then cut a take and have a quick listen, make whatever adjustments, and go for it."

"Alright," they said. "Sounds good."

Trish picked up her bass, feeling nervous now because of Dizzy. Cut it out, she told herself, it'll be fine; but she got flustered trying to tune, fumbling with the keys. Diz winked at her, blew a kiss when no one was looking. "Alright!" he said when they were set. "How about *Blitzkrieg Bop*?"

They nodded, he counted it off, and the room exploded –the whole thing just clicked from the very first. They still couldn't hear, but it was just *right*: Barbi smiling as she pounded out the beat; Trish's bass was throbbing in her hands; and Diz sounded so good over the stripped-down rhythm section, dropping the volume through the verses, cranking the chorus, at the end ripping through one of his New York punk leads. The only problem was they didn't know how to end it, and just crashed to a stop.

"Cool," Diz said. "Hey, Jerry, you get that?"

"Yeah, no problem," the engineer said over the headphones.

"Huh?" Barbi said. "He recorded that?"

"Yeah, I asked him to. Let's go check it out."

It sounded good; everyone was pleased and excited. "Okay," Diz said. "I think I can play *Built for Speed*, do you want to try that?" "Yeah, yeah," they said. "Alright," he said. "How about if we go through it once, and then we'll try to get a take?"

The run-through was fine until the change, where it went completely awry, and finally they had to stop and try to explain it to Diz, who had some trouble understanding; but the second time was fine, and he said, "Do you want to try a take?" "Yeah, okay," they said.

Trish's mouth went dry; she couldn't remember how the song went, or what she was supposed to play. But Barbi counted it off and something happened: though Trish still couldn't remember what she was supposed to play, she was playing it anyway, and the whole band was rocking, maybe better than ever before, and she told herself, Don't think, just keep going! "Alright!" everyone said at the end. "Cool!"

They did a second take just to be sure but the first one was better. The second song was the same: they had to go through it a couple of times to get it right, but got a good take followed by a somewhat inferior one. "How many songs do you want to try to get?" Diz asked. "Three?" "Yeah, yeah, three," they said. "Or maybe even four," Koy said.

They did another plus one of their cover songs, went in the booth to listen. The good takes were just as obvious on playback as they'd been before.

"Okay, we're going to need vocal and guitar overdubs," Diz said. "Koy, do you want to go first or do you want me to?" "You first," Koy said, thinking she wanted another shot before she did her part. "Alright," Diz said to the engineer. "Real quick I'm going to double-track the rhythm guitar on the four good takes. Maybe I'll goose the amp, give it more bottom-end, if that's cool." "Yeah, yeah, go for it," the engineer said. "Hopefully we'll get through that real fast," Diz said. "Then I'm going to switch guitars and we'll put a lead track in. Nothing fancy, just one take to fill it out, and that ought to leave us plenty of time to cut the vocals and do a rough mix, don't you think?" "Oh yeah, yeah," the engineer said.

Diz went back out to the cutting room and Trish followed Koy to the bathroom. Koy stuck a spoonful of coke under Trish's nose and said, "I don't get it, what's all this that Diz is doing?" "Well, I don't completely understand it either," Trish said, "but I think he's said that if you record two guitar tracks it'll sound bigger even at the same volume, because it's like stereo guitars and there's one in each channel." "Oh," Koy said, snorting up a spoonful herself, "*now* I understand." She rolled her eyes and turned to the mirror to touch up her lipstick. "Am I getting fat?" She was watching Trish's face in the mirror.

"No, you're not getting fat," Trish said. She took out her own lipstick to avoid looking Koy in the eyes.

"Tell me the truth."

"No!" Trish said emphatically. "You're not getting fat."

Adjusting her brassiere, Koy wasn't paying attention any more. "You know," she said, still looking in the mirror, "maybe all this is for the best." "Huh?" Trish said. She was tugging down her belt, exposing her navel –Dizzy liked that –and she wasn't really paying attention to Koy either: "What are you talking about?" "This thing with Kaci," Koy said. "Maybe it's for the best. She wasn't happy… and she wasn't really that good." "What are you talking about?" Trish said again. "Of course she's good." "Look," Koy said. "Yeah, sure, she's good. I've known her for a long time and she's gotten a lot better since we started. But she's not *that* good. Listen to how we sound with Dizzy playing." "Dizzy isn't in the band," Trish said. "He doesn't quite fit." "I know he isn't in the band," Koy said. "But we need somebody like that in the band."

Trish sighed. "I think we're going to have trouble finding somebody as good as Kaci, never mind as good as Dizzy," she said. "There's just not that many girl guitar players. I really think we better try to smooth things over with Kaci."

"Hmm," Koy said. "I don't know." She got out the vial again and they each had another snort, and she said, "Go on out there and make sure Barb keeps her cool. I'll be there in a minute."

Trish took her cue and went out as Koy shut herself in a stall. Barbi was sitting in the booth, talking quietly with the engineer when he wasn't cueing up the next take. "This is cool," she said. "I didn't understand before what Diz was trying to do, but, um, Jerry explained it to me, and I can already tell it's going to sound great." "Oh, yeah? Cool," Trish said. "You know, Dizzy really knows what he's doing. We're lucky he could come up here." "Yeah," Barbi said. "Of course, I'm not sure what good it's going to do, really. We may get a great-sounding recording but now we don't have a band." "No," Trish said. "We're still a band. We may have lost our guitar player but we're still a band." Barbi sighed: "I guess you're right... I don't know, Trish. I mean, Kaci and Koy were the band when I first joined... and we had such a hard time, I mean, before we got you, we had such a hard time finding a bass player. You're the fourth one we've had! Of course, one of them only lasted a month; maybe I shouldn't count her. But women musicians aren't exactly a dime a dozen, you know? and, well, I'm *worried*, I don't know how we'll come up with another guitar player."

Trish just nodded; she didn't know what to answer, and besides she was buzzing from the coke and couldn't keep her thoughts straight. There was Lea Zoid, but she was too militantly feminist to play in the super-slut band, and besides, she just wasn't very good-looking, she was too butch; it would never work. There was that chick from Jersey: a mediocre musician, with doubtful taste...Who else? They were going to have to do something: either smooth things over with Kaci, or else find someone new, and fast. They had gigs coming up...

The song ended, and they heard Diz over the monitors: "Okay, how was that?" The engineer hit his mic: "Sounding good, man. What now?" "Roll it back to the first one," Diz's voice said. "I'm going to switch guitars. We'll need to check it, then I'll lay down some leads." "Cool, that's cool," the engineer said.

Koy came floating out of the bathroom, smiling, and Diz went in. "What's going on?" Koy said. They tried to explain it all; she didn't seem to be listening. "How long before I'm supposed to sing?" she asked; they didn't know. She went downstairs to the store.

Diz was in the bathroom just long enough to snort up a big line and another half a bag; he came back all business, got out his Les Paul Junior and played a few riffs while he tweaked the amp and the engineer re-set the levels. The girls were getting bored. The third time through, all Trish could hear were problems, she didn't even listen to the guitar leads, and though she tried to remember that this was only a demo and not an album or something, she was beginning to feel down about the whole thing. Barbi, slumped in a corner of the booth, looked like she felt the same way. Koy came back with a couple bottles of champagne and some plastic cups. "I needed something to wet my throat," she said, "and I thought this might perk us up." The very sound of the cork popping changed the atmosphere: they were all talking at once, even laughing a little. The first glass went straight to Trish's head. Barbi got the hiccups, which made everyone laugh even harder. Even the engineer had some. Dizzy finished the last lead and came out to the booth; Koy poured a big cup for him and said, "Guess I'm up, huh?"

"Go for it," Diz said. "You'll do great."

When the engineer had the big vocal mic set, Koy took one of the bottles with her; she put on the headphones, took a swig, and winked toward the booth, wiggling her hips. "Alright!" she said over the monitors. "I feel good!" Nevertheless, the first take was awful; but since Trish was out in the lobby smoking a cigarette with Barbi, who smoked one too, and Dizzy was in the bathroom again, nobody heard it except the engineer. "Should I do that one again?" she asked. "Yeah, I think so," he said. The second take was pretty much the same, but on the third one she was getting warmed up, and they kept the fourth one. It took three takes to get the second song. In the middle of the third song, she called for more champagne. They were getting low, and Trish sent Dizzy out with the money for more.

By the time he got back they were on the fourth song –the cover song. To Dizzy's way of thinking, it should have been the easiest, but Koy couldn't seem to take it seriously, and kept falling into a cutesy voice that suggested some irony or reservation about it. "What's up with this?" Trish said, quietly.

"I don't know but it's not good," Barbi murmured.

"Uh, do you want to keep that?" the engineer said over the phones to Koy. They heard her say, "I don't know, what do you think? That wasn't too bad, was it?"

"Do it again, re-do it," Barbi and Trish said.

The next take was even worse: Koy started off with the cute voice, kept on that way all the way through. Even the engineer was frowning, which impressed Diz, since they usually remained so impassive. Barbi was looking at

Trish. "Come out here," she said, and got up.

Trish followed her into the hall. "What do you think?" Barbi asked.

"I think she's got to quit screwing around and sing the song!" Trish said.

They waited there until the song ended. Barbi stuck her head in the booth and said, "Before we go on, would you cut the levels in there so we can go in and talk it over?" He nodded.

"Come on," she said to Trish, and went through the doors into the cutting room, the bottle of champagne in her hand.

Koy pulled off her headphones, shook out her hair. Barbi took Koy's cup and refilled it. "Thanks," Koy said. "How does it sound? Should we listen to it?"

"Well," Trish said. "Koy, uh," Barbi said.

"What's the matter?" Koy said. "It doesn't sound good? Tell me!"

Trish opened her mouth, but Koy was so nervous and vulnerable, that Trish fumbled for words.

"Koy, I think you should sing it more seriously," Barbi said.

"What? What does that mean? I mean, I don't get you," Koy said. "What do you mean?"

"I mean, you're singing it in a funny voice; but you should sing it like the other songs, more seriously," Barbi said. "In a serious voice."

"Yeah, like the other songs," Trish said. "Sing it like you mean it."

"But the words are so stupid!" Koy said. "I can't sing it like I mean it. I *don't* mean it."

"You don't have to mean it, you just have to sound like you do," Barbi said. "Otherwise it won't sound good."

"The people who think it's funny will still think it's funny," Trish said.

"What if they don't think it's funny, they just think I'm stupid?"

They had to talk it over quite a while, before Koy finally agreed to do a 'serious' take, but only if they kept an earlier take as well, 'just in case'. And she didn't seem too happy, at that.

"Wow, of all things," Barbi said in the hall. "You'd think, after everything else."

"I've always hated that song," Trish said. "I mean, she's right: it is stupid."

"I wonder if she's been singing in that silly voice all along, like when we play it live," Barbi said, almost to herself.

They went back to the booth, where Dizzy and the engineer were talking trash, but they stopped, looked up expectantly.

"We're going to try it again," Barbi said, "but can we save that last take on a spare track? Like, ah, just in case."

Nobody asked in case of what. The engineer made a couple adjustments, had Koy do another mic check, and was set.

"All right, everybody," Koy's voice said over the monitors. "I'm going to sing it like I mean it."

Barbi and Trish looked at each other, but no one said anything. The engineer rolled it on Koy's cue.

The take was horrible. Trish couldn't believe her ears: Koy apparently had no idea what to do. Finally, somewhere around the end of the first chorus, she settled into it. The second verse was pretty good.

"I wish we could start over like this," Trish said. Barbi nodded.

The engineer punched a button and the music stopped. Koy stopped in the middle of a word. He toggled his talkback mic: "Sorry Koy, we, uh, we had a malfunction. It'll take just a minute to fix. I'm going to roll back to the beginning of the track."

Trish jumped up and hit the button. "Sounding good, Koy, keep it coming!"

"Yeah!" Barbi yelled.

They heard Koy burp. "This stuff's pretty fizzy. Why didn't you leave me the bottle?"

Trish hit the button again. "Bringing it now!"

The next take was better. As the music ended, Koy burped loudly into the mic and said she'd like to listen to that one. In the booth she didn't say much but listened hard.

"Can we keep that one and try another one?" she asked the engineer.

"Sure," he said, "but if we do that it would be best if we could use up that earlier take we kept."

"Okay, fine," Koy said. "Use it up."

They kept the next take, and the engineer was resetting for Koy to record back-up vocals. The other two were getting tired. "Take a break," Diz said. "This is going to take a little while, give your ears a rest before it's time to mix." And he got up and left.

"I'm getting hungry," Barbi said. "This is a lot of work."

"Let's get something," Trish said. "Hey, Jerry, where's good to eat?"

"Salvatore's has good pizza, subs," he said.

"Pizza!" Trish said. "Where is it?"

"The number's by the phone up front," he said. "They deliver."

"Cool," Barbi said. "Would you like something?"

"Yeah! –just a minute," he said, and toggled the talk-back: "Okay, Koy, I'm set for back-up vocals on *Built for Speed*, rolling on your signal." He turned back. "Yes, order me a chicken parmesan sandwich. I'll get you the money in a minute."

Koy was singing along with herself. "No, it's on us," Barbi said. "Chicken parmesan. C'mon!" She dragged Trish out of the booth: "I don't know, that song started and I couldn't listen to it again!"

"Me, neither," Trish said.

They found the number taped next to the phone, ordered two large pizzas and the sandwich, and sat down to wait, burnt-out.

In a bit, Dizzy appeared, obviously high as a kite. They told him about the food. "Oh, great," he said politely but vaguely, and went to look for more champagne.

Night had fallen, and the studio had imperceptibly grown darker. Barbi yawned wide. "Oh wow," she said. "What time is it? It's like we've been here all day." "It's like we've been here forever," Trish said. She yawned too. "We've definitely been here all day."

Barbi stretched out on the couch, Trish and Koy smoked cigarettes; they just sat there, drained by the long effort of concentration, and enervated by the champagne. They livened up a little when the food came. The engineer was already mixing the recording; as soon as he gobbled his chicken parmesan, he went back to it, in his true element now, and like a man possessed. Barbi ate another slice, and declared she was going home: Trish and Koy were to make certain they made a copy for her, and pay her share. And she was gone.

Trish couldn't understand it but that's how it was. She got the vial from Dizzy, snorted up a big line in the bathroom —although she could have done it in the lobby, nobody was around —and went out on her mission. It took a while, but by the time she got back, the demo was done. It wasn't perfect, but it had a hot sound and it rocked.

*       *       *

About a quarter to six —Dizzy had just gotten home from work —the phone rang: Ratso. "Hey man, we have to talk about something."

"Oh yeah?" Diz said. "What's that?"

"It's this," Ratso said. "The sound we've got going now? It just ain't making it."

"It's not?" Diz said. What the fuck was this?

"Nope. There's not enough to it, it's too thin. There's just no question, we need another guitar."

Dizzy tried not to sigh into the receiver. He couldn't believe they were going to have to go through this again, now. What was the point? And he was tired, he'd just gotten home. "Like when we had T-Bone," he said.

"Yeah, like when we had T-Bone," Ratso said.

"Okay," Diz said. "I'll agree. When we had T-Bone was when we sounded the best. But T-Bone was a very special guy. Remember all those losers we tried out? Where are we going to find this guitar player who is like T-Bone?"

"Don't worry about it. It's taken care of."

"Oh yeah?" Diz said. "What does that mean?"

"It means it's taken care of," Ratso said. "Me and Mick have been talking to JT, you remember him, right? And he's coming to our next rehearsal. He's psyched about it, he's ready to do it. He's going to be in the band."

"The hell you say," Diz said.

"He's going to be in the band. We've already talked to him."

"I don't give a shit," Diz said. "I'm not playing with that idiot."

"Look, man, we need another guitar player. It just sounds thin, with only one. The live sound is thin. And when you take a lead, there's nothing there."

Diz couldn't believe he was listening to this. He had to be careful, or he would lose his head. "There's nothing there," he repeated, in spite of himself.

"That's right," Ratso said. "We need another guitar player, it's that simple. And JT is perfect."

"Perfect!" Diz said. "You haven't even played with him. You're out of your mind. Look, I've heard the guy play: he's boring. I'm not playing with him."

"We already talked to him."

"I told you, I don't care. Talk to him again, tell him to forget it. And let me tell you something, Ratso…"

"He's going to play with us."

"Fuck that shit. I won't be there —and neither will my songs. I'm not going to be jerked around like this."

"Look…"

"No, you fucking look. Number one: the guy's a loser. I'm not playing with him. Period. Number two: I don't know where you get off trying to pull this shit, but this better be the last time you call me to *tell* me that somebody's going to join the band, or anything else. Get it? You're not the boss. You're not calling the shots. Now I've got to go, I've got *important* things to do." He hung up.

He was trembling. For the first time, he realized he'd been standing at the window through the whole conversation, glaring down at the corner of Houston and B. He turned away, put down the phone, and sat down on the couch, exhausted. He couldn't remember what he needed to do –if he was supposed to go somewhere, or what. It was just too much. Five minutes later he went down to the little store next door and came back with a quarter-gram of coke.

*       *       *

The buzzer rang. Koy got up, wondering, and answered it. "It's me," Johnny's voice said. "Buzz me in, I'm coming up." He sounded rather strange. Koy had a bad feeling: what was he doing here?

He came in, shut the door hard, and just stood there, glaring at her, obviously furious, almost in a rage. She just looked at him, not sure what to say and waiting for him to begin. He kept starting to say something, then stopping himself, shaking his head.

"No," he said finally. "No."

"What is it, Johnny?" Koy said softly.

He raised a hand to silence her, still shaking his head.

"No, Koy," he said. "You know something? You're not worth it. You're just not worth it! I see that now, I see you're just not worth it."

"What are you talking about?"

"I used to think you were cool. That's what I'm talking about. I used to think you were cool. I thought you cared about me, the way I cared about you."

"I do care about you," Koy said. "What is it, what are you so angry about?"

"I found out about Mick D," he said.

After a horrible silence, he went on: "And you know who told me? *He* did. Yeah, himself. The only reason I didn't beat the shit out of him right then is that I really didn't believe it at the time… But now I see it's true, I see it's really true and you're not worth it, you're just not worth it. You're trash, Koy: you're nothing but a little whore."

She started crying. "Don't say that." She felt like she'd been stabbed in the heart.

"It's true." His expression was frightful. "Nothing but a whore. Sure, go ahead and cry! Cry! Cry your eyes out! I don't care, I've had enough. I'm done with you."

"Johnny," she said.

"Save it!" he said, holding up his hands. She felt trapped. He was back to his cool act. "No," he said. "I'm here to tell you I don't want any more of you. No way. I can't be messing around with you. Forget it, that's it."

Hurt and exasperated, she tried to say something, but he stopped her and, looking nasty, said, "Koy, let me put it in a way that you'll understand. Our *relationship* is *over*. Good-bye." And he walked out the door and slammed it behind him.

Fuck you. The jerk. He could be so horrible, really.

She sat down, exhausted and crying again. She didn't even know why, this was for the best, she hadn't been happy and they couldn't go on the way they had been. But now he was gone because of Mick and she knew she'd really hurt him. The whole thing was bad, and it was all her fault. She'd never meant to hurt him like that.

She dried her eyes, blew her nose, and paced around the room, restless, anxious, oppressed by guilt. Maybe she was cursed, destined to bring only unhappiness and ill fortune upon herself, and those she knew and loved? She thought about Robert… Now this.

After a while she turned on the television, so filled with self-loathing and doubt that she had no idea what she was watching. After a bag, she calmed down enough to flip the channels, trying to distract herself, but she still sat up all night. Because, if she ruined everything she touched, then surely her own life was ruined, too.

*         *         *

Kaci always bought the *Voice* at lunch on Wednesdays and read through the ads while she waited for her food –and for once one sounded pretty good:

> Female vocals, guitar and bass seek 2nd guitar and permanent drummer for all-female rock-n-roll band. Must have own equipment and be dedicated, reliable and ready to rock! We have gear, transportation, original songs and we wanna rock! Do you want it like we do?

The area code was New Jersey but so what, the ad had a lot of positive points and the whole thing sounded just dumb enough to have potential. When she got home she called, left a message. About thirty minutes later the phone rang. "Hello, Kaci?" a woman's voice said. "This is Mercedes, from the Jezebelles."

She seemed nice, very serious and enthusiastic, perhaps even too intensely so; but after all, she was the singer. She'd formed the band with the guitar player, whom she'd known for a while, and with whom she'd written some songs; they had a bass player, who wasn't real experienced but she was really dedicated and she was making lots of progress all the time; they were working with a drummer, he was just filling in, helping them get going until they could find somebody permanent; so, they needed a full-time drummer, and they wanted another guitar player to fill out the sound, play some leads and give the music more punch.

Kaci wasn't sure: their musical tastes were compatible, without being really close. The band hadn't played any gigs yet, which meant they were just trying to get things off the ground, and when Kaci asked if they had any coming up, Mercedes had to say no, although she claimed to have several connections, and could book some as soon as they had the right line-up. But she was excited when Kaci mentioned Dreamwhip, knew they'd played Limelite and even said she'd seen a show at the Underground two years before (Kaci found herself wondering just how bad they –and she –had sounded *that* night),

249

and the end result was that Kaci hung up after agreeing to meet late Saturday afternoon in a midtown studio to jam.

The rest of the week went by. Kaci got through work, and practiced at night, three and four hours at a time, learning a couple songs Mercedes had mentioned, and trying to make sure she was on top of her game. All she could hear were botched licks, muffed notes, and fluctuations in tempo, without even addressing her so-called leads, impossibly limited and simple-minded. Finally, at eleven-thirty Friday night, she more or less gave up, went down to the corner and bought a pint of vodka. A strong drink calmed her down, but there was nothing good on TV; she ended by picking back up her guitar and messing with it till two in the morning, half-watching one meaningless program after another.

Of course she woke up early the next day. The audition wasn't until six o'clock. She didn't know what to do, her fingertips were tender and throbbing slightly, and she didn't think she should hang around there all day, obsessing about it all. Instead she ate something, mostly because she knew she had to, took the subway up to 72nd, and walked over to the Metropolitan Museum.

She'd always loved it, ever since her first trip to the city. During college in Boston, she had profoundly explored the Museum of Fine Arts, a refuge, away from the intensity of Harvard: when she felt overwhelmed by literary language and academic discourse, the multiplicity of exquisite surfaces served as a soothing absence, and she developed a certain habit of it. When she first moved to New York, the number of great museums dazzled her, but in time she found she loved the Metropolitan the best. She'd seen most of it –although the place was so vast and some of the minor collections and salons were subject to such capricious openings that you could hardly say you'd even walked through it all – but she'd become a particular amateur of Egyptian artifacts. Not that she knew much about it –she'd had Western Civ and that was all –but the presentations were good, and after all you didn't have to be an expert to pass through the enormous collection, musing on one curious thing or another.

Today she went backward against the usual sense of the exhibition, passing quickly through Late Antiquity and the Greco-Roman period, pausing only a moment in the long room which housed the Book of the Dead, before turning into the collection of minor artifacts: combs and cosmetics jars, bronze mirrors long-turned black, tiny figurines and images of gods and goddesses for personal and household use. One case held nothing but cats, the beautiful shorthaired Egyptian cat somewhat like a modern Abyssinian. There were cats of every size –from the tiniest of charms and earring pendants, to life-sized cats whose heads bore mirrors or presided over some sacred bowl or saucer –and made from every material: carved from semi-precious stone or granite, cast in bronze or formed in glazed faience, shaped from ash or ebony, bits of polychrome still clinging to the desiccated wood. She lingered over these tiny remnants, so small and so very human, of a people who three or four millennia ago had loved cats so, as much as she. She went on to the maze of mummy cases, a dim labyrinth of vitrines filled with one elaborate set of coffins after another. Her favorites were those from that later period when a three-dimensional face or mask was fashioned on the lid, often in enormous size; but she loved also those, simpler in form, whose every surface was covered with intricate painted designs: hieroglyphs, potent spells and images, Isis spreading her wings in protection, Anubis weighing the souls of the dead.

The time passed pleasantly, but after two-thirty she found herself checking her watch every five minutes, and finally at three she left. She was home in half an hour, showered and made up by four, and now she had to confront the problem she'd been avoiding: what to wear? And though she tried to tell herself that worrying over it too much was something Koy would do, it didn't work: she knew Koy was right to say it always mattered, that you were always making a statement about yourself with what you wore. She fussed over it, got irritated with herself, smoked a cigarette making faces in the mirror –she could just wear her bathrobe, if she took a cab –and ended by putting on a pretty straightforward rock-chick look: black boots, tight black jeans, and a little T-shirt that said *Penthouse* and might or might not have been ironic, depending on your point of view. She'd been in Dreamwhip after all, she had an image to live up to –and screw 'em if they didn't like it. That took till four-thirty. She took out her guitar, tuned up and walked around, playing one riff after another; it sounded terrible. She put it back in its case, checked her bag of gear: cables, fuzz box, extra strings. It was five. She smoked half a cigarette, put on her leather coat, picked up her stuff and left.

The sky was cloudy, the wind had picked up and a light rain was falling. She wished she had the money for a cab but that was out of the question. She went up to 23rd and caught a bus westbound; at least she'd left early, the traffic was a nightmare. At Eighth Avenue, she decided to walk, the transfer wasn't worth the hassle and by the time another bus came she could be there. The rain had slackened to a chilly mist, her hair was ruined, but it hardly mattered, that would be true of everyone, and she set off, going quickly and trying not to feel nervous. The seven blocks took no time, and she turned down 30th, thinking back on the many times Dreamwhip had rehearsed here… But she shook herself: this was no time for nostalgia. Dreamwhip was *over*; this was all about the here and now.

When she got off the elevator she just waved to the guy at the desk, whose name she'd forgotten, and went on back to Studio C. She was feeling more and more nervous, her stomach kept doing little flip-flops, though she kept telling herself to relax, she had no reason to feel uptight. Outside the room she paused, listening, but heard nothing; she shook herself, went through the double doors. A tallish woman in black leather jeans and a ripped Sex Pistols shirt turned toward her, smiling, and came over to shake hands. Her dyed-blonde hair was cut short in a cute way, but she had a vaguely butch air about her. "You must be Kaci, right?"

"Yeah," Kaci said. "And you're Mercedes?" They shook hands.

"Glad you could make it." And she introduced Kaci around. Lisa, the guitar player, was exceedingly pale, her nearly-translucent skin set off by long hair dyed jet black; she wore a velvet camisole top and a mini-skirt, and seemed, in some oddly vampire-like way, exaggeratedly feminine in comparison to the singer. Mika, the bass player, was a stunning Japanese woman whose ultra-chic clothes, a micro-mini and a button-up short-sleeve top, were cut from some futuristic fabric that looked like metal; she was balanced perfectly on little geisha-girl mules, and had some old Danelectro bass. Kaci had never seen anybody who looked so cool –it almost didn't matter how she played.

"And drumming today," Mercedes said, "is Jenna Love, whom we all just met, too –in fact, I talked to her the same night I talked to you! What a coincidence! Anyway, I thought we'd have her come tonight, too, and just see what happens."

"Cool, that's cool," Kaci said. Jenna looked like a cheerleader or sorority girl –big smile, blonde hair in a ponytail –but after shaking hands she ran through the kit and banged out a huge beat like a cave woman. Kaci was surprised at her power.

"Wow, so, like, there's a Marshall," Mercedes said, pointing. "Or I'm sure Jeff could get you a Fender or something else if you'd rather."

"No, no, the Marshall's fine," Kaci said. She turned it on, got out her guitar and tuned up, still feeling uptight, unsure of herself and what they expected of her. The others were screwing around too, checking levels and making little adjustments. Lisa, skronking weird chords from a cheap-looking Strat, seemed especially diffident. Finally Mercedes said, "Well, what are we gonna do?"

Lisa shrugged. Jenna was looking around. "What do you like?" Mika said.

Kaci looked at Mercedes. "Pick something, and let's try it," she said, trying to sound positive.

"Okay," Mercedes said. "Uh, well, just to get going, let's do 'Sonic Reducer'."

Kaci nodded, and without really thinking about it she cranked into the intro. Jenna fell in, then Mika and finally Lisa. Mercedes moved around restlessly, trapped in the obsessive lyrics:

> *Sonic Reducer, ain't no loser*
> *Sonic Reducer, ain't no loser*

After the second chorus Kaci dropped out, stomping on her fuzz box and blasting into a wailing lead. "Yeah, yeah!" Jenna shouted, banging the drums furiously. At the end they slammed to a halt. Kaci grinned; she wasn't nervous anymore.

They played a Stooges song, which was cool, a Pistols song, which turned out okay, and some old rock-n-roll song –Kaci didn't even know what it was, but it sounded terrible. "Why don't you show me some of your originals?" she said.

Jenna agreed, enthusiastic, but Mercedes and Lisa looked slightly consternated: Mercedes suggested one, then another, but Lisa vetoed both, before unwillingly agreeing to a third, and never even told them the key or anything, just launched into it, like she didn't have the slightest idea how to proceed. Mercedes looked dismayed, Mika shrugged and fell in, Jenna picked up the beat, and Kaci guessed at the key, wrongly, struggling to follow the others and feeling irritated. Mercedes sang two verses, listlessly, and looked at Kaci, who waved the band to a halt instead of playing a lead.

"Okay," Kaci said. "We can do that, so is there a change? Or an intro? What's the arrangement?"

"Huh?" Mercedes said.

Oh man, Kaci was thinking, these people don't know anything. "You know," she said. "How many verses are there, what's the chorus, when's the lead, stuff like that."

"Oh," Mercedes said, looking toward Lisa. "Well, like, you know, it's not exactly like, uh, written in stone."

"Well, sure," Kaci said, frustrated by this evasiveness. "But how do you usually do it?"

Lisa was obviously no help on this. Finally Mercedes said, "Well, it's got a verse and a chorus, as you could maybe tell… Actually there's two verses, I just keep doing them over and over."

"Uh-huh," Kaci said, trying to sound encouraging. "And is there, like, a change? Or an intro?"

"There's no change, anyway not right now, but there's like an intro, I guess –I mean, Lisa plays a couple chords to start it. Show 'em, Lisa."

Lisa muffed it at first. "Do it again," Kaci said, trying to follow along. They tried it all together.

"Okay," Kaci said. "Let's try this: do the intro, then verse, chorus, second verse, chorus, then I'll play a lead over a verse, then –Lisa, you want a lead?" Lisa shook her head. "Okay, my lead over a verse, then a last chorus. No, a double last chorus –repeat the last chorus." They were all looking at her. "Well," she said, flushing. "I know it's like every song, but it's a start."

"No, no, that sounds good," Mercedes said. "Let's give it a try."

*What am I doing here?* Kaci was thinking as they counted it off. But she'd been a beginner once, too. She cranked into it like the seasoned rocker she was now, and it went better, now that they had an idea what to do. Unfortunately, it was still a rather ordinary song.

"That needs something," she said at the end. "A change, or an instrumental part, I don't know, but something. Some sort of hook."

Mercedes and Lisa exchanged a look, and it struck Kaci that she ought perhaps to be more diplomatic. She got them to show her another, like the first more or less inchoate until she and Jenna imposed an equally mundane structure, just to get through it. The band faltered when she took a lead, and throughout Kaci found herself working so hard she couldn't tell if this Mercedes could sing or not. At the end she said, "Cool! Hey... check this out: it's something I've been messing around with. It's in *A*." She began the intro to *Put Me in the Trash*. Jenna kicked in like she already knew it; but the other guitarists were useless, and Mercedes acted like she liked it without being much help. After a chorus, Kaci cut it off.

"Man, you wrote that?" Mercedes said.

Kaci shrugged. "It's not really finished," she said. "I mean, you know, it needs some work. The lyrics need a lot of work."

But the others were enthusiastic, and she showed it to them, taught Mercedes the chorus. They tried it: not bad; like she said, it just needed work. Kaci looked at her watch. "Hey, we're running out of time. Let's try that first song again." They played it again, better this time. As Kaci played a lead, the studio guy came in, waved five minutes.

Kaci threw her guitar in its case, dug the little notebook out of her bag and went over to Jenna. "Hey," she said, scribbling down her telephone number. "I really enjoyed playing with you, you're a fine drummer. Here's my number; why don't you give me yours?" While she wrote it down, she could feel the others watching her. Hey man, she thought, you might learn more than *one* thing from me today.

But she pointedly paid one-fourth of the studio fee, as Jenna strolled pleasantly past the desk toward the elevators, looking at the pictures on the walls. Happily surprised, the other Jezebelles objected politely, but took the money. Kaci suggested they tentatively agree to try it again in a week. Mercedes promptly booked the time. "We need to practice anyway."

Down on the street Jenna hung out for a minute, before leaving, giving Kaci a look as if inviting her to come along. Though flattered, Kaci was leery of such free agents, and only said goodbye. "That Jenna," she said to the others, "is some kind of drummer."

"Yeah," Mercedes said. "Do you think she was bored?"

Kaci said carefully, "Well, I think you guys need to get it more together." They were all looking at her. She paused. Did she really want to do this, get involved with these people? "Look," she said. "Let's agree on three or four cover songs that we'll work on for next time. So next week, we'll play them to warm up, then play the songs we played this week, and we'll go from there. And we'll record it, we can record in any of those rooms. But listen, have your friend come in on drums, don't call Jenna. Let's *save* her."

Later, standing at the bus stop, smoking a cigarette she'd bummed from Mika, she really wasn't sure. The fact was, they didn't know anything; they were almost total beginners. Really, she deserved something better than that. But *was* there anything better? And there were *three* of them, including a singer and a bass player...

She'd give it a try. She wasn't going to quit reading the papers. Of course, what would happen was she would get involved with them and along would come something really good. She hoped *Koy* had taught her what to do in that instance.

*               *               *

Koy took the subway uptown to deliver a copy of the demo, and climbed out of the station blinking in the cool autumn sunlight. Midtown always seemed another world: taller, cleaner, more densely concentrated and more jammed with people, above all more saturated with money than downtown. She always liked Rockefeller Center, it had something about it, especially on Fifth Avenue, with St. Patrick's across the street: so utterly New York and yet so different from the New York where she lived. This was the city that tourists knew, or people who'd never been there and had only seen it on TV: you saw limousines and expensive cars everywhere, and people in fabulous clothes speaking every language in the world. But crossing east on Fiftieth, she saw a bum digging through the trash for aluminum cans, and she thought, really, it's just more of the same old thing.

The building was on Madison, a big glossy place with boutiques on the ground floor. She went through a set of double doors and into the lobby, marble and chrome, guarded by an attendant, who made her sign in before directing her to the ninth floor.

She adjusted her appearance in the mirrored elevator as she went up, but the ninth floor wasn't as impressive as downstairs, dim and rather narrow. Suites lined the corridor. The muffled ring of a phone made her realize how quiet it all was. She followed the numbers around a corner and found it: AT Enterprises.

Her mouth went dry. She hesitated, unsure. Was there a buzzer? She didn't see one. She practiced smiling, then opened the door and walked in, smiling. The receptionist, a serene and elegant Japanese woman, looked up from a computer screen and said, "May I help you?"

"Excuse me," Koy said. "Yes, I have a package for Mr. Takahata."

"That's fine. You can leave it with me."

"Mr. Takahata asked me to deliver it to him," Koy said.

"You can leave it with me," she said again. "I'll see that he gets it."

Koy didn't know what else to do so she left it with the woman and went out. She felt let down, but what had she expected? Was Mr. Takahata just going to walk out and hand her a contract? Riding down in the elevator she felt tired, as tired as if she'd done something; yet what had really been accomplished? She'd made a delivery. It might all come to nothing anyway. You shouldn't pin your hopes on just one thing: she needed to remember that. It might all come to nothing. On the other hand, she'd made, what, seven or eight hundred bucks, and that was pretty good.

Back on the street the light had that late-afternoon feeling so persistent in midtown, as if time were already running short, and she headed back for the subway, thinking as she walked about the promo kit, and mostly unaware of the businessmen staring at her. The bio and everything needed to be revised, but how? And she was still pleased with the recording, but a lot of that had to do with Dizzy. So how good was it? This situation with Kaci was a nightmare; where were they going to find a guitarist? The whole thing was a mess, she had a bad feeling about it, and she was glad she'd decided to add the extra picture, one of Robert's soft-core shots of her... They could do what they wanted with *that*.

*      *      *

That night, Koy was going stir-crazy; she couldn't just keep sitting around the house. All she'd done all day was deliver the demo to Mr. Takahata's office; now it was getting dark —and she had to work tomorrow night. Her 'weekend' was almost gone. Tuesday: what could you do on Tuesday?

She went through the paper, half a dozen times, found nothing. Some nights were just so bad, even in New York. But it didn't really matter, she had to get out of the house —see what was happening, talk to somebody.

She messed around, couldn't make up her mind what to wear —till finally it was already 9:30, she couldn't stand it any longer; she got some money, threw on her leather jacket, and ran down the steps. A cab waited at the light, and she jumped in. The driver looked at her.

"Um," Koy said. "Avenue A and… 7th Street."

There had to be some fun somewhere. She would find it.

Traffic was light, and they were there in a couple of minutes. The avenue was pretty quiet. She got out, looked around. The Toilet had something weird she didn't care about, she'd sworn she wasn't going back to that place on the corner after that last time, and right here that left the Fuzz Box. If it were no good, she'd go up to the Inca, or over to Saint Mark's.

The Fuzz Box was empty, but the bottles on the back of the bar looked so appealing that she thought, why not? She'd have one here and move on. Maybe something would happen. But nothing happened, no one came in, the place was completely dead; she drank her vodka and nothing happened with that, either. She pushed back the empty glass and left.

Outside the avenue was even deader than before. She walked up along the edge of the park and crossed on Ninth to the Inca. You could hear the music out on the street but when she opened the door, absolutely no one was inside. She let it close again and turned toward First Avenue. Not a single person on the whole long block and she asked herself, what's the point? She should just head home, buy a couple extra bags on the way and curl up in front of the TV. But the thought of her stupid apartment was just too awful.

At the corner of Saint Mark's some punk kids were panhandling. One of them whistled at her and she smiled, thinking, Loser. The bars were mostly empty, and the few people there either looked just as bored as her or too desperate for words. She went all the way to the corner, but remembered that the Bunker had some band no one would go see. She turned around.

Back on Second Avenue some drunken frat-boys were stumbling along in a pack. One of them yelled something at her and she flipped him off. That was a mistake: they all joined in, their jeers and crude come-ons following her all the way down the block, infuriating.

At First she hesitated, turned downtown toward the Lizmar. If only there was somebody she could call, go hang out with. But the Kamikazis were out of town, she didn't want to see anybody from the band, she avoided Robert's friends like the plague… Funny, she knew so many people, and she didn't seem to have a single friend. What had Robert said that time? Something like, in New York, anybody who wants to be your friend, probably wants something from you.

The avenue got more and more deserted the further she got downtown. Finally she got to Third and thought, I'm getting a drink in the stupid Lizmar whether there's anyone there or not. But the grates were down and the place was shut up tight.

She stood there a couple minutes, trying to think of something, anything. Oh, there were places she could go, but she wanted to hang out, not get hit on. It was hopeless. A cab was coming. She hailed it, climbed in wearily. Her feet hurt –she wasn't used to walking around in these shoes. May as well go home and rest, get some sleep. She had to work the next night.

*   *   *

CBGB might not have been the best idea, but it was close to home on a rainy night, and already she wasn't feeling good. But *something* gave her the heebie-jeebies as she turned from Bleecker onto Bowery, and the doorman stared thoughtfully at her, as if trying to remember her face. Paranoid scenarios flashed through her mind: had he seen her with someone? Had the police been here? Finally he said, "Aren't you in that band, Dreamwhip?"

"Yeah!" Trish said, surprised and dismayed, but trying to smile. "That's right."

"You play the bass."

"That's right."

"Good band." He nodded at the door. "Go on in, it's on us tonight."

"Thank you," Trish said. "That's very nice."

Oh no, she was thinking, inside the door. Now it's no good, he knows me. I can't just walk out with...

She went to the bar, ordered a drink and lit a cigarette. This was terrible. Besides, the place was empty anyway. It was useless –she had to get out of there.

"Hey, alright! Trish!"

She turned around: no way, Larry, she hadn't seen him coming, and here he was, wearing a leopard-print sport-coat and sunglasses on top of his head, swelled-up and strutting, like always. He reeked of expensive men's cologne. His hair was different from when she'd last seen him, maybe two years before, when Dizzy had joined his band, then quit after a month, exasperated. He rather amused Trish, because she couldn't take him seriously, but Dizzy detested the guy.

He kissed her on both cheeks like a European, though he was from Brooklyn, and his goatee tickled her. "So what are you doing here? Come out to see someone?"

"Huh? Oh, yeah," she said. Why did he seem so happy to see her? "You know," she went on vaguely, "returning a favor, a friend's band..."

He was looking around. "And... where's Dizzy?"

"He's, um, at rehearsal. So I'm, uh, out by myself tonight."

"I see that." He asked how she liked playing in Dreamwhip (how he knew that, she couldn't say), didn't listen to her answer, telling her instead about his new project: a heavy blues band, really heavy, called Howling Wolfgang. He was really into it; they had a great guitarist, the guy just rocked; his drummer was good; the bass player if anybody was maybe a little bit weak (and Trish should check them out, you didn't know, if the guy didn't work out, hey, she might be interested) –but the sound was getting tight, really tight; people were really getting into it, as soon as they started playing these tunes, people went crazy, they just went nuts. As he talked, he edged closer and closer, staring at her breasts, and his breath was awful. Trish, despairing, was dying to get out of there. People she knew –it was just too horrible…

But he hardly gave her a chance to talk, just went on and on, she wasn't sure about what; she was trying to think what to do. A guy came in from outside and passed by, absolutely soaking wet: she watched a trail of water form behind him. The one band had finished and the next one was setting up, and if anything, the place had thinned out, people had already left. She felt weak, enervated –and sick now; she had to do something. She fell into a passive and rueful acceptance of the situation.

"Well, hey, are you ready for another drink there?" Larry asked.

"Um, sure." She lit another cigarette, watching him order the drinks, and followed him to a table off to one side, out of the way, where they sat down. Larry was still talking, and she realized with some surprise that now he was telling the story of his recently-broken heart. She tried to act sympathetic, but she couldn't really follow him, and besides she was feeling more and more out of it. Somehow, Larry's girl had done him wrong, and he related woefully his fear that he might never find the one thing that he needed and truly wanted: real love, a woman's love. Trish, irritated now by such a maudlin come-on, was trying to keep herself together, and think of how to do this. She had no doubt Larry would make a move on her, she just didn't know how long it would take him to get up the nerve. She couldn't wait all night.

The next band came on and they weren't just bad, they were way too loud; people were retreating toward the bar; Larry was shouting and she still couldn't hear him. It was ridiculous, and finally she cupped her hand and yelled in his ear, "Come with me, I want to see if someone I know is backstage." He nodded and they picked up their drinks. Trish finished hers and they went back, past the stage. Once beyond the wall of amplifiers, the sound diminished somewhat.

"Wow," Larry said. "That's volume."

Trish nodded, glanced into the first dressing room, a narrow cubbyhole right behind the drummer, the partition vibrating with the beat. Too small. In the second were a couple of guitar cases and an empty sofa. She jumped as he squeezed her ass. He wrapped his arms around her, tried to kiss her. "No," she said. He pulled her closer, smushing her boobs against him. "No!" she said again, to see what he would do. He pushed her head back, kissed her on the throat.

She left him on the sofa. He looked pretty much like he was asleep. Walking out slowly, afraid to stop and rest for fear the band would finish their set, she thanked the doorman again, and turned toward Houston. There'd be no coming back here. It had stopped raining, but she spent the rest of her money on a taxi home anyway.

*    *    *

A week passed after the recording session and everyone was still tired, happy to have a few days free, but after another week, they realized they had to do something. Barbi made an exploratory call to Kaci, who was nice but, if not cold, still not her old self, and who stated firmly that she meant it, she was out, though she wished Barb all the luck in the world. Koy had repeatedly almost swallowed her pride and called Kaci herself, but somehow this made her angry, and she rejected the whole idea, considering any reconciliation impossible, even undesirable.

So they had to find a guitarist. They put ads in the papers, waited for the phone calls to begin, but Koy was plagued by worries, afraid to admit even to herself that they might not find anyone. She tried the grapevine; no one knew anyone, or had any ideas; she went out to clubs, checking out other bands for a guitar player they could steal; nothing turned up. The days kept passing, going by more and more quickly as the band steadily lost momentum.

They rehearsed once with Dizzy, trying to do something, anything, and it went pretty well. Barbi especially was happy. He seemed to know the songs even better than before, and Koy wondered just what was going on; she had her suspicions, but nothing was said. They jammed once with Hiro, from the Kamikazis, pretty much a waste of time: nobody knew any of the same songs, or if they did, Koy didn't know the words. Once, some old acquaintance of Trish came, Lea Zoid, a tough-looking chick, ugly really, with dyed-black hair and the most beat-up guitar Koy had ever seen. Lea wrote her own tunes, tried to teach one to Koy; Koy didn't much like the song; of course the whole thing was impossible in the first place. You couldn't be ugly and be in Dreamwhip.

No one was calling. The ads had run for two weeks, maybe six or seven women had called: three were eliminated immediately, two more were seriously doubtful, one talked a good game but Trish remembered her somehow as being impossibly fat, and there was one 'maybe', whom Koy couldn't succeed in getting on the phone twice. They ran the ads again; no one new called. It looked like no one would.

Koy was getting panicky. This was bad, much worse than she had feared. She didn't know what to do. She talked on the phone to with the others, without coming to any conclusion. Everyone agreed that they ought to have a meeting. Koy set up a date, suspecting all the while that this was wasted effort, that nothing would be resolved, and finally dreading it, lest the situation degrade still further. Everything depended on her. If she lost direction, everything would stop and she knew it, even as she felt paralyzed by indecision, unsure and vacillating.

She didn't really have any friends, anyone to talk to. Finally she called Robert. She didn't know who else to call. He was difficult at first, distant and sometimes sharp; it seemed like he wanted to say I-told-you-so, though about what wasn't clear, but with a general air of being smarter or better informed, and wasn't it funny how after all this time and everything that had happened, she was still so naïve. Finally he mellowed out and said plainly, "Look, you're just wasting your time. Guitar players are a dime a dozen. You could be rehearsing tomorrow if you'd just take on a guy –a guy explicitly temporary, to be replaced as soon as possible. It doesn't matter; do something, *anything*, to keep from doing nothing and so just falling apart."

Koy knew it was good advice, but she didn't want to take it. Dreamwhip was an all-girl band; it had *always* been an all-girl band. Even a temporary substitute seemed a dangerous concession, a dilution of purity and so a reduction in strength. And she was worried it would become permanent: things had a way of doing that. Yet they badly needed a guitar player, and she asked herself if she was being too resistant: should she go with the flow, or risk everything falling to pieces?

They were to meet at the Lizmar Lounge. She was nervous, and bought an extra bag on Clinton, snorting it up on the way. But she got there first and had to wait on the others. Barbi was next, only about ten minutes late if that, but apologetic and out of breath. They just sat and made small talk until Trish arrived, out of breath too, like she'd run all four blocks from her house. Once she'd sat down and wriggled out of her jacket, they all looked at each other. "Well," Koy said finally. "What do you guys think we should do?"

Trish looked at Barbi, who, though seemingly uncomfortable, began to speak: "I guess it's pretty clear we might not find a woman guitar player real quickly. The way I see it, we've got two choices: wait, keep looking, and restart when we find someone, or use a guy as a substitute, temporarily, until we find the right person —but keep going." All very reasonable, and Koy sat listening, nodding her head, thinking that she had heard exactly the same thing from Robert, and she didn't like it any more now than then, and that maybe, in fact, she liked it even less.

Trish had nodded in agreement throughout, and now came what Koy had been more or less expecting: Dizzy had offered to help them until they could find someone else. Trish tendered this offer, of course, and Koy could see that her bass player knew she was on thin ice. Koy scrutinized her: what was she thinking? What was Dizzy thinking?

"I think that if we decide to go that way, then Dizzy is our best choice," she said. "What do you think, Barb?"

"Well, yeah, I guess so," Barbi said. "He's good, and he already knows a bunch of the songs. He's on the demo, after all! And we know him, he's nice."

She paused, took a breath. "I think we should see what happens with him. Right now, I think he's our best choice."

"Yeah, you're right," Koy said. "I mean, like everything you're saying is right. But there's something we haven't talked about yet. Which is, Dizzy is Trish's boyfriend. And that seems to me like a potentially, um, *delicate* situation."

Nobody said anything.

"Don't get me wrong," Koy went on, finally. "I love him to death. He's been very helpful to us. He's a good friend. But I don't want to get involved in something that only makes things worse."

Barbi was nodding her head, but she said, "But it's only temporary. Till we can find somebody permanent, a woman."

"Trish," Koy went on, deliberately. "Are you and he going to get along?"

"Yeah!" Trish said. "I mean, I think so. We can't know till we see." She looked flustered. Jeeze, Koy thought, surely you anticipated this. She waited.

"I think we'll get along fine," Trish said firmly. "He and I have been together a long time. And besides, Barb's right, it's only temporary, and everybody knows it. Dizzy knows it. He's just trying to help us." She sounded slightly indignant.

"I know that," Koy said.

Trish lit a cigarette. Everyone stirred around, sipped their drinks, waiting, giving it time.

"It's a way to keep going," Barbi said.

"What a cursed day that recording session was, anyway," Trish said. "We can't even get the demo made before Kaci quits. Quits! I never thought…"

"Yeah," Koy agreed, vaguely. She was weighing the options, trying to analyze the situation and the meeting itself, convinced that they had reached a critical juncture, and afraid of making the wrong decision. Robert had stressed to her that people wouldn't hang around forever, waiting for something to happen. If she lost Barb… Really, there was no other option, she had no alternative, and she saw clearly it was pointless to struggle any more.

She looked around, looking each of them in the eyes. "Okay, you've convinced me," she said. "Let's use Dizzy as a sub and try to move forward."

\*　　　　　　　\*　　　　　　　\*

They agreed to practice in the next few days, and everyone went home. Koy thought about stopping for a drink somewhere, the Fuzz Box, the Toilet, it didn't matter, and in the old days she would have, but she felt run-down, and sick of it all —the same old places, and never anybody new, and she didn't want to have to tell anyone —again —that the band wasn't playing anywhere, Kaci had quit, and that, in general, they were screwed. Enough people already knew that. Better to lie low until something was happening, till she had something to talk up.

Instead, she zigzagged a block to the Dope House, then turned down Clinton. It was funny: no matter how much she tried not to think about it all, she kept coming back to it anyway. Now more than ever, a guy on guitar seemed like a bad idea —except the alternative was nothing. But she distrusted this Trish-and-Dizzy business —she could imagine any number of bad things that might come out of it —and she told herself she would have to stay on top of it all. They could think what they might; she wasn't losing control of the band.

Even so, a thought occurred to her: Dizzy was a good songwriter, he had written the only Contusions songs that were any good, since that guy Timmy left, and they *were* good songs; maybe she could write some new songs with him, just as she had done with Kaci. Why not? He knew even better what he was doing! And the band could definitely use some new material. He would probably do it, why not? It would only help him, and if they became hits, he'd make money too.

At home nothing was on TV but she left it on anyway, she just couldn't listen to any music. In a way, she regretted that: she could no longer enjoy music like she used to; she no longer felt about it the way she had before she became a musician. Before it had become a part of her, and before she had learned how it could go so right –or so wrong. Before she'd lost her soul to it.

She fixed up a shot. A game: of the Muppets band, which one is the junkie?

Most popular answer: after your fix, you don't care. Second most popular: they all are.

The phone rang, and thinking it probably Trish who would have already talked to Dizzy about his schedule, Koy picked it up.

"Hello, is this Koy?" A woman's voice, perfect diction, the tiniest accent.

"Yes?"

"Koy, this is Manaka, Mr. Takahata's assistant. I apologize for calling so late. Am I disturbing you?"

"No, that's alright," Koy said. "I just got home, I'd been out."

"Ahh… We tried to reach you earlier. Mr. Takahata asks if you would be available for a meeting late tomorrow afternoon? Say at four o'clock? He regrets the inconvenience of such short notice."

"I will be happy to meet with him at four," Koy said. "But I don't know about the other members of the band. I will make every effort…" Oh no! She would have to tell him about Kaci!

"Ah, please, no," Manaka said. "There is no need. Only you need attend. Mr. Takahata was quite clear."

Koy was stunned; she thanked the woman mechanically and got off the phone. She didn't know what to think. What did it mean? What was it all about?

Did they already know about Kaci? But how could they? But it hit her: no. The answer is no. It's over. He's going to tell me no deal. But maybe he wants to get some first, one more time, and then he's going to tell me. Like, you know, We can't do anything right now, but I'll try to put together something else, don't worry, it's going to work out –and then I have to bang him or our demo goes in the garbage can. Except it's probably *already* in the garbage can.

She sank down on the sofa, crushed, looking around at her dumpy little apartment. She had no one to talk to, no one she could call, and everything was going straight to hell.

She just sat there for a long time, trying to pull herself together, to not feel sorry for herself. After a while she found a movie on TV. At the first commercial, she went and got a blanket, and ended by falling asleep, curled up on the couch.

*   *   *

She tried to sleep late but she still woke up too early. The only important thing all day was the meeting, but just waiting for it made time crawl. She got straight, went back to sleep for a while, but she had the weirdest, most restless dreams. When finally she couldn't sleep any more she got out of bed and wandered around in her robe, straightening up and looking at the mail that had piled up; but aside from the bills and a few club invites, most was addressed to "Current Resident", and she didn't like the feeling that gave her.

After a while, she put on some clothes and went downstairs for a cup of coffee, thinking it might get her going. The day was windy, rather cold, and the sky was gray; the sidewalks were packed with the lunchtime crowd; she stood on her step for a moment, watching people pass –hurried, nervous, irritable. New York City. Sometimes it was just too much.

The donut shop wasn't really warm enough but the coffee was good, and she ate a bagel. But other people were waiting for seats, and she left, strolling rather purposelessly down Delancey. She was feeling better –she'd really been feeling low, there for a while, she had to get over that.

She decided to look at some makeup –she had lots of time –and she went into one of the big discount stores. Such places often had good stuff, cheap and in the most outrageous colors, particularly nail polish. But today it was all too garish, and she wandered without stopping through the tube tops and halters, stockings and lingerie. She wasn't in the mood; it was all too trashy.

Out on the street, she was almost drawn into a large knock-off boutique, attracted by the racks of clothes and the pulsing disco music, but she stopped, remembering that she had no money with her: not that she wanted to buy anything there, but rather that she had to go back up and get some, so she could go cop, before the meeting. So she turned back home, and that was when she realized just how much she was dreading the whole thing.

Back home, upstairs, down again with some money, over to Ridge, watching for cops, and there was Carmello. In a minute she was on her way home, the bags in her pocket. If only it were always so easy.

Back in her apartment, it was still a long time till the meeting and she was at loose ends. She turned on the TV, but it was unbearable, so she turned on the radio, and worked on her nails; they didn't really need it, she was just fussing with them, making herself irritable; finally she got up, drew the shades, and lay down on the sofa, hoping that a nap would kill some time, and maybe calm her down. Of course she couldn't go to sleep, she wasn't at all sleepy.

But maybe she dozed for a while, because all of a sudden it was time to get ready. She jumped in the shower, did her makeup, dried her hair, trying to think of something to wear. It wasn't easy, like dressing for your own funeral. Finally she put on her best black cocktail dress, called the car service, touched up her lipstick.

The ride uptown was long, as if a million cars barred her way. It occurred to her that it might have been quicker on the subway, but she hated to walk in the shoes she was wearing. At least in the car she was comfortable. She could go in looking good, and take the train home after, if she wanted to save money.

Back to Madison Avenue, and the place seemed less imposing this time, just another high-rise, a little run-down looking; the shine was off everything today. She signed in, took the elevator –but this time, its dreary mirrors reminded her of a date she had once, out on Long Island, where the guy had a mirrored room. He'd pretty much just wanted to watch, but she was *sure* he'd videotaped her, somehow, and she just knew, if she ever made it, that those videos would be back to haunt her. Of course, right now, it didn't seem to make much difference.

In the office, the receptionist very politely said that Mr. Takahata was running behind schedule, and asked Koy to wait. She sat down on the black leather sofa determined to act patient. There was nothing to do; the place was like a tomb; even the magazines were in Japanese; she flipped through one, unsure what it was about. The office was so quiet, you'd have thought sound were somehow dampened or muffled there; when the phone rang, it rang quietly, and the receptionist's voice was so gentle, like a murmur. She'd forgotten her watch, couldn't see a clock, couldn't tell how long she'd been waiting. It might have been a long time, though she told herself it probably hadn't been long at all.

This may be something they do to you deliberately, she thought. They may have it all figured out, that if they make you wait a certain amount of time, it makes you more docile, easier to manipulate. It was a while longer before the phone buzzed discreetly, and the receptionist approached, perfectly balanced on Italian spike heels. "Mr. Takahata will see you now."

Koy followed her down the hall, to a conference room. She stood, waiting, looking at a print on the wall, a tidal wave crashing down on a village of huts, until he came in, and ceremoniously asked her to take a seat. She did, thinking, Here it comes. What followed was unbelievable, and it shocked Koy so, that at first she had difficulty grasping it. The company proposed to sign her, offering a contract that would be available for review shortly –a contract for recording, production and promotion of two albums, with a two-album option. There would be an attractive and appropriate advance, and she would enjoy all the support and benefits that the company could offer. Even now, marketing was brainstorming, people were already at work; they were behind her every step of the way; in short, the company wanted to see her career go as far as it could go.

*Her* career, that was the key. He made no mention of the band; unsure what her bargaining position was, she didn't know what to say. But she had to know about the others, and finally asked him straightforwardly. He paused, giving the question a certain gravity –but his hands made a little gesture as if brushing something away, and he stated delicately that the contract concerned her alone and that at this time the company was not seeking to sign the other two musicians. So they knew about Kaci —but of course they did, it made perfect sense. She nodded, intending only to indicate that she understood. But she was part of it now, part of their game, and she knew it. Still, she said nothing, and he paused, evaluating her attitude, then continued: as part of the agreement, the company would provide the invaluable help of talented songwriters, with a track record of hits, as well as professional and experienced back-up musicians for both recording and live performances.

She nodded again. She felt sick; she was scared; she didn't know what to do. Evidently he was waiting for some reaction. Stalling, she asked about artistic control —although, in legal terms, she wasn't really sure what that meant; he responded, smiling, with a certain double-talk that she couldn't follow. For the situation was clarifying itself in her own mind: this was it, this was her big chance. She had to remember that, above all. She might not get another one.

He paused. Koy sensed that a whole era of her life was ending, right here and right now. She wondered —without too much hope —if the one that now began would be better. She felt guilty about abandoning the other two, in particular Barbi, but in the end, wasn't it a dog-eat-dog world? Didn't you have to look after your own sweet self first? And Koy wasn't even sure about herself: was the deal any good? Was she getting enough money? Was she giving up too much control? She'd have to have someone read the contract —but whatever it said, was she likely to get a better one?

She looked Mr. Takahata in the eye, smiled, and said that although of course she'd have to review the documents, she felt sure they could work together. And she thanked him.

He seemed genuinely pleased, smiling and making little bows, and proposed a toast. An assistant brought another bottle of French champagne; its *pop!* seemed to let the genie out of the bottle. As they sipped from crystal flutes, he was very flattering and positive, praising her abilities, assuring her of his confidence in her ultimate success. Koy drank two glasses, soaking it all in, thinking that after all she might adjust to her impending stardom —and why not?

He asked her to join him at dinner with yet another important member of the company. The luxury car was waiting downstairs. At the restaurant, she tried not to drink too much, but the others drank like fiends, and she didn't want to refuse too often. Later, most of it was just a blur in her mind. After the restaurant closed, they went up to the new guy's hotel room, and she had to fuck them again –this was a freebie, of course –but by now she didn't care. Let them suck the life out of her! She was getting hers, wasn't she?

*      *      *

Something must have happened at work, or maybe Dizzy was just having one of his days, when he couldn't deal with things, which happened periodically, or maybe he was just exhausted –but she doubted it, because he usually had an answer for *that* –but for whatever reason, he had come home from work, said little, and gone straight to bed. Sometimes he got back up – what time that might be, you couldn't tell –and sometimes he slept around the clock, twelve or thirteen hours, maybe waking up once or twice for a snort of dope, so as not to get sick, before conking back out.

So there she was: seven o'clock, it was getting dark, no idea when or if he'll get up, and she's got to go out herself. And it was raining, it had been raining since six, a steady, soaking rain. Monday night, rain: not a good prospect for the score.

She decided to stall, thinking maybe it would quit. People would come out if it quit. Because right now, nobody was out. She watched the corner of Houston and B for ten minutes straight: not a soul.

She flipped through the TV channels. Of course nothing was on. Not that she could have sat still to watch it. She was getting nervous –starting to, anyway.

She smoked a cigarette, watching the rain, hoping it would lighten up. It didn't, and time kept passing. She didn't know what to do, but she had to go out, soon.

At a quarter to eight she checked on Dizzy, who was sleeping soundly, put on a raincoat, found an umbrella and went out. Down on the street, the rain was much heavier than it looked from the window, and the wind was blowing in gusts. It was atrocious. She set off up Avenue B. The Dope House would never be open yet, she would have to go to Laundromat. Most of the stores were already closed –including the cocaine store, too bad, she had used it before as a back-up, though she didn't like to –and there was no one in the few that were still open. The street was empty all the way to Seventh, where the door to the corner bar opened and a man appeared, glanced up into the rain, grimacing, and sprinted away, around the corner and out of sight.

She turned the other way, was relieved to see the lookouts: at least they were open. But no one else was on the block, and when she copped a bag, the guy said, "Better get more than one. We're going to close soon."

She walked away, really getting worried now. That was bad. She would have to try somewhere else –but where? Delancey and Rivington might already be closed, and she couldn't wait for the Dope House to open. It was this rain, it sucked, it was messing everything up.

Nobody on Avenue B. She looked back along Seventh: they were all gone, vanished; she thought she could see a cop car a block further east. She had to do something. She couldn't just stand there. Besides, she was cold.

She crossed B, opened the door to the bar, had to pull it shut behind her. Two fat old ladies were sitting on stools, drinking beer; the bartender looked at her. No good.

"Got a phone?" she said lamely.

"Customers only," the bartender said.

She nodded and went back out into the rain, even heavier now. The cop car was at the corner, stopped at the light. Act purposeful, she told herself, and turned back toward Houston. But she didn't even know where she was going. This was bad, really bad.

Cold, wet, starting to feel sick, she tried to keep hold of herself, but no one was out, the streets were empty, block after block. It was unreal, like something from a movie, as if she were the last survivor on a dead planet. Still, she had to keep on; she would find something.

The Dope House was still shut up tight, not even the lookouts were around; Second Street was a void; at the next block, the broad scar of Houston Street stretched away in both directions for blocks, little traffic, and no one out on foot, anywhere.

She crossed, the wind driving rain into her face, up under the umbrella. The restaurant where the sellers hung out had its grates down, though the door was open. Closing soon? Clinton looked empty but she couldn't tell. The first block was void. Stanton was empty as well. Rivington, empty, but she went a block west for a look-see. The bodega at the corner was open, but no one was around: not in the block to Delancey, not in the vast schoolyard, nowhere. She turned back, looked again at the store. If only she knew Spanish! But it was too risky.

She went east. A cop was coming as she crossed Clinton. These were different cops than north of Houston, but he'd gotten a good look at her, and besides, she was holding. Things were going from bad to worse. Should she throw the bag away? –but she didn't have any more money and she'd need it. No: she had to find a score.

But there wasn't one, anywhere. She went east along the block: no one, only one deli open and the café where they never stopped playing cards, nobody on the street. Across from the projects, no one was out. She went north, crossed west by the church, went all the way to Ludlow: nothing. The rain was pouring. She felt hopeless, didn't know what to do. And she was freezing –her hands had gone numb and she couldn't stop shivering.

Go home, she told herself. Go home and wait a while. Dry out, get warm. The rain has got to pass, and when it does, people will come out.

Still nothing, all the way back. Once inside, the water streamed off her, forming a puddle; going up the stairs, her boots squeaked.

Dizzy hadn't moved. She changed clothes, lay down on the sofa, restless, couldn't close her eyes. She didn't feel good at all. The rain drummed on the roof, blew against the window. She sat up and smoked a cigarette. If only it would stop! By now it was after nine. She had to get something going, soon. In the mirror, she looked bad. She did what she could, but she was enervated, and lacked concentration; she kept worrying about what to do if nothing worked out.

At nine-thirty she decided the rain was slacking up. She checked Dizzy – still out cold –and looked for a pair of shoes. But she didn't want to ruin any of them, and finally put her boots back on, still soaking wet. She found an old pair of gloves, took a deep breath, and went back downstairs.

Out on the street it was still raining just as hard. The nightmare went on and on, interminably: back up the deserted avenue to Laundromat, closed now; around the block, Sixth and Seventh Streets, then Seventh and Eighth, then Sixth and Seventh again, once more around Seventh and Eighth, nothing; across to Avenue A, where she dragged through every place that didn't have a cover, but the cops were out, beat cops wearing rain parkas and plastic covers on their hats, and she got spooked, and besides there weren't any likely scores anyway, trying to find one in a bar was always bad; up to Thirteenth Street, near T-Bone's old apartment, where there used to be lots of action, including an all-night coke spot –but found nothing and no one, as if the block had been sanitized, exterminated; back down First, couple of clubs there, nothing; then across St. Mark's, feeling sick now, and really desperate –and she must have looked bad, the few people out seemed to avoid her path; no money for the Bunker, she didn't have the strength to try and talk her way in; then back down Third, wishing for someplace dry where she could just sit down for a minute to rest –but of course, no. She crossed slowly east on Second, soaked to the skin, sick now, very sick, the stabbing pain in her guts throbbing with every step, her tongue swollen and hot, her nervous system shorting out, and every fiber in her body screaming for relief. But the Dope House was still closed, the street still empty –and she heard herself moaning, she felt like she might retch. Her eyes were watering and she could hardly see. She stopped at the corner and wiped them, then spit, wanting to spit out the vile taste in her mouth –and went on again, across Houston, down Clinton again, driven on by need past the endurance of the flesh.

The next hour exceeded any mere nightmare: she walked on and on, block after block, meeting no one, seeing no one, hopelessly and utterly alone in the punishment and sickness of withdrawal, wandering a boundless and rain-soaked hell. It was no good: she'd passed through the same spots time after time, crisscrossing the neighborhood; there was nothing out, she wasn't going to find anything. A calm came over her, the calm of despair; the situation was obvious, she had to accept it. She walked home mechanically, secretly –so as not to jinx it –secretly hoping that fate would throw her a score now, at the moment she had abandoned all hope, but it didn't happen. Instead, as she turned painfully onto her block, a sudden nausea overcame her. She stumbled, staggered to the wall, her stomach heaving, sank down and tried to vomit, but nothing came up. She choked, coughed painfully, retched again. The street was reeling; she was dizzy, head spinning. Afraid she might black out, she got to her feet, holding the wall, and trying to spit the taste from her mouth –staggered forward, still holding the wall, then the chain-link fence. She got past the deli, and tripped on the sidewalk grate, but she'd made it home, and she told herself to just get inside, it'll be alright. She jammed the key in the lock and opened the door. Too weak to climb the stairs, she just sat down on them, her head on her knees, holding her stomach; it hurt so bad! But she was cold, freezing cold, and she took a deep breath, got up slowly, and dragged herself upstairs. She didn't know what was going to happen, she couldn't think about it. Inside, she stripped off her wet clothes and wrapped up in a blanket, but her teeth were chattering and she had a terrible tic in one eye.

She must have dozed off for while… When she came to, the need was twice as bad, unbearable, and her arms and legs were trembling uncontrollably; she thought she was having a seizure. In the next room, Dizzy stirred a little.

Was he waking up? She stood, purposefully, letting the blanket fall away, and walked into the bedroom. She felt numb, dissociated, as if watching her own actions performed by someone else.

When it was done she walked to the window and looked out. It was after midnight. The rain had finally stopped, but the streets were as still as death.

*       *       *

It was early evening, just getting dark, and Kaci was walking down Broadway, toward the subway, when she saw Trish —all dolled-up, red lipstick, hair piled on top of her head, leather jacket, *tight* miniskirt and big clunky boots, just dressed to kill and going west quickly on Third Street. Kaci hesitated, almost let her go, but said to herself, No, talk to her.

Trish looked startled when Kaci called out, but smiled when she saw Kaci, and came walking back. Kaci felt at first somewhat embarrassed and shy, and she wondered if Trish felt the same. She didn't want to carry a grudge; she asked about the band.

"Oh," Trish said. "You don't know." She glanced away, down the street. "There is no band. Not any more. Koy got a solo deal. From those Japanese guys she was talking about, who were supposed to be at the Limelite show, remember? I'm still not a hundred per-cent sure who they are, but anyway. No, we never did anything else after the recording session. Isn't that funny? And I'll tell you something else that's funny: that's the recording she used to get the deal." She paused, said, "Of course."

Kaci couldn't believe it. She didn't know what to say, just shook her head.

"Pretty funny," Trish repeated. "So this is what happened: after you left, we couldn't find anybody, and nothing was happening, and Barb and I were saying if we can't find a woman, let's get a guy. Koy was pretty much against that, and we were just stalling out, but Dizzy offered to sub for us, till we could find someone. And the last time I actually saw Koy, the three of us had this meeting, and we agreed that's what we'd do, that Dizzy would sub and we'd play some gigs while still trying to find somebody permanent. So we were supposed to arrange some rehearsals, and I tried to call her, I left messages, and finally a week later she calls me back and says, Sorry…"

"What?" Kaci said. "Sorry, I got a solo deal?"

"That's exactly what she said."

"How can she get a *solo* deal?" Kaci said. She felt affronted, angry; this was outrageous. "I mean, what does she have to offer? That sounds unkind, but think about it: all she can do is sing; her voice is not strong; she doesn't play an instrument; her lyric writing is juvenile…"

"I'm not sure that part matters," Trish said. "In fact, I'm not sure any of it matters. She looks good: that's what's important."

"Of course it's important, but come on! This is music!"

"There's plenty of music," Trish said. "More than enough already. A singer with a look, that's a product. Without us, well, they can do whatever they want with her."

Kaci shook her head. "It all just seems fucked-up to me. The whole thing is just wrong."

Trish shrugged. She was still looking off, past the cars at the intersection, at nothing. "Here's what's really strange. When she told me this stuff, I started to get mad, right? Really mad. But she said, 'I know you hate me, but if you had the offer, you'd do the same thing. I *have* to take this. It's my only chance.' And it was so true, I couldn't get mad."

"Come on!" Kaci scoffed.

Trish shrugged again "The whole situation? Miserable, atrocious. A terrible waste. Be mad at Koy? No. After all, why? She was right: I'd have done the same thing." She looked Kaci right in the eyes. "It wasn't like we were in a very good situation."

Kaci sighed. "I had to get out. I couldn't stay."

Trish nodded, looking away again. "I know," she said. "So I can't be mad at you either. But this company, they were interested, but they knew you were gone and the guitarist on the recording wasn't permanent. So they snagged Koy. A solid business decision."

"Well." Kaci laughed. "I guess."

They were both quiet for a moment.

"Unbelievable," Kaci said. "So, what are you going to do?"

"I don't know yet," Trish answered. "I mean, somebody's going to need a bass player, eventually. I talked to Barb on the phone. At first we were both just stunned, you know? It certainly never occurred to me... that this was how it would turn out. Anyway, Barb and I agreed that we'd still be into playing with each other, and we'd keep our eyes open for an opportunity like that, but I guess we both know that opportunities are probably going to be individual. I mean, that's more likely. But I always enjoyed playing with Barb."

"Oh, absolutely," Kaci said. "She was the best musician in the band."

"Yeah, she's good," Trish said. "She'll be able to take her pick of groups."

It had gotten quite dark by now, but the traffic was still just as dense, bumper to bumper in both directions.

"And what about you?" Trish said. "What are you doing?"

"Well, I haven't been doing much," Kaci said. "I've had to economize because of the rent on the apartment. But I'm moving at the end of this month, to a much smaller and more affordable place, down in your neighborhood, and that's going to help a lot."

"Are you playing with anybody?"

"No," Kaci said. "I mean, I met some people who want to get something going, but it's... it's just getting started. So I don't know. And anyway, I've got a lot of work to do."

"How do you mean?"

"I mean I'm putting in a lot of time practicing at home. I want to get better."

"But Kaci, you're good." Trish looked earnest.

Kaci was about to disagree, but stopped herself. "Thanks," she said. "I still want to get better."

There was another pause.

"How's Dizzy?" Kaci asked.

"Oh, he's okay," Trish said.

"Are the Contusions playing anywhere?"

"No... They're, well, taking some time off, I guess," Trish said.

Was she elusive or just vague? Kaci couldn't tell –but ill at ease, and running out of things to say, she was beginning to regret starting this conversation; and her initial amazement at Koy's *coup* was turning to resentment. Don't say anything you'll regret, she told herself.

Trish was repeating the gossip, but without enthusiasm: band breakups, cancelled gigs, people's drug problems, their trips home or to rehab –and Kaci listened without interest, forgetting it all immediately, yet for all that surprised by the extent of her own isolation.

Trish, too, looked more and more ill at ease, and at length they both stopped talking, just stood together in an awkward silence.

"Well," Kaci said finally. "I guess I'd better go."

"Yeah, me too," Trish said.

"Tell Koy, when you talk to her, that I said good luck."

"Oh, I won't talk to her," Trish said. "She's already gone. She left the day after she called me."

"Left?" Kaci said. "Where did she go?"

"Japan," Trish said. "Oh, yeah. They're doing all this in Japan. The idea is that they'll make a big star out of her in Japan, and then use that as a platform to launch her in the U.S."

"No way," Kaci said.

"She flew to Tokyo the day after she called me." Trish was shaking her head. "That just makes it all the more unreal, doesn't it?"

"Is all this legitimate?" Kaci asked suddenly.

"You've got me," Trish said. "I don't know. But it probably is... because this is what I think will happen: in six months: Koy will have an album out, and we'll still be nowhere."

Kaci just shook her head. They said goodbye, and parted, but Kaci got stuck at the corner, and she glanced back at her former bass player, the last in a series of former bass players in the catastrophic three-year course of Dreamwhip –but Trish had already disappeared from sight.

# Copping Out

## thirteen

He was sitting in the car with the motor running, trying to keep warm, when the girl went past, walking quickly and purposefully down Ridge. He looked at his watch: eleven-ten. That was bad: he hadn't thought it was so late. He got out his cigarettes and lit one, worried; he had to stop this before it got the better of him, he was doing a job here. Okay, he told himself; this one will talk to me. She was cute –a lot of these junkie girls were cute –a punk-rock chick, short blonde hair, leather jacket, heavy boots crunching on the packed snow. Near the end of the block, she went up the stairs into the spot and disappeared. In a couple minutes she re-emerged and headed back the way she had come. When she was about four car-lengths away he turned off the motor and got out, slamming the door and walking to the sidewalk without particularly looking at her. She glanced his way, her face a cold mask, aloof. As she was about to pass he turned and said, "Excuse me." She started. He opened his badge and said, "NYPD, narcotics. I want to talk to you."

Surprise and fear crawled over her face. "Aww, man," she said. "What is this?" Her eyes darted nervously about; she might have run but for fear of making things worse.

"Get in my car," he said, pointing. "I want to ask you a few questions."

"Fuck no, I won't get in your car!" she snarled. "How do I know you're really a cop? Leave me alone!"

She was backing away now. He reached out and took her arm, opening his coat with the other hand. She looked at the gun in its shoulder holster and froze, eyes narrowing like a cat's.

"I showed you my badge," he said mildly, "and if I have to, I'll cuff you and put you in the car. But I'd rather not have to do that." Still holding her arm, he walked her to the car, opened the door.

"What am I charged with?" she said as he guided her into the seat.

"Nothing yet," he said, "but whether it stays that way is up to you. Like I said, I just want to ask you a few questions."

She glared at him, crossing her arms, and he shut the door. He saw her lips move but she stayed put. He got in and started the motor.

"Nothing's gonna happen to you if you're straight with me," he said. "You be straight with me and I'll be straight with you."

"What do you want?" she said. Her voice was tough but her hand trembled slightly.

"I want you to answer some questions."

"I don't have to talk to you," she said. "I know my rights and I know how you cops are. I ain't saying nothing. I don't got to say nothing to you. So why don't you either bust me or let me go?"

That irritated him. He'd been up too long and he didn't like her tone, but he ground his teeth and said calmly: "You don't want me to bust you, and we both know why. You can get dope-sick in the lock-up, or you can talk to me. Answer a few questions, and you walk. Or else we can go over to the precinct, right now, and I'll book you."

"I don't got to say nothing until I talk to a lawyer."

He sighed. "You can talk to a lawyer after twenty-four hours." She didn't answer but he knew that got to her. He tried to wait, but he didn't have much patience left. "Fine," he said, and put the motor in gear.

"Wait a minute," she said. "What do you want to know?"

He put it back in park. "Tell me about that dope spot."

"What's to tell? You can buy dope there."

"What's the brand?"

"It's called 'DOA', usually. Sometimes it's not stamped but it's still the same."

"Is it good?"

She laughed. "What do you know about it? Or maybe you do," she added. "Are you one of *those* cops? Chipping a little on the side?"

She must have seen something cross his face, for she said, more quietly, "Well, yeah, it's good. Why would I be down here freezing my ass off if it wasn't good?"

"Let me see one."

She glared at him and dug around in a pocket, and finally handed him a bag, saying, "Here, knock yourself out."

He ignored her and inspected the bag. Inside a transparent blue seal was a white glassine stamped with a crude image of a coffin and the letters *D.O.A.* He held it to the light: the count was exceptionally good.

"They always this big?"

"Yeah, or bigger," she said. "Maybe you better not do it all at once, you might not be able to handle it."

He sighed. "What do you do?"

"Huh?" she said. "What do you mean, what do you..."

"I mean when you cop," he said, cutting her off. "What do you do when you go up and cop?"

She sighed, looked around. He waited. Finally she said, "You just go up. If they're open, the front door's open. It's an apartment on the second floor."

"What number?"

"I don't know. It's on the left at the top of the stairs on the second floor. You knock and they look through the peephole, and if they know you, they let you in. If they don't know you, they won't answer the door."

"What happens when you go in?"

"You give them the money and tell them how many! What do you think? Are you new at this?"

He told himself to be cool, not let her get to him. "What's it like inside? How many people?"

"There's always three or four, but it's usually just this one guy who takes care of it. Everybody else is just hanging around. It's a funny apartment," she added, "because there's really no furniture except a table and chairs in the kitchen. Besides that it's totally empty. But I'm sure they've got plenty of guns and stuff. Can I go now?"

"No," he said. "How late is it open? When does it open up?"

"I don't know! Till two or so, I guess, and they open up sometime after noon. It depends. Can I go? That's all I know."

He was thinking about what she had told him and didn't answer. Then she said, "Oh, great!" in a low voice, and slid down in the seat. He looked up, glanced in the rear-view mirror. A sector car was slowly rolling up beside them.

It came to a stop. He rolled down the window. Two uniforms were inside, the nearer one shining a light into M's eyes. He squinted against the glare and said, "What's up?"

"What are you doing here?" the cop with the light demanded. He had a funny gargling voice, as if his throat were full of phlegm.

"Detective M, narcotics." He flashed his badge. "I'm working," he added, thinking that was obvious.

"Who's the girl?

"Listen officer, could you take that light out of my eyes?" he said. His own voice sounded tired to him —strained. He needed to get some sleep.

"Who's the girl?" gargle-voice said again. M didn't like that voice, and he didn't much like this cop. What was up with this? Didn't they know anything?

"She's a witness, now for crying out loud, turn off that light!" he said. The uniform looked at his partner and clicked off the light. M could still see bright spots in front of his eyes. He was coming down now, and this was getting on his nerves bad.

"What unit are you assigned to, Officer M?" the cop behind the wheel said. He had a choked voice too, but M didn't stop to think about it.

"That's *Detective* M, buddy!" he said. "Narcotics squad, Special Assignment, Loisaida. Now, if you please, I've had enough of you two, so why don't you just get out of here before I call in your goddamn badges, okay?"

But they just sat there, looking at him, like they didn't acknowledge his authority, and something went through him, something that had nothing to do with the cold. They sat unmoving, their gazes like an insect's, unwavering, never blinking; both were pale, sickly pale; their eyes, almost black, were flat and depthless. M felt abruptly unsure what to do. The corner of his mouth twitched; for some reason, he felt –*afraid*. He looked away, got a grip on himself.

"Do you mind," he said slowly, evenly, "if I get back to work?"

Neither one answered, they just kept staring at him. His nerves jacked sky-high; his hand inched toward his gun... He checked himself, shaken. This was crazy; what was going on?

But the uniform behind the wheel put the sector car in gear and said, "Carry on, detective." His partner never said a word, but his eyes never left M's, even as they drove away.

"Son of a bitch," M muttered.

twelve

Steph was mad. Coming down Third toward the house, after getting out of the car and slamming the door, she realized that the stupid cop had kept her bag of dope. She stopped, half-turned, wanting it back but not wanting to have anything more to do with him; what if he busted her for real this time? He was already pulling away. She tried to tell herself she'd gotten off easy: ten bucks wasn't much to pay for not going to jail, but she knew how these cops were. Good thing he hadn't taken them all.

Shivering in the biting wind, she quickened her pace. He'd given her a ride, but she'd gotten out at the corner, not wanting anyone to see her. Just get upstairs and get straight –then she'd turn on the TV, crawl into bed and warm up. But now she saw somebody in front of the building, carrying a gun. What the hell? That was just asking for trouble.

It was Tiny, holding a pump-action shotgun and keeping a watch up and down the street. Very uptight, his face hard, he saw her coming. "Steph!" he said roughly. "Where have you been?"

"Almost got busted," she said. "What's going on?"

"You better get inside," he said. She'd never seen him so wound up. "Suicide was worried –he went looking for you. Son of a bitch…" he muttered, looking off to the west and squinting. She couldn't tell what he was looking at, but he thumbed the shotgun's safety to off.

"What do you mean?" she said. This scared her; it was all just too weird. "Tiny, where is he? What's going on?"

"There's something bad going down. Real bad. I wish he'd get his ass back here. Said he had to find you. The Prez was pissed, but he left anyway."

"Where did he go? How long has he been gone?"

"How should I know? He went looking for you, half an hour, forty-five minutes ago. Nobody seen you, nobody knew where you were. Now you're back and he's gone… This is a lot of crap."

Any other time she'd have gotten mad –she was Suicide's old lady, nobody talked to her that way –but now she just stood there, watching his eyes flick up and down the block. All of a sudden he looked at her hard. "You said a cop picked you up?" he asked, a funny expression on his face.

"Yeah," she said. "A real son of a bitch."

"What happened? How'd you get away?"

"I don't really know," she said. "I mean, he let me walk. I'm not sure, it was like he freaked out or something, after we saw these other cops… Tiny, what's going on?"

"I don't know," he said. She could see he wasn't going to tell her anything, like he'd closed a door between them. "You better get upstairs. Pack some stuff and be ready to leave. We're pulling out of here."

"Leave?" she said, stunned. "Where are we gonna go?"

He didn't answer: instead he pushed her behind him into the doorway and shouldered the gun. Steph held her breath, heart pounding, but he lowered it again, still glaring into the dark. Without looking at her, he said, "I don't know. Ain't my job to know. My job is to watch the street. Now get your ass upstairs and get packed." With that, he yanked open the door, shoved her inside and slammed it behind her.

Surprised, she hesitated: from here she could hear bangs and thumps and muffled voices all over the building. Her chest felt tight, an oppressive dread settling over her. What was going on? Where was her old man? And what was all this about leaving? Where would they go? It was crazy, she couldn't leave.

She went upstairs, locked the door to their room behind her. First things first: she had to get straight now while she had the chance. She fixed up a shot, then sat with the blanket around her for a while, trying to warm up. But she couldn't relax, thinking about what Tiny had said. Where were they going? She couldn't leave the city: her connections were here. She only had two bags left and she couldn't leave without more. There was just no way; it was impossible. She got up, paced around. What should she do? Where was Suicide? Without wanting to, she kept thinking about the cops she'd seen, the uniform cops on Ridge: their eyes, and the way they talked.

She couldn't sit still; she had to find out something. Patty: Patty would know what was going on, if anybody did; she was the President's old lady, after all. It was worth a try, and anyway she couldn't stand to sit there all alone.

She went out, down one flight to Patty's, paused in front of the door. A lot of noise was coming from the first floor: voices, banging around; she heard a bike cough, start up. It only made her more anxious. She knocked, heard muffled sounds, steps. "Who is it?" a voice said.

"It's me, Steph," she said.

Patty looked out, swung the door open. "Come in." She locked the door again, led them to a battered sofa. "Have a seat," she said, and leaned back, lids closing over pinned-out eyes. Steph sat down, telling herself to be patient. But the noise was louder here, somehow insistent.

"How you doing?" Patty said finally, her voice distant, vague. She sat up, sighing, and lit a cigarette.

"Okay," Steph said. "Look, what's going on?"

"I don't know," Patty said. "I wish I did… The Prez says we're leaving, but I don't know where the hell we're going to go."

A percussive, banging sound came from outside, muffled but unmistakable. Steph jumped to her feet as Patty stubbed out her cigarette, sitting up. "Shit!" she said. "Those were shots!"

Another volley rang out, followed by a pause. They heard indistinct shouts. The shooting started again, steadily.

"No way, this is bad," Steph said. She had a feeling like you get right at the top of the roller-coaster –that you don't want to keep going but there's no stopping it.

"Yeah, we better check it out," Patty said. She stood up, grabbing a leather jacket. "Your place fronts on the street –let's go have a look."

Steph led the way back up. They went to the window without turning on the light. The fire escape blocked the view just below, but red and blue lights flashed up and down the street, and both First and Second Avenues looked blocked off. Steph's stomach knotted up.

"Jeeze," Patty said. "What is going on? This is bad."

Steph just nodded, listening as wailing sirens grew louder and louder. Frowning, lips pursed, Patty silently raised the window. Below them the street was quiet. They put their heads out, peered through the steps. In front of the building, a body lay prone and unmoving before the door: Tiny. Steph felt sick.

"Oh my God," Patty breathed. "That's…"

Above them, a window slammed up. Shots rang out below; a shotgun roared; glass shattered. Steph and Patty ducked back inside, pulling down the window. Bullets slapped against the building; more glass broke; they heard another blast above, more return fire.

Someone was shouting, pounding at the doors on the floor below. Steph looked at Patty and shrugged. She went to the dresser where Suicide kept a gun, but it wasn't there. He must have taken it with him. She reached under the bed and pulled out the baseball bat, hefted it, the weight reassuring in her hands. Steps came up the stairs; someone hammered at the door. She went over to it.

"Who is it," she said, the bat ready.

## eleven

Sitting at a red light at Houston and Allen, M took out a small glass vial, tapped a healthy pile of cocaine onto the back of his hand and snorted it up. He checked what was left: still about half-full. He had another snort, stashed the rest, and turned east onto Houston with the light, nasal membranes stinging as the stuff burned along his nerves.

Almost no one was on the street. Things were so quiet; it was strange. He tried the radio but got nothing but static, and turned it back off.

A siren squalled behind him and he dropped his cigarette. His eyes held the sector car in the rear-view mirror as he moved over to the right, fumbling around on the floorboard. Before he found the cigarette, burning a hole in the floor mat, the cops had shot past toward the East River. Jeeze! —What was he so nervous about? Now his hands were shaking.

Really, if he was smart, he'd go home and get some sleep. He was too wired, he'd been up for too long and he needed some rest. But that wasn't going to happen and he knew it. All sorts of weird thoughts were going through his head. Something was going on, something strange. Maybe it wasn't exactly his assignment, but he wanted to know.

His heart was hammering and he was grinding his teeth: the cheap cocaine had wound up his nerves and he needed to come down. Of a sudden, he had an idea, felt his pocket, and took out the bag he'd been looking at on Ridge when the sector car pulled up. He'd forgotten about it, but now it would do him some good. He changed lanes and turned left up Avenue C.

Here traffic was still light but at least people were out on the street and it didn't seem quite so dead. The spots were open and people were buying and selling. Yet he sensed an air of paranoia, like an electric current, buzzing. Every person on the street looked uptight, moving hurriedly along the dimly-lit sidewalk; each one turned a pale face toward the car, giving him a nervous scrutiny as he passed; and in the mirror he saw other figures emerge from the shadows, as if they had hidden at the very sound of his approach, before he'd ever seen them. Disquieted, he pulled into an open parking space near Seventh and cut the lights, leaving the motor running.

As he opened the bag of DOA he asked himself if he hadn't really screwed up this time. He knew he ought to call in but he was already so long overdue –they'd dismiss him for sure this time. So he might as well wait. If he got something, maybe it wouldn't be so bad. There wasn't much to lose by waiting. He snorted up the bag: it *was* good! Relief flooded his nerves; he slumped down in the seat, tired now.

He opened his eyes with a start, disoriented. How long had he been nodded out? The car was stifling hot and he was covered with a fine sweat. He turned down the heater, cracked the window. It couldn't have been long, though he didn't remember what time it had been before. He took a little snort of coke, to perk up.

Awake again, he sat there, smoking a cigarette, thinking about how burnt-out he was. The radio was still nothing but static. A sector car went by going south and he could almost feel the uniforms inside checking him out. That was the last thing he needed, but he ignored them and they went on. He watched in the rear-view mirror as the car turned into the dead-end at Fourth. It disappeared from sight but in a minute came back, pulled over at the corner and shut off its lights.

His skin was crawling; he wondered if maybe he should get out of there.

But he was curious —as long as it didn't involve him. He didn't want to talk to any more uniforms right now. That scene on Ridge had given him a bad feeling —nothing he could put into words, or that made any sense. But he couldn't forget those cops: their strange, gargling voices, and weird unblinking eyes.

In the mirror, the sector car didn't move, just sat there, but something ahead caught his eye: a beat cop coming down the avenue. He sat back, sinking down in the seat. Without taking his eyes away, he took out the vial of coke and had another snort.

The light was bad —was he seeing right? —but the cop had something *wrong* about him. M squinted, trying to see; his flesh crawled. The way the cop walked, and carried himself, it was shocking, weirdly repellant. He had a nightstick in his hand, going steadily forward, not looking around, his face never moving at all. M found him loathsome, and he shook himself, struggling against the impulse to put the car in gear and take off.

Just then some junkie came around the corner of Seventh, going fast, and ran right into him. M's mouth went dry. The cop grabbed him, threw him up against the wall, cuffed him and shook him down. But now a second one came around the corner, saw what was happening and turned to run. The cop threw the first one down on the sidewalk —M winced as the perp's head hit concrete – and ran after the other one, up Avenue C.

M looked back, saw the sector car flip on its lights and jolt into gear, wheels lunging on the slippery pavement. It sloughed onto the avenue, fishtailed, straightened, and came on, engine roaring. The beat cop grabbed the second perp by the shoulder, lost his footing and slipped. He fell, hard, but bounced back up like he hadn't even felt it. The perp turned, and pulled something from his pants —a knife.

"Shit," M said. He saw the blade spring open with slow-motion clarity. The perp braced himself, lunged, thrust it into the cop's belly. The cop stumbled, slid sideways —*but didn't go down.* The sector car went past with a wail, slid to a halt broadside in the avenue, and its uniforms spilled out. M watched, stunned, as all of them fell on the perp, stomping and kicking, clubbing him with their sticks. There was a lot of blood when the man's skull shattered, a reddish smear mixed with globs of gray spreading slowly on the dirty ice and snow.

ten

"It's Joker," a voice shouted, fist still pounding. "Open up!"

Steph lowered the bat and looked at Patty –surprised, she saw a knife in Patty's hand –and when Patty nodded, Steph opened the door.

"Get it together, we're splitting," Joker said, pushing past them to the window and opening it up. A frigid wind poured in. Below, gunfire continued, intermittent. "What's going on?" Patty said. Joker didn't answer. He had a big automatic in one hand and was looking for a target. "Joker?" Patty said.

"Tiny…" Steph said hesitantly. "Is he…"

Joker turned to her. "Tiny's dead," he said, his voice harsh. Steph flinched, he looked so bad –livid and drawn, lips snarled back from his teeth, which were grinding so hard she could hear it; his speed-freak eyes were like sapphires set in a skull. "It's the cops," he said, white flecks forming at the corners of his mouth. "They got Third sealed off. We're trapped here like rats. C'mon, I'm supposed to get you together, we're going over the roof."

"What do you mean?" Patty demanded. "Going where?"

"My van's on Fourth, if we can get to it –shit!" They all ducked as glass shattered above them. Joker leaned out and fired a shot, the report deafening. He fired again, pulled back. "So we're going over to Fourth while the boys hold 'em off. Move it, we're going, now!"

"Wait a minute," Patty said. "I ain't going off without…"

"Save it!" Joker shouted. "I'm just doing what I'm told. And they told me to get you bitches out of here! So let's move it!"

*He's losing it*, Steph thought. But Joker made a visible effort to get control of himself. "I don't like it either," he said, "but it's what the Prez told me to do. They're gonna meet us by Forsyth Park. We're going first and they're gonna cover us. So be on the roof in two minutes. I've got to find Jenna. Let's move!" Before they could argue, he left.

Steph and Patty looked at each other, shook their heads. "I better get some stuff," Patty said, and left.

Steph looked around, feeling panicky. What should she take? Where were they going? She peeked out the window again: the shooting had stopped, but searchlights were playing along the street; somehow this lull suggested things were about to get much worse. This was a nightmare –how could she leave the city? And where was Suicide?

She heard steps, running feet on the stairs, and Joker, shouting again. What now? They had a little money stashed away for an emergency. She put it and the last two packs of cigarettes in her coat, with the dope and her works.

Joker banged through the door. "Ready?" he snapped, but went straight to the window. Steph saw Jenna standing in the hall. She looked ready to cry. Muttering, Joker leaned out the window, holding the sill with one hand; he fired, grunted with satisfaction. A searchlight picked him out, flooding the room with light. He ducked back and threw himself down as gunfire raked the room, shattering the windows and hammering into the walls and ceiling. Steph screamed and hit the floor, covering her face as the air filled with bits of plaster and shards of wood. Then she was crawling toward the door. Joker was behind her, shouting, "Go! Go! Get out of here!"

In the hall she scrambled to her feet. Somehow she still had the bat in her hands. Shouts and gunfire rang through the building. "The roof," Joker gasped, wiping debris from his face and spitting. He gave her a push but she was already going, her mind a blur. She took the steps two at a time, coughing, her eyes smarting from the burnt powder heavy in the air. As they reached the roof hatch a sharp detonation came from below, then a crash.

"What was that?" Steph said.

"Special Weapons," Joker said. "They've blown the door."

On the roof Patty, Nikki and Jenna were standing together, shivering in the freezing wind. But Joker went to the parapet, looked over.

"Joker, come on!" Patty shouted.

A sustained burst of gunfire from the street drowned her out. Steph turned around to see Joker rise up, gripping the pistol with both hands, and fire off round after round. Again a searchlight picked him out, and something snatched hold of him, spinning him around and knocking him back. He staggered, sat down hard, dropping the gun, and hunched forward in pain.

Steph and Patty cried out and ran to him. Joker got heavily to his feet, teeth clenched and blood on his hands. He reeled to a low masonry wall and sat down. He was white as a corpse.

"Damn it, Joker," Patty was saying over and over, and Steph, surprised, saw tears in her eyes. Joker was groaning.

"Let me see it," Steph said. "How bad is it?"

It was bad: a bullet through his left arm and another through the shoulder. The arm was shattered, and he was losing blood fast. She looked at Patty hard, but said soothingly, "Joker baby, you're gonna be okay, but listen to me, we got to get you out of here."

"I fucked up," Joker said.

Gunfire hammered along the street, insanely loud.

"It's okay," Steph said. "We just got to stick together and we'll be okay. Now where's the van?" He tried to answer but the shots drowned him out.

"Fourth Street," he said again, his breath rasping. "Near Second Avenue."

"Alright," she said. She could tell he was hurting bad. "Just hang in there, baby." She stood up and shouted in Patty's ear. "We've got to do something. He's losing too much blood. But I think we better get out of here now. How do we get to Fourth?"

"Down the fire escape," Patty said. "The back door to the building behind us doesn't lock. We went out that way the last time we got raided."

"Okay," Steph said. She picked up Joker's gun and handed the bat to Nikki. "You two start down first. We'll bring him down after." She turned back to Patty: "Let's get him up."

Steph got under his good arm and they raised him to his feet. Somehow they got him down the fire escape. His eyes kept rolling up in his head and Steph was afraid he would pass out, but he held on. They staggered across the courtyard and through the hallway of the building behind. Steph, glancing back, saw a trail of blood behind them. Something rose in her throat; she swallowed hard.

Nikki and Jenna were waiting at the street door, looking out. "See anything?" Patty said. They shook their heads.

"Joker, your keys in your pocket?" Steph said. He nodded.

"Nikki, take his keys, and you and Jenna go get the van. We'll wait here till you pull up," Steph said. Nikki's face was ashen but she did as she was told, Jenna following as if lost. Steph and Patty leaned Joker against the wall of the vestibule and waited. They could still hear gunfire, muffled but heavy.

"Joker, you alright?" Steph said. He nodded, but he looked bad.

"C'mon, hurry up," Patty murmured, watching for the van.

Joker's lips writhed. "In my shirt pocket –a vial. I need a hit."

Steph understood. She felt his pockets till she found a little vial, half full of pinkish-white powder, and a rolled-up bill, soaked in blood. She poured a pile on the back of her hand, held it to his nose; he snorted it up, said thickly, "The rest." She did as he said, incredulous: that much speed would have killed anyone else. But Joker's lips snarled back in a wolfish grin. "Okay," he mumbled. A horn honked: the van.

They limped out –he was moving more under his own power now –and got him into the back. Nikki was driving. "Keep a good look-out," Steph said to her. "I want to try and take care of him before we start moving, but if you see any cops, yell so I'll know and take off."

She turned to Joker. "Okay baby, we got to get this jacket off," she said. He nodded. She slipped it from his right shoulder and eased it off the other arm. He gasped, clenched his teeth. "That's good," Steph murmured. "Easy... Easy..."

The shoulder wound was clean but the arm looked very bad, worse than she'd expected. The bone was shattered, and he was bleeding out. She didn't know how he could take it; if it weren't for the speed he'd have been unconscious, in shock. "You're gonna be okay, baby," she said, trying to keep her voice steady. "We're gonna take care of you." He nodded, his eyes hard, but he was starting to shiver.

Patty was kneeling next to her, frowning. "We've got to get that bleeding stopped," she said.

"His belt," Steph said. She unbuckled it, pulled it free.

"I really fucked up this time," Joker croaked.

"Don't try to talk," Steph said. "Just listen... We'll use this for a tourniquet. It ain't gonna feel good but we've got to do it, and when we get the bleeding stopped we're going to get you to the hospital."

"Forget that," Joker said. "Cops'll get us, sure." His eyes kept rolling up in his head. When they pulled the belt tight around his upper arm he grunted and said, "No hospital. We go to Forsythe Park. Doc'll patch me up when he gets there. Okay?"

Steph looked at Patty, who said quietly, "I hate to say it but he's right. We can't take him to the hospital."

"There's a car turning up Fourth behind us," Nikki said.

"Is it a cop?" Patty said.

"Let's go," Joker said thickly. "Move it."

Nikki put the van in gear and they were moving. "Where are we going?" she said, looking in the rear-view mirror. Patty was watching out the back.

"Is it a cop?" Steph said.

"Can't tell," Patty said. "Might be... I'm not sure."

Steph crawled up to the front and leaned up between the seats. "Okay," she said. "Make a right at the light. We're going to Forsythe Park, but I want to get a look at the house." She turned to Jenna and said, "Trade places with me."

"It's a cop," Patty said tensely.

"Easy," Steph said to Nikki, sliding into the passenger seat. "Don't roll the light. Don't give them a reason to stop us." She opened the glove box, poked around. "Just be cool."

At the bottom of all the junk was a box of shells. She ejected the clip of Joker's gun and reloaded it. Nikki looked over. "Shit!" she said. "What are you doing?"

"Easy, easy, be cool," Steph said.

The light turned green and Steph popped the cartridge back into the gun. "Okay," she said. "Let's go –but easy." They were moving, Steph looking down First Avenue, when Nikki said, "Shit! No way!" Steph glanced in the side mirror and saw blue lights. A siren cranked up. "What do I do?" Nikki said

"Pull over and slow down, but don't stop till I tell you to." Steph looked down at the gun, clicked the safety off. Her hands were trembling. She took a deep breath.

But the cop car went around them, engine winding, and screeched to a halt at Third, behind the others. Two cops got out, pulling their guns, and ran herky-jerky down the block, out of sight.

Nikki was gripping the wheel, her face blanched, knuckles white. Steph glanced back at Patty, kneeling by Joker and stroking his hair. She touched Nikki's shoulder. "Alright," she said. "We're cool... Cross over Third, slow, let's try and see what's going on."

Nikki nodded, gave it a little gas. At the corner, there must have been a dozen cop cars jammed together, lights all flashing crazily at once. The signal turned green. They rolled slowly through the intersection, but couldn't see anything. "What now?" Nikki said. Steph was trying to think, unsure if maybe they should just get out of there, but she said, "Pull up here. Keep the motor running. I'm gonna have a look-see." She stuck the gun inside her coat and zipped up. "I won't be long. Whatever you do, don't go off without me."

"Don't worry," Patty said. "We won't."

Steph jumped out and slammed the door as a volley of gunshots rang out. She crept back to the corner but no one was there, just the sector cars parked at crazy angles, doors standing open and the motors still running. Where were the cops? Careful, she told herself –if they grab you, you're dead.

She peeked around the corner. The block was brilliantly illuminated, brighter than day, huge floodlights trained on the building. Cops were everywhere, firing from behind cover. The clubhouse windows were dark but here and there she saw a muzzle flash. Now the firing intensified, a hammering din that rang up and down the street like a subway train, as a choking stench filled the cold air, burnt powder and seared metal. Somewhere, a loudspeaker droned something about laying down weapons to surrender, the words almost unintelligible, the voice so distorted it hardly sounded human at all. Something inside Steph went very cold at the sound of that garbled voice…

Tear-gas cannons thumped, launching canister after canister into every floor. In moments a thick yellowish smoke began to seep from the building's shattered windows. But a flaming missile sailed from an upper window, smacked onto the street and exploded: a Molotov cocktail.

"No…" Steph said. This was crazy…

A second one flew out, landed with a pop next to two of the cops, spattering one with flaming gasoline. His uniform caught fire and blazed up like a torch. He dropped his shotgun and staggered away, out of sight –silently.

Now the cops rolled something toward the door. Two muffled explosion followed, one after another, then a tremendous detonation that rocked the street. Windows blew out all along the block, the air filled with broken glass. Steph saw jets of flame and secondary blasts rip through the house from bottom to top, and she screamed, her voice lost in the maelstrom. A wave of intense heat surged past her. Unable to take any more, crying and cursing, she turned and ran back to the van.

nine

M wheeled the car onto Ridge and rolled down the darkened street, looking for a place to park. He wanted to cop. Two doors past the all-night coke spot a Cadillac pulled out and drove away without lights, and he pulled his car into the vacant space.

He cut the motor, checked the rear-view mirror. The lookouts on the corner were watching Houston. He could see the steam of their breath, their faces hidden by ski masks, or shielded by fur caps and upturned collars, and they were shuffling their feet, hands thrust into pockets. He wondered if they knew anything. He told himself again he should forget it, just pack it in and go home. But what he'd seen… wouldn't just go away. He felt like he should have done something —what, he didn't know —and though he didn't understand what was happening, he couldn't ignore it. He had to find out.

Out on the street, the wind cut right through him. He tugged the ski cap down over his ears but his eyes were already watering, his sinuses running. He pulled a wadded tissue from his pocket, blew his nose; it stained red with blood; he threw it away into the street. Coughing, he choked, spit out phlegm. This was crazy, he was falling apart.

As he approached the spot the lookouts turned, recognized him, and turned away again. M rapped on the door twice. A face looked through the little window. The door opened and slammed shut behind him.

"No way," the lookout muttered, nodding at M. "It's freezing out there."

"How's it going," M said to the dealer.

"Yo, man, what's up?" the dealer said. "What you want?"

"Two dimes." M handed him a twenty. The dealer gave him two small plastic zipper bags rolled into cylinders. "Alright, thanks," M said, and left.

Out on the street his nose started running again. He wiped it with the back of his hand, walked to the corner, where he saw a guy he knew: one of the lookouts, a tall Puerto Rican with a beard. He caught the guy's eye and said, "Hey man, what's happening?"

"Yo, man," the guy said. "What's up." He kept scanning Houston. The street was empty, no traffic at all, like Sunday morning –strange. M said, "Listen man, can I ask you something?" The guy glanced at him, raised his eyebrows. "You hear about anything... *weird* going down?"

The lookout shook his head.

"I mean, I don't know, but it seems like people are spooked, you know?" M said.

The lookout cleared his throat, spit. "Pressure Point, man," he said. "Think they doing a sweep tonight."

"Oh yeah?" M waited a second and said, "Hot out?"

The guy stamped his feet. "Well," he said, "it feels hot but there's nobody out, you know what I mean? And anybody who shows up just runs in and out and they're gone. I don't know but I don't like it. You better get what you want now, 'cause I think we're going to close up early. Especially if it starts to snow."

"Alright, thanks," M said. "Take it easy."

"Yeah," the guy said. "You be careful."

M headed west on Houston, crossed to the north side at Attorney, and turned up Avenue B. Except for the lookouts at the corner of Second, clustered about a fire burning in a fifty-gallon drum, the avenue was utterly deserted, spectrally calm. But he was disappointed when he turned the corner and saw the dope house closed. One man stood in front of the building, heavily bundled up and staring into space. He never looked around, but as M went past, he hissed: "Keep walking. Five minutes. Keep walking."

M kept walking. Halfway up the block two guys were standing in a doorway, smoking cigarettes and looking back toward the building. M got out a cigarette and walked up to them. They watched him approach, so nervous and suspicious they might have run away.

"Hey," M said. He coughed, spit out phlegm. "You got a light?"

The taller of the two, cadaverously pale, reluctantly produced a lighter. "Here," he said in a rasping voice. He kept his bare hands loose and ready at his sides, as if ready to ward off a blow.

M lit his cigarette and returned the lighter with a nod. "Been waiting long?" he said, blowing smoke.

"About ten minutes," the tall one said.

"Seems like an hour," the other one said. He was short and fat, a greasy little guy.

"Told me five minutes," M said. He coughed, spit again. "I wish they'd hurry up. I need to get straight."

This seemed to reassure them, a little. Back at the building, nothing was happening. The tall one said, "Me too. But now Louie here, he ain't *sick*, he just got the junkie jitters."

"Screw you, Dave," Louie muttered.

"He's got, like, an *overactive imagination*," Dave went on. "You should hear…"

"Hey, I think they're opening up," Louie said.

He was right, something was happening: the lookout was up by the door, and all along the street furtive men and women appeared from nowhere, converging on the spot. M hadn't suspected so many. Dave and Louie pushed past him and hustled down the sidewalk without another word. Already people were spilling back out of the building and hurrying away.

Though the place was working fast, even once they let him in, a line of five or six buyers waited ahead of him. All of them were fidgeting, scratching, folding and unfolding their money. Each took a quick look at him as he joined the line, but turned back, anxious and impatient, as if by watching, they could hurry the seller.

This man, his movements so deliberate he was painfully slow, stood on the first step of the stairway, carefully counting the money, then dealing the bags one at a time into the buyer's hand; his expression never changed, as over and over again he repeated the same gestures, in the same sequence. But a shout went up outside, repeated up and down the street. The lookout banged the door open. "Move it!" he roared. "Walk! Walk!"

Cursing and moaning, the line of buyers stumbled back out and scattered in the street, M among them. "What's up?" he said, going down the steps.

"Cop car," someone said.

"Walk! Walk!" the lookout barked.

*What now?* M thought. He shuffled away from the building, stalling, and watched two or three others cross the street to a ruinous tenement, where they ducked under a sidewalk shed, and disappeared. Probably a shooting gallery: he'd try it.

He crossed the street at an even pace as the sector car turned the corner from Avenue B. He glanced toward it, then away, pulling out a cigarette and lighting it as he avoided a patch of slushy filth half-frozen in the gutter. The dope house was completely silent; all the workers had vanished, as well as the buyers. The sector car rolled slowly by, giving him the once-over, but didn't stop, and he kept walking, on past the end of the sidewalk shed. When the cops were out of sight, he threw the cigarette away and turned back. The windows of the tenement were sealed with concrete block, but the heavy steel door swung open on its hinges. He went in, pulled it shut behind him. The place was pitch black, but somewhere ahead was a low murmur of voices, and the air smelled of smoke. He heard steps approach; a flashlight picked him out, played over him.

"Hey man," a voice said, a certain threat in its tone. "You want something?"

Dazzled by the light, he made out a huge black man, dressed in an expensive leather coat, a ski cap perched on his shaven head. He carried an aluminum baseball bat in his left hand, tapping it on the floor as he walked like a cane.

"Looking for a place to get off," M said.

The big man just looked at him.

"Too hot out there," M said. "I'll pay."

"Two dollars," the big man said. He leaned down and looked in M's face. "Been here before?"

"No," M said, holding out the money.

The other nodded, like he'd known the answer already. "Don't be starting no trouble." He hit the bat on the floor with a little *bonk*.

M shrugged. "Just came in to get off. I don't want no trouble."

The big man seemed satisfied. "Want to rent a rig?"

"No, I'm alright," M said.

"Straight back, to the left," he said, pointing with the bat.

M went back and to the left, and came into the shooting gallery itself, a big empty room like the back of a store. A fire was burning in a metal tub, and huddled around it on bits of filthy, cast-off furniture —broken chairs, derelict sofas, hideously stained mattresses —were ten or eleven wretched-looking junkies. A couple of candles were burning here and there for cooking up, and the air was choked with smoke and a mingled stench of urine, excrement and unwashed bodies. Trash was everywhere: empty glassine bags, broken syringes, spent matches, burnt-out lighters, cigarette butts, plastic drink containers. One guy was shooting up as M walked in: he popped the needle from his arm, giggling, as blood spattered the floor, and lay back, sighing, eyes rolling up in his head. One or two others were nodded out —or overdosed —but mostly they were just sitting there, staring at nothing; and though one girl whose face was spotted with pus-covered sores glanced up at M through pinned-out eyes, none of them moved or said a word.

He sat down on a backless kitchen chair that wobbled beneath him, got out one of the dimes he'd bought on Ridge, and did up half. The coke was like

Drano, ripping through his sinuses and bringing tears to his eyes. His nose started running; he dabbed at it with a tissue that stained red. The jolt hit him like an electric shock. The stuff must've been almost pure speed; his howling nerves jacked up into overdrive, and he began grinding his teeth. A noxious taste of gasoline dripped down the back of his throat. The stuff was awful. He snorted the rest of the bag and got out a cigarette.

Glancing around, he saw that the others, or anyway the conscious ones, had been watching him, but they looked away, avoiding his eyes, except for one hideous junkie, who grimaced a toothless mouth and said, "Hey man, you got a cigarette?"

"Sure," M said. The junkie took it with a leprous claw-like hand. They sat smoking in silence. The guy coughed and spit after every puff. Finally M said: "Unreal how cold it is tonight."

"You said it," the junkie rasped. "It's too cold. Too cold and too weird. I ain't going home tonight. I *can't* go home. I hope old Boss Man up front don't try and throw me out 'cause I got nowhere to go."

"Oh yeah?" M said. His nerves were buzzing, and he wasn't really paying attention.

"Yeah man, the fucking cops…" He choked on his own vehemence, broke up coughing. "The cops torched our squat, man."

"What?" M said, listening now.

"Yeah man, for real… I ain't shitting you! They busted in, drug everybody out and set it on fire!"

"Where?" M said. "What happened?"

"Up on Thirteenth, between C and D. I been living there more than a year now, and last time anybody even hassled us was the end of summer. I came down here as it got dark, I had to cop for me and my old lady. She's in bad shape, man, she's real sick, she can't even get out of bed." He sniffled, his eyes watering, but rage was building up in him as he went on: "So I came out to cop, right? And I'm standing on the corner half a block away talking to this guy I know, who was telling me to watch my ass 'cause there'd been sweeps all over the neighborhood, when all of a sudden a bunch of cop cars and one of those big weapons trucks turns the corner and stops in front of our building, and they bust in and start dragging everybody out! People were yelling and screaming, there was shooting and —oh fuck man, I don't know."

"What the hell," M said softly. The guy was clenching and unclenching his fists, staring into space. In a second he went on: "I seen my buddy Jésus jump out the second floor, he tried to run for it. They caught him and beat his head in. And then they just threw him in the van."

They sat there for a minute. M got out his cigarettes and gave the guy another one. Finally he said, as gently as he could, "What about your old lady?"

"I don't know, man." The guy's mouth was all twisted up. "I don't know. I seen them carry her out. She looked dead. I don't know if she was or not. She looked dead." He coughed again. "They threw her in the van too. I couldn't do nothing. I just stood there. I would've killed them if I could have. But I'm a cripple." He turned toward M, snarling. "I was in 'Nam. Got my leg messed up. Got a plastic knee ain't worth a shit, got to walk with a crutch. I was going nuts! I seen 'em throw her in the van and I just went *off*. My buddy dragged me away." His eyes went dead. "I should've done something."

"I'm sorry, man," M said. "That's awful."

"I should've done something," the guy said again.

M just shook his head; he didn't know what to say. They sat there for a while like that, the junkie slowly smoking his cigarette, M grinding his teeth and wiping his nose with the back of his hand. He was so tired; he couldn't think straight. It was all too much. He couldn't make sense of it. Finally he said, "Did you notice anything strange about those cops?"

"Huh?" the junkie said. He had gotten out his works and was emptying a bag into a blackened spoon. He added a few drops of filthy water and cooked it up.

"The cops," M said. "Was there anything strange about them? I mean, did they look funny, or act, like, weird?"

The guy didn't answer, concentrating: he drew the liquefied dope up into the syringe, and rolled down one filthy sock, looking for a vein in his ankle. It took a while. M sat watching him, appalled but fascinated; he had never gotten over a horror of needles. The junkie probed for a time in the grayish flesh, smiled vaguely when he found a vein, and shot the plunger home. You could see the stuff go through him. M was dying for a bag himself: the wretched coke was fraying his nerves to the breaking point.

The junkie leaned back, eyes closed, and said slowly, "No man, I didn't see nothing. Just what I told you. What do you care anyway? I didn't see nothing."

"I did," said a voice like a little girl's. M looked up: a black woman, so skinny her flesh was like tissue paper over bone. Her hair was falling out but she had been pretty once. She hadn't even moved before; M hadn't thought she was awake.

"Yeah?" he said.

"I seen these motherfucking cops that looked more dead than alive." He turned toward her as she went on: "I mean, they looked bad. My girlfriend and I, we were working down on Houston and Eldridge. It was a slow night, and we were so cold we were about to freeze to death. I felt like the blood was turning to ice in my veins. So we were walking up and down the block just trying to keep warm." She shivered, and pulled her shabby fun-fur close around her. M saw now her ragged hooker's clothes: gold metallic miniskirt over run-marred stockings, white go-go boots yellow with age. "So I told Charlene I was gonna go cop me a bag to keep warm, did she want to come? And she said no, she's too broke, she's got to stay and try and make some money. But I got a little money and I tell her I'll front her one, that I'll be back quick. But I guess it took maybe fifteen minutes, over on Ludlow, and when I come back around Eldridge I stopped, 'cause there's a police car stopped at the corner and Charlene is bent over, talking in the window with the cops. You got another cigarette, honey?"

He gave her one and lit it for her, and she said, "Thank you. You're a gentleman." She blew out smoke, looking off into space for a moment, before going on: "Now these no good police are *pigs*, you understand? I mean, *pigs*. You don't know what it's like out there. They're always hassling us. I hate 'em. Twice –I tell you, twice –they busted me, and when they got me in the van they took me down to East River Park and raped me. When they were done they just put me out and laughed as they drove off. I hate those suckers more than anything in the whole world.

"But now Charlene, maybe she's smarter than me, I don't know –but when they start to hassle her, she just gets in the car and gives them a blow job or a quickie and they leave her alone. I won't do it. I just won't. But anyway I'm figuring that must be what's going on, the cops are horny and they looking for a freebie.

"So I just hung back, you know, 'cause I didn't want no part of *that*. And I see her look scared, and start to back away from the car, and these two cops get out and they look like death warmed over –I mean, completely pale, and they just look *bad*, and both of them are walking funny, all stiff, like their legs don't work right. So Charlene, she's going, 'No, no, leave me alone,' and she starts to try and run, right? and one of the cops yells something, only I don't know if you'll understand what I'm saying, but his voice was *messed up*. A chill went through me when I heard him, I don't know why. So I hid in this doorway, 'cause I'm scared for Charlene, she's my girlfriend you know, but she's already in a fix and all I can think of is I don't want them to come after *me*."

"What was his voice like?" M said.

"I don't know how to tell you," she said. "Like something was wrong with his throat or something. Like it wouldn't work right –something wrong, *bad* wrong. It don't sound like much but it sure scared the hell out of me."

"And what happened to Charlene?" Strange memories were stirring in his mind, a creep running down his spine.

The girl's eyes narrowed to slits, and she said slowly, "Charlene tried to run but she slipped, and when she fell down they was all over her. First they beat her with their sticks, and then they throw her in the car and take her away. I wanted to kill them. They hurt her bad. She was screaming something awful."

She stopped, but went on quietly: "I wanted to kill them. And I'm not a violent person. I don't believe in violence. But if I'd had a gun I would've blown their fucking brains out."

He nodded, trying to think but the coke buzz wouldn't let him. All he could think was he needed a bag.

"They had no reason to hurt her like that," the girl said. "She would've given them what they wanted."

"I don't know," M said after a minute. "Maybe that wasn't what they wanted." He opened the other dime –not that he needed it.

A muffled shout came from the front of the building. He jumped, heart thumping. Everyone looked around stupidly. "Oh, man!" a voice groaned. "Fuck this," the crippled vet muttered, picking up his crutch and getting to his feet. M just sat there like an idiot, holding the coke and a straw in his hands. The others stirred themselves, the place suddenly tense. A gunshot rang out; sirens howled. The big man appeared, baseball bat gripped like a club.

"Five-O!" he barked. "Get out of here!"

M did the whole dime in one snort and stood up. He shouldn't have done it: a huge head-rush hit him, black spots exploding before his eyes. He swayed, almost fell.

The big man was inside the doorway when the first cop appeared. He swung hard, hit the cop square across the forehead, *smack!* The skull crushed in like a cantaloupe.

M scrambled away through a ruined, half-filled door, bile rising in his throat. He looked back, saw a shotgun blast cut the big man in half, blood spraying everywhere –and then, following the others, he slipped through another door and was outside, running for his life. Heart hammering, nerves screaming, his only thought was to get back to the car. He crossed a broad open lot at a dead run, heading toward Houston –dodged through a hole in a chain-link fence –crossed the broad traffic artery at a slant, going east –and slowed to a walk at Clinton, gasping for breath, the freezing air burning his lungs. The streets were empty, but he saw blue lights ahead. He slowed still more, squinting and trying to make it out. The cops were on Ridge —he could see the rear of a sector car, parked right in front of the coke spot. That was bad. He looked back but saw nothing —hesitated, starting to shiver now in the frigid air, the sweat freezing on his skin —but he had only one option, down Attorney: he'd have to try to get to the car from the south. All down the long block, passing the endless file of empty taxis, he felt horribly exposed and alone. Finally, at Stanton, he turned east again, steps ringing along the empty blocks, and stopped at the corner of Ridge, putting his head around. His heart sank: the cops were parked halfway down the block, well past where he'd left the car — what an idiot he'd been to park right next to the spot! —and they were busting the place. It was no good —there was no way. He let his breath out, furious with himself, and leaned back against the building, exhaustion and too much cocaine about to rip him apart. The car would have to wait —he'd have to come back when they were gone. He had no other choice. He took a breath, trying to pull himself together, and gave a start: coming his way was a sector car, rolling east on Stanton, straight toward him. He dodged around the corner, tried to melt into a doorway. The car went by with painful slowness —looking for him —he held his breath, for fear the steam would betray him —blood pounding like surf, black spots boiling in his eyes —but then it passed, and he gasped for air, reeling.

He had to get out of here —away from this trap —the car would wait, he needed a bag. He couldn't go on like this, he needed some dope —and this goal, crystallizing in his mind, supplanted all others, gave him a purpose. He'd cop some dope, then come back for the car. Keep moving. Cop a couple bags and come back.

He took a last look up Ridge —the bust still going down —and turned back, east on Stanton again. The street ahead was empty once more, but now snow had begun to fall, fat wet flakes as big as your fist.

eight

Steph jumped into the van, slammed the door and gasped, "Go, go!" Nikki took one look at her and jerked the van into gear; Third Street fell behind them. Steph unzipped her coat and the gun dropped into her lap. She took out a cigarette and looked down at her shaking hands.

"What happened back there?" Patty demanded. For a minute Steph couldn't answer, just shook her head, trying to get her breath and wiping her eyes. The others were looking at her.

"It was awful," she said. "They blew it up –the house blew up."

"What?" the others all said at once. "What do you mean?"

"They were all shooting," Steph said. "The SWAT team was there. They were firing off teargas. It looked bad. Then –oh Jeeze this is so fucked-up! – somebody in the house threw these Molotov cocktails. And one of the cops got hit, it just torched him, and the other cops went crazy after that." She was trying to get the cigarette lit. "They threw these grenades in, and all of a sudden the whole place blew up. It just exploded from top to bottom."

They were all staring at her. She could guess what they were thinking. Her eyes teared up again. "Nobody could have survived it. I mean it just blew up, the whole thing."

They came to a stop. Nikki was crying too. Jenna looked stunned, and

Patty was just looking at her, like she didn't believe it or something. "Do you think anyone got away?" she asked carefully.

"I don't know," Steph said. "I just don't know. Nobody who was in there… I just don't know." Trying to pull herself together, she looked around. "We've got to get moving," she said. "Nikki…"

"Where to?" Nikki's mouth was quivering but she looked determined.

"Cross Houston," Steph said. "We'll go down Allen, and cross at… Fuck, where are we going?" She turned. "Joker, where are we supposed to meet?"

He looked almost dead: horribly pale, his eyes were filmed over, and beads of sweat were running down his face. "Forsythe and Hester," he said thickly. "By the old toilets there."

"Okay," Steph said. "Hester. I don't think that goes through to Allen. We may have to go around to Bowery. Just take it easy, we don't want to attract any attention." She had the gun in her hand and was looking around in every direction. The streets were empty but they could hear sirens everywhere.

Patty crawled up close, crouching by the transmission well and saying urgently, "Look, I'm not sure we should do this at all. Why are we gonna wait around Forsythe Park? There may not be anybody coming. We've got to think about getting out of the city."

"You don't know that," Nikki said. "We've got to wait for them. Some of them are coming. I know they are."

Steph didn't answer. After a moment Patty went on: "This town is a death trap. It's an island! We don't even know if the bridges and tunnels are open. I don't know if any of the boys made it or not… But the longer we wait, the more likely we'll get trapped here."

"Where would we go?" Steph said. "You talk about leaving but we don't have anywhere to go."

"My brother lives in Jersey City," Patty said. "He's cool, he'll put us up. It's close, and the Prez would look for us there."

"And what about Roach? He don't know where your brother lives," Nikki said angrily.

Looking at Steph, Patty said, "We can cop there."

"I don't know," Steph said. She felt numb; her voice was like someone else talking. "The Prez told Joker to meet in Forsythe Park..."

"Steph, they may all be dead!" Patty's voice was hoarse.

"They're *not* dead!" Nikki said.

"We've got to look after ourselves now," Patty said.

Steph looked back. "Jenna, what do you say?

"I don't know." Jenna spoke slowly, as if stunned. "I just... I don't know."

"We've got to wait," Nikki said. "They told us to meet them and that's what we've got to do, we've got to wait for them."

"We've got to look after ourselves, now."

"What if some of them got out first, like we did?" Nikki demanded. "They'll come looking for us. We've got to be there."

Patty shook her head. "It's stupid. If we sit around waiting we're as good as dead."

"I think... I think we'd better wait a while." Steph tried to make her voice firm. "We've got to give them a chance."

"That's right," Nikki said.

"You're making a mistake." Patty lowered her voice: "And I'll tell you something else: Joker will be first." She turned, went back to him.

They drove on, Steph wondering if Patty was right. The streets were strangely empty. They turned onto Bowery. To the north she thought she saw fires burning, but she wasn't sure; she couldn't tell anything for sure. Cops were parked at Canal, blocking the bridge approaches; no one was crossing. Steph got a sudden panicky feeling –her chest tight, she could hardly breathe –when it struck her that Patty might be right, that it might *already* be too late to get away. If the bridges and tunnels were sealed off there wouldn't be any getting out of Manhattan at all.

Joker moaned and she looked around: his head lolled over to one side, his tongue sticking out between his teeth. Patty was stroking his hair, her eyes like slits and her mouth set in a tight line.

"Okay, here we are," Nikki said. Steph looked up to see Hester dead-ending into Forsyth Park ahead. To the right, Christie ended in a cul-de-sac in front of a low, bunker-like school; an empty plaza was in front of them, the wretched, narrow park stretching away to the north, its trees bare and the crumbling brick walkways empty and dark. Steph pointed to a low structure off to the left where the park's elevation terraced down.

"Pull it down by those steps," she said. "We'll get Joker out and down to the building, and you find someplace to park as close as you can. We're going to need this van."

They stopped at the curb. Steph zipped the gun back into her coat. "Cut the lights," she said, checking the street in both directions. "Ready?" she said to Patty, who nodded. "Alright, let's go!"

She jumped out and slammed the door. Patty had the rear door open and one arm around Joker's shoulders, cradling his head in the crook of her elbow. "Get the tire iron," she told Jenna. "Try to get that door open." Jenna did what she was told, her mouth screwed up like she was about to cry again.

"Fuck," Patty muttered.

"Take it easy," Steph said. "We're all scared. C'mon Joker, here we go."

They got him out of the van as gently as they could, but he was like a dead weight. They moved painfully down the steps and across a broken level space to the ruined bathrooms. Jenna was standing there, looking at the padlock and chain that sealed the door. "It's all locked up," she said.

"Break it open with the tire iron!" Patty gasped. "What are you waiting for?"

Jenna smacked the tool against the lock, to no effect. Patty sighed, said, "Can you hold him?" to Steph, and let go of the wounded man. She took the tire iron and bashed the lock hard, twice: no good. Muttering, she reversed the tool and wrenched it against the chain like a lever. Mortar crumbled, fell; she gouged more out; masonry gave way, the chain and lock clattered free, and the door swung open. Patty stepped back, breathing hard, and gestured with the tool. Steph staggered past her, Joker's good arm slung around her shoulder, into the crypt-like blackness, and they slowly lowered him to the filthy tiled floor. Steph gagged at the dank and rancid air.

"Jeeze!" she said, looking around. Patty knelt next to Joker, supporting his head. Steph couldn't tell if he was still conscious.

"Now what?" Patty said, as if to herself.

"Jenna, stay by the door, watch for Nikki," Steph said, trying to sound calm. She crouched next to Patty and said, "How is he?"

"Not good," Patty said. "I think we better find some way to build a fire."

"Think we can risk it?"

"I don't think we have a choice," Patty said. "If we don't keep him warm… there's no way he'll make it."

An old trash can stood outside. They dragged it in, went out into the frozen park and gathered newspapers and fallen sticks and limbs. When they got back Nikki was inside with the other two. "I parked just past the corner," she said. "The first spot I came to, about a block away."

"That's cool," Steph said. She started making a fire as Patty went back for another armload of wood. When it caught pretty well they tried to make Joker comfortable. After that they could only wait, anxious, keeping a lookout at the door. Nobody had much to say. The fire only took the chill off, the warmed air rank and nauseating. As it burned, Steph gathered more fuel, just to have something to do. Out in the frozen park, it felt like the temperature had dropped still further. Around them, the city was silent, save for the echoing sirens, and here, in this forgotten place, it seemed to her less and less likely that anyone would ever come. But she didn't want to say so: she didn't know what they would do then.

Time crawled. Despite the fire it was getting colder. Steph was staring into the flames when she heard sobbing, and looked around. It was Jenna. Steph went and sat down next to her, putting her arm around the girl's shoulders. Jenna was trying not to cry but she couldn't stop. "Oh God," she sobbed. "Oh God… What are we gonna do?"

"Easy," Steph murmured. "It's okay."

Jenna shuddered, but settled down. After a little while, she said, "I'm scared."

"I know," Steph said. "Listen… I'm sorry about Tiny. He was a friend of mine, and he didn't deserve that… But he's gone now, and you've got to think about yourself. You've got to be strong and keep it together. Tiny would've wanted that… You understand? It's just us now and we've got to look after one other."

Jenna nodded, biting her lip.

"Take it easy," Steph said. "We're gonna be okay."

She squeezed the girl's shoulder again, got up and went to Patty, who was staring tight-lipped out the door. "Now it's gonna snow?" Steph said. The ground was already covered, the park so quiet you could hear the whisper of the flakes drifting through the trees and settling to the earth.

"Yep," Patty said. "Ain't that great." Turning to Steph, she said, "Listen, I don't know what you wanna do and I ain't gonna try to tell you. You've got to decide for yourself. But my brother lives in Jersey City. The Prez has been there, he'd know where to find me –if he's still alive." She shook herself and went on: "I've got no way to know. And I've got to think about myself right now, nobody else is going to. You… we don't know what's happened to Suicide, where he is or whether he knows to meet you here. He wasn't at the club, so maybe he's okay. I don't know. You've got to decide for yourself. But you can come with me if you want. You'd be welcome there. The city looks like a death trap to me, and I don't want to get stuck here. And there's another thing." She lowered her voice. "We can cop there. The stuff isn't as good as in the city, but you can get it. And that's going to become an issue pretty soon – we both know it."

Steph nodded, trying to think. In her heart she knew Patty was right about it all. "What about Joker?"

Patty just looked back at him and shook her head.

Steph nodded. "We have to talk to the other two," she said. "I don't know what they want… We've got to think about them, too."

"They're big girls," Patty said. "I'm sorry, I really am, but I have to think about myself. You better do the same."

"We have to look out one other."

"I have to look after myself."

"Look," Steph said, pissed off now and about to let Patty know it –but an awful groan came from behind them. She turned, saw Nikki, bent double in pain, her face white and twisted. Steph's first thought was that Nikki was dope-sick. But she wasn't on the stuff –was she? Dread seized her, an awful prescience.

"Nikki?" Patty said. Nikki tried to say something, but couldn't. She fell to her knees, gagged, and threw up. They froze, horrified by the black, jelly-like vomit that splattered to the floor. "Oh Jesus," Nikki moaned, her voice choked. She vomited again.

"Goddamn," Patty said, going to her, but even as she knelt down, Nikki's eyes rolled up and she fainted, sinking over sideways until her head lay with her cheek to the floor, black goo seeping from her lips. "Shit!" Patty said. "What in hell?"

Steph hadn't moved, unwilling to go any closer. "I don't know," she said slowly –but didn't she? Wasn't she just afraid to acknowledge what she was thinking?

Nikki began twitching and jerking spasmodically. Her head tossed from side to side; awful convulsions wracked her body. Patty tried to hold her still. "Help me, Steph," she said. "If we don't keep her mouth free, she'll choke to death."

Steph swallowed hard. She crouched next to them, but Nikki's limbs were jerking and flailing as if from electric shook. Patty peeled her lips back, but she couldn't force the jaws apart. "Goddamn it!" Patty said. "I can't… I don't know what to do!"

Nikki went limp. Patty felt for a pulse, then just shook her head. They let her go and she slumped to the floor, a dead weight. Steph drew back. *How can she be dead?* Steph was thinking. *My God, what is going to happen to us?*

Patty closed Nikki's eyes and stood up. Jenna was drawn up against the wall; she seemed withdrawn, as if watching something she didn't understand. Patty's fists were clenched, her mouth a tight grim line. Steph couldn't think straight, her mind wouldn't work. But Patty gasped. "Steph!" she said under her breath. "Didn't I close her eyes?"

"Huh?" Steph said

"Her eyes –Nikki's eyes. Didn't I close them?"

"I –I think so. Why?"

"Because they're open now."

It was impossible, but they *were* open –and now a convulsion went through Nikki, and she sat up –slowly, awkwardly, the dead girl sat up. She looked at them.

"Nikki?" Patty said.

"Nikki, are you okay?" Steph said. "We thought you were… You were sick, are you okay?"

Nikki didn't answer, just sat looking at them –and Steph felt something go through her, a shudder of revulsion, at the sight of Nikki's eyes. They were different now –*changed* –like something had gone out of them, all the life and color –gone dead black.

"Nikki, say something," Patty said. "How do you feel?" Nikki didn't answer, just looked at them, no expression on her face, not even blinking –but one hand reached out, fumblingly, found the baseball bat and dragged it closer, fingers closing on it.

Steph looked at Patty; their eyes met. What she'd seen back on Ridge was going through Steph's mind, but what could she say? "Keep an eye on her," Patty said lowly. Steph nodded. Patty went to Joker and knelt down.

"How is he?" Steph said.

Patty got up, shaking her head. "He's dead," she said.

No one said anything. Jenna picked at her fingernails and stared at the floor. Patty stood on one side of the room, away from Nikki, who sat immobile and silent, the bat gripped in one hand. Joker lay as they'd left him, at once a reproach and an omen. Steph couldn't look at him, sure now that his death only announced more disaster, that there was little chance of getting out of this nightmare alive. Maybe he was the lucky one: it was over for him. Feeling numb, incapable of making a decision, she rechecked the gun, but despair bore down on her. It was hopeless; she had no idea what to do.

She went to the door and looked out at the park shrouded in snow, like a dead world. But behind her came a creak of leather, the scrape of boots on the floor. Goose flesh rose on Steph's skin. She turned: Jenna, moaning, one hand to her mouth, pointed to Joker. He was sitting up.

"Joker," Patty whispered. Steph's legs felt weak, like she couldn't hold herself up. This couldn't be happening, it was impossible…

"You're… Are you okay?" Patty said. "You better take it easy. We thought… Jeeze, we were afraid…" She didn't finish. Joker was struggling heavily to his feet. *Don't get up*, Steph thought crazily. You *can't* get up, you're *dead*. But he got up, looking from one to another of them, his eyes staring, never blinking, flat and black as two tiny pools of dirty motor oil.

"Joker?" Patty said again. "You okay?"

His mouth moved but only a choking sound came out.

Steph looked around. Jenna huddled against the wall, trembling, her mouth like a wound in her face. "Oh no," she moaned softly, "no, no…" Joker rocked slightly from foot to foot, as if he had forgotten how to stand; he put out a hand to steady himself, still watching them. Patty was standing quite still. "Steph," she said. "I think we better get out of here."

Joker's eyes narrowed. A gurgle came out of his throat; his hand stretched toward them, blood-stained fingers twitching; he took a tentative step, almost lost his balance, recovered.

"Shit!" Steph said. "Come on!" Patty hissed. She was sidling toward the door.

Steph looked back. Jenna cowered there, a pitiful, pleading look on her face. "Jenna, come on!" Steph said. She grabbed the girl's arm and yanked. "We've got to get out of here. Move!" Steph shoved her toward the door. She turned, pulled out the gun and aimed it at Joker. "I'm sorry, Joker," she said. Her voice quavered. "I don't know if you can understand me or not, and I don't want to do this but I will. I'll shoot you. We're getting out of here. Stay back or I'll shoot you, I swear I will."

His mouth twisted and he took a tentative step. Steph thumbed the safety off. "I'm telling you, stay back!" she said. He opened his mouth; a gargling sound came out, like a laugh.

"Okay," Steph said out of the side of her mouth. "Let's go."

"Ready when you are," Patty said. Steph heard the switchblade open with a *snick*. "We've got to find that van —aww, shit!"

It hit Steph: the van. Nikki had the keys, and she was sitting there with Joker in between them. Steph's heart sank: *That's it —we're dead*, she thought.

"Forget it," she started to say. But Patty darted forward, dodging around Joker's outstretched hand. He grabbed at her and caught her sleeve. Patty threw her weight the other way and slashed the knife across his face, opening his cheek from ear to mouth. Gurgling, he swung a fist at her. She ducked and he lost his balance, staggered against the trashcan and knocked it over. With a crash, burning embers scattered across the floor and ash boiled up in a choking cloud. Now Nikki got up, heavily, holding the bat in front of her, as Joker clambered to his feet and lurched forward, grasping for Patty. She stumbled back and ran into the wall. Coughing, her eyes burning, Steph gripped the gun with both hands and stepped forward, trying not to think. She brought the barrel up to the back of Joker's skull and fired twice, the reports deafening. The back of his head blew off, bits of bone and brain spattering the wall, and he collapsed. The stink of powder and burned flesh filled the air, but there was little blood.

Trembling all over, her ears ringing, arms and legs tingling like they'd gone to sleep, Steph felt sick. She wanted to throw up, or hurt herself —most of all, to take it back. But Joker was dead this time. Jenna and Patty stared open-mouthed. Steph lowered the gun, and it slipped from her hands, fell clattering across the floor. Patty started to say something, but stopped, shook her head.

So tired now, like her body weighed a thousand pounds, Steph turned away from Joker and leaned against the wall. She would have given anything to forget about what she'd done. A shudder went through her.

"You alright?" Patty said.

"Yeah," Steph said. "Let's get out of here."

"Okay," Patty said. She looked around. "Oh no," she said. "Where's Nikki?"

Steph jerked around, saw Joker's body, and Jenna, standing against the wall and picking at her fingernails –but Nikki was gone.

"Where'd she go?" Steph said, panicky. She went to the door. The park was as empty as before, but there were footprints in the gathering snow.

"Gone," Patty said. "So much for the van. We better get out of here."

Steph looked around at the hellish little room. "Patty?" she said. "What do you think was the matter with Nikki?"

"I don't know," Patty said. "Was she dope-sick?"

"That didn't look like any withdrawal I ever saw," Steph said. "Besides, Nikki wasn't on the stuff, was she?"

"No," Patty said. "She never touched the shit."

"That's right," Jenna said. "I asked her once did she want to try it and she said no, she was scared of it."

They both turned and looked at her. "You?" Patty said. Jenna shrugged, looking at the floor. "Tiny didn't know," she said. "Nobody knew. Tiny... He would've flipped out." Tears were running down her face.

Steph was trying to understand. "Jenna... When did you last fix up?"

"This afternoon."

"You got any left?"

Jenna shook her head. "I needed to go out and cop but things were getting weird and nobody would let me leave. I was going to sneak out but that's when it all went crazy." She looked up into Steph's eyes. "I need to get straight... I already don't feel so good."

Steph looked at Patty. "You said we could cop over in Jersey City, where your brother lives? In the daytime or just at night?"

"I don't know," Patty said. "I mean, I've only ever done it at night. In the day I'd come back to the city."

"We'd better get going," Steph said. "It's already late. I don't think we can wait until tomorrow night."

"I agree with you," Patty said. "But there's something you're not saying."

Steph shrugged, didn't answer.

"C'mon Steph. Talk to me."

Steph shook her head. "I don't know exactly," she said, slowly. "But Nikki wasn't a junkie. And neither was Joker –he was a speed freak, he looked down on dope. Whatever happened to them, it hasn't happened to us –yet. But I think we better cop and fix up as soon as we can."

Patty looked away, as if thinking it over. Finally she said, "We don't know if the PATH trains are running. If they're not, we'll have to walk. It's a long way, and the tunnels are dark. You up for it?"

"I don't think we have much choice," Steph said.

"What about her?" She pointed her chin at Jenna.

"She'll make it," Steph said. She took Jenna's arm. "Okay: Jersey City. You set? We better get going. We're gonna have to walk."

Jenna nodded and wiped her eyes. Steph zipped up her coat, dreading what might happen next, but glad enough to get moving, to leave this horrid place. She looked one last time at Joker's body, but wished she hadn't.

"If only we knew if the subways were running," Patty was saying. "That would save a lot of walking."

"Think we could risk it?" Steph answered, thinking about everything that had taken place here.

"I don't know," Patty said. "I guess we could try to get the F or the D at Broadway-Lafayette, it's more or less on the way... The main thing is, we've got to be real careful, we've got to avoid the cops."

"Once we're across the Bowery," Steph said, trying to think, "we take Spring or Prince to Lafayette. It's safer to avoid Houston."

"Okay," Patty said. "All set? Whatever we do, remember, stay alert."

"Right," Steph said. Jenna nodded. Patty swung open the door –but they stopped, dazzled, lights shining in their eyes: cops –uniform cops, with flashlights. "Shit!" Patty said.

Two of them, maybe twenty of thirty feet away, and the sector car parked on Christie, lights on and the motor running. Behind them, a figure –Nikki?

One of the cops opened his mouth; a gurgling sound came out. The other one was unlimbering his nightstick.

"No way," Steph said. "They're not getting me."

"Me either," Patty answered. "Run for it... Ready?"

But Jenna, like a trapped animal, turned and ducked back into the bathroom.

"Jenna, what the fuck!" Steph said. "C'mon, let's get out of here!"

Jenna reappeared. She had Joker's gun in her hands, was pointing it at the cops. Patty and Steph were edging away. "Jenna, don't be a fool," Patty hissed. "Come *on!*" But Jenna stopped still, the gun at shoulder height. The cops were still coming.

"Keep away from me!" Her voice rose, hysterical. "Keep away or I'll kill you!"

"Jenna!" Steph yelled.

One of the cops made a rush at her, herky-jerky, terrifying. Jenna emptied the gun. The bullets slammed into him, throwing him off balance. He caught himself and chopped her down, then leaned into it, the nightstick pounding her skull.

Steph cried out but Patty yanked her arm: "Come on!" They ran. Steph looked back: now both cops were after them, moving all wrong but coming fast.

"Goddamn," Patty said, gasping for breath. "If we get separated..."

"Yeah?"

"Meet me at the PATH station on West Ninth, on the outbound platform." She looked back. "Run!"

But ahead another sector car pulled up, siren howling, blue lights reflecting over the snow. Cursing, Patty bolted toward Christie but Steph saw the cops from the car cut her off; she ducked back toward Forsythe. One followed her, swinging wide, and trying to force her back toward the car. She cut back south, running hard, making for Rivington. As she went up the park steps she looked back, saw a cop throw his stick between Patty's ankles as she ran. Patty tripped, fell forward, and he dropped heavily on top of her. Behind Steph, the cop lost his balance, slid, fell, got clumsily to his feet. Seeing Steph out of reach, he turned back toward his partners.

Steph stopped, filled with horror and dread. Patty wriggled free. The knife flashed in the dim light –Steph saw it stab into the cop's gut. He knocked Patty back with one fist. She went sprawling and he was on her like the wound was nothing. Then the others were there. They began to beat her with their sticks.

Steph choked. She turned –nothing she could do –and staggered away, legs weak. At the corner of Rivington she looked back once more, saw them carrying Patty, limp, to the sector car.

She was alone. Oh God. *Now* I've had it.

seven

Desperate for some dope, M slipped around the corner of Fourth onto Avenue D, trying to look everywhere at once and wishing he had eyes in the back of his head. A few others were out on the street, watchful furtive figures hugging the walls and moving from shadow to shadow. The sound of the rare passing car could be heard for blocks, menacing.

When he was maybe halfway to the spot there came a *whoop!* from behind him, the siren of a sector car starting up, and the few people on the street vanished like smoke. M slipped into a crumbling doorway and flattened against the wall. Siren wailing, the car's lights illuminated the towering projects like lightning flashes before it disappeared around a corner a few blocks north. M exhaled sharply; he hadn't even realized he'd been holding his breath. This was messed up. He had to get his car back.

As he headed up the street again he saw that the other wraiths had also reappeared, silent shadows swiftly converging on the spot: an abandoned and burnt-out tenement between Fifth and Sixth. Though its once-ornate windows were crudely sealed with concrete blocks, the entrance, atop a flight of crumbling, trash-littered steps, gaped open like a mouth, engorging and disgorging a steady flow of customers. M took his place in the jumpy, nervous line waiting on the street below. No one spoke, just eyed one another tensely, and peered restlessly up and down the long avenue. M looked at them: a bunch of pitiful junkies, some shivering in threadbare clothes, hands thrust into pockets and stamping the heavy wet snow from their feet –and others, partly coated with it, like livestock, oblivious to everything except the prospect of the next fix. One wretch didn't even have shoes. What am I doing here? he asked himself. But his nerves were wound way too tight and he needed some dope, bad.

He lit a cigarette, trying to hold it inside his palm, away from the snow. The line moved with painful slowness as the lookout, hidden in the darkened foyer, signaled one buyer at a time to enter. It was taking too long; M was sure they'd all get picked up here. He kept looking up and down the street, expecting a sector car to roll into sight at any moment.

But now he was next, the lookout gesturing to him. He threw away the cigarette and went up the steps fast. "Hurry up, hurry up," the lookout said. M went past him and down the hall, feet uncertain on the broken floor. The place was an utter ruin, littered with rubble and trash. Here and there candles burning in coffee cans cast a weird flickering light on the scabrous, crumbling walls. About halfway down he came to the stairwell, its steps blocked by heavy beams and a jumble of broken furniture; he stopped and looked up, waiting. Several flights up, he saw a light, and movement; from the darkness a small box descended, hanging from the end of a cord. He caught it, turned it over, saw two compartments, one marked "C" and one "D". He put two twenties in the "D" side and tugged at the line; the box flew up and out of sight. After a moment it came down again. He scooped out his four bags and turned back toward the door, sticking three in his pocket and holding the other between his fingers. "Hurry up, hurry up," the lookout chanted again as he went down the steps and out onto the street, walking away fast.

He hesitated at the corner, uncertain. Avenue D felt wrong –too exposed –but he wanted to get away from the spot, and Fifth was mostly vacant lots, a long open stretch back to Avenue C. He turned toward Fourth: he could cross west there with some cover and, with luck, make it down across Houston back to Ridge. He wanted to get back to the car, he'd feel much safer in the car, but his nerves were too wound up; he had to do the bag first. Once he did the bag, he'd be okay. But the snow was no good: the stuff might get wet, or he'd drop it. He took a quick glance around, began rattling doorknobs. The third door he tried was unlocked, and he found himself in a dingy hallway, lit by a single flickering fluorescent tube. He paused, listening: no sound, nothing, the building was quiet. He turned the bag over in his fingers: the blue glassine was stamped with a tombstone that read "R.I.P." He pulled off the scotch tape, ripped away the top half, and did up the bitter powder in one snort; and as he sagged against the wall, leaning his head back and closing his eyes, the warmth oozed down his spine, muscles relaxing as the jagged cocaine edge faded like a fire doused with water. He breathed deeply; fine, that was much better; he could think again, focus on something besides his own short-circuiting nerves. He lit a cigarette, and looked at his watch: one-thirty.

The car. He had to get back to the car; he would decide what to do next once he was back in the car. He snorted up a second bag for good measure, and went over it again: Fourth over to C, down to Houston and over to Ridge.

But he wasn't really thinking very clearly, he was only thinking about getting back to the car, and he went back to the door and walked straight out without even checking the street. But now a sector car was rolling up the avenue toward him. He stuck his hands in his pockets and hustled on his way, hunching his neck against the wind-driven snow, his heart pounding. All he could think was, No, no, just keep going. In the glare of the headlights he couldn't see the uniforms at all. He glanced straight at the windshield –he didn't have anything to hide, he was just out minding his own business –and turned the corner west on Fourth without another look, just a guy going someplace and wanting to get there quick. But he was listening hard, thinking what to do if they came after him. There was a slow gentle *swish*, wheels passing through snow, soft, louder, quite clear, then muffled again, and gone. They'd gone on. He risked a look around; the car hadn't turned, it had gone past. He breathed out through clenched teeth, lips cracking painfully. That had been close, way too close. He'd better be more careful. Moving as fast as he could on the slick, snow-packed sidewalk, he hurried on, his steps crunching faintly along the dead-silent block, the black nightmare city looming all around. He was just starting to cross the street to the south side when headlights flashed, turning, tires swishing again, and the sector car turned onto the street ahead of him.

Maybe they weren't looking for him. He hesitated between two parked cars, went ahead and crossed the street; keeping the same pace, his eyes roved, looking for a way to escape. But they were already pulling up, the car sliding to a stop beside him, and even through the window he could see the cop's black unblinking eyes fixed on him. The window rolled down: "Hold it!" a voice croaked. His stomach knotted into a ball, but the surge of fear made him angry, and adrenaline pumped through him. *Fuck this*, he thought. *You're not getting me.* He ran. The doors of the sector car opened and the cops jumped out, shouting.

He kept going, slipping and sliding. Just ahead was an empty lot between two derelict tenements; maybe he could get through to Third. One of the cops was following, the other turning back to the car. M dodged around the corner of the first tenement and through the rubble-strewn lot. He heard footfalls behind him –the bastard was coming fast. M gasped for breath, icy air searing his lungs and pain stabbing his sides. He leapt over a foundation and ducked behind the westward building, as sirens approached from the south and east. They were trying to cut him off.

He clattered through a narrow passage, found himself in a dead end, a tiny box of a courtyard half-filled with junk and garbage, every window barred and nothing but sealed metal doors. He turned back, but the uniform was there, blocking the way. Sirens moaned on all sides.

"What the fuck do you want?" M's voice was choked with rage and fear.

"You're under arrest," the uniform said. The words were so garbled, M could barely understand them. The uniform came toward him, one hand reaching out, nightstick in the other.

M pulled his gun. "Don't come any closer," he said. But the uniform kept coming. M ground his teeth, swung the gun up and fired a shot into the cop's chest. The impact knocked him back a little; he kept coming. M fired again.

The uniform shook it off, didn't go down. An animal cry coming from his throat, M fired point blank in the cop's face –and now his blood froze. The uniform just stood there, stopped in his tracks but not dead, despite the holes the shots had torn in him.

"Dear God," M said.

Footsteps coming, close now. He panicked, turned round, round again – trapped like a rat –clambered up on a blind windowsill and grasped the bottom rung of the fire escape. But the uniforms were already there. They shouldered aside the wounded man, and grabbed M's legs, dragging him free, the frozen iron ripping his hands. He slammed to the ground and the breath went out of him. Stunned, he struggled to his hands and knees, spitting out heavy wet snow. A nightstick fell hard on his back; he grunted in pain. The second blow cracked a rib in his side; then they hit him on the head –again –again. He groaned, the pain intense. His skull split open –black spots exploded before his eyes–

six

Steph headed east on Houston. Goddamn it was cold. She'd had no idea it might snow, and now, here she was, freezing, and wandering the streets. Her hands and feet ached, her face was numb, her nose was running like crazy and when she coughed it was like a knife in her chest. The miserable snow was so wet and heavy it seemed to melt on her, then re-freeze. And she had no idea where to go or what to do.

She felt outrage, disbelief; at the same time her mind wouldn't work, she couldn't understand anything. How could this be happening? It wasn't *right*, you couldn't explain it. She kept trying to think, to come up with a plan, but she was scared to death, and two awful thoughts wouldn't leave her alone: she was homeless now, she had nowhere to go, and she needed some dope. Her fear was almost paralyzing, all she could do was push it away; right now she had to get through the night —stay away from the cops, and find someplace out of the cold where she could get straight. Tomorrow…

Dope: she only had two bags left, and little money. The thought of running out, now, was worse than anything else… Panic gripped her; she fought it down. If she could make it till morning —she could cop in the morning. She had to believe that.

There was a rumble up ahead, she saw lights: something coming her way, west on Houston. Her heart jumped. In this eerie absence of traffic, anything was dangerous. She slipped into a doorway, huddling in the shallow alcove and peeking around the corner, scared and trying to think what to do.

But it was only a garbage truck, with a snowplow attached to the front, like they always sent out to clear the streets. As it drew near the *swish* of the snow thrown to one side overlay the noise of the diesel motor. Maybe they would help her! But she pressed herself into the corner, keeping still.

As the thing went past, leaving a filthy sodden track in its wake, the driver turned his head, uncannily sensing her presence. She gasped at the sight of his face, immobile and pallid. Time stopped for an instant as his flat dead eyes locked on hers, and she couldn't move. But he looked away again, turning back to the street ahead. She went limp, knees sagging, heart pounding like it would burst. He'd seen her —what should she do?

Still the truck never slowed, not even for the red light at Christie, and it disappeared into the gloom going toward the Bowery, taillights vanishing into the night. As the sound faded, she got hold of herself again, and set off, hurrying east again.

She crossed Orchard, Ludlow, Essex. She was hurting now, lungs aching from the freezing air, but she saw lights coming down Avenue A. It might be a cop; she kept going. Her legs weak, the stitch in her side now a gouging pain, she pushed herself on, crossing to the north side of Houston. A shooting gallery was somewhere around here —she'd seen it before —but now everything was dark. She had a bad feeling, went on, slowing down in spite of herself, exhausted and almost in despair. The sidewalks here were very slick; near the corner of Avenue B she slipped and fell to her hands and knees and for a moment couldn't get up. But behind her she heard a motor, tires cutting through snow. She looked back: a sector car turning her way, onto Houston.

She scrambled to her feet, adrenaline pumping, and ducked around the corner, trying to get out of sight. But where? Behind a car? And then —right across Avenue B in front of her —she saw it: the side door to a gas station, half open and partly blocked by drifting snow.

Was it a trap? —but she had nowhere else to go, on the street she was as good as dead. She pushed her way in, tried to shut the door but the snow blocked it —and now the cop car was right there. She held perfectly still, listening: it decelerated, passed by slowly, then abruptly it was gone. But they were looking for her, she was sure of it. She kicked snow out of the way, got the door closed, but it wouldn't lock. And her footprints led right here. For the first time she hoped it would keep snowing.

She turned, got out her lighter, picked her way about the garage by the flickering light. A dented, rust-eaten sedan sat on the skids, its hood up and motor disassembled, some of the parts sitting in a reeking tub of kerosene off to one side. She walked over to the interior door, tried the knob: locked. It wasn't going to be real warm in here. She wondered why the one door was open, anyway. She didn't like it —it was too much like a trap. Still, it was better than nothing.

The lighter was burning her fingers. She felt her way to the car, opened the door and got in. What now? She shivered, unzipped her coat and put her frozen hands under her armpits to warm them. Though it was cold in the garage, out of the wind her body warmth melted the snow caked on her clothes and boots, soaking them. She needed a fix but could she take a chance on it here? She was so tired, she knew she would nod out immediately. It wasn't safe, but where could she go? Not back out *there*.

She got out a cigarette and was about to light it when she heard footsteps: someone right outside. Her heart beat furiously; the crazy notion went through her head that you could hear it through the wall. She held her breath.

Whoever it was passed by, headed toward Second, then stopped.

After a long still moment that lasted forever, the steps continued on, the sound gradually fading away. Steph let out her breath, leaning her head back on the seat.

She had to do something —but what? Barricade the door? Get out of there and look for someplace else? But where? She climbed out of the car. There was a heavy wheeled crank for pulling motors: it might block the door shut.

But now the steps were coming back, very close already. She waited; they stopped outside the door. Her mouth went dry. She crouched behind the car, held perfectly still as the doorknob rattled. The door shoved open, and dim light from the street outlined a beat cop —one of *them*. A shudder went through her. He got out his flashlight and swept the room. The beam caught her, held. He unlimbered his nightstick.

Quick but awkward, all wrong, he strode forward, trying to corner her. She dodged around the other side of the car, trying to keep it between them. "Stay away from me," she said. "I'll fuck you up!" Clever, he stayed with her, she couldn't reach the door; he never said a word, matching her step for step, relentless and silent. "Stay away from me, you son of a bitch," she kept saying. "I'll fuck you up!" But she was almost panicked, revolted by his grotesquely pale face and dead black eyes.

She bumped hard against something —a workbench —fumbled over it, knocking parts and tools to the floor with a clatter. Her fingers closed on a heavy wrench. She tugged it off the table and gripped it in both hands like a club. "Okay, man," she hissed. "Come on… I'll fuck you up!"

He never answered, just came for her, reaching out one hand. She feinted, jumped forward and smashed the wrench against his knee with all the strength she had. With a *crunch!* the bone shattered, his leg folded, and she grunted in satisfaction as he fell to the floor, still silent. She backed away, watching, appalled, as he tried to stand, fell, tried again, fell. Nothing human could have put any weight on that leg, but he didn't seem to feel anything, finally just gave up and dragged himself toward her, reaching out for her ankles. She kicked at his hand but he caught her boot, tried to throw her off balance. She chopped at his wrist and he let go, catching at her with the other hand, crawling after her like a crippled spider.

She stomped down one wrist, swung the wrench back and hit him across the temple with all her strength. He didn't even blink —she was starting to freak out —his head just rolled back and he kept coming. She lost it. "Die, you son of a bitch!" she screamed. "Die! Die! Why won't you fucking die!" She flailed at him, swinging the wrench like an axe —smashed one eye to a pulp —a wave of nausea ripped through her. He grabbed an ankle, tripped her. The wrench tumbled from her hands.

She kicked free, scrambled away —crashed into something, fell. He crawled after her. *Why aren't you dead?* she thought hopelessly. *Why won't you die?* Her foot banged against a metal can; liquid sloshed. She snatched it up, laughing now —tore off the cap, and splashed him with it, dodging back from his grasping hands, dousing him with it. The stench of gasoline filled the air. She threw the empty can aside, pulled out her lighter and sparked it.

"Fuck you," she hissed, and touched the flame to him.

five

He came to a little as they pulled him from the back of the sector car and dragged him across the frozen parking lot into Central Booking. Then he lay prone on the floor in the holding pen. He didn't know how long he'd been there; it was all as vague and disconnected as a dream. He came to again, confused, sick with pain, sprawled in a heap of stinking bodies. A door opened, and a dead weight fell on him, hard –it hurt so bad he might have vomited; he groaned through cracked lips, sticky with dried blood. He was chilled to the bone, and his eyes were swollen almost shut, so he couldn't see anything. He tried to move but his hands were cuffed behind his back.

Bumping motion, a jarring stop, and now he realized where he was: the back of a police van. Pull yourself together, he told himself dully, and tried to spit out the vile taste in his mouth, but his tongue was swollen and dry.

The doors opened, cop hands grabbed him, dragged him out. It was still snowing, and the wind cut like an icy knife. He'd never felt such pain. It was all he could do to stand. The cops lined up the vanload of prisoners, poking and prodding with their sticks, uncuffing them one at a time. The others were appalling, every one a wretched junkie. An emaciated Caucasian started coughing and couldn't stop; he choked, gagged, fell and lay on the ground moaning, wracked by convulsions. One of the cops kicked him hard across the head. He lay still, and they marched the rest of them away. M saw a massive building looming above, and realized they were at the Tombs. He looked back at the body face down next to the van –snow was already beginning to cover it –before they passed under a portal and were inside.

They shuffled through a labyrinth of corridors, up and down half-lit stairways, the buzzing electric locks at each security door jarring him from exhausted, trancelike agony. Everywhere it reeked of urine and vomit, and the revolting stench of filthy human flesh. At length the stumbling procession halted. One of the cops unlocked a cell; they were herded in; the door slammed shut behind them.

M looked dully around. A single flickering fluorescent tube, buzzing incessantly, cast a dirty light. They were in a mid-sized holding cell, with concrete benches against the walls and a steel toilet in the middle of the floor. M pushed his way to a bench, sat down.

He leaned back against the wall, closed his eyes. What now? He tried to think but he hurt so bad he couldn't. Pain stabbed at his ribs like the point of a knife. He passed his hands over his aching head: the flesh was pulpy and damp; his jaw was swollen, a couple of teeth were loose; he had a long cut over one brow. He scraped away the caked blood with a fingernail. He couldn't believe he was still alive, and wondered vaguely why he was there, what they would do with him. Things had stopped making sense so long ago –it was useless to try to figure them out now. And he was so tired. If only he could rest for a while. Probably nothing would happen until morning. He felt in his pocket but the other two bags were gone. That was the icing on the cake.

A few of the prisoners had been thrashing about, or muttering to themselves, but the cell grew quiet. He closed his eyes again, drifting off. Suddenly he started awake, unsure for a moment where he was, or what was happening. Most of the others were dozing, one or two whimpering as they slept. To one side, a skeletal Puerto Rican was holding his stomach, moaning and swaying from side to side; next to him was a huge black man, big as a linebacker, elbows on his knees and resting his chin on his hands, a look like pure murder on his face. From somewhere in the distance came a scream, a drawn-out howl of agony that echoed hollowly through the building. M winced. What was going on? A second scream broke off with a choking blubber. The black man sat up, with a gesture like snapping someone's neck. His face contorted; he turned to the Puerto Rican and bellowed: "Shut up!"

The other man didn't seem to hear him; his eyes were clenched shut, he kept moaning and rocking from side to side. "Shut the fuck up!" the black man yelled, even louder. The Puerto Rican was still oblivious. The black man popped him in the head, yelling, "Shut up!" He hit him again, then again: "I said shut up!" M watched, silent.

The Puerto Rican fell sliding off the bench and vomited, quietly. The smell was loathsome. The big man got up, crossed the cell; the men there made room for him, and he sat as before, staring at nothing. After the fit passed, the Puerto Rican lay with his face in the black pool he had disgorged, twitching.

The cell quieted again, but M, awake now, sat there, pointlessly looking at his watch every five minutes as time slowed to a crawl. The others were sunken in torpor, silent in their misery, or unconscious, all of them passing through various stages of dope-sickness. M's eyes were closing again, when he saw the black man furtively remove one shoe.

M didn't move, curious and watchful. The man pulled something from the sneaker's tongue, stuck it in his mouth and chewed; a visible shudder went through him.

Glassines, M realized: the guy had squirreled away his empty bags in case he got desperate.

The guy chewed up two or three more, sucking out dust and residue from the empty bags; he giggled, spat a wad of paper into the middle of the floor. A scrawny little junkie turned to see, desperate longing on his face, but the big man gave him a look and carried on, snorting and giggling to himself. The other turned away, despair on his face.

Soon the floor was littered with spitballs and the guy shut up and just sat there with his eyes rolled up in his head. Some of the others were eyeing his shoes, obviously wondering how much he had in there and calculating their chances of getting it away. Every few minutes, the big man snorted, shook himself, and glared about the cell; the others looked quickly away, while he slipped back into a stupor. But the stuff wore off quickly, and he had to keep getting out more.

He was noisily sucking on another wad when the cops reappeared, four of them. The tension in the cell disappeared like smoke before a sudden gust of fear. The big man swallowed what was left of the bag. The cops' eyes were fixed, as inhuman as the glare of insects; they unlocked the door and came through with their nightsticks ready, going straight for him. He flinched back, shook himself, leapt at them. A cop went down and the big junkie got him by the throat, but a second one kicked him across the jaw, breaking it, and he howled in pain and let go. They went to work with the sticks. The sound of the blows was sickening: they swung the heavy clubs two-handed like axes, splitting skin, rupturing blood vessels, shattering bone. When the beating stopped the black man lay unmoving in a pool of gore, his head a bloody ruin. It took three of them to drag him away.

No one else in the cell had moved. The other cop looked around, prodded the dope-sick Puerto Rican on the floor with the bloody tip of his stick. M had thought the guy was dead. But the junkie rose slowly to his feet, unsteady but silent, and followed the cop out the door. What was worse –M had only half-seen –but weren't the man's eyes now a flat and depthless black?

Aching and exhausted, he just sat there, trying to think. None of it made any sense, but it had to be the dope. The cops knew it. That's why he and the others were here, to run out their metabolic clock. The dope blocked whatever it was, whatever was caused it all. As soon as your body metabolized the dope… it got you, whatever *it* was. He wondered how long he had… How long had it been? How long did it take –eight hours? twelve?

He looked around the cell in horror and despair. His throat and chest were tight, he could hardly breathe. He had to get out of there –but how? It was hopeless: he was a prisoner…

One of the other junkies moaned in his sleep, sat up. His teeth clenched, he was shaking; sweat covered his face; he clutched his abdomen. "Jesus," he groaned. "Ahh... Jesus!" He gagged, tried to vomit, but only a gob of spit and phlegm came up. M heard him praying, the words interrupted by heaves and coughs that wracked his entire body. M couldn't look away, this man's agony like a rehearsal of his own imminent future.

"Aaagghhh," the junkie moaned, choking. "Aagghh Jesus Christ!" He thrashed about, beating his temples with his fists, and fell to his knees, pounding his head against the concrete floor. "Jesus!" he gasped between moans. "Agghh Jesus Christ!"

It went on longer than M would have thought possible. The junkie collapsed at last, unconscious or exhausted, gashes and lesions all over his forehead, and lay there, his breathing stertorous, while his whole body convulsed horribly, as from electric shock. When the fit ended, he vomited up a blackish liquid, and lay still.

Nothing happened for a while. M must have dozed off; when he opened his eyes, the junkie was sitting up, quite calm and still. As sensing M's look, he turned and stared —stared from black depthless eyes. M drew back involuntarily, looking away.

He felt like he'd been sucked into a whirlpool. He hadn't thought he could go down any further. But this was too much. He hugged his knees to his chest, trying to stay warm. If only they'd just killed him —it would have been better to die. Instead, his body was a ticking time bomb, and when it went off, he'd end up like that. He couldn't accept it —yet there it was, undeniable, like all the things he'd seen, the absurd, unbelievable things he'd seen —and done—

Exhausted, he slept again, a fitful, restless sleep... Trying to cop, he hurried stumbling through darkened labyrinthine streets, a jumbled rotting ghetto where nightmare revelation jeered behind every door and death skulked behind, dogging his steps... Sweating, shaking, shivering with cold, he turned corner after corner, only to be forced back, or driven into furtive byways and detours, by flashing blue lights and beat cops... At last, his relief so great he could have sobbed from joy, he saw his connection, and copped; and greedily, gratefully clutching the precious bag, he ran until he could hide, ripped the thing open… A scream rang out, he jerked his head up: he was still in the cell, he'd been dreaming.

The junkie who'd *changed* was gone. Through the course of the night, as he slipped in and out of enervating, nightmare-filled sleep, the others vanished, one by one, until apart from M, only two were left: two filthy, burnt-out addicts, sitting in silence, waiting dully for this nightmare to end, and the next one to begin. M had long since gone numb, prey to hopeless despair; he barely noticed the hideous screams that periodically rang through the echoing corridors; he scarcely even looked at his watch. Its time no longer had any meaning, being measured in hours and minutes. For him, time was marked by the slow dull pulse of the blood moving sluggishly through his veins, by the steady, inevitable metabolizing of the drug within him, the only barrier that remained between sanity and madness, between life –and what?

Morning must have come, for he couldn't sleep any more, and he just sat there, like the others, not looking around, just staring at the floor, and waiting. They might have been there forever, three cadavers entombed in a forgotten vault, and he had begun to wish it would go ahead and happen, just get it over with. What difference did it make now? Instead the cell door opened, the cops motioning with their sticks for him and the other two to get up and get moving. He stood up, uncaring, and shuffled out. They cuffed him again. It didn't matter: he was ready to die.

He followed them back through the stinking labyrinth, wondering dully, and without real interest, where they were going and what would happen to them there. The Tombs were empty now. Cell after cell was vacant, though still littered with bits of trash and cigarette butts, here and there a ragged coat or crumpled hat, and on the floor congealing pools of blood and black vomit. It was quiet –only a whisper of voices somewhere far away, the sound of dripping water, the pace of their own steps. He remembered all the prisoners the night before, the cells full of junkies: where had they all gone? Revolt came over him:

he had to do something. It was now or never.

He looked back but a guard jabbed him hard in the ribs. He pictured himself smashing the thing's head against the wall. Be cool, take it easy, he told himself. You've got to keep it together.

They went up a couple flights of stairs, passed through a door and were outside. A van waited, back door open and the engine running. Dawn soon, bitterly cold, though the snow had stopped. The other two prisoners didn't even pause, just climbed in, and M followed. The door slammed behind them and the van took off. They stumbled against each other, and fell onto the bench seats. As they went around a corner, the door to the driver's compartment slid open with a bang, and slowly closed again. *No way!* he thought. *It's not even locked!*

He looked out through the small rear window. They were heading south, parallel to Centre, passing behind the Tombs. No way to know how much time they had. He had to act fast; this might be his only chance. He felt his pants pocket with his elbow –Yes! –and made up his mind.

"Hey," he said lowly, looking at the others. "Listen to me. I think we can get out of here but you've got to help me."

"Do what?" one of them said. "What are we gonna do?"

"First we're gonna get out of these cuffs," M said. "We've got to be cool about it. One of you get the keys out of my pocket. I think I have a key that will open them."

"Okay," the guy said. "Let's try it." M scooted over next to him as the guy turned his back; the other was watching eagerly. "Keep watch!" he hissed.

They wriggled around until the other guy could reach M's pocket. He couldn't get his fingers very far inside, with painful slowness pulling the whole pocket inside out before he could get the key ring. Then the van was bumping and rattling so hard he dropped them. M, cursing his luck, slid to his knees, trying to reach them –sure the driver would figure out what they were up to. But his blood was pumping, hope giving him nervous energy. Finally he got hold of the keys, unlocked the other's cuffs; in moments they were all loose.

The others looked at him expectantly. He could tell they were going to be a lot of help, and said, "Okay, be ready to back me up if I yell. Then bail as soon as we get stopped and get the hell away from the van."

They nodded. He took a deep breath; his heart was racing and he'd broken out in a cold sweat. He glanced toward the rear window —was that City Hall Park? He rose up and moved toward the door. Okay —easy —easy—

He slammed the door open and threw himself forward. The cop at the wheel turned, taken by surprise. He let off the gas and stepped on the brake as M grabbed his head and smacked it against the side window, hard. The wheel spun as the brakes locked up. M was trying to bash the cop's head again but the van was skidding sideways —his hands round the cop's throat, the cop trying to hold the wheel with one hand and push M away with the other —then they hit something broadside, slammed to a stop. M lurched forward. Bone snapped sickeningly under his fingers; the cop went limp; the motor died. M got up fast, wanting away from the thing whose head was now grotesquely askew from its body.

The door slid open again, the two junkies peeping out. "Beat it," M croaked. Without a word, they jumped out the back door. When he climbed heavily down and looked around, they had vanished.

four

Steph touched the lighter to the cop's gas-drenched uniform and the flame caught. It ran slowly for a moment as he looked at it, not seeming to comprehend, and then he went up like a torch. Steph slowly backed away, glaring into his eyes. "How you like that, motherfucker?" she hissed.

He opened his mouth, moved his jaws; some gargled sounds came out, as he dragged himself toward her. She couldn't believe it: even his hair was on fire, the flames searing his skin, which blistered and turned black –but he stretched out a burning hand, still trying to reach her.

"What are you?" she whispered, backing away from the single-minded horror that wouldn't give up. The air filled with acrid smoke; her eyes watering, she started coughing, couldn't stop. The place was suddenly very hot. Pools of flame appeared on the floor –the whole building was about to go up.

*Get out of here!* She dodged his arms, skirted the flames to the door, and looked back. His head, immobile, was no more than a burning skull, eyeballs melted away.

Which way? The street was empty; falling snowflakes whispered to the ground. She hesitated, looked around, crossed Houston. Now the whole garage was burning, smoke boiling from the open door, the flames' red light reflected on the snow-covered sidewalk.

*Move!* A siren screamed in the distance. Inside the gas station, something exploded, and the windows blew out, spraying glass. Steph turned to run as the underground tanks detonated —a deep blast, then a roar like ripping concrete. The street lit up for a second, illuminated in a huge flash, and a wave of hot air threw Steph forward on her face. She scrambled up, skidded away down Clinton, burning debris and blackened hunks raining down about her.

At Stanton she came to a stop, panting and out of breath, rubbing her skinned palms together. "Goddamn," she muttered. Back at Houston was a dancing blaze of fire. She heard a minor explosion, like an aftershock, and then sirens again. She had to keep moving —they'd be here any time.

Now blue lights turned up Clinton from Delancey, coming toward her fast. She ducked around the corner and into a doorway on the south side; seconds later the cop zoomed past.

The night had come alive with wailing sirens. She shook her head: this was bad. Her hands and feet hurt and she was still freezing, her teeth starting to chatter. What was worse, she was starting to feel sick —dope-sick —she had to find somewhere to hole up and get straight. But where? She looked around, set off into the biting wind again. There had to be someplace she could hide.

Cop cars were coming from every direction now. Ducking in and out of doorways, trying to stay out of sight, she moved west on Stanton; crossed Suffolk and Norfolk; finally, driven back at Essex, she turned north again on Norfolk. Traffic was heavy on Houston: sector cars, heavy equipment trucks, and fire-fighting equipment; and it looked like something else was happening to the south, near Delancey and Rivington. Boxed in here, panicky, she had to find someplace now —she *had* to get off the street.

She picked her way up Norfolk, looking for an unbolted entrance, a broken window, trying the car doors. Better to freeze than get picked up by *them*. But there was nothing. A sector car turned up the block, and she threw herself between two parked vans, scooting up close to the wheels and watching the tires roll slowly past. Despairing, she could have given up right then. Tears came to her eyes, freezing in the lashes —but she remembered what had happened at Forsyth Park, and the thing she had fought in the gas station. They didn't have her yet, and she still had two bags. Filled with revulsion, determined to stay alive, she got up and went on.

But everything was locked up tight, not a sign of life anywhere. She looked speculatively at the elementary school, but the windows were wire glass. No good, it was just no good. Out of ideas, as hopeless and void as the nightmare city all around her, she saw ahead the ruined synagogue, steel door ajar on its hinges. There was something about the place she didn't like, that made her leery... A siren squawked behind her: a sector car, coming up Norfolk fast. That did it. She ran up the snow-covered steps and slipped through.

Once inside, her repugnance grew, and she paused, watching at the door. After the cops went past without slowing and disappeared around the corner, she was reluctant to go any further. The interior was very dim, only the vaguest light seeping in from the street lamps outside, so that its shape and extent were vague and uncertain, and a curious hush seemed to fill the place.

She got out a cigarette and lit it with shaking hands, telling herself to take it easy, just have a look around and make sure there was nobody there. She held the lighter up like a torch and took a few tentative steps into the nave. It was empty: she was alone beneath the high vaulted ceiling. The synagogue was no more than a shell, now: no pews, no furniture or decor of any kind, not even any trash —like it had been swept clean. She'd thought this was a shooting gallery, but now it seemed more like... something else. She wasn't sure; but as long as it was deserted, she ought to be safe until morning.

Near where the altar might have stood, the place was cold and drafty, and she turned back to the entrance, where she'd seen a door to one side. This opened on a set of stairs. Holding up the lighter, she made her way down the steps to another door, leading to a hallway, and came finally to a small room, cold but quiet and still. Like an office, it held a beat-up desk heaped with books and papers, some bookshelves, and an old swivel chair. A box of candles lay on the desk; she lit one, sat down. Dust coated everything: no one had been here for a long time, so maybe it was safe. Just sitting down was good, but she was so cold: her arms, legs, her whole body was shivering. She saw a metal waste can, and thought, *Why not? It's my night for setting fires.* The dry papers caught immediately, and soon the fire was warm, wonderfully warm. When the papers were gone she ripped pages out of the books and fed them to the flames. Some of the books were so old and tough she had to break them apart on the edge of the desk first; they were written in languages she couldn't even identify and the few illustrations were simply bizarre. She found it better not to look at them, but they made excellent fuel. In a little she warmed up, her circulation got going, and she out her works and cooked up a shot. She needed this. She had never needed it so bad in her life. It seemed as if her junk-starved cells had never felt such relief. Once she was straight, the whole awful night began to seem fuzzy and unreal. Now there was nothing but to wait for morning. Feeling safe enough, she smoked another cigarette, curled up in the chair with her jacket pulled tight around her, and went to sleep.

three

M half-stumbled, half-fell down the ice-covered steps of the entrance to the Fulton Street subway station. His broken rib was an agony and every muscle in his body ached but he was moving as fast as he could, on metabolic time. Below ground the illumination was poor, most of the lights out or broken, and it was still freezing cold but at least there was less wind. As best as he could tell, the place was deserted. Still, he crept through the maze of passages cautiously, watching his back, peeping around each corner and bend, listening intently, but he heard nothing, all was quiet, but for the hum of the generators.

When he reached the turnstiles he could barely see: the only light was that of early dawn filtering through the sidewalk grates. It appeared that a struggle had taken place at the token booths. The doors had been forced, and hung open on their hinges; here and there bullet holes starred the plexiglass; spent shell casings lay scattered about the floor, inside and out of the booth, amidst spatters and pools of blood. M didn't want to think about it, and kept going.

If he could get down onto the tracks, he figured he could follow them one way or another back to Loisaida, and his car, his miserable car. Why he had ever… he couldn't remember, couldn't imagine now why he'd ever gotten out of the car in the first place; he must have been out of his mind. He was full of rage, at himself, at the whole world, and he had to force himself to keep calm, to concentrate –to try and figure out what the hell he was going to do.

At least down in the tunnels he should be safer than out on the street. This far downtown, he didn't know the subway lines well… But he thought if he followed the 6 line to Broadway-Lafayette, he could get over to the F, and it would be just a short stretch to Second Avenue; he could get leave the station at Allen, at the far end, and from there go above ground to Ridge. He would just have to be very careful.

He squeezed through a turnstile and went down the steps to the platform, moving by feel. It was like descending into a pit. Even the emergency lights were out, and he wondered if the tracks still had power. He didn't want to get electrocuted; it would be tricky in the tunnels. Halfway down the stairs he froze, startled by a sound that took a moment to identify: the rumble, distant and muted, of an approaching train. He was astonished: the trains were running? In seconds, the rapidly mounting noise clarified itself: a downtown train, on the far side of the platform. He hesitated: should he get on it? These trains reversed direction, somewhere way downtown; but he didn't like the idea of going the wrong way, and what about the driver, or passengers? It was too late anyway: he saw a light in the tunnel, the headlight's beam splashing across the tile wall. Now as the noise grew incredibly loud, he realized it wasn't slowing for the station. Roaring, it fairly exploded out of the tunnel, running way too fast. M couldn't see the conductor, but every car, brilliantly illuminated, was completely empty. The light from the windows threw weird flickering shadows through the big empty station, eerily consonant with the motor's roar and the screeching wheels. Seconds later, it disappeared again into the tunnel, and the station went dark, the noise fading gradually.

So the tracks were electrified, but the rest –it was beyond understanding, incomprehensible, like so much else. Drained, out of strength, he swayed, gripped the handrail, sat down hard. His body ached as never before, cold intensifying the bruising; his nose was running, head pounding. He put his face in his hands and rubbed his eyes. If only he had some dope.

Okay! He had to think. What now? —but he couldn't, his brain had gone numb, his mind as empty as the station around him, filled only with despair. He coughed, rib stabbing him, and spit out phlegm that tasted like blood. He spit again, but the taste wouldn't go away. He ran shaky hands over his face, through his lank oily hair, scratching the itchy scalp. He couldn't take much more. Something had to give. He was about to come apart. How to pick a way through the tunnels if the trains were still running? But he didn't have any choice: going up on the streets was too dangerous, and he had to get moving. He didn't know how long he had.

The thought scared him. "Okay," he said out loud, got heavily to his feet. He was alright. He could make it. He would go on as he'd planned, through the tunnels. If a train was coming, he'd hear it and get out of the way. You could get off to the side; the subway crews worked down there all the time. He would just have to be careful about the third rail. As long as he kept it together, he'd be fine.

Down on the platform he couldn't see anything. He fumbled in his jacket, inside the pocket where the lining was ripped: Yes! A lighter! He pulled it out, flicked it: low but still working.

He held the flame above his head. The light was pitiful, just a vague glow that only carried a few feet, but better than nothing. He shuffled to the edge of the platform, looked down. Rats scurried away. He sat down on the edge, peered into the gloom below, trying to see the third rail, about to drop down onto the tracks when something, more felt than heard, stopped him where he was. He looked around, saw nothing, but he could hear it now: an approaching train. Foul, warmish air blew over his face. He stood again, squinting into the gloom below the station. There: an uptown train, running without lights but intermittently visible in the sparks thrown from arcing electrical connections. Judging from the sound, it was moving pretty slowly.

*I'll take it.* The downtown train had been running its lights: this might be a different train. Revulsion went through him: who —or *what* —was driving it? He thrust the thought from his mind.

The rumble of the wheels intensified; the bulk of the train suddenly emerged from the tunnel and rolled slowly forward with no sign of stopping. It was a J.

The first car passed him, not slowing. He began to run as the second car passed —but now the train accelerated, the lead car already about to re-enter the tunnel, wheels clattering over the rails and pulling away even as he ran harder and harder. The third car passed, doors closed —he'd have to get on between cars. Gasping, running as hard as he could, he jumped for the platform of the next-to-last car, reaching out for the ladder. The train lurched; he landed wrong, stumbled, fell, clutching at the safety chain —caught himself —and the car plunged into the sheer blackness of the tunnel.

His heart pounding, he clung to the back of the swaying car, trying to catch his breath. The train hammered over a long rough spot, still accelerating, gaining speed every moment. His hands were going numb, the din about to deafen him. He couldn't stay there, he had to get inside —check a map.

Apprehensive, he pulled himself up close to the door and opened it. A rush of lukewarm air hit him in the face. He slipped through, and fell against the bulkhead as the train lurched and the door slammed shut behind him. In the sudden relative quiet he could hear his own heart pounding. Now the lights flashed on, blinding him. He hunkered down, squinting and shielding his eyes, but the car was empty. The lights flickered, dimmed, went off again.

Now the car was swaying wildly. He pulled himself up, bracing his feet. Beyond the windows a station rushed past, cold dim daylight filtering down on graffiti-covered walls. For a moment he saw dark lumpish forms —bodies— lying prone and unmoving on the platform. Then they were gone. Find the map, he told himself. At this speed, he didn't have long.

He pulled his way forward by the seatbacks, stumbling and staggering against the momentum of the train. It was shaking and rattling like it would come apart. Metal howled, the hammering wheels jarring his bones. How much more could the thing take?

The lights came back on. He saw where the map should be: gone, the frame empty. He'd have to go on to the next car. The windows brightened suddenly: a station. He leaned over, looking out: Canal.

The platforms were brilliantly lit. Between the racing uprights, he saw a figure standing alone, turning to look at the train: a uniformed transit cop, his skin grotesquely pale, his face an empty malignant stare. Their eyes locked together. M shuddered, couldn't look away –till like a blow to the head, the car passed into the tunnel and the windows went black again. The station fell behind.

The lights flickered, went out. The air brakes slammed on, throwing him to the floor. He struggled back up, the car bucking and jerking as the train slowed down fast, then coasted along, lights slowly blinking back on. He moved to the forward door, opened it, and crossed to the next car. It looked empty. He punched the button and went through.

The door slammed shut behind him. The train was accelerating once more. The lights flickered, went out again. The car swayed drunkenly, the din unbearable. He hauled himself forward by feel, guessing at where the map would be, and wondering what he would do if the train didn't stop: jump? He wasn't going to have much time to decide.

As he approached the forward end of the car, his nostrils caught an acrid stench, raw and nauseating. When the lights came on again, he saw blood everywhere, spattered across the floor in pools and half-congealed rivulets, splashed on the walls, sprayed across the ceiling, puddling in the convex plastic seats. He swallowed hard, staring: what had happened here? It was smeared across the plexiglass protecting the map. He wiped the worst away on his sleeve. In the poor light, the tiny print was impossible to read, the color-coding indistinguishable. He leaned closer, trying to make it out. The J train went on to Brooklyn, then Queens; the last Manhattan stop was Essex Street.

The windows brightened, the noise opening up: Bowery. Not much time. How to get off? Wasn't there an emergency brake? He looked around, as if the answer could be read on the graffiti-scarred windows, or in the blood soiling the walls and floor. Then the door slammed open.

The *thing* –a transit cop –fixed its eyes on him, reached for its nightstick. M had had enough of *that*. He moved first, leaping forward and throwing a block that knocked the thing off balance. It toppled backward, its head slamming against the metal door. Adrenaline pumping, M stomped the wrist that fumbled for the gun, and kicked the thing hard across the temple. The lights were flickering crazily on and off. He saw its head driven to one side by the blow, roll around, the eyes closing, opening again. The thing twisted to one side, clutching at him, trying to throw him off balance. He kicked it again. Its lips writhed back in a mocking snarl.

He was gasping for breath now, his heart was hammering, his mind nothing but a red rage. He wanted to tear the thing apart with his bare hands, but it wouldn't die, couldn't even be hurt or slowed. He stomped down at its throat; it caught his boot. The train hit a rough spot, jumping and shaking, and braked hard. M lost his balance, fell; the thing scrabbled to its knees, pulling the gun. *This is it!*

He threw himself at the gun hand, smashed it back against a hand-pole. The gun went off like a cannon, 9mm shell ricocheting through the metal car; but he felt the wrist break, and the gun fell clattering to the floor. He snatched it up, wheeled, and at extreme close range put two shots, one after another, into the thing's right orbital.

It fell back. There wasn't much blood. It still faintly moved.

"Fuck you," M said, but he turned away, sick with revulsion and fear.

He checked the clip: four rounds. Reluctantly, he turned back, sat down on the seat nearest the body and searched it. He found two spare clips, put them in his pocket. All the time, he was trying not to look at the appalling wreck that had once been a cop, and a human being, like him. What was left of its face was scorched black from the muzzle blast, but the thing's one good eye still glared up at him.

Sighing, numbed and empty, he turned away, the gun like a hundred pounds in his hand. But now the door at the forward end of the car slammed open and two of them came through, one behind the other. They hardly glanced at the dead one on the floor, just headed straight for him, unlimbering their sticks. Was there hate in their empty eyes? Or just his own abhorrence, mirrored there?

He raised the gun and fired off two rounds. The first went wild, but the second took the lead cop full in the chest. The impact knocked it back against the other; they both fell, got back up and came for him again. Useless —he was wasting ammo.

He stuck the gun in his belt, smacked the door's button, and darted through when it slid open. Between cars the noise was roaring. He entered the next car and ran stumbling to the other end. As he went through the rear door, the forward one opened behind him.

Only one more car: what now? They were right behind! He looked around —trapped —and on impulse crawled up the handrails to the roof, holding on for dear life. It was a mistake: the jerking, bumping train felt like it was trying to shake him off; dust and grit whipped into his face, blinding him; the wind tore at his clothes, tugging at him, trying to pluck him loose. He could sense the roof racing past, just over his head.

The door below banged open. He struck out, kicking down as the thing came through —and even as he did it he realized he should have waited for the second. It was too late. Time seemed to dilate, as in a film when the action decelerates to slow motion: he saw his foot strike the thing hard between the shoulder blades, the force and impact almost throwing M from his perch; the thing toppled forward, taken by surprise and hurled off balance; its outstretched grasping hands missed the chain of the guard rail, slapped against the step, grabbing vainly, unable to hold; the tumbling body slipped down between the cars, visible there for a fraction of a second —head twisting, black depthless eyes seeking M —then disappeared. The wheels of the last car slashed over it, cutting it to pieces.

The second cop ducked back into the car below. M struggled to keep hold, fear and adrenaline giving him strength. One slip…

The tunnel ahead was brightening —the train was coming into Essex

Street. This is it, he told himself. One way or another, I'm getting *off*. His chest tightened. The noise of the wheels boomed in his ears like a rolling explosion. He tensed, ready to jump, took a deep breath. Okay... Get ready...

The train roared into the station and he blinked, dazzled by the sudden light. Move! Move! —and he jumped down from the ladder and hit the swaying step hard, off-balance; caught himself; threw one leg over the chain guard, holding tight to the hand rail; looked down at the concrete platform flying by, a blur like the runway seen from the window of a plane about to land; and he hesitated, his stomach knotting, dreading the fall...

Next to him the door slammed open and the other cop grabbed his arm and pulled, jerking him off balance. He threw his weight the other way, but the thing wouldn't let go; he couldn't break its grip. The station was rushing past, he could see it from the corners of his eyes; and time was collapsing, the seconds speeding up like a film projected too fast, though his movements were agonizingly slow, and ineffective, like in a dream. The thing's face leered into his, empty black eyes glinting with hate, lips snarled back in maddening triumph. M let go of the chain rail —only the thing's grip holding him now —and chopped down hard across its arm, twisting and pulling —no good —it held on, its mouth moving, laughing at him, dragging him inexorably back.

Infuriated, he pulled the 9mm automatic from his belt, fired point-blank into the thing's face. The hollow-point shell tore a gaping hole but the thing didn't let go. M brought the gun down, muzzle against the inner tendons of its wrist, fired again. Powder and burned flesh seared his nostrils, the thing's grip went slack, and he fell back, away from the train. A sickening moment of free-fall —he hit the platform hard —tried to roll —his head smacked concrete —he blacked out—

two

When he came to, he got up slowly, painfully, running a hand over his aching head and looking around at the station. The gun was lying on the platform a few feet away. When he bent over to pick it up, he thought he would pass out again. He limped toward the exit, waves of pain passing through him, went out the revolving door and slowly up the steps of the frozen escalator. Snow was drifted ankle deep at the exit door, and he saw no sign that anyone had passed that way recently. As he reached the top another train roared through the station without stopping, headed downtown at furious speed. He didn't even turn. The brute insanity of it all was exhausting; his dulled mind couldn't handle it.

Essex, though freshly plowed, was appallingly empty, and he paused on the threshold, uncertain, bracing himself. The Seventh Precinct was too close, he had to get away from Delancey; north on Essex was the only way. He stuck the gun in his belt, zipped up his coat, and set off warily, already shivering. It was hatefully cold. Shining from a bright and clear sky, rays magnified tenfold by the snowfall, the winter sun made it impossible to see, and the wind was blowing ice crystals that stung his eyes and abraded his skin. He put his hands in his pockets, trying to walk quickly, but the frozen sidewalk was hard going, and he kept turning to look back. Within half a block his nose was running uncontrollably and his feet had gone numb; every muscle in his body ached. He heard himself cursing over and over, like someone else speaking. He shook himself; he had to pull himself together.

At the corner of Rivington he peeped around the corner and ducked back as a sector car rolled southbound through the intersection a block east. Fear clutched at him: which way was it going? He crossed, heading north, then went east: Norfolk was one-way, and if he went up it maybe he could find cover before the cops came around again. No matter what, he had to get off Essex.

Norfolk was empty and he turned north again, hugging the storefronts on the west side and feeling terribly exposed by the vast empty playground opposite. But there was nothing in sight, no cops, no occupied cars, no people at all, and every door was locked, every storefront shuttered. He had never seen the city so utterly empty, so completely devoid of life. He didn't know where, but he had to cop, soon. It was cop some dope or die.

At Stanton he skirted a chain link fence around an empty lot and paused, squinting and straining his eyes, hoping desperately for an open door, a broken window. Maybe further up Norfolk, he wasn't sure: was there a door ajar? He crossed over. From the west came the sound of a car. He started, looked around: nothing in sight but –he couldn't believe it –the coke store between Norfolk and Essex was open. He laughed out loud and turned. The whole city had gone insane but this place was open for business. Well, that was fine with him, he could use it.

He rapped on the glass and the lock buzzed. The little store was soothingly warm, and he sighed with relief. The counter guy was young; he looked high as a kite.

"Cold out," M said. The guy just nodded, bored.

"Quiet morning?" M said.

"Yeah," the guy said, yawning. "Nobody around."

*Imagine that*, M thought.

"And the TV is broken," the guy said. He turned on an old black and white set that sat on the counter, flipped through the dial. "Look. It comes on but nothing." Every station was static.

"Why don't you play the radio?" M said.

"That's just it!" the guy shouted, laughing and slapping the counter with his hand. M flinched. "It's broken too. How many you want?"

"Two," M said, reaching for his wallet –but of course it was gone. The guy ducked beneath the counter to get the stuff. *The hell with it.* He pulled out the gun, feeling bad about it, and brought it down on the guy's head as he came up. He slumped to the floor. M tensed, listening, ready to fire; nothing happened. He went around behind the counter, checked the back room: empty. The counter guy was still breathing. M felt better about it: at least he hadn't killed him.

He knelt, picked up the two bags the guy had dropped, and dug around until he found the stash: eighteen or twenty in all. He put all but one in his pocket, opened it up and dumped in on the counter. The count was big. He mashed it up into one long line, rolled a bill from the register into a tube, and did it up in two snorts. The stuff slammed into his brain like a runaway train.

He sighed with satisfaction, filled with new life, and looked down at the open register full of money, mostly tens and twenties. That would buy a lot of dope. He scooped it up and put it in his pockets.

The guy on the floor moaned, stirred a little. M zipped up his coat and went to the door. He had to get moving, he couldn't stay here. The place was too hot; he was a sitting duck.

He cracked the door, looked both ways –clear –and he was back on the street, moving quickly along the slippery sidewalk. He was up again, wired and ready to go, but twice as sensitive to the cold; he could hardly take it. The wind was blowing even harder now, just cutting through him, and the clouds of ice particles burned his face and hands like frozen fire.

His head was pounding, his nasal passages seared by the cheap drugs. He was trying to hurry now and that was a mistake: as he crossed diagonally through the intersection of Stanton and Norfolk, a sector car rolled through Stanton and Suffolk a block away. The brakes locked up and the car slid past the corner. M took off at a run. He heard the cop throw it into reverse, wheels spinning; he turned up Norfolk, out of sight for a moment. He had to find somewhere to hide, now.

He was cursing: nothing, the whole street bolted, shuttered, grated, locked tight. The cop's motor was roaring; he had only seconds now; he was slipping and sliding, his hand on the gun, ready to shoot it out for all the good it would do. To his right, he saw the old synagogue —and maybe his one chance: between it, and the neighboring tenement, a narrow foot passage lead away from the street. The wrought-iron gate stood ajar. He fled down the narrow cleft, and when the sector car cruised past, swish of tires in the snow, he was flat against a rear wall, gasping for breath in the frigid air, his heart about to burst.

The cop car crawled up the street and finally passed from earshot. He'd lost them. He looked around: in front of him was a small building hidden from the street, only four stories tall and much older than the tenements looming higher on all sides. Though intact, it had the desolate air of being abandoned. Or at least he hoped so. It would do. Anywhere to hole up for a minute, get out of the wind, let things cool off.

He hefted the gun, scanned about in all directions —no one —and cautiously picked his way to the entrance. It had no knob, just a round hole in the metal where the knob had been, and the door swung open at his touch. He stepped through, closed it gently behind him. The corridor was very dim, and he waited, listening, as his eyes adjusted to the dark, but heard nothing: no voices or sounds of movement, no noise at all. Even the sound of the wind was distant and extenuated, the surrounding buildings sheltering this place —a dead building in a dead city.

He went up the stairs with extreme caution, nerves jangling, his steps seeming to ring through the whole structure. The gun in his hand, he was so jacked up he might have shot anything that moved. But the place was empty. At the third floor, he paused, enervated and indecisive, his head swimming as he leaned against the wall. A slight breeze of cold air came down the stairwell.

He'd thought to go to the top, but maybe the roof was bad. Better to stop here. He looked around at the five doors on the landing. Did anyone live here?

On the west side was a shabby, frail-looking door, of laminated wood. He tried the knob: locked, but flimsy. He looked around and raised the gun, grinding his teeth —took a deep breath, reared back and slammed his foot against it, dropping into a firing stance as the door banged open.

Nothing happened. He waited a beat, stepped over the threshold, swinging the gun in a covering arc, and kicked the door closed again. Nothing: a jumble of cast-off furniture and trash, dust everywhere. He swept the rest of the apartment: two other tiny rooms, a bedroom and a kitchen, claw-footed bathtub against one wall, the toilet in a closet. The place was clear —he was alone, no one there. He lowered the gun, his hands shaking. A line would do him some good, he'd have a line.

He sat down on the ratty sofa, gun beside him, and rubbed his eyes —then remembered the door and heaved himself to his feet again. The lock was useless now, of course. He cast about, hardly able to think, and finally found a battered folding chair, collapsed it, and wedged it under the knob. It wouldn't hold much but it would make a lot of noise, and that was the best he could do right now. He flopped back down beside the gun.

Okay, he told himself. Take it easy. Relax. One thing at a time. He leaned back, rubbed his eyes again; if only he had a cigarette. Instead he got out two bags of coke and dumped both on a rickety table. The stuff was mostly rocks, one as big as a marble. He went into the kitchen and found an old butter knife in the back of a drawer, chopped the stuff into big fat lines and snorted them up one after another.

It hit his bloodstream fast and hard. For a while he got up and paced around, walking from room to room, looking out the filmy windows at nothing, his mind an incoherent jumble. But it wore off fast. Afraid to sleep, he did another whole bag, the stuff really burning now, clogging his nose, some of it falling back out again, his upper lip dusted with it. He went back in the kitchen and ran some water on his fingers, held his head back so the water ran down his nose, the back of his throat burning now and his whole mouth and head tasting like cheap cocaine; when he straightened up the water dripped back out of his nose and he wiped it away and saw his fingers pink with diluted blood. He wiped them on his pants. Somehow even more tired now than before, he went back to the couch and lay down, holding the gun across his chest. His eyes closed, waves of fatigue passing over him as, still cranking, he dropped into a shallow, nervous sleep.

one

Shivering, Steph awoke in the strange room, now dark again, the air like the inside of a refrigerator. For a moment, she was confused —couldn't remember where she was, or how she'd gotten there —and then it all came back in an awful rush. She pulled her coat around her and lit a cigarette. Her limbs were stiff, she ached like she'd been beaten up, and she needed to get straight. But this was her last bag. She cooked up a shot, booted it, and slumped back in the chair, closing her eyes as relief coursed through her veins. When she woke up again she had no idea how long she'd been nodded out, and right away she got a panicky feeling: the stuff hadn't seemed very strong. What if... She had to score some more. She felt okay, but it wouldn't last. Time to get moving —no way to know where she could cop. Still, someplace *had* to be open.

She felt her way back up the stairs to the door. Outside, it was quiet, very quiet, the streets as empty as Christmas morning. She didn't like it; it was all wrong. The air was frigid, painful to breathe, but the snow had stopped and the sun was shining, its light sparkling over the snow-covered streets. She wondered what time it was, and hesitated in the doorway, looking left and right, trying to think. Where should she go —who would be open? It was too cold to just walk around hoping to get lucky. No reason to go north: the main spots, the Dope House, Laundromat, wouldn't open until dark, if then; Thirteenth was too far, and uncertain anyway; Avenue D was only a last resort. To get to Ludlow she'd have to cross Delancey, and the Seventh precinct was right there –no good. Clinton was closest, but the quality was so uneven and you ran the risk of getting beat –a risk she couldn't take. She'd have to try Ridge. If DOA wasn't open, maybe somebody would be on the corner of Rivington.

She got out her money and counted it: not much, but she couldn't think about it now; the first thing was to go out and cop. She took a deep breath. The most important thing was to be careful. Put her radar up. She shuddered, memories from the night before coming unwanted into her mind as she picked her way down the slick, snow covered steps.

She turned south toward Stanton, keeping a sharp eye and staying close to the wall. The crunch of her boots in the snow was loud in her ears and she worried someone would hear. It was bitterly cold: the icy air tightened the skin of her face, gusts of wind brought tears to the corners of her eyes that tried to freeze; she wiped them away, put her hands back in her pockets. It was only five blocks. If DOA was open, maybe they would let her warm up inside for a while. Maybe even stay. She didn't follow the thought, but she was getting desperate… She'd been almost that desperate before.

*I must look like hell.* She veered toward a parked car, examined her face in the side mirror. She looked bad alright: pale, dark circles under her eyes, nose red and runny… She put on some lipstick, numb hands almost smearing it. It didn't help much.

Behind her came the sound of a vehicle on Houston. She ducked behind a parked car, peered around the fender. It passed, going east: a sector car. *They* were still out there. She'd better be careful.

She waited until the sound faded to nothing, turned the corner and made her way east on Stanton, looking in all directions and straining her ears. Suffolk was quiet and empty, the block-long stretch of vacant lots like a graveyard buried in snow. At the far corner, the old polytechnic school loomed, a gothic fortress. None of the sellers were out. She was feeling more and more uneasy.

Clinton too was empty, and she stopped at the corner for a moment, looking at the long lines of parked cars covered in snow. The street showed tire-tracks but the sidewalks were undisturbed. Was it still too early? But even when the sellers weren't out, the buyers usually were, dope-sick men and women impatient and nervous. Most days, you could cop at dawn, but here it was, broad daylight, and no one out at all.

Now a car turned up the street off Delancey. She panicked: without waiting to see, she fled east on Stanton, pushing at entrance doors as she passed. Like a miracle, one opened, and she jumped inside. But the inner door was locked. Trapped now, she crouched down, staying low and peering warily through the wire glass. She could hear it coming, slow and purposeful. She held her breath, trying to slow the pounding of her heart.

A sector car rolled into view. Had they seen her? She ducked down; what to do if it stopped? But there was nowhere to go–

It stopped. Her blood went cold. She pressed herself against the door, trembling and trying to make herself small. Above the noise of the idling motor she heard both doors open and shut, then footsteps crunching in the snow. Her arms and legs were tingling and she could see the vapor rising from her own breath. She tried to stop –they'd find her–

The steps came nearer; a door rattled. *They know I'm here and they're looking for me!* Steps, another door, more steps –close now. The foyer dimmed, a shadow in the window above…

Static spewed, a garbled voice squawked: the cop's radio. She was shaking violently, clenching her teeth. The radio spluttered again, and the footsteps retreated, the car doors opened, shut again, and the car drove away, tires slicing through the snow.

Steph couldn't believe it. Unsteady, little tears in the corner of each eye, she rose up, peeked out the window. The street was empty again. She leaned against the wall, drained now, trying to pull herself together. How much more of this she could take? But she had to cop. After that… After that she didn't know what she would do.

The street was still empty. She eased open the door, looked both ways, slipped out, and headed east as quickly as she could. Her tracks were clear in the untouched snow; anyone could have seen where she'd been. How she'd gotten away… She put it out of her mind.

Attorney was quiet, the garages all closed and empty taxis parked up and down the block. Ahead, she saw a figure appear at the corner of Ridge.

She ducked into a doorway, peeked around. He wasn't a cop: a man in jeans, boots, a heavy snow jacket, the fur-lined hood zipped completely over his head, walking back and forth with the purposeful idleness of the seller. *Yes! Thank God!*

She looked around, headed straight for him. He saw her half a block away, looked her over, and went back to watching the street. She smiled as she came up. He grinned: a young Puerto Rican with a long knife scar seaming one cheek and several teeth missing. He looked high as a kite.

"Hi," she said. He just kept grinning, looking back and forth from her to the street. Finally he said, "What's up?"

"Looking for *manteca*," she said. "What you got?"

"R.I.P. How many?"

"One, I guess," she said. "I was looking for DOA"

"They ain't open," he said.

She hesitated, thinking that might or might not be true.

"You want it or not?" he said.

"Yeah," she said. "Give me one." She gave him the money; he passed her a plastic-covered glassine. "Okay," she said. "See you later."

"Won't be here long," he said. "Too fucking cold."

She went on down the street, but he'd told her the truth: DOA wasn't open. At least she'd gotten something. Maybe she should have gotten two, but it might be beat —though it sure looked like *he* had gotten off.

Rivington was empty when she reached the corner, mute tenements and shuttered storefronts stretching away in both directions. A frigid wind was blowing, clouds of ice particles stinging her face. She turned back west, moving warily but going as fast as she could. Past the playground the street was still empty but someone had been there, for the snow was trampled and dirty. Clinton was clear and she turned north, wanting to avoid the big empty school grounds between Norfolk and Suffolk, but halfway up the block she heard a siren in the distance. She ducked into a doorway, but it passed away to the north. Freezing, she pushed on.

At Stanton she peeped around the corner: still nothing. That was good, she was almost there —and she slipped along the crosstown block like a ghost, every step bringing her that much closer. She wondered about the time: it felt early, and maybe DOA would open up later… Suffolk was clear, and she crossed to the north side of the street, where she could plainly see her own tracks going east. She scuffed through them, hoping to obscure her own trail a little. Only a block to go, if only her luck would hold —and she told herself not to even think about it. But still everything was cool, here was Norfolk, no cops in sight, and in a minute she'd be there…

At the steps of the synagogue she heard the sound, faint at first, so unexpected that it took her a moment to identify it. She paused and it hit her – no way –was it her imagination? But it came closer: a motorcycle engine, the rumble of a chopper. One of the boys? *Oh God, please!* She took off at a run toward Houston, slipping and sliding, the cops forgotten, desperate to get there, because if it was one of them she'd be alright —she wouldn't be alone any more…

The bike passed, going east, before she got to the corner. Her heart leapt into her throat: it was *him!* It was Suicide! He was alive, *alive* –it was all going to be okay! She waved her arms, cried out, "Hey! Hey!" at the top of her lungs, still running.

He'd seen her! Twisting around, he turned his head toward her, mirrored sunglasses reflecting snow. The rumbling bike made a tight circle, sliding a little on the snow-covered street, straightened out and came back fast. She was clapping her hands and laughing, blinking back tears of relief. "Suicide!" she shouted, her voice drowned by the motor. "I can't believe it! Suicide! Oh, God,

I'm so glad to see you!"

He rolled up to the curb, shut it down and climbed off. She threw herself on him, hugging him tight: "I'm so glad to see you. I've been so scared. Oh, you don't know, it's been awful… I thought…"

He took hold of her arms, hard.

"Hey," she said. "Look out, that hurts… Are you okay?"

He didn't answer.

"Suicide, baby… are you okay?"

He opened his mouth. A gargling sound came out. "No-o-o…" she moaned, twisting, trying to pull away. He wouldn't let go. She beat at him with her fists, striking his face, knocking away the mirror-shades. He glared down at her from flat, black eyes.

She started to scream.

zero

When M came to, he had the shakes bad, and when the first thing he did was chop another big line and snort it up, it didn't help things much. He couldn't believe he'd fallen asleep –he was just lucky… He couldn't think about it. The first thing to do was get some dope: that was obvious. The clock might be running down *right now*, he wasn't going to let it happen to *him*. He had enough cash for at least a couple of bundles, and if he could just get the car… After that his thoughts ran into a brick wall; he had no idea what he would do then. But first things first.

He got a drink from the kitchen faucet, took a piss in the wretched bathroom, went back to the couch and did another big line. Totally wired, he paced up and down through the narrow rooms, looking out the dingy windows and scratching himself, his nasal passages on fire. The coke was all he could taste now, the stuff falling back out of his nose and sprinkling down the front of his shirt. He checked the gun, loaded a fresh clip, and counted the money: four hundred sixty dollars. That was fine, he'd get four bundles. He folded together four hundred –he wasn't going to waste time bargaining, he'd pay full price, what did he care –and put it in his pants, stuck the rest in his shirt pocket. Plenty left for gas, when it came to that. If it came to that.

He told himself to get moving, stood up, decided he'd have one more line. He cut another huge rail, looked at it. It was pointless. He snorted it up anyway.

Now he was grinding his teeth like a son of a bitch and his temples were starting to throb. He stood up, stuck the gun in his belt, looked around: did he have everything? Maybe; he wasn't sure. But he was wasting time, he had to get going.

He took the folding chair from under the doorknob, eased open the door. Of course the hall was empty. Shaking from all the coke, he sniffled, coughed, spit out a huge lump of phlegm, began to shiver and couldn't stop. *You are a mess,* he thought.

He eased back down the stairwell with his hand on the butt of the gun, but the building was as quiet and empty as a tomb. At the front door he realized he had no idea where to cop. He looked at his watch, but the hands hadn't moved since the last time he looked at it. He shook it: broken. Maybe Ridge, if they were open; at least that was close to the car. He'd take anything at this point, but he wanted his damned car back.

When he went out the door the icy air smacked him in the face; the mucus ran from his nose over his lip. He wiped it away with the back of his hand and saw blood smeared there. "Fuck this," he mumbled out loud.

Fuck everything, just go and cop. He trudged wearily back the way he had come, aching all over and already starting to come down off the coke. But just as he turned between buildings, somebody —a woman —passed in front of him, going up the sidewalk on Norfolk. He flattened himself against the wall, hand on the gun, but she was familiar. He *knew* her —but how?

It hit him —she was the junkie chick, the girl he'd stopped —what, last night? —when the whole nightmare was just beginning. The blonde from Ridge, with the DOA. She might still be okay —he had to catch her—

She was already out of sight. He almost called out, though she might not be that happy to see him… But if she'd been through anything like he had, they could help one other. He hustled to the sidewalk, not even thinking to check the street. She was at the corner of Houston, waving her arms in the air, and he heard the sound of a motor. He stopped, unsure what to do, as a biker came into sight, riding a big chopper.

M hung back, apprehensive. They hadn't seen him; he wasn't sure he wanted them to. The bike came to a stop, the guy climbed off and the girl threw herself on him. *Her old man*, M thought. This may not be so good... The biker was tall and skinny, dressed in leather, his colors over the jacket. He seemed to move funny... A chill went through M.

The girl started screaming and he knew he was right. He took off running toward them, tugging the gun from his belt. The biker was holding her as she struggled, hitting at him, thrashing around; she couldn't get free. Trying not to fall, M thumbed off the safety. *If you had any brains*, he thought, *you'd stay out of this*. But pent-up rage and fear had taken hold of him; he was cranked on adrenaline and cheap cocaine, the helpless frustration of it all. *She* was still normal –*he* wouldn't let that *thing* get her–

The biker pinned her arms behind her back and dragged her toward his machine. She struggled, kicking against his knees and shins, but he ignored her, didn't even feel it. She was screaming and cursing at the top of her lungs. When she saw M coming she yelled, "Help! Help me!"

Maybe thirty feet away, M slid to a stop, went into a crouch with the gun aimed at the thing's head. "Hold it!" he yelled hoarsely. "N.Y.P.D.! Let her go!"

The thing paid no attention. He tried to steady the gun but his hands were shaking. Loathing boiled within him. He wanted to blow its head off but he couldn't get a shot. "I said let her go!"

The thing turned, looked at him, a sort of sneer on its face. He looked into its eyes: empty black pools of nothing, a depthless blank; the void he saw in them was nauseating. His stomach heaved; a burning taste of vomit seeped back up his throat. He winced, blinked his eyes, sight wavering.

"Shoot!" the girl cried, trying to throw herself down. "Shoot him!"

He blinked, sighted again, exhaled, squeezed the trigger. The bullet caught it in the shoulder, knocked it back off balance. The girl twisted and jerked free. She fell to her knees, scrambled up and ran toward him. As she went past, he fired twice more, gnashing his teeth together in wired rage. The shots hit the thing dead in the chest, knocked it backwards to the ground. He turned to follow the girl. She slipped and fell in front of him; he grabbed her by the wrist, jerked her up, and ran, dragging her along behind. She was saying something but he couldn't hear, ears ringing from the gunshots.

He looked back. The thing was getting to its feet. He fired again, missed –kept going. Sobbing, the girl was trying to keep up. He was already winded, each breath a stabbing frozen agony, pain searing his sides. Behind them the chopper's motor coughed, caught and revved. He let go of the girl's wrist, yelled, "Run!" into her ear, and turned to see the thing straddle the bike and roll it up over the curb. It slid on the snow, straightened; the thing opened up the throttle. M heard the girl shriek. He turned: she was right behind him, shivering, her eyes glazed. "Run!" he yelled. "Go, go!"

*Fuck it*, he thought, turning back. The thing was bearing down on him, the bike's motor a hammering roar. He went into a firing stance, sighting down the barrel of the automatic. "Come on!" he muttered, teeth clenched. "I'm gonna waste you!"

As it neared the synagogue, the thing popped a wheelie, M dead in its path. Its face was a leering skull, pallid skin taut over jutting bone, eyes shining with poisonous life. "Fuck... you... you... bastard," M grunted, squeezing the trigger at each word, aiming for the bike. The rear tire blew; the bike sheered over and went down, slamming the thing down with it, pinning it between the frame and the synagogue steps. Motor still racing, the rear wheel spun the bike around in a semicircle, raking it against concrete, the thing struggling to free its crushed leg. The tank ripped open in a spray of sparks and the gasoline exploded, the detonation shattering. M threw himself down, covering his face; fragments of metal rained down all around. He moaned, pain jabbing through each ear; he felt dizzy; the explosion must have burst his eardrums. He got to his hands and knees, then to his feet, looked around. The girl was leaning against the synagogue fence, crying. The thing, charred and blackened, was still moving weakly, amidst the wreckage. M gagged, bent over and threw up.

Shuddering, he spit, trying to get the taste out of his mouth, and straightened slowly. He'd dropped the gun. Hands shaking, he picked it up, ejected the empty clip and threw it away, loaded another one. His soul was poisoned, tainted by everything that had happened, everything they had done to him, everything he had done. But he had to finish it.

Without looking at the girl he walked back to the wreck and looked down at the thing still feebly stirring, one fist clenching and unclenching. The fire had died quickly but the air was filled with a sickening burnt smell, scorched flesh and gasoline; the snow, melted in a broad circle, was already starting to re-freeze. The thing's skin, reddish-black, was shriveled and cracked; the lips were burnt away, exposing the clenched teeth, yellow and rotten; the eyes gone, it still seemed to glare up at him from the empty sockets. The girl's sobs were the only sound he could hear, muffled and vague. He couldn't look at her. With a sigh, he brought the muzzle point-blank to the thing's forehead, pulled the trigger. There was a dull report, and the skull disintegrated; fragments of bone scattered; the bullet ricocheted away. The thing slumped, stopped moving.

He turned away, went slowly back to the girl. He didn't know what to do. He could barely hold himself up, and he was absolutely drained, just an empty shell; he didn't know how much longer he could go on. But they couldn't just stand there. The girl's face was pale as death, she looked exhausted and weak. He felt sorry for her. "Are you okay?" he said. His voice sounded strange, buzzing in his ears.

She nodded, looking away, shivering uncontrollably. M was freezing too, his hands and feet numb, and his nerves bad; he felt exposed and uptight. They were too vulnerable here. He hesitated, said, "Look, we ought to try and get inside somewhere, out of the cold."

She nodded again, saying, "Yeah, I… Come on."

He was thinking of the apartment building but she led him to the synagogue instead. Neither of them looked at the wreck; they went quickly up the steps and into the ruined building. M felt a little warmer out of the wind, and he followed her, looking around with dull curiosity. As she led him down a set of stairs, holding up a lighter to show the way, he said, "You been holed up in here?"

"Yeah," she said. "Do you know what time it is?"

"No," he said. "My watch is broken." The girl just nodded. They came into a room like an office, with a desk and chair, some books and papers lying around. The place smelled like burnt trash. The girl sat down and began ripping pages out of a book, crumpling them into a waste can.

"That's a good idea," he said. "I'll help you." He dumped out a crate of books and sat down on it, and they fed them into the fire. The smoke stung his eyes and nostrils but he was glad to feel some warmth. They sat a while in silence. M was numb, he couldn't imagine how she felt. She took out a cigarette.

"Hey, could you spare one of those?" he asked. She just handed him the pack. "Thanks," he said, and sat there looking at it between drags.

"Look," she said abruptly. "I remember you from last night, so… I guess you remember me." She looked him in the eyes. "I hope you don't care, but no matter what, I've got to get straight." She pulled out her works and lay them on the desk.

"Hey," he said. She looked up. "What's your name?"

"Steph," she said.

"Listen, Steph," he said. "I guess you know that stuff's all that's keeping us alive." She nodded. "How many you do you have?"

"One," she said. "That, and thirty bucks… Then I don't know what's going to happen."

"Look at this," he said, pulling the wad of money from his pocket. "I need a bag, too —bad. Split that one with me, and then we'll go cop, and we'll both be good, as long as it lasts."

She looked at him for a long time, as if trying to decide if she could trust him.

"How much you got?" she said at last.

"Four hundred," he said, riffling the bills.

"Why do you want to share that with me?"

"Because I need some right now," he said. "I'm scared of what's gonna happen if I don't. And because I don't want to be alone." She didn't answer, but she didn't want to be alone either. Four bundles was a lot of dope –but could she trust him? He'd already ripped her off for one, and he *was* a cop…

"Look," he said. "We can help each other. I've got the money… You know that place on Ridge, and my car is right near there. But we've got to do something… before… like, I don't want it to happen to me… and I'm not sure how long it's been…"

She thought about it happening again, right there, and made up her mind. "Okay…" she said, "but, like, you've got your own works, right?"

"No," he said. "I'm not into needles. I'll just snort it up."

She looked at him in disbelief, but he was serious. She shrugged, said, "Okay."

The bag wasn't real big but not tiny either, and the stuff was a pale beige: that could be good. She cut it in half, trying to be fair, and scraped her part into the spoon. "Okay," she said, cooking it up.

He snorted the line up in one go and straightened, his head back, holding his nose and trying not to sneeze. Nothing happened for a second, then warm relief oozed down his spine. He sat down, closing his eyes and sighing. Thank God: he'd never needed it so bad in his life. When he opened his eyes again she was looking at him.

"You do yours?" he said.

"Ten minutes ago," she said. She was smoking another cigarette. "You nodded out."

He pointed to the pack and she nodded.

"Feel better?" she said.

He nodded back. They sat there a while in silence. He kept thinking about the biker-thing he'd killed –Steph's old man, he guessed. He couldn't bring himself to ask. He couldn't think of anything to say. There wasn't anything to say. He was so tired, and even the dope hadn't eased the pain of his aching, bruised body.

She was watching him, curled up small, picking at her chapped lips with a finger. The half-bag had helped, but how much had it done for him? She didn't want to take any chances. Survival was all that mattered now. Everything else had died inside her: she couldn't think, she couldn't feel, she didn't care.

He stirred himself, stood up; rubbed his eyes and scratched his itching scalp; looked again at his useless watch. "What time did you tell me they opened up over there?"

"By now, I guess," she said. "If they're going to open at all."

He nodded. "Maybe we'd better go."

"That's probably a good idea."

He looked around: the gun was at his feet; when had he put it down there? He picked it up, checked it: that's right, he had reloaded. He stuck it in his belt, felt aimlessly through his pockets.

Steph picked up her pack of cigarettes –two left –and stashed them away. She was feeling more and more nervous. She didn't really want to go down to the spot with this cop. Sure, they needed the dope –but him taking the gun was just a bad idea. But what choice did she have now? Still, she couldn't believe it when he sat back down and took out a big bag of cocaine.

"You want a line?" he said, crushing the stuff up on the desk.

"No," she said. "You think that stuff's a good idea? It'll bring you down off the dope."

"Naww," he said. "Besides, right now I don't think I can do this without it." He honked up half the gram in one loud snort.

*Great, a cokehead*, she thought. *Those four bundles are really going to last us a long time.*

She couldn't believe how bad he looked: pale, dirty and ragged, cut and bruised, spotted here and there with dried blood. His hands were trembling and his face twitched; he obviously hadn't slept in days. When he glanced at her his eyes were wired tight. *This is hopeless*, she thought. *We're already as good as dead.*

He looked at the other line. No point in wasting it. He snorted it up. "Let's go".

Steph zipped up her coat and led the way back out of the synagogue. Night had fallen. It was even colder than before, if that were possible. The streets were utterly empty and very dark; for some reason, most of the streetlamps were out. The quiet now was palpable, impossible to ignore.

They slipped down Norfolk to Stanton, went east. Steph's teeth chattered at every gust of wind. M felt something warm on his upper lip; he wiped it away: blood. Suffolk was empty, no sound of a car anywhere. They trudged on, moving as fast as possible. The way was hard going, the frigid air difficult to breathe. Clinton, too, was deserted: no cops, no sellers, no junkies, no nothing. He was grinding his teeth: this was starting to be very bad. They kept going. Attorney: nothing. They heard a car behind them, to the west, and ducked into a doorway. It passed, going north, without slowing down, blocks away.

"I couldn't tell," he said.

"Me neither," Steph said. "C'mon, it's freezing."

Ridge was empty. It didn't look good at all.

"Up here," he said, turning the wrong way. Steph looked at him. "My car," he said.

It was still there, he couldn't believe it. That was the first decent thing that had happened since… since all of it. Maybe his luck was starting to change.

"Maybe I should start it," he said. "Warm it up."

"I think when you start that thing, you better be ready to *go*," Steph said.

He thought about it. "Maybe you're right."

"Come on," Steph said. "Let's get this over with, then we can do one while the car's warming up. Unless," she added, "you want to wait while I go."

He shook his head. "No," he said. "I think we better both go."

*He doesn't trust me.* She didn't blame him; she didn't trust him, either.

They turned back, stopped again at the corner and looked warily around: still clear.

"Okay," he said. "Tell me again how you do it."

"If the front door's open, you just go in," Steph said, thinking how they'd had this same conversation the night before under very different circumstances. "It's on the second floor. You knock on the door and they look at you through the peephole, and if they know you're cool they open up and you go in. That's it."

"You think they got lookouts?"

"Probably, but I don't really know. They know me; I just hope we don't have any trouble because of you –though you don't look much like a cop right now." She laughed, but went on: "Whatever you do, don't let them see that damned gun. This place is serious, they wouldn't think twice about killing us."

He nodded, checked the money.

"Okay," he said. "You do the talking. Just tell 'em I'm your friend, and we want four bundles."

Steph nodded. *Jesus*, she thought, *you want to tell me how to shake my ass too?* I've probably been doing this longer than *you* have.

He was still watching over his shoulder, but the street was absolutely empty. What if the place wasn't open? They'd have to find another spot fast. Lots of places didn't open up till midnight –but they couldn't wait until midnight. Maybe the girl knew another place. Even if they couldn't get it all –if they could just score a few, or even a couple would do.

They were there. He looked around, followed her up the half-flight of steps. She pushed on the door. It opened. They went in, shut it behind them. The building was quiet. He looked at her. She pointed to the stairs. He nodded. She went up first, he followed, out of habit watching the sway of her hips, grinning as he ground his teeth. She was cute –he'd thought that the first time he saw her.

She stopped before a door at the top of the stairs, gave him a heads-up, tried to smile and knocked sharply. Nothing happened. "Come on," she muttered, and knocked again.

They heard steps. His nerves were jumping and he was sweating; he hadn't even noticed that the building was warm. After a pause, the door opened.

A big Puerto Rican stood in the doorway. The room was dark but there was light behind him from another room. M couldn't see back there, couldn't tell what was going on. The dealer frowned at Steph, then looked at him, eyes narrowing. "Yeah?" he said. "What you want?"

Steph was taken back. "*Holà*," she said quietly. "*Yo quiero manteca.* DOA."

"Who's he?" the big guy said, pointing his chin at M. Steph smiled a little, looking into the dealer's eyes. "He's my friend," she said. "He's okay." She didn't feel good about saying it, but she wanted him to believe her, bad. The Puerto Rican looked hard at M. A long time seemed to pass.

"Okay, how many?" he said.

"Four bundles," Steph said.

"Okay," he said, glancing back. "Come in here, don't stand in the hall." He stepped aside.

M didn't like this, but he followed Steph through the door. The big guy was holding it; they went past him and stopped in the middle of the empty room; he pushed it to, not really shutting it. Another, smaller man came up behind him, said, "How many?"

"Four bundles," Steph said.

He nodded, his eyes shifting from side to side. "Okay," he said, turning away. "Wait a minute." He went back to the kitchen and disappeared from sight.

Steph heard him say something in Spanish; she couldn't understand it. A drawer opened, then shut. The big guy waited next to them. M kept looking back and forth; this didn't feel right, and he didn't like the look on Steph's face. Steph was shifting her weight from foot to foot, trying not to look nervous, trying to smile. The smaller man came back, bundles in his hand: "Okay, four hundred."

M pulled the money from his pocket and handed it to him. The seller counted it quickly but carefully. "Okay," he said. "Here you go."

M took them, mumbling thanks, and the guy turned away. M looked at Steph and nodded. She grinned —she couldn't believe it, they had it! —and turned to go. M stuffed the bags in a pocket and turned to follow her. The big guy was looking past them, hadn't opened the door. M sensed what was coming, but didn't want to believe it. Behind them, the seller said: "Okay, hold it."

*It's a rip-off!* Steph thought —and she jumped for the door, yanked it open. Startled, the big guy grabbed her wrist and pulled her back, hard. Despairing, M tugged the gun from his belt and turned quick. A third guy stood there, holding a small automatic pistol: he fired —missed —fired again. The second shot hit M high in the left shoulder, slapping him back off balance. The wound was searing; his vision starred; he swung the 9mm up, fury going through him like a rush, and fired. His shot took the other man in the chest, slamming him back against the wall. M spun, stuck the gun in the big guy's belly and fired two, three times, the slugs ripping up through the body cavity. The big guy sagged backwards, moaning pitifully and clutching at his midsection, then collapsed.

Steph jerked her arm free and stumbled out the door, horrified and sick inside. "Go!" M yelled. The third guy was pulling a gun. Backing out the door, M fired and missed, then grabbed Steph and pushed her ahead of him down the steps.

The seller appeared in the doorway, ducked back, took aim and fired. The bullet smacked into the wall next to M's head. "Move!" he said to Steph. He took aim, fired. The seller bounced into sight. They both fired again. The seller toppled, shot through the eye, but something hit M in the stomach —a red-hot fist punching through his guts and out the small of his back, knocking the breath out of him. He groaned; black spots exploded in front of his eyes; his knees buckled, legs unable to support him; he fell. The pain was awful. He tasted blood in his mouth.

Below him, Steph cried out and came running back. She knelt beside him, hands fluttering. He tried to get up and couldn't. His face was deathly pale and he was gnashing his teeth. "Don't move," she said. What should she do? My God!

"The keys," she blurted. She had a sickening feeling that all this had happened before. "Gimme the keys and I'll go get the car."

He was trying to say something. Flecks of blood appeared on his lips. Now sirens moaned in the distance. She couldn't think about it.

"Come on!" she said. "We've got to get out of here!" She started searching his pockets.

He shook his head a little. "Here," he said thickly. He was trying to hand her something. She took it: not the keys, but the bundles of dope. She just looked at them.

"Go," he said, and added, with an effort: "I... I'm not gonna make it." His eyes closed.

The sirens –she couldn't ignore them –the sirens were getting closer.

"Go," he whispered.

She crouched there a moment, not really seeing him –thinking about Joker, and Patty, and Suicide. But the sirens were coming down the street. She pocketed the bundles and picked up the gun he had dropped. It was awful, all of it. It made her sick –she'd never get over it.

Sirens screaming now, and she heard brakes locking up, tires sliding on snow. "Bye," she whispered. She squeezed his hand, and went down the steps fast without looking back. Car doors slammed as she reached the bottom. No way out the front, and she turned to the back: a door. As she ran to it she tugged free one of the bags from the bundle, ripped the plastic sleeve open with her teeth and threw it away. The door wasn't locked. She went through and pushed it closed behind her. Footsteps pounded in the hall, going up the stairs in a rush. She tore the bag open and stuck it under a nostril, snorting as hard as she could. The stuff burned her nose; tears came to her eyes.

*Get out of here!* She looked around. There was nowhere to go, just a square space hemmed in by buildings: a metal door, two blank walls. She tried the door: locked. The fire escapes were cranked up out of reach. She was trapped.

More sirens now, coming closer. *Hide!* —but there was nowhere to go. Despair took hold of her, and exhaustion: it was hopeless. She looked back up at DOA. A figure was outlined in one lighted window, but it moved away. *Saw me*, Steph said to herself. *That's it.*

Hands trembling, trying not to think about what was happening, she tore open another bag and snorted it up. Feet on the stairs again, pounding down: they were coming. She snorted up a third bag, was about to open another when the first of *them* banged open the door. She swung up the gun, aimed straight at his chest, fired. He kept coming. She emptied the gun, reports like explosions in the narrow space. It didn't stop him.

Tears came to the corners of her eyes; she blinked them away. "Fuck you!" she yelled, threw the gun aside. More were behind him now: five or six, pushing their way into the courtyard, glaring at her. Hands trembling, looking at their horrible eyes, she ripped open one more bag and did it up; it hit her hard, she staggered a little. "Fuck you," she said again, and spit. They were all around her now, encircling her, and the one she had shot was unlimbering his stick.